LORD PETER WIMSEY
INVESTIGATES

SELECTED SHORT STORIES

DOROTHY L. SAYERS

LORD PETER WIMSEY INVESTIGATES

SELECTED SHORT STORIES

With an introduction by
DAVID STUART DAVIES

MACMILLAN COLLECTOR'S LIBRARY

Lord Peter Views the Body first published in Great Britain in 1928 by Victor Gollancz Ltd
Hangman's Holiday first published in Great Britain in 1933 by Victor Gollancz Ltd
In the Teeth of the Evidence first published in Great Britain in 1939 by Victor Gollancz Ltd
Striding Folly first published in Great Britain in 1971 by Victor Gollancz Ltd

This collection first published by Macmillan Collector's Library 2018
an imprint of Pan Macmillan
The Smithson, 6 Briset Street, London ECIM 5NR
EU representative: Macmillan Publishers Ireland Ltd, 1st Floor,
The Liffey Trust Centre, 117–126 Sheriff Street Upper,
Dublin 1, DOI YC43
Associated companies throughout the world
www.panmacmillan.com

ISBN 978-1-5098-6864-3

Introduction copyright © David Stuart Davies 2018

Copyright © Dorothy L. Sayers 1928, 1933, 1939, 1971

The right of Dorothy L. Sayers to be identified as the
author of this work has been asserted by her in accordance
with the Copyright, Designs and Patents Act 1988.

Published by arrangement with Hodder & Stoughton Ltd

3 5 7 9 8 6 4

A CIP catalogue record for this book is available from the British Library.

Casing design and endpaper pattern by Andrew Davidson
Typeset in 8.5/10.5 pt Plantin Std by Jouve (UK), Milton Keynes
Printed and bound in China by Imago

MIX
Paper | Supporting
responsible forestry
FSC® C116313

Visit www.panmacmillan.com to read more about all our books
and to buy them. You will also find features, author interviews and
news of any author events, and you can sign up for e-newsletters
so that you're always first to hear about our new releases.

Contents

Introduction

DAVID STUART DAVIES

The period between the two world wars is generally regarded as the Golden Age of crime fiction. It was during this time that there emerged a varied cast of private detectives and amateur investigators who captured the imagination of readers with their brilliance in solving baffling mysteries. It was the era of G. K. Chesterton's Father Brown, Agatha Christie's Hercule Poirot and Miss Marple, John Dickson Carr's Dr Fell and Margery Allingham's Mr Campion, among others. Each had their own varied individual characteristics and idiosyncratic methods of investigating murder and mayhem. Perhaps the most interesting of these colourful sleuths was Lord Peter Wimsey, who was unlike the other crime-solvers in many ways. He was aristocratic, wealthy, a dilettante and at times could appear to be a silly ass. Indeed, on occasion there seemed to be a definite touch of the Bertie Woosters about him. This led both readers and criminals alike to be fooled by his frothy and casual demeanour. He was, in fact, sharp of brain and very cunning.

Lord Peter was the creation of Dorothy Leigh Sayers, who was born in 1893. It was from her father, a clergyman and a classical scholar, that she inherited her love of literature and writing. From a very early age she displayed a ferocious intellect as well as a loud and flamboyant character, and by the age of seven she had learned Latin and French. She later won a scholarship to study at Oxford and was a Gilchrist scholar at

Somerville College from 1912 to 1915. She was one of the first women graduates, gaining a Higher in Modern Languages. At college, she was remembered for her bizarre dress sense and a penchant for holding conversations in a booming voice.

After university, Sayers tried teaching for a while, but this did not suit her – she found coping with students who were not on her intellectual level too trying. There followed a spell in a publisher's office before she went to work for an advertising firm, Benson's, where she coined the immortal slogan: 'Guinness is good for you'. Also while at Benson's, she handled the Colman's Mustard account, and came up with the idea of a set of cartoon characters of British colonel types who gathered around to praise the product at the Mustard Club. Some historians regard this as one of her early contributions to the mystery field: the inspiration for the character Colonel Mustard in the board game *Cluedo*.

Sayers began working out the ideas for her first novel some time in 1920–1. The seeds of the plot for *Whose Body?* can be seen in a letter that Sayers wrote to her mother on 22 January 1921:

> My detective story begins brightly, with a fat lady found dead in her bath with nothing on but her pince-nez. Now why did she wear pince-nez in her bath? If you can guess, you will be in a position to lay hands upon the murderer, but he's a very cool and cunning fellow . . .*

The crime was solved by her newly hatched detective, Lord Peter Death Bredon Wimsey. She maintained

---

* Reynolds, Barbara, *Dorothy L. Sayers: Her Life and Soul* (London: Hodder & Stoughton, 1993).

that she did not 'remember inventing Lord Peter', that he just 'walked in complete with spats' into her imagination. However, prior to her work on *Whose Body?* she had tried to be recruited on to the rota of writers producing the Sexton Blake novels. Blake was a popular detective, 'the office boy's Sherlock Holmes' who had his own series of paperback novels penned by a variety of authors. Having asked a friend to send her a selection of these to read and research, Sayers then devised a short story in which Blake hears about a man in London named Lord Peter Wimsey and asks who he is. Blake is given the following information:

> Younger son of the Duke of Peterborough. Harmless sort of fellow. Distinguished himself in the war. Rides his own horse in the Grand National. Authority on first editions. I've seen his photograph somewhere. Fair-haired, big nose, aristocratic sort of man whose socks match his tie. No politics.

If the story was ever submitted to the publishers of Sexton Blake, it was certainly not printed. However, the idea of this character stayed with her and was eventually developed and refined.

In a very real sense, Wimsey was the true love of Sayers' life. She made him a charming and charismatic superman and there is apparently nothing that Lord Peter is ever called on to do that is beyond him. In his endeavours, he is often assisted by his valet and former batman Mervyn Bunter, and his good friend and later brother-in-law Inspector/Chief Inspector Charles Parker. Of all the sleuths of the Golden Age, Wimsey is the most fleshed out and rounded. Sayers knew her man well and had so strong an affection for her character that she created a detailed background and biography for him.

Wimsey, born in 1890, is the younger son of Mortimer Gerald Wimsey, 15th Duke of Denver. He was educated at Eton and Balliol College, Oxford, where he excelled at cricket and in his studies, achieving first-class honours in modern history. About to get married on the eve of his First World War service, he postponed the wedding because he felt that it would be unfair to his betrothed 'if he were to come back mutilated. Sadly, returning on leave he found the girl had married someone else.' (It can be said that his affected manner of g-dropping on certain words, his 'old bean' dialogue and his penchant for silly humour, such as ad-libbing doggerel in unsuitable situations, was mainly a defence and antidote to the pains of a broken heart.)

Wimsey returned to the front and almost lost his life behind enemy lines, earning the Distinguished Service Order in the process. He suffered 'a nervous breakdown' as a result of his combat experiences and was subject to recurring bouts of headache and nightmares.

After the war, Lord Peter became resident in a plush apartment at 110A Piccadilly, where he was looked after by Bunter, who had served under him. As a man of moneyed leisure he began to follow a variety of interests, including history, rare books and music – he was also an accomplished pianist. His main passion, however, was criminology, and the witty aristocrat soon became the leading amateur detective in London. Unlike Holmes and Poirot, he never accepts any fee for his services.

Wimsey investigates his first recorded case, *Whose Body?* (1923), at the request of his mother. The bizarre nature of the crime, the aforementioned fat lady found dead in a bath wearing only her pince-nez, and the intricate train of events that stemmed from this discovery, were typical of Sayers' carefully crafted, convoluted mysteries. The crimes were far more outré and complicated than those of Agatha Christie, for example.

Sayers submitted the manuscript of *Whose Body?* to several publishers, all of whom turned it down. Finally, an American publishing house, Boni & Liveright, accepted the book, on condition that the author delete certain passages in order to reduce the length, which they considered a little unwieldy. As a result, the most English of detectives was first published in America in May 1923 and in the UK six months later.

More Wimsey novels followed, with the settings and characters often drawn from the author's own life and experiences. There was the fishing and painting community in Scotland (*The Five Red Herrings*, 1931); an advertising agency where Wimsey goes undercover to solve a murder and proves to be rather talented at coming up with catchy slogans (*Murder Must Advertise*, 1933); the fen country, a favorite haunt of Sayers (*The Nine Tailors*, 1934) and academic Oxford (*Gaudy Night*, 1935).

Her detective fiction relied on what she considered an essential ingredient in the genre, namely 'a vivid conviction of fact', which allowed the reader to be induced into accepting the imaginary scenario without question. It is the magic art of presenting fabrication as reality. Another aspect of her novels is the vivid reflection of the social, economic and cultural life of her time. Of course, Sayers has been accused of snobbery, particularly in presenting a louche aristocrat as her hero. Yet Wimsey, who is far from elitist, is such a likeable and friendly fellow that his persona dilutes such criticism. Beneath his external frivolity, which is a self-defensive disguise, he is vulnerable and very human. The society that Sayers presents in her novels is one mixed with various classes, and indeed Wimsey marries a commoner and his sister marries a Scotland Yard inspector.

Sayers' desire to raise the artistic standing of the detective story to that of a novel of manners and literary merit caused her to change and develop Wimsey's character, in order to make him both a three-dimensional hero and indeed a plausible marriage partner. The later novels saw less of the Wooster-ish behaviour and more of a rounder, mellower individual, with greater sensitivity than the majority of fictional detectives – at least those of the Golden Age such as Poirot, who throughout his long career remains a concoction of mannerisms and habits. Wimsey matures with the passage of time.

The real turning point in the detective career of Lord Peter Wimsey, and a large move forward in giving the character greater depth, is the introduction of Harriet Vane, with whom he falls in love in *Strong Poison* (1930). It seems that with Vane, a highly intelligent mystery writer, Sayers was consciously writing herself into the stories in order to have a relationship and later a romance with Wimsey.

In *Strong Poison*, Wimsey is attempting to clear Harriet of the accusation that she murdered her lover. Sayers' treatment of the relationship between Wimsey and Vane in this and in later novels, and her obvious sympathy for Harriet, who is seen to be largely on trial because she is unconventional and female, does much to reveal the moral hypocrisy of the era.

Some readers felt that the love interest distracted from the purity of the detective story form, pulling the books out of shape and making them too long and dull, while others thought that Harriet was not worthy of their hero. Sayers was inundated with letters begging her not to let Peter marry that 'horrid girl'. However, the author liked the dimension that the Peter and Harriet relationship added to the traditional mystery story, and allowed the two to marry. But first she teased her readers with the courtship. After Wimsey proves Harriet's innocence in *Strong Poison*, in the following novel, *Have His Carcase* (1932), she collaborates with him to solve a murder but still finds Lord Peter to be overbearing and superficial. However, he eventually wins her round and she returns his love in *Gaudy Night* (1935) and then marries him in *Busman's Honeymoon* (1937), which had the ominous subtitle, *A Love Story with Detective Interruptions*. With their marriage, it seemed that Wimsey's career as a detective was cast into the shadows. It appeared that Sayers had done with him, or it may be that she was running out of steam in creating novel-length mysteries for her detective.

According to Sayers' friend and biographer Barbara Reynolds*, Sayers had begun work in 1936 on *Thrones, Dominations*, a murder mystery novel in which the Wimsey marriage was to be contrasted with those of two other couples. Apparently, she worked on it for some months, but does not appear to have done so thereafter. Reynolds suggests that this is due at least in part to the constitutional crisis of that year surrounding Edward VIII and his relationship with Wallis Simpson. The events of December 1936 onwards overtook the story, with the abdication altering how Sayers' potential audience would interpret a tale of contrasting marriages. In 1938, she declared in a letter that she had

* *Dorothy L. Sayers: Her Life and Soul* (Hodder & Stoughton, 1993).

come to dislike the book, and had 'great difficulty doing anything about it'. The novel was eventually completed by Jill Paton Walsh and published in 1998.

In later life, Dorothy L. Sayers stated: 'I wrote the Peter Wimsey books when I was young and had no money. I made some money and stopped writing them and began to write what I always wanted to write.'

After the last Wimsey novel, she devoted the rest of her writing career to poetry, plays and essays, primarily on religious themes, including a translation of Dante's *Divine Comedy*, which she considered her best work.

In her claim to have been done with detective novels, Sayers does protest a little too much. She had been adding some short stories to the Wimsey canon during the time she wrote the eleven novels. There were twelve stories published in a collection called *Lord Peter Views the Body* in 1928, and *Hangman's Holiday* in 1933 contained four stories. After Sayers had brought the curtain down on Lord Peter's novel career, further short stories continued to appear. There were two in a collection called *In the Teeth of the Evidence* in 1939. Also published the same year were two of the three final Wimsey investigations, 'Striding Folly' and 'The Haunted Policeman', which appeared in *Detection Medley* (Hutchinson & Co. Ltd), edited by her close friend and fellow crime writer John Rhode. The final Wimsey short story, 'Talboys', was written in 1942, but was never published at the time and only discovered years later. It first appeared in print in 1972. Although by the mid-1930s Sayers had lost interest in writing crime novels, she still harboured a lingering fascination for her titled sleuth for some years.

It was in the short stories that Sayers was able to experiment with the mystery story form. While some of these narratives do follow the tried and trusted linear format of the genre, which involves the crime followed by its detection and then the solution, as in 'The Necklace of Pearls', others approach the construction of the narrative in a more recherché fashion, such as 'The Incredible Elopement of Lord Peter Wimsey', which is a really spooky entry into the canon, having elements which would grace an effective horror tale. In several of the stories, Wimsey appears as a shadowy figure and is not identified clearly until the closing moments of the narrative. In this fashion, Sayers cleverly adds a further conundrum for the reader. As well as the crime to be solved, we are uncertain where Lord Peter fits into the mystery jigsaw.

The stories in the collection that you hold in your hand are not only the best and most effective of the bunch, but also cover the breadth of Lord Peter Wimsey's literary career, from the lightly sketched fellow, still in Wodehouse mode, of 'In Teeth of Evidence', to the mature and happily married middle-aged sleuth we encounter in 'The Haunted Policeman', where Peter views his first born with incredulity, and 'Talboys', when Wimsey is now aged fifty-two and the father of three children.

It is a lively assembly of stories featuring a detective who not only aged, developed and matured but, thanks to Sayers' acuity and storytelling skills, still retained that twinkle in the eye and the brilliance of mind that can spot a clue a mile off.

THE NECKLACE OF PEARLS

Sir Septimus Shale was accustomed to assert his authority once in the year and once only. He allowed his young and fashionable wife to fill his house with diagrammatic furniture made of steel; to collect advanced artists and anti-grammatical poets; to believe in cocktails and relativity and to dress as extravagantly as she pleased; but he did insist on an old-fashioned Christmas. He was a simple-hearted man, who really liked plum-pudding and cracker mottoes, and he could not get it out of his head that other people, 'at bottom,' enjoyed these things also. At Christmas, therefore, he firmly retired to his country house in Essex, called in the servants to hang holly and mistletoe upon the cubist electric fittings; loaded the steel sideboard with delicacies from Fortnum & Mason; hung up stockings at the heads of the polished walnut bedsteads; and even, on this occasion only, had the electric radiators removed from the modernist grates and installed wood fires and a Yule log. He then gathered his family and friends about him, filled them with as much Dickensian good fare as he could persuade them to swallow, and, after their Christmas dinner, set them down to play 'Charades' and 'Clumps' and 'Animal, Vegetable and Mineral' in the drawing-room, concluding these diversions by 'Hide-and-Seek' in the dark all over the house. Because Sir Septimus was a very rich man, his guests fell in with this invariable programme, and if they were bored, they did not tell him so.

Another charming and traditional custom which he followed was that of presenting to his daughter Margharita a pearl on each successive birthday – this anniversary happening to coincide with Christmas Eve. The pearls now numbered twenty, and the collection was beginning to enjoy a certain celebrity, and had been photographed in the Society papers. Though not sensationally large – each one being about the size of a marrowfat pea – the pearls were of very great value. They were of exquisite colour and perfect shape and matched to a hair's-weight. On this particular Christmas Eve, the presentation of the twenty-first pearl had been the occasion of a very special ceremony. There was a dance and there were speeches. On the Christmas night following, the more restricted family party took place, with the turkey and the Victorian games. There were eleven guests, in addition to Sir Septimus and Lady Shale and their daughter, nearly all related or connected to them in some way: John Shale, a brother, with his wife and their son and daughter Henry and Betty; Betty's fiancé, Oswald Truegood, a young man with parliamentary ambitions; George Comphrey, a cousin of Lady Shale's, aged about thirty and known as a man about town; Lavinia Prescott, asked on George's account; Joyce Trivett, asked on Henry Shale's account; Richard and Beryl Dennison, distant relations of Lady Shale, who lived a gay and expensive life in town on nobody precisely knew what resources; and Lord Peter Wimsey, asked, in a touching spirit of unreasonable hope, on Margharita's account. There were also, of course, William Norgate, secretary to Sir Septimus, and Miss Tomkins, secretary to Lady Shale, who had to be there because, without their calm efficiency, the Christmas arrangements could not have been carried through.

Dinner was over – a seemingly endless succession of soup, fish, turkey, roast beef, plum-pudding, mince-pies, crystallised fruit, nuts and five kinds of wine, presided over by Sir Septimus, all smiles, by Lady Shale all mocking deprecation, and by Margharita, pretty and bored, with the necklace of twenty-one pearls gleaming softly on her slender throat. Gorged and dyspeptic and longing only for the horizontal position, the company had been shepherded into the drawing-room and set to play 'Musical Chairs' (Miss Tomkins at the piano), 'Hunt the Slipper' (slipper provided by Miss Tomkins), and 'Dumb Crambo' (costumes by Miss Tomkins and Mr William Norgate). The back drawing-room (for Sir Septimus clung to these old-fashioned names) provided an admirable dressing-room, being screened by folding doors from the large drawing-room in which the audience sat on aluminium chairs, scrabbling uneasy toes on a floor of black glass under the tremendous illumination of electricity reflected from a brass ceiling.

It was William Norgate who, after taking the temperature of the meeting, suggested to Lady Shale that they should play at something less athletic. Lady Shale agreed and, as usual, suggested bridge. Sir Septimus, as usual, blew the suggestion aside.

'Bridge? Nonsense! Nonsense! Play bridge every day of your lives. This is Christmas time. Something we can all play together. How about "Animal, Vegetable and Mineral"?'

This intellectual pastime was a favourite with Sir Septimus; he was rather good at putting pregnant questions. After a brief discussion, it became evident that this game was an inevitable part of the programme. The party settled down to it, Sir Septimus undertaking to 'go out' first and set the thing going.

3

Presently they had guessed among other things Miss Tomkins's mother's photograph, a gramophone record of 'I want to be happy' (much scientific research into the exact composition of records, settled by William Norgate out of the *Encyclopaedia Britannica*), the smallest stickleback in the stream at the bottom of the garden, the new planet Pluto, the scarf worn by Mrs Dennison (very confusing, because it was not silk, which would be animal or artificial silk, which would be vegetable, but made of spun glass – mineral, a very clever choice of subject), and had failed to guess the Prime Minister's wireless speech – which was voted not fair, since nobody could decide whether it was animal by nature or a kind of gas. It was decided that they should do one more word and then go on to 'Hide-and-Seek.' Oswald Truegood had retired into the back room and shut the door behind him while the party discussed the next subject of examination, when suddenly Sir Septimus broke in on the argument by calling to his daughter.

'Hullo, Margy! What have you done with your necklace?'

'I took it off, Dad, because I thought it might get broken in "Dumb Crambo." It's over here on this table. No, it isn't. Did you take it, Mother?'

'No, I didn't. If I'd seen it, I should have. You are a careless child.'

'I believe you've got it yourself, Dad. You're teasing.'

Sir Septimus denied the accusation with some energy. Everybody got up and began to hunt about. There were not many places in that bare and polished room where a necklace could be hidden. After ten minutes' fruitless investigation, Richard Dennison, who had been seated next to the table where the pearls had been placed, began to look rather uncomfortable.

'Awkward, you know,' he remarked to Wimsey.

At this moment, Oswald Truegood put his head through the folding-doors and asked whether they hadn't settled on something by now, because he was getting the fidgets.

This directed the attention of the searchers to the inner room. Margharita must have been mistaken. She had taken it in there, and it had got mixed up with the dressing-up clothes somehow. The room was ransacked. Everything was lifted up and shaken. The thing began to look serious. After half an hour of desperate energy it became apparent that the pearls were nowhere to be found.

'They must be somewhere in these two rooms, you know,' said Wimsey. 'The back drawing-room has no door and nobody could have gone out of the front drawing-room without being seen. Unless the windows—'

No. The windows were all guarded on the outside by heavy shutters which it needed two footmen to take down and replace. The pearls had not gone out that way. In fact, the mere suggestion that they had left the drawing-room at all was disagreeable. Because – because—

It was William Norgate, efficient as ever, who coldly and boldly faced the issue.

'I think, Sir Septimus, it would be a relief to the minds of everybody present if we could all be searched.'

Sir Septimus was horrified, but the guests, having found a leader, backed up Norgate. The door was locked, and the search was conducted – the ladies in the inner room and the men in the outer.

Nothing resulted from it except some very interesting information about the belongings habitually carried about by the average man and woman. It was natural that Lord Peter Wimsey should possess a pair of forceps, a pocket lens and a small folding foot-rule – was he not a Sherlock Holmes in high life? But that Oswald Truegood should have two liver-pills in a screw of paper and Henry Shale a pocket edition of *The Odes of Horace* was unexpected. Why did John Shale distend the pockets of his dress-suit with a stump of red sealing-wax, an ugly little mascot and a five-shilling piece? George Comphrey had a pair of folding scissors, and three wrapped lumps of sugar, of the sort served in restaurants and dining-cars – evidence of a not uncommon form of kleptomania; but that the tidy and exact Norgate should burden himself with a reel of white cotton, three separate lengths of string and twelve safety-pins on a card seemed really remarkable till one remembered that he had superintended all the Christmas decorations. Richard Dennison, amid some confusion and laughter, was found to cherish a lady's garter, a powder-compact and half a potato; the last-named, he said, was a prophylactic against rheumatism (to which, he was subject), while the other objects belonged to his wife. On the ladies' side, the more striking exhibits were a little book on palmistry, three invisible hair-pins and a baby's photograph (Miss Tomkins); a Chinese trick cigarette-case with a secret compartment (Beryl Dennison); a *very* private letter and an outfit for mending stocking-ladders (Lavinia Prescott); and a pair of eyebrow tweezers and a small packet of white powder, said to be for headaches (Betty Shale). An agitating moment followed the production from Joyce Trivett's handbag of a small string of pearls – but it was promptly remembered that these had come out of one of the crackers at dinner-time, and they were, in fact, synthetic. In short, the search was unproductive of anything beyond a general shamefacedness and the discomfort always produced by undressing and re-dressing in a hurry at the wrong time of the day.

It was then that somebody, very grudgingly and halt-ingly, mentioned the horrid word 'Police.' Sir Septimus, naturally, was appalled by the idea. It was disgusting. He would not allow it. The pearls must be somewhere. They must search the rooms again. Could not Lord Peter Wimsey, with his experience of – er – mysterious happenings, do something to assist them?

'Eh?' said his lordship. 'Oh, by Jove, – yes – by all means, certainly. That is to say, provided nobody supposes – eh, what? I mean to say, you don't know that I'm not a suspicious character, do you, what?'

Lady Shale interposed with authority.

'We don't think *anybody* ought to be suspected,' she said, 'but, if we did, we'd know it couldn't be you. You know *far* too much about crimes to want to commit one.'

'All right,' said Wimsey. 'But after the way the place has been gone over –' He shrugged his shoulders.

'Yes, I'm afraid you won't be able to find any foot-prints,' said Margharita. 'But we may have overlooked something.'

Wimsey nodded.

'I'll try. Do you all mind sitting down on your chairs in the outer room and staying there. All except one of you – I'd better have a witness to anything I do or find. Sir Septimus – you'd be the best person, I think.'

He shepherded them to their places and began a slow circuit of the two rooms, exploring every surface, gazing up to the polished brazen ceiling and crawling on hands and knees in the approved fashion across the

7

black and shining desert of the floors. Sir Septimus followed, staring when Wimsey stared, bending with his hands upon his knees when Wimsey crawled, and puffing at intervals with astonishment and chagrin. Their progress rather resembled that of a man taking out a very inquisitive puppy for a very leisurely constitutional. Fortunately, Lady Shale's taste in furnishing made investigation easier; there were scarcely any nooks or corners where anything could be concealed.

They reached the inner drawing-room, and here the dressing-up clothes were again minutely examined, but without result. Finally, Wimsey lay down flat on his stomach to squint under a steel cabinet which was one of the very few pieces of furniture which possessed short legs. Something about it seemed to catch his attention. He rolled up his sleeve and plunged his arm into the cavity, kicked convulsively in the effort to reach farther than was humanly possible, pulled out from his pocket and extended his folding foot-rule, fished with it under the cabinet and eventually succeeded in extracting what he sought.

It was a very minute object – in fact, a pin. Not an ordinary pin, but one resembling those used by entomologists to impale extremely small moths on the setting-board. It was about three-quarters of an inch in length, as fine as a very fine needle, with a sharp point and a particularly small head.

'Bless my soul!' said Sir Septimus. 'What's that?'

'Does anybody here happen to collect moths or beetles or anything?' asked Wimsey, squatting on his haunches and examining the pin.

'I'm pretty sure they don't,' replied Sir Septimus. 'I'll ask them.'

'Don't do that.' Wimsey bent his head and stared at the floor, from which his own face stared meditatively back at him.

'I see,' said Wimsey presently. 'That's how it was done. All right, Sir Septimus. I know where the pearls are, but I don't know who took them. Perhaps it would be as well – for everybody's satisfaction – just to find out. In the meantime they are perfectly safe. Don't tell anyone that we've found this pin or that we've discovered anything. Send all these people to bed. Lock the drawing-room door and keep the key, and we'll get our man – or woman – by breakfast-time.'

'God bless my soul,' said Sir Septimus, very much puzzled.

Lord Peter Wimsey kept careful watch that night upon the drawing-room door. Nobody, however, came near it. Either the thief suspected a trap or he felt confident that any time would do to recover the pearls. Wimsey, however, did not feel that he was wasting his time. He was making a list of people who had been left alone in the back drawing-room during the playing of 'Animal, Vegetable and Mineral.' The list ran as follows.

> Sir Septimus Shale
> Lavinia Prescott
> William Norgate
> Joyce Trivett and Henry Shale (together,
>   because they had claimed to be incapable of
>   guessing anything unaided)
> Mrs Dennison
> Betty Shale
> George Comphrey

Richard Dennison
Miss Tomkins
Oswald Truegood.

He also made out a list of the persons to whom pearls might be useful or desirable. Unfortunately, this list agreed in almost all respects with the first (always excepting Sir Septimus) and so was not very helpful. The two secretaries had both come well recommended, but that was exactly what they would have done had they come with ulterior designs; the Dennisons were notorious livers from hand to mouth; Betty Shale carried mysterious white powders in her handbag, and was known to be in with a rather rapid set in town; Henry was a harmless dilettante, but Joyce Trivett could twist him round her little finger and was what Jane Austen liked to call 'expensive and dissipated'; Comphrey speculated; Oswald Truegood was rather frequently present at Epsom and Newmarket – the search for motives was only too fatally easy.

When the second housemaid and the under-footman appeared in the passage with household implements, Wimsey abandoned his vigil, but he was down early to breakfast. Sir Septimus with his wife and daughter were down before him, and a certain air of tension made itself felt. Wimsey, standing on the hearth before the fire, made conversation about the weather and politics.

The party assembled gradually, but, as though by common consent, nothing was said about pearls until after breakfast, when Oswald Truegood took the bull by the horns.

'Well now!' said he. 'How's the detective getting along? Got your man, Wimsey?'

'Not yet,' said Wimsey easily.

Sir Septimus, looking at Wimsey as though for his cue, cleared his throat and dashed into speech.

'All very tiresome,' he said, 'all very unpleasant. Hr'rm. Nothing for it but the police, I'm afraid. Just at Christmas, too. Hr'rm. Spoilt the party. Can't stand seeing all this stuff about the place.' He waved his hand towards the festoons of evergreens and coloured paper that adorned the walls. 'Take it all down, eh, what? No heart in it. Hr'rm. Burn the lot.'

'What a pity, when we worked so hard over it,' said Joyce.

'Oh, leave it, Uncle,' said Henry Shale. 'You're bothering too much about the pearls. They're sure to turn up.'

'Shall I ring for James?' suggested William Norgate.

'No,' interrupted Comphrey, 'let's do it ourselves. It'll give us something to do and take our minds off our troubles.'

'That's right,' said Sir Septimus. 'Start right away. Hate the sight of it.'

He savagely hauled a great branch of holly down from the mantelpiece and flung it, crackling, into the fire.

'That's the stuff,' said Richard Dennison. 'Make a good old blaze!' He leapt up from the table and snatched the mistletoe from the chandelier. 'Here goes! One more kiss for somebody before it's too late.'

'Isn't it unlucky to take it down before the New Year?' suggested Miss Tomkins.

'Unlucky be hanged. We'll have it all down. Off the stairs and out of the drawing-room too. Somebody go and collect it.'

'Isn't the drawing-room locked?' asked Oswald.

'No. Lord Peter says the pearls aren't there, wherever

else they are, so it's unlocked. That's right isn't it Wimsey?'

'Quite right. The pearls were taken out of these rooms. I can't yet tell you how, but I'm positive of it. In fact, I'll pledge my reputation that wherever they are, they're not up there.'

'Oh, well,' said Comphrey, 'in that case, have at it! Come along, Lavinia – you and Dennison do the drawing-room and I'll do the back room. We'll have a race.'

'But if the police are coming in,' said Dennison, 'oughtn't everything to be left just as it is?'

'Damn the police!' shouted Sir Septimus. 'They don't want evergreens.'

Oswald and Margharita were already pulling the holly and ivy from the staircase, amid peals of laughter. The party dispersed. Wimsey went quietly upstairs and into the drawing-room, where the work of demolition was taking place at a great rate, George having bet the other two ten shillings to a tanner that they would not finish their part of the job before he finished his.

'You mustn't help,' said Lavinia, laughing to Wimsey. 'It wouldn't be fair.'

Wimsey said nothing, but waited till the room was clear. Then he followed them down again to the hall, where the fire was sending up a great roaring and spluttering, suggestive of Guy Fawkes night. He whispered to Sir Septimus, who went forward and touched George Comphrey on the shoulder.

'Lord Peter wants to say something to you, my boy,' he said.

Comphrey started and went with him a little reluctantly, as it seemed. He was not looking very well.

'Mr Comphrey,' said Wimsey, 'I fancy these are some

of your property.' He held out the palm of his hand, in which rested twenty-two fine, small-headed pins.

'Ingenious,' said Wimsey, 'but something less ingenious would have served his turn better. It was very unlucky, Sir Septimus, that you should have mentioned the pearls when you did. Of course, he hoped that the loss wouldn't be discovered till we'd chucked guessing games and taken to "Hide-and-Seek". Then the pearls might have been anywhere in the house, we shouldn't have locked the drawing-room door, and he could have recovered them at his leisure. He had had this possibility in his mind when he came here, obviously, and that was why he brought the pins, and Miss Shale's taking off the necklace to play "Dumb Crambo" gave him his opportunity.

'He had spent Christmas here before, and knew perfectly well that "Animal, Vegetable and Mineral" would form part of the entertainment. He had only to gather up the necklace from the table when it came to his turn to retire, and he knew he could count on at least five minutes by himself while we were all arguing about the choice of a word. He had only to snip the pearls on the string with his pocket-scissors, burn the string in the grate and fasten the pearls to the mistletoe with the fine pins. The mistletoe was hung on the chandelier pretty high – it's a lofty room – but he could easily reach it by standing on the glass table, which wouldn't show footmarks, and it was almost certain that nobody would think of examining the mistletoe for extra berries. I shouldn't have thought of it myself if I hadn't found the pin which he had dropped. That gave me the idea that the pearls had been separated and the rest was easy. I took the pearls off the mistletoe last night – the clasp was there, too, pinned among the holly-leaves. Here they are. Comphrey must have got a nasty shock this morning. I knew he was our man when he suggested that the guests should tackle the decorations themselves and that he should do the back drawing-room – but I wish I had seen his face when he came to the mistletoe and found the pearls gone.'

'And you worked it all out when you found the pin?' said Sir Septimus.

'Yes; I knew then where the pearls had gone to.'

'But you never even looked at the mistletoe.'

'I saw it reflected in the black glass floor, and it struck me then how much the mistletoe berries looked like pearls.'

THE QUEEN'S SQUARE

'You Jack o' Di'monds, you Jack o' Di'monds,' said Mark Sambourne, shaking a reproachful head, 'I know you of old.' He rummaged beneath the white satin of his costume, panelled with gigantic oblongs and spotted to represent a set of dominoes. 'Hang this fancy rig! Where the blazes has the fellow put my pockets? You rob my pocket, yes, you rob-a my pocket, you rob my pocket of silver and go-ho-hold. How much do you make it?' He extracted a fountain-pen and a cheque-book.

'Five-seventeen-six,' said Lord Peter Wimsey. 'That's right, isn't it, partner?' His huge blue-and-scarlet sleeves rustled as he turned to Lady Hermione Creethorpe, who, in her Queen of Clubs costume, looked a very redoubtable virgin, as, indeed, she was.

'Quite right,' said the old lady, 'and I consider that very cheap.'

'We haven't been playing long,' said Wimsey apologetically.

'It would have been more, Auntie,' observed Mrs Wrayburn, 'if you hadn't been greedy. You shouldn't have doubled those four spades of mine.'

Lady Hermione snorted, and Wimsey hastily cut in:

'It's a pity we've got to stop, but Deverill will never forgive us if we're not there to dance Sir Roger. He feels strongly about it. What's the time? Twenty past one. Sir Roger is timed to start sharp at half-past. I suppose we'd better tootle back to the ballroom.'

'I suppose we had,' agreed Mrs Wrayburn. She stood up, displaying her dress, boldly patterned with red and black points of a backgammon board. 'It's very good of you,' she added, as Lady Hermione's voluminous skirts swept through the hall ahead of them, 'to chuck your dancing to give Auntie her bridge. She does so hate to miss it.'

'Not at all,' replied Wimsey. 'It's a pleasure. And in any case I was jolly glad of a rest. These costumes are dashed hot for dancing in.'

'You make a splendid Jack of Diamonds, though. Such a good idea of Lady Deverill's, to make everybody come as a game. It cuts out all those wearisome pierrots and columbines.' They skirted the south-west angle of the ballroom and emerged into the south corridor, lit by a great hanging lantern in four lurid colours. Under the arcading they paused and stood watching the floor, where Sir Charles Deverill's guests were fox-trotting to a lively tune discoursed by the band in the musicians' gallery at the far end. 'Hullo, Giles!' added Mrs Wrayburn, 'you look hot.'

'I am hot,' said Giles Pomfret. 'I wish to goodness I hadn't been so clever about this infernal costume. It's a beautiful billiard-table, but I can't sit down in it.' He mopped his heated brow, crowned with an elegant green lamp-shade. 'The only rest I can get is to hitch my behind on a radiator, and as they're all in full blast, it's not very cooling. Thank goodness, I can always make these damned sandwich boards an excuse to get out of dancing.' He propped himself against the nearest column, looking martyred.

'Nina Hartford comes off best,' said Mrs Wrayburn. 'Waterpolo – so sensible – just a bathing-dress and a ball; though I must say it would look better on a less *Restor-*

ation figure. You playing-cards are much the prettiest, and I think the chess-pieces run you close. There goes Gerda Bellingham, dancing with her husband – isn't she *too* marvellous in that red wig? And the bustle and everything – my dear, so attractive. I'm glad they didn't make themselves too Lewis Carroll; Charmian Grayle is the sweetest White Queen – where is she, by the way?'

'I don't like that young woman,' said Lady Hermione; 'she's fast.'

'Dear lady!'

'I've no doubt you think me old-fashioned. Well, I'm glad I am. I say she's fast, and, what's more, heartless. I was watching her before supper, and I'm sorry for Tony Lee. She's been flirting as hard as she can go with Harry Vibart – not to give it a worse name – and she's got Jim Playfair on a string, too. She can't even leave Frank Bellingham alone, though she's staying in his house.'

'Oh, I say, Lady H!' protested Sambourne, 'you're a bit hard on Miss Grayle. I mean, she's an awfully sporting kid and all that.'

'I detest that word "sporting",' snapped Lady Hermione. 'Nowadays it merely means drunk and disorderly. And she's not such a kid either, young man. In three years' time she'll be a hag, if she goes on at this rate.'

'Dear Lady Hermione,' said Wimsey, 'we can't all be untouched by time, like you.'

'You could,' retorted the old lady, 'if you looked after your stomachs and your morals. Here comes Frank Bellingham – looking for a drink, no doubt. Young people today seem to be positively pickled in gin.'

The fox-trot had come to an end, and the Red King was threading his way towards them through a group of applauding couples.

'Hullo, Bellingham!' said Wimsey. 'Your crown's crooked. Allow me.' He set wig and head-dress to rights with skilful fingers. 'Not that I blame you. What crown is safe in these Bolshevik days?'

'Thanks,' said Bellingham. 'I say, I want a drink.'

'What did I tell you?' said Lady Hermione.

'Buzz along, then, old man,' said Wimsey. 'You've got four minutes. Mind you turn up in time for Sir Roger.'

'Right you are. Oh, I'm dancing it with Gerda, by the way. If you see her, you might tell her where I've gone to.'

'We will. Lady Hermione, you're honouring me, of course?'

'Nonsense! You're not expecting me to dance at my age? The Old Maid ought to be a wallflower.'

'Nothing of the sort. If only I'd had the luck to be born earlier, you and I should have appeared side by side, as Matrimony. Of course you're going to dance it with me – unless you mean to throw me over for one of these youngsters.'

'I've no use for youngsters,' said Lady Hermione. 'No guts. Spindle-shanks.' She darted a swift glance at Wimsey's scarlet hose. 'You at least have some suggestion of calves. I can stand up with you without blushing for you.'

Wimsey bowled his scarlet cap and curled wig in deep reverence over the gnarled knuckles extended to him.

'You make me the happiest of men. We'll show them all how to do it. Right hand, left hand, both hands across, back to back, round you go and up the middle. There's Deverill going down to tell the band to begin. Punctual old bird, isn't he? Just two minutes to go . . . What's the matter, Miss Carstairs? Lost your partner?'

'Yes – have you seen Tony Lee anywhere?'

'The White King? Not a sign. Nor the White Queen either, I expect they're together somewhere.'

'Probably. Poor old Jimmie Playfair is sitting patiently in the north corridor, looking like Casabianca.'

'You'd better go along and console him,' said Wimsey, laughing.

Joan Carstairs made a face and disappeared in the direction of the buffet, just as Sir Charles Deverill, giver of the party, bustled up to Wimsey and his companions resplendent in a Chinese costume patterned with red and green dragons, bamboos, circles and characters and carrying on his shoulder a stuffed bird with an enormous tail.

'Now, now,' he exclaimed, 'come along, come along, come along! All ready for Sir Roger. Got your partner Wimsey? Ah, yes, Lady Hermione – splendid. You must come and stand next to your dear mother and me Wimsey. Don't be late, don't be late. We want to dance it right through. The waits will begin at two o'clock I hope they will arrive in good time. Dear me, dear me! Why aren't the servants in yet? I told Watson – I must go and speak to him.'

He darted away, and Wimsey, laughing, led his partner up to the top of the room, where his mother, the Dowager Duchess of Denver, stood waiting, magnificent as the Queen of Spades.

'Ah! here you are,' said the Duchess placidly. 'Dear Sir Charles – he was getting quite flustered. Such a man for punctuality – he ought to have been a Royalty. A delightful party, Hermione, isn't it? Sir Roger and the waits – quite medieval – and a Yule-log in the hall with the steam-radiators and everything – so oppressive!'

'Tumty, tumty, tiddledy, tumty, tumty, tiddledy,' sang Lord Peter, as the band broke into the old tune.

'I do adore this music. Foot it featly here and these – oh! there's Gerda Bellingham. Just a moment! Mrs Bellingham – hi! your royal spouse awaits your Red Majesty's pleasure in the buffet. Do hurry him up. He's only got half a minute.'

The Red Queen smiled at him, her pale face and black eyes startlingly brilliant beneath her scarlet wig and gown.

'I'll bring him up to scratch all right,' she said, and passed on, laughing.

'So she will,' said the Dowager. 'You'll see that young man in the Cabinet before very long. Such a handsome couple on a public platform, and very sound, I'm told, about pigs, and that's so important, the British breakfast-table being what it is.'

Sir Charles Deverill, looking a trifle heated, came hurrying back and took his place at the head of the double line of guests, which now extended three-quarters of the way down the ballroom. At the lower end, just in front of the Musicians' Gallery, the staff had filed in, to form a second Sir Roger, at right angles to the main set. The clock chimed the half-hour. Sir Charles, craning an anxious neck, counted the dancers.

'Eighteen couples. We're two couples short. How vexatious! Who are missing?'

'The Bellinghams?' said Wimsey. 'No, they're here. It's the White King and Queen, Badminton and Diabolo.'

'There's Badminton!' cried Mrs Wrayburn, signalling frantically across the room. 'Jim! Jim! Bother! He's gone back again. He's waiting for Charmian Grayle.'

'Well, we can't wait any longer,' said Sir Charles peevishly. 'Duchess, will you lead off?'

The Dowager obediently threw her black velvet train over her arm and skipped away down the centre, displaying an uncommonly neat pair of scarlet ankles. The two lines of dancers, breaking into the hop-and-skip step of the country dance, jigged sympathetically. Below them, the cross lines of black and white and livery coats followed their example with respect. Sir Charles Deverill dancing solemnly down after the Duchess, joined hands with Nina Hartford from the far end of the line. Tumty, tumty, tiddledy, tumty, tumty, tiddledy . . . the first couple turned outward and led the dancers down. Wimsey, catching the hand of Lady Hermione, stooped with her beneath the arch and came triumphantly up to the top of the room, in a magnificent rustle of silk and satin. 'My love,' sighed Wimsey, 'was clad in the black velvet, and I myself in cramoisie.' The old lady, well pleased, rapped him over the knuckles with her gilt sceptre. Hands clapped merrily.

'Down we go again,' said Wimsey, and the Queen of Clubs and Emperor of the great Mahjongg dynasty twirled and capered in the centre. The Queen of Spades danced up to meet her Jack of Diamonds. 'Bézique,' said Wimsey; 'double Bézique,' as he gave both his hands to the Dowager. Tumty, tumty, tiddledy. He again gave his hand to the Queen of Clubs and led her down. Under their lifted arms the other seventeen couples passed. Then Lady Deverill and her partner followed them down – then five more couples.

'We're working nicely to time,' said Sir Charles, with his eye on the clock. 'I worked it out at two minutes per couple. Ah! here's one of the missing pairs.' He waved an agitated arm. 'Come into the centre – come along – in here.'

A man whose head was decorated with a huge shuttlecock, and Joan Carstairs, dressed as a Diabolo, had emerged from the north corridor. Sir Charles, like a fussy rooster with two frightened hens, guided and pushed them into place between two couples who had not yet done their 'hands across', and heaved a sigh of relief. It would have worried him to see them miss their turn. The clock chimed a quarter to two.

'I say, Playfair, have you seen Charmian Grayle or Tony Lee anywhere about?' asked Giles Pomfret of the Badminton costume. 'Sir Charles is quite upset because we aren't complete.'

'Not a sign of 'em. I was supposed to be dancing this with Charmian, but she vanished – upstairs and hasn't come down again. Then Joan came barging along looking for Tony, and we thought we'd better see it through together.'

'Here are the waits coming in,' broke in Joan Carstairs. 'Aren't they sweet? Too-too-truly-rural!'

Between the columns on the north side of the ballroom the waits could be seen filing into place in the corridor, under the command of the Vicar. Sir Roger jigged on his exhausting way. Hands across. Down the centre and up again. Giles Pomfret, groaning, scrambled in his sandwich-boards beneath the lengthening arch of hands for the fifteenth time. Tumty, tiddledy. The nineteenth couple wove their way through the dance. Once again, Sir Charles and the Dowager Duchess, both as fresh as paint, stood at the top of the room. The clapping was loudly renewed; the orchestra fell silent; the guests broke up into groups; the servants arranged themselves in a neat line at the lower end of the room; the clock struck two; and the Vicar, receiving a signal from Sir Charles, held his tuning-fork to his ear and gave forth a sonorous A. The waits burst shrilly into the opening bars of 'Good King Wenceslas'.

It was just as the night was growing darker and the wind blowing stronger that a figure came thrusting its way through the ranks of the singers, and hurried across to where Sir Charles stood; Tony Lee, with his face as white as his costume.

'Charmian . . . in the tapestry room . . . dead . . . strangled.'

Superintendent Johnson sat in the library, taking down the evidence of the haggard revellers, who were ushered in upon him one by one. First, Tony Lee, his haunted eyes like dark hollows in a mask of grey paper.

'Miss Grayle had promised to dance with me the last dance before Sir Roger; it was a fox-trot. I waited for her in the passage under the musicians' gallery. She never came. I did not search for her. I did not see her dancing with anyone else. When the dance was nearly over, I went out into the garden, by way of the service door under the musicians' stair. I stayed in the garden till Sir Roger de Coverley was over—'

'Was anybody with you, sir?'

'No, nobody.'

'You stayed alone in the garden from – yes, from 1.20 to past 2 o'clock. Rather disagreeable, was it not, sir, with the snow on the ground?' The Superintendent glanced keenly from Tony's stained and sodden white shoes to his stained face.

'I didn't notice. The room was hot – I wanted air. I saw the waits arrive at about 1.40 – I daresay they saw me. I came in a little after 2 o'clock—'

'By the service door again, sir?'

'No; by the garden door on the other side of the house at the end of the passage which runs along beside the tapestry room. I heard singing going on in the ball-room and saw two men sitting in the little recess at the foot of the staircase on the left-hand side of the passage. I think one of them was the gardener. I went into the tapestry room—'

'With any particular purpose in mind, sir?'

'No – except that I wasn't keen on rejoining the party. I wanted to be quiet.' He paused; the Superin-tendent said nothing. 'Then I went into the tapestry room. The light was out. I switched it on and saw – Miss Grayle. She was lying close against the radiator. I thought she had fainted. I went over to her and found she was – dead. I only waited long enough to be sure, and then I went into the ballroom and gave the alarm.'

'Thank you, sir. Now, may I ask, what were your relations with Miss Grayle?'

'I – I admired her very much.'

'Engaged to her, sir?'

'No, not exactly.'

'No quarrel – misunderstanding – anything of that sort?'

'Oh, no!'

Superintendent Johnson looked at him again, and again said nothing, but his experienced mind informed him:

'He's lying.'

Aloud he only thanked and dismissed Tony. The White King stumbled drearily out, and the Red King took his place.

'Miss Grayle,' said Frank Bellingham, 'is a friend of my wife and myself; she was staying at our house. Mr Lee is also our guest. We all came in one party. I believe

there was some kind of understanding between Miss
Grayle and Mr Lee – no actual engagement. She was a
very bright, lively, popular girl. I have known her for
about six years, and my wife has known her since our
marriage. I know of no one who could have borne a
grudge against Miss Grayle. I danced with her the last
dance but two – it was a waltz. After that came a fox-
trot and then Sir Roger. She left me at the end of the
waltz; I think she said she was going upstairs to tidy.
I think she went out by the door at the upper end of
the ballroom. I never saw her again. The ladies'
dressing-room is on the second floor, next door to the
picture-gallery. You reach it by the staircase that goes
up from the garden-passage. You have to pass the door
of the tapestry room to get there. The only other way
to the dressing-room is by the stair at the east end of
the ballroom, which goes up to the picture-gallery. You
would then have to pass through the picture-gallery to
get to the dressing-room. I know the house well; my
wife and I have often stayed here.'

Next came Lady Hermione, whose evidence, delivered at great length, amounted to this:

'Charmian Grayle was a minx and no loss to anybody. I am not surprised that someone has strangled
her. Women like that ought to be strangled. I would
cheerfully have strangled her myself. She has been
making Tony Lee's life a burden to him for the last six
weeks. I saw her flirting with Mr Vibart tonight on purpose to make Mr Lee jealous. She made eyes at Mr
Bellingham and Mr Playfair. She made eyes at everybody. I should think at least half a dozen people had
very good reason to wish her dead.'

Mr Vibart, who arrived dressed in a gaudy Polo cos
tume, and still ludicrously clutching a hobby-hor

said that he had danced several times that evening with Miss Grayle. She was a damn sportin' girl, rattlin' good fun. Well, a bit hot, perhaps, but, dash it all, the poor kid was dead. He might have kissed her once or twice, perhaps, but no harm in that. Well, perhaps poor old Lee did take it a bit hard. Miss Grayle liked pulling Tony's leg. He himself had liked Miss Grayle and was dashed cut-up about the whole beastly business.

Mrs Bellingham confirmed her husband's evidence. Miss Grayle had been their guest, and they were all on the very best of terms. She felt sure that Mr Lee and Miss Grayle had been very fond of one another. She had not seen Miss Grayle during the last three dances, but had attached no importance to that. If she had thought about it at all, she would have supposed Miss Grayle was sitting out with somebody. She herself had not been up to the dressing-room since about midnight, and had not seen Miss Grayle go upstairs. She had first missed Miss Grayle when they all stood up for Sir Roger.

Mrs Wrayburn mentioned that she had seen Miss Carstairs in the ballroom looking for Mr Lee, just as Sir Charles Deverill went down to speak to the band. Miss Carstairs had then mentioned that Mr Playfair was in the north corridor, waiting for Miss Grayle. She could say for certain that the time was then 1.28. She had seen Mr Playfair himself at 1.30. He had looked in from the corridor and gone out again. The whole party had then been standing up together, except Miss Grayle, Miss Carstairs, Mr Lee and Mr Playfair. She knew that, because Sir Charles had counted the couples.

Then came Jim Playfair, with a most valuable piece of evidence.

Grayle was engaged to me for Sir Roger de ... went to wait for her in the north corridor as

26

soon as the previous dance was over. That was at 1.25. I sat on the settee in the eastern half of the corridor. I saw Sir Charles go down to speak to the band. Almost immediately afterwards, I saw Miss Grayle come out of the passage under the musicians' gallery and go up the stairs at the end of the corridor. I called out: "Hurry up! they're just going to begin." I do not think she heard me; she did not reply. I am quite sure I saw her. The staircase has open banisters. There is no light in that corner except from the swinging lantern in the corridor, but that is very powerful. I could not be mistaken in the costume. I waited for Miss Grayle till the dance was half over; then I gave it up and joined forces with Miss Carstairs, who had also mislaid her partner.'

The maid in attendance on the dressing-room was next examined. She and the gardener were the only two servants who had not danced Sir Roger. She had not quitted the dressing-room at any time since supper, except that she might have gone as far as the door. Miss Grayle had certainly not entered the dressing-room during the last hour of the dance.

The Vicar, much worried and distressed, said that his party had arrived by the garden door at 1.40. He had noticed a man in a white costume smoking a cigarette in the garden. The waits had removed their outer clothing in the garden passage and then gone out to take up their position in the north corridor. Nobody had passed them till Mr Lee had come in with his sad news.

Mr Ephraim Dodd, the sexton, made an important addition to this evidence. This aged gentleman was, as he confessed, no singer, but was accustomed to go round with the waits to carry the lantern and collecting-box. He had taken a seat in the garden passage 'to rest me pore feet.' He had seen the gentleman come in from the garden 'all in white with a crown on 'is 'ead.' The choir were then singing 'Bring me flesh and bring me wine.' The gentleman had looked about a bit, 'made a face, like,' and gone into the room at the foot of the stairs. He hadn't been absent 'more nor a minute,' when. he 'come out faster than he gone in,' and had rushed immediately into the ballroom.

In addition to all this, there was, of course, the evidence of Dr Pattison. He was a guest at the dance, and had hastened to view the body of Miss Grayle as soon as the alarm was given. He was of opinion that she had been brutally strangled by someone standing in front of her. She was a tall, strong girl, and he thought it would have needed a man's strength to overpower her. When he saw her at five minutes past two he concluded that she must have been killed within the last hour, but not within the last five minutes or so. The body was still quite warm, but, since it had fallen close to the hot radiator, they could not rely very much upon that indication.

Superintendent Johnson rubbed a thoughtful ear and turned to Lord Peter Wimsey, who had been able to confirm much of the previous evidence and, in particular, the exact times at which various incidents had occurred. The Superintendent knew Wimsey well, and made no bones about taking him into his confidence.

'You see how it stands, my lord. If the poor young lady was killed when Dr Pattison says, it narrows it down a good bit. She was last seen dancing with Mr Bellingham at – call it 1.20. At 2 o'clock she was dead. That gives us forty minutes. But if we're to believe Mr Playfair, it narrows it down still further. He says he saw her alive just after Sir Charles went down to speak to the band, which you put at 1.28. That means that there's only five people who could possibly have done it, because all the rest were in the ballroom after that, dancing Sir Roger. There's the maid in the dressing-room; between you and me, sir, I think we can leave her out. She's a little slip of a thing, and it's not clear what motive she could have had. Besides, I've known her from a child, and she isn't the sort to do it. Then there's the gardener; I haven't seen him yet, but there again, he's a man I know well, and I'd as soon suspect myself. Well now, there's this Mr Tony Lee, Miss Carstairs, and Mr Playfair himself. The girl's the least probable, for physical reasons, and besides, strangling isn't a woman's crime – not as a rule. But Mr Lee – that's a queer story, if you like. What was he doing all that time out in the garden by himself?'

'It sounds to me,' said Wimsey, 'as if Miss Grayle had given him the push and he had gone into the garden to eat worms.'

'Exactly, my lord; and that's where his motive might come in.'

'So it might,' said Wimsey, 'but look here. There's a couple of inches of snow on the ground. If you can confirm the time at which he went out, you ought to be able to see, from his tracks, whether he came in again before Ephraim Dodd saw him. Also, where he went in the interval and whether he was alone.'

'That's a good idea, my lord. I'll send my sergeant to make inquiries.'

'Then there's Mr Bellingham. Suppose he killed her after the end of his waltz with her. Did anyone see him in the interval between that and the fox-trot?'

'Quite, my lord. I've thought of that. But you see where *that* leads. It means that Mr Playfair must have been in a conspiracy with him to do it. And from all we hear, that doesn't seem likely.'

'No more it does. In fact, I happen to know that Mr Bellingham and Mr Playfair were not on the best of terms. You can wash that out.'

'I think so, my lord. And that brings us to Mr Playfair. It's him we're relying on for the time. We haven't found anyone who saw Miss Grayle during the dance before his – that was the fox-trot. What was to prevent him doing it then? Wait a bit. What does he say himself? Says he danced the fox-trot with the Duchess of Denver.' The Superintendent's face fell, and he hunted through his notes again. 'She confirms that. Says she was with him during the interval and danced the whole dance with him. Well, my lord, I suppose we can take Her Grace's word for it.'

'I think you can,' said Wimsey, smiling. 'I've known my mother practically since my birth, and have always found her very reliable.'

'Yes, my lord. Well, that brings us to the end of the fox-trot. After that, Miss Carstairs saw Mr Playfair waiting in the north corridor. She says she noticed him several times during the interval and spoke to him. And Mrs Wrayburn saw him there at 1.30 or thereabouts. Then at 1.45 he and Miss Carstairs came and joined the company. Now, is there anyone who can check all these points? That's the next thing we've got to see to.'

Within a very few minutes, abundant confirmation was forthcoming. Mervyn Bunter, Lord Peter's personal man, said that he had been helping to take refreshments along to the buffet. Throughout the interval between the waltz and the fox-trot, Mr Lee had been standing by the service door beneath the musicians' stair, and half-way through the fox-trot he had been seen to go out into the garden by way of the servants' hall. The police-sergeant had examined the tracks in the snow and found that Mr Lee had not been joined by any other person, and that there was only the one set of his footprints, leaving the house by the servants' hall and returning by the garden door near the tapestry room. Several persons were also found who had seen Mr Bellingham in the interval between the waltz and the fox-trot, and who were able to say that he had danced the fox-trot through with Mrs Bellingham, Joan Carstairs had also been seen continuously throughout the waltz and the fox-trot, and during the following interval and the beginning of Sir Roger. Moreover, the servants who had danced at the lower end of the room were positive that from 1.29 to 1.45 Mr Playfair had sat continuously on the settee in the north corridor, except for the few seconds during which he had glanced into the ballroom. They were also certain that during that time no one had gone up the staircase at the lower end of the corridor, while Mr Dodd was equally positive that, after 1.40, nobody except Mr Lee had entered the garden passage or the tapestry room.

Finally, the circle was closed by William Hoggarty, the gardener. He asserted with the most obvious sincerity that from 1.30 to 1.40 he had been stationed in the garden passage to receive the waits and marshal them to their places. During that time, no one had come down the stair from the picture-gallery or entered the tapestry room. From 1.40 onwards, he had sat beside Mr Dodd in the passage and nobody had passed him except Mr Lee.

These points being settled, there was no further reason to doubt Jim Playfair's evidence, since his partners were able to prove his whereabouts during the waltz, the fox-trot and the intervening interval. At 1.28 or just after, he had seen Charmian Grayle alive. At 2.00 she had been found dead in the tapestry room. During that interval, no one had been seen to enter the room, and every person had been accounted for.

At 6 o'clock, the exhausted guests had been allowed to go to their rooms, accommodation being provided in the house for those who, like the Bellinghams, had come from a distance, since the Superintendent had announced his intention of interrogating them all afresh later in the day.

This new inquiry produced no result. Lord Peter Wimsey did not take part in it. He and Bunter (who was an expert photographer) occupied themselves in photographing the ballroom and adjacent rooms and corridors from every imaginable point of view, for, as Lord Peter said, 'You never know what may turn out to be relevant.' Late in the afternoon they retired together to the cellar, where with dishes, chemicals and safe-light hastily procured from the local chemist, they proceeded to develop the plates.

'That's the lot, my lord,' observed Bunter at length, sloshing the final plate in the water and tipping it into the hypo. 'You can switch the light on now, my lord.'

Wimsey did so, blinking in the sudden white glare.

'A very hefty bit of work,' said he. 'Hullo! What's that plateful of blood you've got there?'

'That's the red backing they put on these plates, my lord, to obviate halation. You may have observed me washing it off before inserting the plate in the developing-dish. Halation, my lord, is a phenomenon—'

Wimsey was not attending.

'But why didn't I notice it before?' he demanded. 'That stuff looked to me exactly like clear water.'

'So it would, my lord, in the red safe-light. The appearance of whiteness is produced,' added Bunter sententiously, 'by the reflection of *all* the available light. When all the available light is red, red and white are, naturally, indistinguishable. Similarly, in a green light—'

'Good God!' said Wimsey. 'Wait a moment, Bunter, I must think this out . . . Here! damn those plates – let them be. I want you upstairs.'

He led the way at a canter to the ballroom, dark now, with the windows in the south corridor already curtained and only the dimness of the December evening filtering through the high windows of the clerestory above the arcading. He first turned on the three great chandeliers in the ballroom itself. Owing to the heavy oak panelling that rose to the roof at both ends and all four angles of the room, these threw no light at all upon the staircase at the lower end of the north corridor. Next, he turned on the light in the four-sided hanging lantern, which hung in the north corridor above and between the two settees. A vivid shaft of green light immediately flooded the lower half of the corridor and the staircase; the upper half was bathed in strong amber, while the remaining sides of the lantern showed red towards the ballroom and blue towards the corridor wall.

Wimsey shook his head.

'Not much room for error there. Unless – I know! Run, Bunter, and ask Miss Carstairs and Mr Playfair to come here a moment.'

While Bunter was gone, Wimsey borrowed a stepladder from the kitchen and carefully examined the fixing of the lantern. It was a temporary affair, the lantern being supported by a hook screwed into a beam and lit by means of a flex run from the socket of a permanent fixture at a little distance.

'Now, you two,' said Wimsey, when the two guests arrived, 'I want to make a little experiment. Will you sit down on this settee, Playfair, as you did last night. And you, Miss Carstairs – I picked you out to help because you're wearing a white dress. Will you go up the stairs at the end of the corridor as Miss Grayle did last night. I want to know whether it looks the same to Playfair as it did then – bar all the other people, of course.'

He watched them as they carried out this manoeuvre. Jim Playfair looked puzzled.

'It doesn't seem quite the same, somehow. I don't know what the difference is, but there is a difference.'

Joan, returning, agreed with him.

'I was sitting on that other settee part of the time,' she said, 'and it looks different to me. I think it's darker.'

'Lighter,' said Jim.

'Good!' said Wimsey. 'That's what I wanted you to say. Now, Bunter, swing that lantern through a quarter-turn to the left.'

The moment this was done, Joan gave a little cry.

'That's it! That's it! The blue light! I remember thinking how frosty-faced those poor waits looked as they came in.'

'And you, Playfair?'

'That's right,' said Jim, satisfied. 'The light was red last night. *I* remember thinking how warm and cosy it looked.'

Wimsey laughed.

'We're on to it, Bunter. What's the chessboard rule? *The Queen stands on a square of her own colour.* Find the

34

maid who looked after the dressing-room, and ask her whether Mrs Bellingham was there last night between the fox-trot and Sir Roger.'

In five minutes Bunter was back with his report.

'The maid says, my lord, that Mrs Bellingham did not come into the dressing-room at that time. But she saw her come out of the picture-gallery and run downstairs towards the tapestry room just as the band struck up Sir Roger.'

'And that,' said Wimsey, 'was at 1.29.'

'Mrs Bellingham?' said Jim. 'But you said you saw her yourself in the ballroom before 1.30. She couldn't have had time to commit the murder.'

'No, she couldn't,' said Wimsey. 'But Charmian Grayle was dead long before that. It was the Red Queen, not the White, you saw upon the staircase. Find out why Mrs Bellingham lied about her movements, and then we shall know the truth.'

'A very sad affair, my lord,' said Superintendent Johnson, some hours later. 'Mr Bellingham came across with it like a gentleman as soon as we told him we had evidence against his wife. It appears that Miss Grayle knew certain facts about him which would have been very damaging to his political career. She'd been getting money out of him for years. Earlier in the evening she surprised him by making fresh demands. During the last waltz they had together, they went into the tapestry room and a quarrel took place. He lost his temper and laid hands on her. He says he never meant to hurt her seriously, but she started to scream and he took hold of her throat to silence her and – sort of accidentally – throttled her. When he found what he'd done, he left her there and came away, feeling, as he says, all of a

35

daze. He had the next dance with his wife. He told her what had happened, and then discovered that he'd left the little sceptre affair he was carrying in the room with the body. Mrs Bellingham – she's a brave woman – undertook to fetch it back. She slipped through the dark passage under the musicians' gallery – which was empty – and up the stair to the picture-gallery. She did not hear Mr Playfair speak to her. She ran through the gallery and down the other stair, secured the sceptre and hid it under her own dress. Later, she heard from Mr Playfair about what he saw, and realised that in the red light he had mistaken her for the White Queen: In the early hours of this morning, she slipped downstairs and managed to get the lantern shifted round. Of course, she's an accessory after the fact, but she's the kind of wife a man would like to have. I hope they let her off light.'

'Amen!' said Lord Peter Wimsey.

THE IMAGE IN THE MIRROR

The little man with the cow-lick seemed so absorbed in the book that Wimsey had not the heart to claim his property, but, drawing up the other arm-chair and placing his drink within easy reach, did his best to entertain himself with the Dunlop Book, which graced, as usual, one of the tables in the lounge.

The little man read on, his elbows squared upon the arms of his chair, his ruffled red head bent anxiously over the test. He breathed heavily, and when he came to the turn of the page, he set the thick volume down on his knee and used both hands for his task. Not what is called 'a great reader', Wimsey decided.

When he reached the end of the story, he turned laboriously back, and read one passage over again with attention. Then he laid the book, still open, upon the table, and in so doing caught Wimsey's eye.

'I beg your pardon, sir,' he said in his rather thin Cockney voice, 'is this your book?'

'It doesn't matter at all,' said Wimsey graciously, 'I know it by heart. I only brought it along with me because it's handy for reading a few pages when you're stuck in a place like this for the night. You can always take it up and find something entertaining.'

'This chap Wells,' pursued the red-haired man, 'he's what you'd call a very clever writer, isn't he? It's wonderful how he makes it all so real, and yet some of the things he says, you wouldn't hardly think they could be really possible. Take this story now; would you say, sir, a thing like that could actually happen to a person, as it might be you – or me?'

Wimsey twisted his head round so as to get a view of the page.

'*The Plattner Experiment*,' he said, 'that's the one about the schoolmaster who was blown into the fourth dimension and came back with his right and left sides reversed. Well, no, I don't suppose such a thing would really occur in real life, though of course it's very fascinating to play with the idea of a fourth dimension.'

'Well –' He paused and looked up shyly at Wimsey. 'I don't rightly understand about this fourth dimension. I didn't know there was such a place, but he makes it all very clear no doubt to them that know science. But this right-and-left business, now, I know that's a fact. By experience, if you'll believe me.'

Wimsey extended his cigarette-case. The little man made an instinctive motion towards it with his left hand and then seemed to check himself and stretched his right across.

'There, you see. I'm always left-handed when I don't think about it. Same as this Plattner. I fight against it, but it doesn't seem any use. But I wouldn't mind that – it's a small thing and plenty of people are left-handed and think nothing of it. No. It's the dretful anxiety of not knowing what I mayn't be doing when I'm in this fourth dimension or whatever it is.'

He sighed deeply.

'I'm worried, that's what I am, worried to death.'

'Suppose you tell me about it,' said Wimsey.

'I don't like telling people about it, because they might think I had a slate loose. But it's fairly getting on my nerves. Every morning when I wake up I wonder what I've been doing in the night and whether it's the day of the month it ought to be. I can't get any peace till I see the morning paper, and even then I can't be sure . . .

'Well, I'll tell you, if you won't take it as a bore or a liberty. It all began –' He broke off and glanced nervously about the room. 'There's nobody to see. If you wouldn't mind, sir, putting your hand just here a minute—'

He unbuttoned his rather regrettable double-breasted waist-coat, and laid a hand on the part of his anatomy usually considered to indicate the site of his heart.

'By all means,' said Wimsey, doing as he was requested.

'Do you feel anything?'

'I don't know that I do,' said Wimsey. 'What ought I to feel? A swelling or anything? If you mean your pulse, the wrist is a better place.'

'Oh, you can feel it *there*, all right,' said the little man. 'Just try the other side of the chest, sir.'

Wimsey obediently moved his hand across.

'I seem to detect a little flutter,' he said after a pause.

'You do? Well, you wouldn't expect to find it that side and not the other, would you? Well, that's where it is. I've got my heart on the right side, that's what I wanted you to feel for yourself.'

'Did it get displaced in an illness?' asked Wimsey sympathetically.

'In a manner of speaking. But that's not all. My liver's got round the wrong side, too, and my organs. I've had a doctor see it, and he told me I was all reversed. I've got my appendix on my left side – that is, I had till they took it away. If we was private, now, I could show you the scar. It was a great surprise to the surgeon

39

when they told him about me. He said afterwards it made it quite awkward for him, coming left-handed to the operation, as you might say.'

'It's unusual, certainly,' said Wimsey, 'but I believe such cases do occur sometimes.'

'Not the way it occurred to me. It happened in an air-raid.'

'In an air-raid?' said Wimsey, aghast.

'Yes – and if that was all it had done to me I'd put up with it and be thankful. Eighteen I was then, and I'd just been called up. Previous to that I'd been working in the packing department at Crichton's – you've heard of them, I expect – Crichton's for Admirable Advertising, with offices in Holborn. My mother was living in Brixton, and I'd come up to town on leave from the training-camp. I'd been seeing one or two of my old pals, and I thought I'd finish the evening by going to see a film at the Stoll. It was after supper – I had just time to get into the last house, so I cut across from Leicester Square through Covent Garden Market. Well, I was getting along when whallop! A bomb came down it seemed to me right under my feet, and everything went black for a bit.'

'That was the raid that blew up Odham's, I suppose.'

'Yes, it was January 28th, 1918. Well, as I say, everything went right out. Next thing as I knew, I was walking in some place in broad daylight, with green grass all round me and trees and water to the side of me, and knowing no more about how I got there than the man in the moon.'

'Good Lord!' said Wimsey. 'And was it the fourth dimension, do you think?'

'Well, no, it wasn't. It was Hyde Park, as I come to when I had my wits about me. I was along the bank of the Serpentine and there was a seat with some women sitting on it, and children playing about.'

'Had the explosion damaged you?'

'Nothing to see or feel, except that I had a big bruise on one hip and shoulder as if I'd been chucked up against something. I was fairly staggered. The air-raid had gone right out of my mind, don't you see, and I couldn't imagine how I came there, and why I wasn't at Crichton's. I looked at my watch, but that had stopped. I was feeling hungry. I felt in my pocket and found some money there but it wasn't as much as I should have had – not by a long way. But I felt I must have a bit of something, so I got out of the Park by the Marble Arch gate, and went into a Lyons. I ordered two poached on toast and a pot of tea and while I was waiting I took up a paper that somebody had left on the seat. Well, that finished me. The last thing I remembered was starting off to see that film on the 28th – and here was the date on the paper – January 30th! I'd lost a whole day and two nights somewhere!'

'Shock,' suggested Wimsey. The little man took the suggestion and put his own meaning on it.

'Shock? I should think it was. I was scared out of my life. The girl who brought my eggs must have thought I was barmy. I asked her what day of the week it was and she said "Friday". There wasn't any mistake.

'Well, I don't want to make this bit too long because that's not the end by a long chalk. I got my meal down somehow, and went to see a doctor. He asked me what I remembered doing last, and I told him about the film and he asked whether I was out in the air-raid. Well, then it came back to me, and I remembered the bomb

41

falling, but nothing more. He said I'd had a nervous shock and lost my memory a bit, and that it often happened and I wasn't to worry. And then he said he'd look me over to see if I'd got hurt at all. So he started in with his stethoscope, and all of a sudden he said to me:

'"Why, you keep your heart on the wrong side, my lad!"

'"Do I?" said I. "That's the first I've head of it."

'Well, he looked me over pretty thoroughly, and then he told me what I've told you, that I was all reversed inside, and he asked a lot of questions about my family. I told him I was an only child and my father was dead – killed by a motor-lorry, he was, when I was a kid of ten – and I lived with my mother in Brixton and all that. And he said I was an unusual case, but there was nothing to worry about. Bar being wrong side round I was sound as a bell, and he told me to go home and take things quietly for a day or two.

'Well, I did, and I felt all right, and I thought that was the end of it, though I'd overstayed my leave and had a bit of a job explaining myself to the R.T.O. It wasn't till several months afterwards the draft was called up, and I went along for my farewell leave. I was having a cup of coffee in the Mirror Hall at the Strand Corner House – you know it, down the steps?'

Wimsey nodded.

'All the big looking-glasses all round. I happened to look into the one near me, and I saw a young lady smiling at me as if she knew me. I saw her reflection, that is, if you understand me. Well, I couldn't make it out, for I had never seen her before, and I didn't take any notice, thinking she'd mistook me for somebody else. Besides, though I wasn't so very old then, I thought I knew her sort, and my mother had always brought me up strict. I looked away and went on with my coffee, and all of a sudden a voice said quite close to me:

'"Hullo, Ginger – aren't you going to say good evening?"

'I looked up and there she was. Pretty, too, if she hadn't been painted up too much.

'"I'm afraid," I said, rather stiff, "you have the advantage of me, miss."

'"Oh, Ginger," says she, "Mr Duckworthy, and after Wednesday night!" A kind of mocking way she had of speaking.

'I hadn't thought so much of her calling me Ginger, because that's what any girl would say to a fellow with my sort of hair, but when she got my name off so pat, I tell you it did give me a turn.

'"You seem to think we're acquainted, miss," said I.

'"Well, I should rather say so, shouldn't you?" said she.

'There! I needn't go into it all. From what she said I found out she thought she'd met me one night and taken me home with her. And what frightened me most of all, she said it had happened on the night of the big raid.

'"It *was* you," she said, staring into my face a little puzzled like. "Of course it was you. I knew you in a minute when I saw your face in the glass."

'Of course, I couldn't say that it hadn't been. I knew no more of what I'd been and done that night than the babe unborn. But it upset me cruelly, because I was an innocent sort of lad in those days and hadn't ever gone with girls, and it seemed to me if I'd done a thing like that I ought to know about it. It seemed to me I'd been doing wrong and not getting full value for my money either.

'I made some excuse to get rid of her, and I wondered what else I'd been doing. She couldn't tell me farther than the morning of the 29th, and it worried me a bit wondering if I'd done any other queer things.'

'It must have,' said Wimsey, and put his finger on the bell. When the waiter arrived, he ordered drinks for two and disposed himself to listen to the rest of Mr Duckworthy's adventures.

'I didn't think much about it, though,' went on the little man; 'we went abroad and I saw my first corpse and dodged my first shell and had my first dose of the trenches, and I hadn't much time for what they call introspection.

'The next queer thing that happened was in the C.C.S. at Ypres. I'd got a blighty one near Caudry in September during the advance from Cambrai – half buried, I was, in a mine explosion and laid out unconscious near twenty-four hours it must have been. When I came to, I was wandering about somewhere behind the lines with a nasty hole in my shoulder. Somebody had bandaged it up for me, but I hadn't any recollection of that. I walked a long way, not knowing where I was, till at last I fetched up in an aid-post. They fixed me up and sent me down the line to a base hospital. I was pretty feverish, and the next thing I knew, I was in bed with a nurse looking after me. The bloke in the next bed to mine was asleep. I got talking to a chap in the next bed beyond him, and he told me where I was, when all of a sudden the other man woke up and says:

'"My God," he says, "your dirty ginger-haired swine, it's you, is it? What have you done with them vallables?"

'I tell you, I was struck all of a heap. Never seen the man in my life. But he went on at me and made such a row, the nurse came running in to see what was up. All the men were sitting up in bed listening – you never saw anything like it.

'The upshot was, as soon as I could understand what this fellow was driving at, that he'd been sharing a shell-hole with a chap that he said was me, and that this chap and he had talked together a bit and then, when he was weak and helpless, the chap had looted his money and watch and revolver and what not and gone off with them. A nasty, dirty trick, and I couldn't blame him for making a row about it, if true. But I said and stand to it, it wasn't me, but some other fellow of the same name. He said he recognised me – said he and this other chap had been together a whole day, and he knew every feature in his face and couldn't be mistaken. However, it seemed this bloke had said he belonged to the Blankshires, and I was able to show my papers and prove I belonged to the Buffs, and eventually the bloke apologised and said he must have made a mistake. He died, anyhow, a few days after, and we all agreed he must have been wandering a bit. The two divisions were fighting side by side in that dust-up and it was possible for them to get mixed up. I tried afterwards to find out whether by any chance I had a double in the Blankshires, but they sent me back home, and before I was fit again the Armistice was signed, and I didn't take any more trouble.

'I went back to my old job after the war, and things seemed to settle down a bit. I got engaged when I was twenty-one to a regular good girl, and I thought everything in the garden was lovely. And then, one day – up it all went! My mother was dead then, and I was living by myself in lodgings. Well, one day I got a letter from my intended, saying that she had seen me down at

Southend on the Sunday, and that was enough for her. All was over between us.

'Now, it was most unfortunate that I'd had to put off seeing her that week-end, owing to an attack of influenza. It's a cruel thing to be ill all alone in lodgings, and nobody to look after you. You might die there all on your own and nobody the wiser. Just an unfurnished room I had, you see, and no attendance, and not a soul came near me, though I was pretty bad. But my young lady she said as she had seen me down at Southend with another young woman, and she would take no excuse. Of course, I said, what was *she* doing down at Southend without me, anyhow, and that tore it. She sent me back the ring, and the episode, as they say, was closed.

'But the thing that troubled me was, I was getting that shaky in my mind, how did I know I hadn't been to Southend without knowing it? I thought I'd been half sick and half asleep in my lodgings, but it was misty-like to me. And knowing the things I had done other times – well, there! I hadn't any clear recollection one way or another, except fever-dreams. I had a vague recollection of wandering and walking somewhere for hours together. Delirious, I thought I was, but it might have been sleepwalking for all I knew. I hadn't a leg to stand on by way of evidence. I felt it very hard, losing my intended like that, but I could have got over that if it hadn't been for the fear of myself and my brain giving way or something.

'You may think this is all foolishness and I was just being mixed up with some other fellow of the same name that happened to be very like me. But now I'll tell you something.

'Terrible dreams I got to having about that time. There was one thing as always haunted me – a thing

46

that had frightened me as a little chap. My mother, though she was a good, strict woman, liked to go to a cinema now and again. Of course, in those days they weren't like what they are now, and I expect we should think those old pictures pretty crude if we was to see them, but we thought a lot of them at that time. When I was about seven or eight I should think, she took me with her to see a thing – I remember the name now – *The Student of Prague*, it was called. I've forgotten the story, but it was a costume piece, about a young fellow at the university who sold himself to the devil, and one day his reflection came stalking out of the mirror on its own, and went about committing dreadful crimes, so that everybody thought it was him. At least, I think it was that, but I forget the details, it's so long ago. But what I shan't forget in a hurry is the fright it gave me to see that dretful figure come out of the mirror. It was that ghastly to see it, I cried and yelled, and after a time mother had to take me out. For months and years after that I used to dream of it. I'd dream I was looking in a great long glass, same as the student in the picture, and after a bit I'd see my reflection smiling at me and I'd walk up to the mirror holding out my left hand, it might be, and seeing myself walking to meet me with its right hand out. And just as it came up to me, it would suddenly – that was the awful moment – turn its back on me and walk away into the mirror again, grinning over its shoulder, and suddenly I'd know that *it* was the real person and *I* was only the reflection, and I'd make a dash after it into the mirror, and then everything would go grey and misty round me and with the horror of it I'd wake up all of a perspiration.'

'Uncommonly disagreeable,' said Wimsey. 'That legend of the *Doppelganger,* it's one of the oldest and the most widespread and never fails to terrify me. When *I* was a kid, my nurse had a trick that frightened me. If we'd been out, and she was asked if we'd met anybody, she used to say, "Oh, no – we saw nobody nicer than ourselves." I used to toddle after her in terror of coming round a corner and seeing a horrid and similar pair pouncing out at us. Of course I'd have rather died than tell a soul how the thing terrified me. Rum little beam, kids.'

The little man nodded thoughtfully.

'Well,' he went on, 'about that time the nightmare came back. At first it was only at intervals, you know, but it grew on me. At last it started coming every night. I hadn't hardly closed my eyes before there was the long mirror and the thing coming grinning along, always with its hand out as if it meant to catch hold of me and pull me through the glass. Sometimes I'd wake up with the shock, but sometimes the dream went on, and I'd be stumbling for hours through a queer sort of world – all mist and half-lights, and the walls would be all crooked, like they are in that picture of "Dr Caligari". Lunatic, that's what it was. Many's the time I've sat up all night for fear of going to sleep. I didn't know, you see. I used to lock the bedroom door and hide the key for fear – you see, I didn't know what I might be doing. But then I read in a book that sleepwalkers can remember the places where they've hidden things when they were awake. So that was no use.'

'Why didn't you get someone to share the room with you?'

'Well, I did.' He hesitated. 'I got a woman – she was a good kid. The dream went away then. I had blessed peace for three years. I was fond of that girl. Damned fond of her. Then she died.'

He gulped down the last of his whisky and blinked.

'Influenza, it was. Pneumonia. It kind of broke me up. Pretty she was, too . . .

'After that, I was alone again. I felt bad about it. I couldn't – I didn't like – but the dreams came back. Worse. I dreamed about doing things – well! That doesn't matter now.

'And one day it came in broad daylight . . .

'I was going along Holborn at lunch-time. I was still at Crichton's. Head of the packing department I was then, and doing pretty well. It was a wet beast of a day, I remember – dark and drizzling. I wanted a hair-cut. There's a barber's shop on the south side, about half way along – one of those places where you go down a passage and there's a door at the end with a mirror and the name written across it in gold letters. You know what I mean.

'I went in there. There was a light in the passage, so I could see quite plainly. As I got up to the mirror I could see my reflection coming to meet me, and all of a sudden the awful dream-feeling came over me. I told myself it was all nonsense and put my hand out to the door-handle – my left hand, because the handle was that side and I was still apt to be left-handed when I didn't think about it.

'The reflection, of course, put out its right hand – that was all right, of course – and I saw my own figure in my old squash hat and burberry – but the face – oh, my God! It was grinning at me – and then just like in the dream, it suddenly turned its back and walked away from me looking over its shoulder—

'I had my hand on the door, and it opened, and I felt myself stumbling and falling over the threshold.

49

'After that, I don't remember anything more. I woke up in my own bed and there was a doctor with me. He told me I had fainted in the street, and they'd found some letters on me with my address and taken me home.

'I told the doctor all about it, and he said I was in a highly nervous condition and ought to find a change of work and get out in the open air more.

'They were very decent to me at Crichton's. They put me on to inspecting their outdoor publicity. You know. One goes round from town to town inspecting the hoardings and seeing what posters are damaged or badly placed and reporting on them. They gave me a Morgan to run about in. I'm on that job now.

'The dreams are better. But I still have them. Only a few nights ago it came to me. One of the worst I've ever had. Fighting and strangling in a black, misty place. I'd tracked the devil – my other self – and got him down. I can feel my fingers on his throat now – killing myself.

'That was in London. I'm always worse in London. Then I came up here . . .

'You see why that book interested me. The fourth dimension . . . it's not a thing I ever heard of, but this man Wells seems to know all about it. You're educated now. Daresay you've been to college and all that. What do you think about it, eh?'

'I should think, you know,' said Wimsey, 'it was more likely your doctor was right. Nerves and all that.'

'Yes, but that doesn't account for me having got twisted round the way I am, now, does it? Legends, you talked of. Well, there's some people think those medeeval johnnies knew quite a lot. I don't say I believe in devils and all that. But maybe some of them may have been afflicted, same as me. It stands to reason they wouldn't talk such a lot about it if they hadn't felt it, if you see what I mean. But what I'd like to know is, can't I get back any way? I tell you, it's a weight on my mind. I never know, you see.'

'I shouldn't worry too much, if I were you,' said Wimsey. 'I'd stick to the fresh-air life. And I'd get married. Then you'd have a check on your movements, don't you see. And the dreams might go again.'

'Yes. Yes. I've thought of that. But – did you read about that man the other day? Strangled his wife in his sleep, that's what he did. Now, supposing I – that would be a terrible thing to happen to a man, wouldn't it? Those dreams . . .'

He shook his head and stared thoughtfully into the fire. Wimsey, after a short interval of silence, got up and went out into the bar. The landlady and the waiter and the barmaid were there, their heads close together over the evening paper. They were talking animatedly, but stopped abruptly at the sound of Wimsey's footsteps.

Ten minutes later, Wimsey returned to the lounge. The little man had gone. Taking up his motoring-coat, which he had flung on a chair, Wimsey went upstairs to his bedroom. He undressed slowly and thoughtfully, put on his pyjamas and dressing-gown, and then, pulling a copy of the *Evening News* from his motoring coat pocket, he studied a front-page item attentively for some time. Presently he appeared to come to some decision, for he got up and opened his door cautiously. The passage was empty and dark. Wimsey switched on a torch and walked quietly along, watching the floor. Opposite one of the doors he stopped, contemplating a pair of shoes which stood waiting to be cleaned. Then he softly tried the door. It was locked. He tapped cautiously.

A red head emerged.

'May I come in a moment?' said Wimsey, in a whisper.

The little man stepped back, and Wimsey followed him in.

'What's up?' said Mr Duckworthy.

'I want to talk to you,' said Wimsey. 'Get back into bed, because it may take some time.'

The little man looked at him, scared, but did as he was told. Wimsey gathered the folds of his dressing-gown closely about him, screwed his monocle more firmly into his eye, and sat down on the edge of the bed. He looked at Mr Duckworthy a few minutes without speaking, and then said:

'Look here. You've told me a queerish story tonight. For some reason I believe you. Possibly it only shows what a silly ass I am, but I was born like that, so it's past praying for. Nice, trusting nature and so on. Have you seen the paper this evening?'

He pushed the *Evening News* into Mr Duckworthy's hand and bent the monocle on him more glassily than ever.

On the front page was a photograph. Underneath was a panel in bold type, boxed for greater emphasis:

'The police at Scotland Yard are anxious to get in touch with the original of this photograph, which was found in the handbag of Miss Jessie Haynes, whose dead body was found strangled on Barnes Common last Thursday morning. The photograph bears on the back the words "J. H. with love from R. D." Anybody recognising the photograph is asked to communicate immediately with Scotland Yard or any police station.'

Mr Duckworthy looked, and grew so white that Wimsey thought he was going to faint.

'Well?' said Wimsey.

'Oh, God, sir! Oh, God! It's come at last.' He whimpered and pushed the paper away, shuddering. 'I've always known something of this would happen. But as sure as I'm born I knew nothing about it.'

'It's you all right, I suppose?'

'The photograph's me all right. Though how it came there I *don't* know. I haven't had one taken for donkey's years, on my oath I haven't – except once in a staff group at Crichton's. But I tell you, sir, honest-to-God, there's times when I don't know what I'm doing, and that's a fact.'

Wimsey examined the portrait feature by feature.

'Your nose, now – it has a slight twist – if you'll excuse my referring to it – to the right, and so it has in the photograph. The left eyelid droops a little. That's correct, too. The forehead here seems to have a distinct bulge on the left side – unless that's an accident in the printing.'

'No!' Mr Duckworthy swept his tousled cow-lick aside. 'It's very conspicuous – unsightly, I always think, so I wear the hair over it.'

With the ginger lock pushed back, his resemblance to the photograph was more startling than before.

'My mouth's crooked, too.'

'So it is. Slants up to the left. Very attractive, a one-sided smile, I always think – on a face of your type, that is. I have known such things to look positively sinister.'

Mr Duckworthy smiled a faint, crooked smile.

'Do you know this girl, Jessie Haynes?'

53

'Not in my right sense, I don't, sir. Never heard of her except, of course, that I read about the murder in the papers. Strangled – oh, my God!' He pushed his hands out in front of him and stared woefully at them.

'What can I do? If I was to get away—'

'You can't. They've recognised you down in the bar. The police will probably be here in a few minutes. No' – as Duckworthy made an attempt to get out of bed – 'don't do that. It's no good, and it would only get you into worse trouble. Keep quiet and answer one or two questions. First of all, do you know who I am? No, how should you? My name's Wimsey – Lord Peter Wimsey—'

'The detective?'

'If you like to call it that. Now, listen. Where was it you lived at Brixton?'

The little man gave the address.

'Your mother's dead. Any other relatives?'

'There was an aunt. She came from somewhere in Surrey, I think. Aunt Susan, I used to call her. I haven't seen her since I was a kid.'

'Married?'

'Yes – oh, yes – Mrs Susan Brown.'

'Right. Were you left-handed as a child?'

'Well, yes, I was, at first. But mother broke me of it.'

'And the tendency came back after the air-raid. And were you ever ill as a child? To have the doctor, I mean?'

'I had measles once, when I was about four.'

'Remember the doctor's name?'

'They took me to the hospital.'

'Oh, of course. Do you remember the name of the barber in Holborn?'

This question came so unexpectedly as to stagger the wits of Mr Duckworthy, but after a while he said he thought it was Biggs or Briggs.

Wimsey sat thoughtfully for a moment, and then said:

'I think that's all. Except – oh, yes! What is your Christian name?'

'Robert.'

'And you assure me that, so far as you know, you had no hand in this business?'

'That,' said the little man, 'that I swear to. As far as I know, you know. Oh, my Lord! If only it was possible to prove an alibi! That's my only chance. But I'm so afraid, you see, that I *may* have done it. Do you think – do you think they would hang me for that?'

'Not if you could prove you knew nothing about it,' said Wimsey. He did not add that, even so, his acquaintance might probably pass the rest of his life at Broadmoor.

'And you know,' said Mr Duckworthy, 'if I'm to go about all my life killing people without knowing it, it would be much better that they should hang me and be done with it. It's a terrible thing to think of.'

'Yes, but you may not have done it, you know.'

'I hope not, I'm sure,' said Mr Duckworthy. 'I say – what's that?'

'The police, I fancy,' said Wimsey lightly. He stood up as a knock came at the door, and said heartily, 'Come in!'

The landlord, who entered first, seemed rather taken aback by Wimsey's presence.

'Come right in,' said Wimsey hospitably. 'Come in, sergeant; come in, officer. What can we do for you?'

'Don't,' said the landlord, 'don't make a row if you can help it.'

The police sergeant paid no attention to either of them, but stalked across to the bed and confronted the shrinking Mr Duckworthy.

'It's the man all right,' said he. 'Now, Mr Duckworthy, you'll excuse this late visit, but as you may have seen by the papers, we've been looking for a person answering your description, and there's no time like the present. We want—'

'I didn't do it,' cried Mr Duckworthy wildly. 'I know nothing about it—'

The officer pulled out his note-book and wrote: 'He said before any question was asked him, "I didn't do it."'

'You seem to know all about it,' said the sergeant.

'Of course he does,' said Wimsey; 'we've been having a little informal chat about it.'

'You have, have you? And who might you be – sir?' The last word appeared to be screwed out of the sergeant forcibly by the action of the monocle.

'I'm so sorry,' said Wimsey, 'I haven't a card on me at the moment. I am Lord Peter Wimsey.'

'Oh, indeed,' said the sergeant, 'And may I ask, my lord, what you know about this here?'

'You may, and I may answer if I like, you know. I know nothing at all about the murder. About Mr Duckworthy I know what he has told me and no more. I dare say he will tell you, too, if you ask him nicely. But no third degree, you know, sergeant. No Savidgery.'

Baulked by this painful reminder, the sergeant said, in a voice of annoyance:

'It's my duty to ask him what he knows about this.'

'I quite agree,' said Wimsey. 'As a good citizen, it's his duty to answer you. But it's a gloomy time of night, don't you think? Why not wait till the morning? Mr Duckworthy won't run away.'

'I'm not so sure of that.'

'Oh, but I am. I will undertake to produce him whenever you want him. Won't that do? You're not charging him with anything, I suppose?'

'Not yet,' said the sergeant.

'Splendid. Then it's all quite friendly and pleasant, isn't it? How about a drink?'

The sergeant refused this kindly offer with some gruffness in his manner.

'On the waggon?' inquired Wimsey sympathetically. 'Bad luck. Kidneys? Or liver, eh?'

The sergeant made no reply.

'Well, we are charmed to have had the pleasure of seeing you,' pursued Wimsey. 'You'll look us up in the morning, won't you? I've got to get back to town fairly early, but I'll drop in at the police-station on my way. You will find Mr Duckworthy in the lounge, here. It will be more comfortable for you than at your place. Must you be going? Well, good night, all.'

Later, Wimsey returned to Mr Duckworthy, after seeing the police off the premises.

'Listen,' he said, 'I'm going up to town to do what I can. I'll send you up a solicitor first thing in the morning. Tell him what you've told me, and tell the police what he tells you to tell them and no more. Remember, they can't force you to say anything or to go down to the police-station unless they charge you. If they do charge you, go quietly and say nothing. And whatever you do, don't run away, because if you do, you're done for.'

Wimsey arrived in town the following afternoon, and walked down Holborn, looking for a barber's shop. He found it without much difficulty. It lay, as Mr Duckworthy had described it, at the end of a narrow passage, and it had a long mirror in the door, with the name Briggs scrawled across it in gold letters. Wimsey stared at his own reflection distastefully.

'Check number one,' said he, mechanically setting his tie to rights. 'Have I been led up the garden? Or is it a case of fourth dimensional mystery? "The animals went in four by four, *vive la compagnie*! The camel he got stuck in the door." There is something intensely unpleasant about making a camel of one's self. It goes for days without a drink and its table-manners are objectionable. But there is no doubt that this door is made of looking-glass. Was it always so, I wonder? On, Wimsey, on. I cannot bear to be shaved again. Perhaps a haircut might be managed.'

He pushed the door open, keeping a stern eye on his reflection to see that it played him no trick.

Of his conversation with the barber, which was lively and varied, only one passage is deserving of record.

'It's some time since I was in here,' said Wimsey. 'Keep it short behind the ears. Been redecorated, haven't you?'

'Yes, sir. Looks quite smart, doesn't it?'

'The mirror on the outside of the door – that's new too, isn't it?'

'Oh, no, sir. That's been there ever since we took over.'

'Has it? Then it's longer ago than I thought. Was it there three years ago?'

'Oh yes, sir. Ten years Mr Briggs has been here, sir.'

'And the mirror too?'

'Oh, yes, sir.'

'Then it's my memory that's wrong. Senile decay setting in. "All, all are gone, the old familiar landmarks." No, thank you, if I go grey I'll go grey decently. I don't want any hair-tonics today, thank you. No, nor even an electric comb. I've had shocks enough.'

It worried him, though. So much so that when he emerged, he walked back a few yards along the street, and was suddenly struck by seeing the glass door of a teashop. It also lay at the end of a dark passage and had a gold name written across it. The name was 'The BRIDGET Tea-shop', but the door was of plain glass. Wimsey looked at it for a few moments and then went in. He did not approach the tea-tables, but accosted the cashier, who sat at a little glass desk inside the door.

Here he went straight to the point and asked whether the young lady remembered the circumstances of a man's having fainted in the doorway some years previously.

The cashier could not say; she had only been there three months, but she thought one of the waitresses might remember. The waitress was produced, and after some consideration, thought she did recollect something of the sort. Wimsey thanked her, said he was a journalist – which seemed to be accepted as an excuse for eccentric questions – parted with half a crown, and withdrew.

His next visit was to Carmelite House. Wimsey had friends in every newspaper office in Fleet Street, and made his way without difficulty to the room where photographs are filed for reference. The original of the 'J. D.' portrait was produced for his inspection.

'One of yours?' he asked.

'Oh, no. Sent out by Scotland Yard. Why? Anything wrong with it?'

'Nothing. I wanted the name of the original photographer, that's all.'

'Oh! Well, you'll have to ask them there. Nothing more I can do for you?'

'Nothing, thanks.'

Scotland Yard was easy. Chief-Inspector Parker was Wimsey's closest friend. An inquiry of him soon furnished the photographer's name, which was inscribed at the foot of the print. Wimsey voyaged off at once in search of the establishment, where his name readily secured an interview with the proprietor.

As he had expected, Scotland Yard had been there before him. All information at the disposal of the firm had already been given. It amounted to very little. The photograph had been taken a couple of years previously, and nothing particular was remembered about the sitter. It was a small establishment, doing a rapid business in cheap portraits, and with no pretensions to artistic refinements.

Wimsey asked to see the original negative, which, after some search, was produced.

Wimsey looked it over, laid it down, and pulled from his pocket the copy of the *Evening News* in which the print had appeared.

'Look at this,' he said.

The proprietor looked, then looked back at the negative

'Well, I'm dashed,' he said. 'That's funny.'

'It was done in the enlarging lantern, I take it,' said Wimsey.

'Yes. It must have been put in the wrong way round. Now, fancy that happening. You know, sir, we often have to work against time, and I suppose – but it's very careless. I shall have to inquire into it.'

'Get me a print of it right way round,' said Wimsey.

'Yes, sir, certainly, sir. At once.'

'And send one to Scotland Yard.'

'Yes, sir. Queer it should have been just this particular one, isn't it, sir? I wonder the party didn't notice. But we generally take three or four positions, and he might not remember, you know.'

'You'd better see if you've got any other positions and let me have them too.'

'I've done that already, sir, but there are none. No doubt this one was selected and the others destroyed. We don't keep all the rejected negatives, you know, sir. We haven't the space to file them. But I'll get three prints off at once.'

'Do,' said Wimsey. 'The sooner the better. Quick-dry them. And don't do any work on the prints.'

'No, sir. You shall have them in an hour or two, sir. But it's astonishing to me that the party didn't complain.'

'It's not astonishing,' said Wimsey. 'He probably thought it was the best likeness of the lot. And so it would be – to him. Don't you see – that's the only view he could ever take of his own face. That photograph, with the left and right sides reversed, is the face he sees in the mirror every day – the only face he can really recognise as his. "Wad the gods and giftie gie us", and all that.'

'Well, that's quite true, sir. And I'm much obliged to you for pointing the mistake out.'

Wimsey reiterated the need for haste, and departed. A brief visit to Somerset House followed; after which he called it a day and went home.

★

Inquiry in Brixton, in and about the address mentioned by Mr Duckworthy, eventually put Wimsey on to the track of persons who had known him and his mother. An aged lady who had kept a small greengrocery in the same street for the last forty years remembered all about them. She had the encyclopaedic memory of the almost illiterate, and was positive as to the date of their arrival.

'Thirty-two years ago, if we lives another month,' she said. 'Michaelmas it was they come. She was a nice-looking young woman, too, and my daughter, as was expecting her first took a lot of interest in the sweet little boy.'

'The boy was not born here?'

'Why, no, sir. Born somewheres on the south side, he was but I remember she never rightly said where – only that it was round about the New Cut. She was one of the quiet sort and kep' herself to herself. Never one to talk, she wasn't. Why even to my daughter, as might 'ave good reason for bein' interested, she wouldn't say much about 'ow she got through 'er bad time. Chlorry-form she said she 'ad, I know, and she disremembered about it, but it's my belief it 'ad gone 'ard with 'er and she didn't care to think overmuch about it. 'Er 'usband – a nice man 'e was, too – 'e says to me, "Don't remind 'er of it, Mrs 'Arbottle, don't remind 'er of it." Whether she was frightened or whether she was 'urt by it I don't know, but she didn't 'ave no more children. "Lor!" I says to 'er time and again, "you'll get used to it, my dear, when you've 'ad nine of 'em same as me," and she smiled but she never 'ad no more, none the more for that.'

'I suppose it does take some getting used to,' said Wimsey, 'but nine of them don't seem to have hurt *you*

Mrs Harbottle, if I may say so. You look extremely flourishing.'

'I keeps my 'ealth, sir, I am glad to say, though stouter than I used to be. Nine of them does 'ave a kind of spreading action on the figure. You wouldn't believe, sir, to look at me, as I'd a eighteen-inch waist when I was a girl. Many's the time me pore mother broke the laces on me, with 'er knee in me back and me 'olding on to the bed-post.'

'One must suffer to be beautiful,' said Wimsey politely. 'How old was the baby, then, when Mrs Duckworthy came to live in Brixton?'

'Three weeks old, 'e was, sir – a darling dear – and a lot of 'air on 'is 'ead. Black 'air it was then, but it turned into the brightest red you ever see – like them carrots there. It wasn't so pretty as 'is ma's, though much the same colour. He didn't favour 'er in the face, neither, nor yet 'is dad. She said 'e took after some of 'er side of the family.'

'Did you ever see any of the rest of the family?'

'Only 'er sister, Mrs Susan Brown. A big, stern, 'ard-faced woman she was – not like 'er sister. Lived in Evesham she did, as well I remembers, for I was gettin' my grass from them at the time. I never sees a bunch o' grass now but what I think of Mrs Susan Brown. Stiff, she was, with a small 'ead, very like a stick o' grass.'

Wimsey thanked Mrs Harbottle in a suitable manner and took the next train to Evesham. He was beginning to wonder where the chase might lead him, but discovered, much to his relief, that Mrs Susan Brown was well known in the town, being a pillar of the Methodist Chapel and a person well respected.

She was upright still, with smooth, dark hair parted in the middle and drawn tightly back – a woman broad in the base and narrow in the shoulder – not, indeed, unlike the stick of asparagus to which Mrs Harbottle had compared her. She received Wimsey with stern civility, but disclaimed all knowledge of her nephew's movements. The hint that he was in a position of some embarrassment, and even danger, did not appear to surprise her.

'There was bad blood in him,' she said. 'My sister Hetty was softer by half than she ought to have been.'

'Ah!' said Wimsey. 'Well, we can't all be people of strong character, though it must be a source of great satisfaction to those that are. I don't want to be a trouble to you, madam, and I know I'm given to twaddling rather, being a trifle on the soft side myself – so I'll get to the point. I see by the register at Somerset House that your nephew, Robert Duckworthy, was born in Southwark, the son of Alfred and Hester Duckworthy. Wonderful system they have there. But of course – being only human – it breaks down now and again – doesn't it?'

She folded her wrinkled hands over one another on the edge of the table, and he saw a kind of shadow flicker over her sharp dark eyes.

'If I'm not bothering you too much – in what name was the other registered?'

The hands trembled a little, but she said steadily:

'I don't understand you.'

'I'm frightfully sorry. Never was good at explaining myself. There were twin boys, weren't there? Under what name did they register the other? I'm sorry to be a nuisance, but it's really rather important.'

'What makes you suppose that there were twins?'

'Oh, I don't suppose it. I wouldn't have bothered you for a supposition. I know there was a twin brother.

What became – at least, I do know more or less what became of him—'

'It died,' she said hurriedly.

'I hate to seem contradictory,' said Wimsey. 'Most unattractive behaviour. But it didn't die, you know. In fact, it's alive now. It's only the name I want to know, you know.'

'And why should I tell you anything, young man?'

'Because,' said Wimsey, 'if you will pardon the mention of anything so disagreeable to a refined taste, there's been a murder committed and your nephew Robert is suspected. As a matter of fact, I happen to know that the murder was done by the brother. That's why I want to get hold of him, don't you see. It would be such a relief to my mind – I am naturally nice-minded – if you would help me to find him. Because, if not, I shall have to go to the police, and then you might be subpoena'd as a witness, and I shouldn't like – I really shouldn't like – to see you in the witness-box at a murder trial. So much unpleasant publicity, don't you know. Whereas, if we can lay hands on the brother quickly, you and Robert need never come into it at all.'

Mrs Brown sat in grim thought for a few minutes.

'Very well,' she said, 'I will tell you.'

'Of course,' said Wimsey to Chief-Inspector Parker a few days later, 'the whole thing was quite obvious when one had heard about the reversal of friend Duckworthy's interior economy.'

'No doubt, no doubt,' said Parker. 'Nothing could be simpler. But all the same, you are aching to tell me how you deduced it and I am willing to be instructed. Are all twins wrong-sided? And are all wrong-sided people twins?'

'Yes. No. Or rather, no, yes. Dissimilar twins and some kinds of similar twins may both be quite normal. But the kind of similar twins that result from the splitting of a single cell *may* come out as looking-glass twins. It depends on the line of fission in the original cell. You can do it artificially with tadpoles and a bit of horsehair.'

'I will make a note to do it at once,' said Parker gravely.

'In fact, I've read somewhere that a person with a reversed inside practically always turns out to be one of a pair of similar twins. So you see, while poor old R.D. was burbling on about the *Student of Prague* and the fourth dimension, I was expecting the twin-brother.

'Apparently what happened was this. There were three sisters of the name of Dart – Susan, Hester and Emily. Susan married a man called Brown; Hester married a man called Duckworthy; Emily was unmarried. By one of those cheery little ironies of which life is so full, the only sister who had a baby, or who was apparently capable of having babies, was the unmarried Emily. By way of compensation, she overdid it and had twins.

'When this catastrophe was about to occur, Emily (deserted, of course, by the father) confided in her sisters, the parents being dead. Susan was a tartar – besides, she had married above her station and was climbing steadily on a ladder of good works. She delivered herself of a few texts and washed her hands of the business. Hester was a kind-hearted soul. She offered to adopt the infant, when produced, and bring it up as her own. Well, the baby came, and, as I said before, it was twins.

'That was a bit too much for Duckworthy. He had agreed to one baby, but twins were more than he had bargained for. Hester was allowed to pick her twin and being a kindly soul, she picked the weaklier-looking one, which was our Robert – the mirror-image twin. Emily had to keep the other, and, as soon as she was strong enough, decamped with him to Australia, after which she was no more heard of.

'Emily's twin was registered in her own name of Dart and baptised Richard. Robert and Richard were two pretty men. Robert was registered as Hester Duckworthy's own child – there were no tiresome rules in those days requiring notification of births by doctors and midwives, so one could do as one liked about these matters. The Duckworthys, complete with baby, moved to Brixton, where Robert was looked upon as being a perfectly genuine little Duckworthy.

'Apparently Emily died in Australia, and Richard, then a boy of fifteen, worked his passage home to London. He does not seem to have been a nice little boy. Two years afterwards, his path crossed that of Brother Robert and produced the episode of the air-raid night.

'Hester may have known about the wrong-sidedness of Robert, or she may not. Anyway, he wasn't told. I imagine that the shock of the explosion caused him to revert more strongly to his natural left-handed tendency. It also seems to have induced a new tendency to amnesia under similar shock-conditions. The whole thing preyed on his mind, and he became more and more vague and somnambulant.

'I rather think that Richard may have discovered the existence of his double and turned it to account. That explains the central incident of the mirror. I think Robert must have mistaken the glass door of the tea-shop for the door of the barber's shop. It really was Richard who came to meet him, and who retired again so hurriedly for fear of being seen and noted. Circumstances played into his hands, of course – but these meetings do take place, and the fact that they were both wearing soft hats and burberries is not astonishing on a dark, wet day.

'And then there is the photograph. No doubt the original mistake was the photographer's, but I shouldn't be surprised if Richard welcomed it and chose that particular print on that account. Though that would mean, of course, that he knew about the wrong-sidedness of Robert. I don't know how he could have done that, but he may have had opportunities for inquiry. It was known in the Army, and rumours may have got round. But I won't press that point.

'There's one rather queer thing, and that is that Robert should have had that dream about strangling, on the very night, as far as one could make out, that Richard was engaged in doing away with Jessie Haynes. They say that similar twins are always in close sympathy with one another – that each knows what the other is thinking about, for instance, and contracts the same illness on the same day and all that. Richard was the stronger twin of the two, and perhaps he dominated Robert more than Robert did him. I'm sure I don't know. Daresay it's all bosh. The point is that you've found him all right.'

'Yes. Once we'd got the clue there was no difficulty.'

'Well, let's toddle round to the Cri and have one.' Wimsey got up and set his tie to rights before the glass.

'All the same,' he said, 'there's something queer about mirrors. Uncanny, a bit, don't you think so?'

IN THE TEETH OF THE EVIDENCE

'Well, old son,' said Mr Lamplough, 'and what can we do for you today?'

'Oh, some of your whizz-bang business, I suppose,' said Lord Peter Wimsey, seating himself resentfully in the green velvet torture-chair and making a face in the direction of the drill, 'Jolly old left-hand upper grinder come to bits on me. I was only eating an omelette, too. Can't understand why they always pick these moments. If I'd been cracking nuts or chewing peppermint jumbles I could understand it.'

'Yes?' said Mr Lamplough, soothingly. He drew an electric bulb, complete with mirror, as though by magic out of a kind of Maskelyne-and-Devant contraption on Lord Peter's left; a trail of flex followed it, issuing apparently from the bowels of the earth. 'Any pain?'

'No *pain*,' said Wimsey irritably, 'unless you count a sharp edge fit to saw your tongue off. Point is, why should it go pop like that? I wasn't doing anything to it.'

'No?' said Mr Lamplough, his manner hovering between the professional and the friendly, for he was an old Winchester man and a member of one of Wimsey's clubs, and had frequently met him on the cricket-field in the days of their youth. 'Well, if you'll stop talking half a moment, we'll have a look at it. Ah!'

'Don't say "Ah!" like that, as if you'd found pyorrhoea and necrosis of the jaw and were gloating over it, you damned old ghoul. Just carve it out and stop it up and be hanged to you. And, by the way, what have you

69

been up to? Why should I meet an inspector of police on your doorstep? You needn't pretend he came to have his bridge-work attended to, because I saw his sergeant waiting for him outside.'

'Well, it was rather curious,' said Mr Lamplough, dexterously gagging his friend with one hand and dabbing cotton-wool into the offending cavity with the other. 'I suppose I oughtn't to tell you, but if I don't, you'll get it all out of your friends at Scotland Yard. They wanted to see my predecessor's books. Possibly you noticed that bit in the papers about a dental man being found dead in a blazing garage on Wimbledon Common?'

'Yonk – ugh?' said Lord Peter Wimsey.

'Last night,' said Mr Lamplough. 'Pooped off about nine pipemma, and it took them three hours to put it out. One of those wooden garages – and the big job was to keep the blaze away from the house. Fortunately it's at the end of the row, with nobody at home. Apparently this man Prendergast was all alone there – just going off for a holiday or something – and he contrived to set himself and his car and his garage alight last night and was burnt to death. In fact, when they found him, he was so badly charred that they couldn't be sure it was he. So, being sticklers for routine, they had a look at his teeth.'

'Oh, yes?' said Wimsey, watching Mr Lamplough fitting a new drill into its socket. 'Didn't anybody have a go at putting the fire out?'

'Oh, yes – but as it was a wooden shed, full of petrol, it simply went up like a bonfire. Just a little bit over this way, please. That's splendid.' Gr-r-r, whizz, gr-r-r. 'As a matter of fact, they seem to think it might just possibly be suicide. The man's married, with three children, and immured and all that sort of thing.' Whizz, gr-r-r, buzz, gr-r-r, whizz. 'His family's down at Worthing, staying with his mother-in-law or something. Tell me if I hurt you.' Gr-r-r. 'And I don't suppose he was doing any too well. Still, of course, he may easily have had an accident when filling up. I gather he was starting off that night to join them.'

'A – ow – oo – oo – uh – ihi – ih?' inquired Wimsey naturally enough.

'How do I come into it?' said Mr Lamplough, who, from long experience was expert in the interpretation of mumblings. 'Well, only because the chap whose practice I took over here did this fellow Prendergast's dental work for him.' Whizz. 'He died, but left his books behind him for my guidance, in case any of his old patients should feel inclined to trust me.' Gr-r-r, whizz. 'I'm sorry. Did you feel that? As a matter of fact, some of them actually do. I suppose it's an instinct to trundle round to the same old place when you're in pain, like the dying elephants. Will you rinse, please?'

'I see,' said Wimsey, when he had finished washing out chips of himself and exploring his ravaged molar with his tongue. 'How odd it is that these cavities always seem so large. I feel as if I could put my head into this one. Still, I suppose you know what you're about. And are Prendergast's teeth all right?'

'Haven't had time to hunt through the ledger, yet, but I've said I'll go down and have a look at them as soon as I've finished with you. It's my lunch-time anyway, and my two o'clock patient isn't coming, thank goodness. She usually brings five spoilt children, and they all want to sit round and watch, and play with the apparatus. One of them got loose last time and tried to electrocute itself on the X-ray plant next door. And she thinks that children should be done at half-price. A little wider if you can manage it.' Gr-r-r. 'Yes, that's very nice. Now we can dress that and put in a temporary. Rinse please.'

'Yes,' said Wimsey, 'and for goodness' sake make it firm and not too much of your foul oil of cloves. I don't want bits to come out in the middle of dinner. You can't imagine the nastiness of caviar flavoured with cloves.'

'No?' said Mr Lamplough. 'You may find this a little cold.' Squirt, swish. 'Rinse, please. You may notice it when the dressing goes in. Oh, you did notice it? Good. That shows that the nerve's all right. Only a little longer now. There! Yes, you may get down now. Another rinse? Certainly. When would you like to come in again?'

'Don't be silly, old horse,' said Wimsey. 'I am coming out to Wimbledon with you straight away. You'll get there twice as fast if I drive you. I've never had a corpse-in-blazing-garage before, and I want to learn.'

There is nothing really attractive about corpses in blazing garages. Even Wimsey's war experience did not quite reconcile him to the object that lay on the mortuary slab in the police station. Charred out of all resemblance to humanity, it turned even the police surgeon pale, while Mr Lamplough was so overcome that he had to lay down the books he had brought with him and retire into the open to recover himself. Meanwhile Wimsey, having put himself on terms of mutual confidence and esteem with the police officials, thoughtfully turned over the little pile of blackened odds and ends that represented the contents of Mr Prendergast's pockets. There was nothing remarkable about them. The leather note-case still held the remains of a thickish wad of notes – doubtless cash in hand for the holiday at Worthing. The handsome gold watch (obviously a presentation) had stopped at seven minutes past nine. Wimsey remarked on its good state of preservation. Sheltered between the left arm and the body – that seemed to be the explanation.

'Looks as though the first sudden blaze had regularly overcome him,' said the police inspector. 'He evidently made no attempt to get out. He'd simply fallen forward over the wheel, with his head on the dashboard. That's why the face is so disfigured. I'll show you the remains of the car presently if you're interested, my lord. If the other gentleman's feeling better we may as well take the body first.'

Taking the body was a long and unpleasant job. Mr Lamplough, nerving himself with an effort and producing a pair of forceps and a probe, went gingerly over the jaws – reduced almost to their bony structure by the furnace heat to which they had been exposed – while the police surgeon checked entries in the ledger. Mr Prendergast had a dental history extending back over ten years in the ledger and had already had two or three fillings done before that time. These had been noted at the time when he first came to Mr Lamplough's predecessor.

At the end of a long examination, the surgeon looked up from the notes he had been making.

'Well, now,' he said, 'let's check that again. Allowing for renewal of old work, I think we've got a pretty accurate picture of the present state of his mouth. There ought to be nine fillings in all. Small amalgam filling in right lower back wisdom tooth; big amalgam ditto in right lower back molar; amalgam fillings in right upper first and second bicuspids at point of contact; right upper incisor crowned – that all right?'

'I expect so,' said Mr Lamplough, 'except that the right upper incisor seems to be missing altogether, but possibly the crown came loose and fell out.' He probed delicately. 'The jaw is very brittle – I can't make anything of the canal – but there's nothing against it.'

'We may find the crown in the garage,' suggested the Inspector.

'Fused porcelain filling in left upper canine,' went on the surgeon; 'amalgam fillings in left upper first bicuspid and lower second bicuspid and left lower thirteen-year-old molar. That seems to be all. No teeth missing and no artificials. How old was this man, Inspector?'

'About forty-five, Doc.'

'My age. I only wish I had as good a set of teeth,' said the surgeon. Mr Lamplough agreed with him.

'Then I take it, this is Mr Prendergast all right,' said the Inspector.

'Not a doubt of it, I should say,' replied Mr Lamplough; 'though I should like to find that missing crown.'

'We'd better go round to the house, then,' said the Inspector. 'Well, yes, thank you, my lord, I shouldn't mind a lift in that. Some car. Well, the only point now is, whether it was accident or suicide. Round to the right, my lord, and then second on the left – I'll tell you as we go.'

'A bit out of the way for a dental man,' observed Mr Lamplough, as they emerged upon some scattered houses near the Common.

The Inspector made a grimace.

'I thought the same, sir, but it appears Mrs Prendergast persuaded him to come here. So good for the children. Not so good for the practice, though. If you ask me, I should say Mrs P. was the biggest argument we have for suicide. Here we are.'

The last sentence was scarcely necessary. There was a little crowd about the gate of a small detached villa at the end of a row of similar houses. From a pile of dismal debris in the garden a smell of burning still rose, disgustingly. The Inspector pushed through the gate with his companions, pursued by the comments of the bystanders.

'That's the Inspector . . . that's Dr Maggs . . . that'll be another doctor, him with the little bag . . . who's the bloke in the eye-glass? . . . Looks a proper nobleman, don't he, Florrie? . . . Why he'll be the insurance bloke . . . Coo! look at his grand car . . . that's where the money goes . . . That's a Rolls, that is . . . no, silly, it's a Daimler . . . Ow, well, it's all advertisement these days.'

Wimsey giggled indecorously all the way up the garden path. The sight of the skeleton car amid the sodden and fire-blackened remains of the garage sobered him. Two police constables, crouched over the ruin with a sieve, stood up and saluted.

'How are you getting on, Jenkins?'

'Haven't got anything very much yet, sir, bar an ivory cigarette-holder. This gentleman' – indicating a stout, bald man in spectacles, who was squatting among the damaged coachwork – 'is Mr Tolley, from the motor-works, come with a note from the Superintendent, sir.'

'Ah, yes. Can you give an opinion about this, Mr Tolley? Dr Maggs you know. Mr Lamplough, Lord Peter Wimsey. By the way, Jenkins, Mr Lamplough has been going into the corpse's dentistry, and he's looking for a lost tooth. You might see if you can find it. Now, Mr Tolley?'

'Can't see much doubt about how it happened,' said Mr Tolley, picking his teeth thoughtfully. 'Regular death-traps, these little saloons, when anything goes wrong unexpectedly. There's a front tank, you see, and it looks as though there might have been a bit of a leak behind the dash, somewhere. Possibly the seam of the tank had got strained a bit, or the union had come loose. It's loose now, as a matter of fact, but that's not unusual after a fire, Rouse case or no Rouse case. You can get quite a lot of slow dripping from a damaged tank or pipe, and there seems to have been a coconut mat round the controls, which would prevent you from noticing. There'd be a smell, of course, but these little garages do often get to smell of petrol, and he kept several cans of the stuff here. More than the legal amount – but *that's* not unusual either. Looks to me as though he'd filled up his tank – there are two empty tins near the bonnet, with the caps loose – got in, shut the door, started up the car, perhaps, and then lit a cigarette. Then, if there were any petrol fumes about from a leak, the whole show would go up in his face – whoosh!'

'How was the ignition?'

'Off. He may never have switched it on, but it's quite likely he switched it off again when the flame went up. Silly thing to do, but lots of people *do* do it. The proper thing, of course, is to switch off the petrol and leave the engine running so as to empty the carburettor, but you don't always think straight when you're being burnt alive. Or he may have meant to turn off the petrol and been overcome before he could manage it. The tank's over here to the left, you see.'

'On the other hand,' said Wimsey, 'he may have committed suicide and faked the accident.'

'Nasty way of committing suicide.'

'Suppose he'd taken poison first.'

'He'd have had to stay alive long enough to fire the car.'

'That's true. Suppose he'd shot himself – would the flash from the – no, that's silly – you'd have found the weapon in the case. Or a hypodermic? Same objection. Prussic acid might have done it – I mean, he might just have had time to take a tablet and then fire the car. Prussic acid's pretty quick, but it isn't absolutely instantaneous.'

'I'll have a look for it anyway,' said Dr Maggs.

They were interrupted by the constable.

'Excuse me, sir, but I think we've found the tooth. Mr Lamplough says this is it.'

Between his pudgy finger and thumb he held up a small, bony object, from which a small stalk of metal still protruded.

'That's a right upper incisor crown all right by the look of it,' said Mr Lamplough. 'I suppose the cement gave way with the heat. Some cements are sensitive to heat, some, on the other hand, to damp. Well, that settles it, doesn't it?'

'Yes – well, we shall have to break it to the widow. Not that she can be in very much doubt, I imagine.'

Mrs Prendergast – a very much made-up lady with a face set in lines of habitual peevishness – received the news with a burst of loud sobs. She informed them, when she was sufficiently recovered, that Arthur had always been careless about petrol, that he smoked too much, that she had often warned him about the danger of small saloons, that she had told him he ought to get a bigger car, that the one he had was not really large enough for her and the whole family, that he *would* drive at night, though she had always said it was dangerous, and that if he'd listened to her, it would never have happened.

'Poor Arthur was not a good driver. Only last week, when he was taking us down to Worthing, he drove the car right up on a bank in trying to pass a lorry, and frightened us all dreadfully.'

'Ah!' said the Inspector. 'No doubt that's how the tank got strained.' Very cautiously he inquired whether Mr Prendergast could have had any reason for taking his own life. The widow was indignant. It was true that the practice had been declining of late, but Arthur would never have been so wicked as to do such a thing. Why, only three months ago, he had taken out a life-insurance for £500 and he'd never have invalidated it by committing suicide within the term stipulated by the policy. Inconsiderate of her as Arthur was, and whatever injuries he had done her as a wife, he wouldn't rob his innocent children.

The Inspector pricked up his ears at the word 'injuries'. What injuries?

Oh, well, of course, she'd known all the time that Arthur was carrying on with that Mrs Fielding. You couldn't deceive her with all this stuff about teeth needing continual attention. And it was all very well to say that Mrs Fielding's house was better run than her own. *That* wasn't surprising – a rich widow with no children and no responsibilities, of course she could afford to have everything nice. You couldn't expect a busy wife to do miracles on such a small housekeeping allowance. If Arthur had wanted things different, he should have been more generous, and it was easy enough for Mrs Fielding to attract men, dressed up like a fashion plate and no better than she should be. She'd told Arthur that if it didn't stop she'd divorce him. And since then he'd taken to spending all his evenings in Town, and what was he doing there—

The Inspector stemmed the torrent by asking for Mrs Fielding's address.

'I'm sure I don't know,' said Mrs Prendergast. 'She did live at Number 57, but she went abroad after I made it clear I wasn't going to stand any more of it. It's very nice to be some people, with plenty of money to spend. I've never been abroad since our honeymoon, and that was only to Boulogne.'

At the end of this conversation, the Inspector sought Dr Maggs and begged him to be thorough in his search for prussic acid.

The remaining testimony was that of Gladys, the general servant. She had left Mr Prendergast's house the day before at 6 o'clock. She was to have taken a week's holiday while the Prendergasts were at Worthing. She had thought that Mr Prendergast had seemed worried and nervous the last few days, but that had not surprised her, because she knew he disliked staying with his wife's people. She (Gladys) had finished her work and put out a cold supper and then gone home with her employer's permission. He had a patient – a gentleman from Australia, or some such a place, who wanted his teeth attended to in a hurry before going off on his travels again. Mr Prendergast had explained that he would be working late, and would shut up the house himself, and she need not wait. Further inquiry showed that Mr Prendergast had 'scarcely touched' his supper, being, presumably, in a hurry to get off. Apparently, then, the patient had been the last person to see Mr Prendergast alive.

The dentist's appointment-book was next examined. The patient figured there as 'Mr Williams 5.30', and the address-book placed Mr Williams at a small hotel in Bloomsbury. The manager of the hotel said that Mr Williams had stayed there for a week. He had given no address except 'Adelaide', and had mentioned that he was revisiting the old country for the first time after twenty years and had no friends in London. Unfortunately, he could not be interviewed. At about half-past ten the previous night, a messenger had called, bringing his card, to pay his bill and remove his luggage. No address had been left for forwarding letters. It was not a district messenger, but a man in a slouch hat and heavy dark overcoat. The night-porter had not seen his face very clearly, as only one light was on in the hall. He had told them to hurry up, as Mr Williams wanted to catch the boat-train from Waterloo. Inquiry at the booking-office showed that a Mr Williams had actually travelled on that train, being booked to Paris. The ticket had been taken that same night. So Mr Williams had disappeared into the blue, and even if they could trace him, it seemed unlikely that he could throw much light on Mr Prendergast's state of mind immediately previous to the disaster. It seemed a little odd, at first, that Mr Williams, from Adelaide, staying in Bloomsbury, should have travelled to Wimbledon to get his teeth attended to, but the simple explanation was the likeliest: namely, that the friendless Williams had struck up an acquaintance with Prendergast in a cafe or some such place, and that a casual mention of his dental necessities had led to a project of mutual profit and assistance.

After which, nothing seemed to be left but for the coroner to bring in a verdict of Death by Misadventure and for the widow to send in her claim to the Insurance Company, when Dr Maggs upset the whole scheme of things by announcing that he had discovered traces of a large injection of hyoscine in the body, and what about it? The Inspector, on hearing this, observed callously that he was not surprised. If ever a man had an excuse for suicide, he thought it was Mrs Prendergast's husband. He thought that it would be desirable to make a careful search among the scorched laurels surrounding what had been Mr Prendergast's garage. Lord Peter Wimsey agreed, but committed himself to the prophecy that the syringe would not be found.

Lord Peter Wimsey was entirely wrong. The syringe was found next day, in a position suggesting that it had been thrown out of the window of the garage after use. Traces of the poison were discovered to be present in it. 'It's a slow-working drug,' observed Dr Maggs. 'No doubt he jabbed himself, threw the syringe away, hoping it would never be looked for, and then, before he lost consciousness, climbed into the car and set light to it. A clumsy way of doing it.'

'A damned ingenious way of doing it,' said Wimsey. 'I don't believe in that syringe, somehow.' He rang up his dentist. 'Lamplough, old horse,' he said, 'I wish you'd do something for me. I wish you'd go over those teeth again. No – not my teeth; Prendergast's.'

'Oh, blow it!' said Mr Lamplough, uneasily.

'No, but I wish you would,' said his lordship.

The body was still unburied. Mr Lamplough, grumbling very much, went down to Wimbledon with Wimsey, and again went through his distasteful task. This time he started on the left side.

'Lower thirteen-year-old molar and second bicuspid filled amalgam. The fire's got at those a bit, but they're all right. First upper bicuspid – bicuspids are stupid sort of teeth always the first to go. That filling looks to have been rather carelessly put in – not what I should call good work; it seems to extend over the next tooth – possibly the fire did that. Left upper canine, cast porcelain filling on anterior face—'

'Half a jiff,' said Wimsey, 'Maggs's note says "fused porcelain". Is it the same thing?'

'No. Different process. Well, I suppose it's fused porcelain – difficult to see. I should have said it was cast, myself, but that's as maybe.'

'Let's verify it in the ledger. I wish Maggs had put the dates in – goodness knows how far I shall have to hunt back, and I don't understand this chap's writing or his dashed abbreviations.'

'You won't have to go back very far if it's cast. The stuff only came in about 1928, from America. There was quite a rage for it then, but for some reason it didn't take on extraordinarily well over here. But some men use it.'

'Oh, then it isn't cast,' said Wimsey. 'There's nothing here about canines, back to '28. Let's make sure; '27, '26, '25, '24, '23. Here you are. Canine, something or other.'

'That's it,' said Lamplough, coming to look over his shoulder. 'Fused porcelain. I must be wrong, then. Easily see by taking it out. The grain's different, and so is the way it's put in.'

'How, different?'

'Well,' said Mr Lamplough, 'one's a cast, you see.'

'And the other's fused. I did grasp that much. Well, go ahead and take it out.'

'Can't very well; not here.'

'Then take it home and do it there. Don't you see, Lamplough, how important it is? If it is cast porcelain, or whatever you call it, it *can't* have been done in '23.

82

And if it was removed later, then another dentist must have done it. And he may have done other things – and in that case, those things ought to be there, and they're not. Don't you *see?*'

'I see you're getting rather agitato,' said Mr Lamplough; 'all I can say is, I refuse to have this thing taken along to my surgery. Corpses aren't popular in Harley Street.'

In the end, the body was removed, by permission, to the dental department of the local hospital. Here Mr Lamplough, assisted by the staff dental expert, Dr Maggs, and the police, delicately extracted the filling from the canine.

'If that,' said he triumphantly, 'is not cast porcelain I will extract all my own teeth without an anaesthetic and swallow them. What do you say, Benton?'

The hospital dentist agreed with him. Mr Lamplough, who had suddenly developed an eager interest in the problem, nodded, and inserted a careful probe between the upper right bicuspids, with their adjacent fillings.

'Come and look at this, Benton. Allowing for the action of the fire and all this muck, wouldn't you have said this was a very recent filling? There, at the point of contact. Might have been done yesterday. And – here – wait a minute. Where's the lower jaw gone to? Get that fitted up. Give me a bit of carbon. Look at the tremendous bite there ought to be here, with that big molar coming down onto it. That filling's miles too high for the job. Wimsey – when was this bottom right-hand back molar filled?'

'Two years ago,' said Wimsey.

'That's impossible,' said the two dentists together, and Mr Benton added:

'If you clean away the mess, you'll see it's a new filling. Never been bitten on, I should say. Look here, Mr Lamplough, there's something odd here.'

'Odd? I should say there was. I never thought about it when I was checking it up yesterday, but look at this old cavity in the lateral here. Why didn't he have that filled when all this other work was done? Now it's cleaned out you can see it plainly. Have you got a long probe? It's quite deep and must have given him jip. I say, Inspector, I want to have some of these fillings out. Do you mind?'

'Go ahead,' said the Inspector, 'we've got plenty of witnesses.'

With Mr Benton supporting the grisly patient, and Mr Lamplough manipulating the drill, the filling of one of the molars was speedily drilled out, and Mr Lamplough said: 'Oh, gosh!' – which, as Lord Peter remarked, just showed you what a dentist meant when he said 'Ah!'

'Try the bicuspids,' suggested Mr Benton.

'Or this thirteen-year-old,' chimed in his colleague.

'Hold hard, gentlemen,' protested the Inspector, 'don't spoil the specimen altogether.'

Mr Lamplough drilled away without heeding him. Another filling came out, and Mr Lamplough said 'Gosh!' again.

'It's all right,' said Wimsey, grinning, 'you can get out your warrant, Inspector.'

'What's that, my lord?'

'Murder,' said Wimsey.

'Why?' said the Inspector. 'Do these gentlemen mean that Mr Prendergast got a new dentist who poisoned his teeth for him?'

'No,' said Mr Lamplough; 'at least, not what you mean by poisoning. But I've never seen such work in my life. Why, in two places the man hasn't even troubled to clear out the decay at all. He's just enlarged the cavity and stopped it up again anyhow. Why this chap didn't get thundering abscesses I don't know.'

'Perhaps,' said Wimsey, 'the stoppings were put in too recently. Hullo! What now?'

'This one's all right. No decay here. Doesn't look as if there ever had been, either. But one can't tell about that.'

'I dare say there never was. Get your warrant out, Inspector.'

'For the murder of Mr Prendergast? And against whom?'

'No. Against Arthur Prendergast for the murder of one Mr Williams, and, incidentally, for arson and attempted fraud. And against Mrs Fielding too, if you like, for conspiracy. Though you mayn't be able to prove that part of it.'

It turned out, when they found Mr Prendergast in Rouen, that he had thought out the scheme well in advance. The one thing he had had to wait for had been to find a patient of his own height and build, with a good set of teeth and few home ties. When the unhappy Williams had fallen into his clutches, he had few preparations to make. Mrs Prendergast had to be packed off to Worthing – a journey she was ready enough to take at anytime – and the maid given a holiday. Then the necessary dental accessories had to be prepared and the victim invited out to tea at Wimbledon. Then the murder – a stunning blow from behind, followed by an injection. Then, the slow and horrid process of faking the teeth to correspond with Mr Prendergast's own. Next, the exchange of clothes and the body carried down and placed in the car. The hypodermic put where it might be overlooked on a casual inspection and yet might plausibly be found if the presence of the drug should be discovered; ready, in the one case, to support a verdict of Accident and, in the second, of Suicide. Then the car soaked in petrol, the union loosened, the cans left about. The garage door and window left open, to lend colour to the story and provide a draught, and, finally, light set to the car by means of a train of petrol laid through the garage door. Then, flight to the station through the winter darkness and so by underground to London. The risk of being recognised on the underground was small, in Williams's hat and clothes and with a scarf wound about the lower part of the face. The next step was to pick up Williams's luggage and take the boat train to join the wealthy and enamoured Mrs Fielding in France. After which, Williams and Mrs Williams could have returned to England, or not, as they pleased.

'Quite a student of criminology,' remarked Wimsey, at the conclusion of this little adventure. 'He'd studied Rouse and Furnace all right, and profited by their mistakes. Pity he overlooked that matter of the cast porcelain. Makes a quicker job, does it, Lamplough? Well, more haste, less speed. I do wonder, though, at what point of the proceedings Williams actually died.'

'Shut up,' said Mr Lamplough, 'and, by the way, I've still got to finish that filling for you.'

THE ENTERTAINING EPISODE OF THE ARTICLE IN QUESTION

The unprofessional detective career of Lord Peter Wimsey was regulated (though the word has no particular propriety in this connection) by a persistent and undignified inquisitiveness. The habit of asking silly questions – natural, though irritating, in the immature male – remained with him long after his immaculate man, Bunter, had become attached to his service to shave the bristles from his chin and see to the due purchase and housing of Napoleon brandies and Villar y Villar cigars. At the age of thirty-two his sister Mary christened him Elephant's Child. It was his idiotic enquiries (before his brother, the Duke of Denver, who grew scarlet with mortification) as to what the Woolsack was really stuffed with that led the then Lord Chancellor idly to investigate the article in question, and to discover, tucked deep within its recesses, that famous diamond necklace of the Marchioness of Writtle, which had disappeared on the day Parliament was opened and been safely secreted by one of the cleaners. It was by a continual and personal badgering of the Chief Engineer at 2LO on the question of 'Why is Oscillation and How is it Done?' that his lordship incidentally unmasked the great Ploffsky gang of Anarchist conspirators, who were accustomed to converse in code by a methodical system of howls, superimposed (to the great annoyance of listeners in British and European stations) upon the London wave-length and duly relayed by 5XX over a radius of some five or six hundred miles. He annoyed persons of more leisure than decorum by suddenly taking into his head to descend to the Underground by way of the stairs, though the only exciting thing he ever actually found there were the blood-stained boots of the Sloane Square murderer; on the other hand when the drains were taken up at Glegg's Folly, it was by hanging about and hindering the plumbers at their job that he accidentally made the discovery which hanged that detestable poisoner, William Girdlestone Chitty.

Accordingly, it was with no surprise at all that the reliable Bunter, one April morning, received the announcement of an abrupt change of plan.

They had arrived at the Gare St Lazare in good time to register the luggage. Their three months' trip to Italy had been purely for enjoyment, and had been followed by a pleasant fortnight in Paris. They were now intending to pay a short visit to the Duc de Sainte-Croix in Rouen on their way back to England. Lord Peter paced the Salle des Pas Perdus for some time, buying an illustrated paper or two and eyeing the crowd. He bent an appreciative eye on a slim, shingled creature with the face of a Paris *gamin*, but was forced to admit to himself that her ankles were a trifle on the thick side; he assisted an elderly lady who was explaining to the bookstall clerk that she wanted a map of Paris and not a *carte postale*, consumed a quick cognac at one of the little green tables at the far end, and then decided he had better go down and see how Bunter was getting on.

In half an hour Bunter and his porter had worked themselves up to the second place in the enormous queue – for, as usual, one of the weighing-machines was out of order. In front of them stood an agitated little group – the young woman Lord Peter had noticed in the Salle des Pas Perdus, a sallow-faced man of about thirty, their porter, and the registration official, who was peering eagerly through his little *guichet*.

'Mais je te répète que je ne les ai pas,' said the sallow man heatedly. 'Voyons, voyons. C'est bien toi qui les as pris, n'est-ce pas? Eh bien, alors, comment veux-tu que je les aie, moi?'

'Mais non, mais non, je te les ai bien donné là-haut, avant d'aller chercher les journaux.'

'Je t'assure que non. Enfin, c'est évident! J'ai cherché partout, que diable! Tu ne m'as rien donné, du tout, du tout.'

'Mais, puisque je t'ai dit d'aller faire enrégistrer les bagages! Ne faut-il pas que je t'aie bien remis les billets? Me prends-tu pour un imbécile? Va! On n'est pas dépourvu de sens! Mais regarde l'heure! Le train part à 11 h. 20 m. Cherche un peu, au moins.'

'Mais puisque j'ai cherché partout – le gilet, rien! Jacquet rien, rien! Le pardessus – rien! rien! rien! C'est toi—'

Here the porter, urged by the frantic cries and stamping of the queue, and the repeated insults of Lord Peter's porter, flung himself into the discussion.

'P't-être qu' m'sieur a bouté les billets dans son pantalon,' he suggested.

'Triple idiot!' snapped the traveller, 'je vous le demande – est-ce qu'on a jamais entendu parler de mettre des billets dans son pantalon? Jamais—'

The French porter is a Republican, and, moreover, extremely ill-paid. The large tolerance of his English colleague is not for him.

'Ah!' said he, dropping two heavy bags and looking round for moral support. 'Vous dîtes? En voilà du joli!

Allons, mon p'tit, ce n'est pas parce qu'on porte un faux col qu'on a le droit d'insulter les gens.'

The discussion might have become a full-blown row, had not the young man discovered the missing tickets – incidentally, they were in his trousers-pocket after all – and continued the registration of his luggage, to the undisguised satisfaction of the crowd.

'Bunter,' said his lordship, who had turned his back on the group and was lighting a cigarette, 'I am going to change the tickets. We shall go straight on to London. Have you got that snapshot affair of yours with you?'

'Yes, my lord.'

'The one you can work from your pocket without anyone noticing?'

'Yes, my lord.'

'Get me a picture of those two.'

'Yes, my lord.'

'I will see to the luggage. Wire to the Duc that I am unexpectedly called home.'

'Very good my lord.'

Lord Peter did not allude to the matter again till Bunter was putting his trousers in the press in their cabin on board the *Normannia*. Beyond ascertaining that the young man and woman who had aroused his curiosity were on the boat as second-class passengers, he had sedulously avoided contact with them.

'Did you get that photograph?'

'I hope so, my lord. As your lordship knows, the aim from the breast-pocket tends to be unreliable. I have made three attempts, and trust that one at least may prove to be not unsuccessful.'

'How soon can you develop them?'

'At once, if your lordship pleases. I have all the materials in my suit case.'

'What fun!' said Lord Peter, eagerly tying himself into a pair of mauve silk pyjamas. 'May I hold the bottles and things?'

Mr Bunter poured 3 ounces of water into an 8-ounce measure, and handed his master a glass rod and a minute packet.

'If your lordship would be so good as to stir the contents of the white packet slowly into the water,' he said, bolting the door, 'and, when dissolved, add the contents of the blue packet.'

'Just like a Seidlitz powder,' said his lordship happily. 'Does it fizz?'

'Not much, my lord,' replied the expert, shaking a quantity of hypo crystals into the hand-basin.

'That's a pity,' said Lord Peter. 'I say, Bunter, it's no end of a bore to dissolve.'

'Yes, my lord,' returned Bunter sedately. 'I have always found that part of the process exceptionally tedious, my lord.'

Lord Peter jabbed viciously with the glass rod.

'Just you wait,' he said, in a vindictive tone, 'till we get to Waterloo.'

Three days later Lord Peter Wimsey sat in his book-lined sitting-room at 110A Piccadilly. The tall bunches of daffodils on the table smiled in the spring sunshine, and nodded to the breeze which danced in from the open window. The door opened, and his lordship glanced up from a handsome edition of the *Contes de La Fontaine*, whose handsome hand-coloured Fragonard plates he was examining with the aid of a lens.

'Morning, Bunter. Anything doing?'

'I have ascertained, my lord, that the young person

in question has entered the service of the elder Duchess of Medway. Her name is Célestine Berger.'

'You are less accurate than usual, Bunter. Nobody off the stage is called Célestine. You should say "under the name of Célestine Berger". And the man?'

'He is domiciled at this address in Guildford Street, Bloomsbury, my lord.'

'Excellent, my Bunter. Now give me *Who's Who*. Was it a very tiresome job?'

'Not exceptionally so, my lord.'

'One of these days I suppose I shall give you something to do which you *will* jib at,' said his lordship, 'and you will leave me and I shall cut my throat. Thanks. Run away and play. I shall lunch at the club.'

The book which Bunter had handed his employer indeed bore the words *Who's Who* embossed upon its cover, but it was to be found in no public library and in no bookseller's shop. It was a bulky manuscript, closely filled, in part with the small print–like handwriting of Mr Bunter, in part with Lord Peter's neat and altogether illegible hand. It contained biographies of the most unexpected people, and the most unexpected facts about the most obvious people. Lord Peter turned to a very long entry under the name of the Dowager Duchess of Medway. It appeared to make satisfactory reading, for after a time he smiled, closed the book, and went to the telephone.

'Yes – this is the Duchess of Medway. Who is it?'

The deep, harsh old voice pleased Lord Peter. He could see the imperious face and upright figure of what had been the most famous beauty in the London of the 'sixties.

'It's Peter Wimsey, duchess.'

'Indeed, and how do you do, young man? Back from your Continental jaunting?'

'Just home – and longing to lay my devotion at the feet of the most fascinating lady in England.'

'God bless my soul, child, what do you want?' demanded the duchess. 'Boys like you don't flatter a woman for nothing.'

'I want to tell you my sins, duchess.'

'You should have lived in the great days,' said the voice appreciatively. 'Your talents are wasted on the young fry.'

'That is why I want to talk to you, duchess.'

'Well, my dear, if you've committed any sins worth hearing I shall enjoy your visit.'

'You are as exquisite in kindness as in charm. I am coming this afternoon.'

'I will be at home to you and no one else. There.'

'Dear lady, I kiss your hands,' said Lord Peter, and he heard a deep chuckle as the duchess rang off.

'You may say what you like, duchess,' said Lord Peter from his reverential position on the fender-stool, 'but you are the youngest grandmother in London, not excepting my own mother.'

'Dear Honoria is the merest child,' said the duchess. 'I have twenty years more experience of life, and have arrived at the age when we boast of them. I have every intention of being a great-grandmother before I die. Sylvia is being married in a fortnight's time, to that stupid son of Attenbury's.'

'Abcock?'

'Yes. He keeps the worst hunters I ever saw, and doesn't know still champagne from sauternes. But Sylvia is stupid, too, poor child, so I dare say they will get on

93

charmingly. In my day one had to have either brains or beauty to get on – preferably both. Nowadays nothing seems to be required but a total lack of figure. But all the sense went out of society with the House of Lords' veto. I except you, Peter. You have talents. It is a pity you do not employ them in politics.'

'Dear lady, God forbid.'

'Perhaps you are right, as things are. There were giants in my day. Dear Dizzy. I remember so well, when his wife died, how hard we all tried to get him – Medway had died the year before – but he was wrapped up in that stupid Bradford woman, who had never even read a line of one of his books, and couldn't have understood 'em if she had. And now we have Abcock standing for Midhurst, and married to Sylvia!'

'You haven't invited me to the wedding, duchess dear. I'm so hurt,' sighed his lordship.

'Bless you, child, *I* didn't send out the invitations, but I suppose your brother and that tiresome wife of his will be there. You must come, of course, if you want to. I had no idea you had a passion for weddings.'

'Hadn't you?' said Peter. 'I have a passion for this one. I want to see Lady Sylvia wearing white satin and the family lace and diamonds, and to sentimentalise over the days when my fox-terrier bit the stuffing out of her doll.'

'Very well, my dear, you shall. Come early and give me your support. As for the diamonds, if it weren't a family tradition, Sylvia shouldn't wear them. She has the impudence to complain of them.'

'I thought they were some of the finest in existence.'

'So they are. But she says the setting are ugly and old-fashioned, and she doesn't like diamonds, and they won't go with her dress. Such nonsense. Whoever heard of a girl not liking diamonds? She wants to be something romantic and moonshiny in pearls. I have no patience with her.'

'I'll promise to admire them,' said Peter – 'use the privilege of early acquaintance and tell her she's an ass and so on. I'd love to have a view of them. When do they come out of cold storage?'

'Mr Whitehead will bring them up from the Bank the night before,' said the duchess, 'and they'll go into the safe in my room. Come round at twelve o'clock and you shall have a private view of them.'

'That would be delightful. Mind they don't disappear in the night, won't you?'

'Oh, my dear, the house is going to be over-run with policemen. Such a nuisance. I suppose it can't be helped.'

'Oh, I think it's a good thing,' said Peter. 'I have rather an unwholesome weakness for policemen.'

On the morning of the wedding-day, Lord Peter emerged from Bunter's hands a marvel of sleek brilliance. His primrose-coloured hair was so exquisite a work of art that to eclipse it with his glossy hat was like shutting up the sun in a shrine of polished jet; his spats, light trousers, and exquisitely polished shoes formed a tone-symphony in monochrome. It was only by the most impassioned pleading that he persuaded his tyrant to allow him to place two small photographs and a thin, foreign letter in his breast-pocket. Mr Bunter, likewise immaculately attired, stepped into the taxi after him. At noon precisely they were deposited beneath the striped awning which adorned the door of the Duchess of Medway's house in Park Lane. Bunter promptly disappeared in the direction of the back entrance, while his lordship mounted the steps and asked to see the dowager.

The majority of the guests had not yet arrived, but the house was full of agitated people, flitting hither and thither, with flowers and prayer-books, while a clatter of dishes and cutlery from the dining-room proclaimed the laying of a sumptuous breakfast. Lord Peter was shown into the morning-room while the footman went to announce him, and here he found a very close friend and devoted colleague, Detective-Inspector Parker, mounting guard in plain clothes over a costly collection of white elephants. Lord Peter greeted him with an affectionate handgrip.

'All serene so far?' he enquired.

'Perfectly O.K.'

'You got my note?'

'Sure thing. I've got three of our men shadowing your friend in Guildford Street. The girl is very much in evidence here. Does the old lady's wig and that sort of thing. Bit of a coming-on disposition, isn't she?'

'You surprise me,' said Lord Peter. 'No' – as his friend grinned sardonically – 'you really do. Not seriously? That would throw all my calculations out.'

'Oh, no! Saucy with her eyes and her tongue, that's all.'

'Do her job well?'

'I've heard no complaints. What put you on to this?'

'Pure accident. Of course I may be mistaken.'

'Did you receive any information from Paris?'

'I wish you wouldn't use that phrase,' said Lord Peter peevishly. 'It's so of the Yard – yardy. One of these days it'll give you away.'

'Sorry,' said Parker. 'Second nature, I suppose.'

'Those are the things to beware of,' returned his lordship, with an earnestness that seemed a little out of place. 'One can keep guard on everything but just those second-nature tricks.' He moved across to the window, which overlooked the tradesmen's entrance. 'Hullo!' he said, 'here's our bird.'

Parker joined him, and saw the neat, shingled head of the French girl from the Gare St Lazare, topped by a neat black bandeau and bow. A man with a basket full of white narcissi had rung the bell, and appeared to be trying to make a sale. Parker gently opened the window, and they heard Célestine say with a marked French accent, 'No, nossing today, sank you.' The man insisted in the monotonous whine of his type, thrusting a big bunch of the white flowers upon her, but she pushed them back into the basket with an angry exclamation and flitted away, tossing her head and slapping the door smartly to. The man moved off muttering. As he did so a thin, unhealthy-looking lounger in a check cap detached himself from a lamp post opposite and mouched along the street after him, at the same time casting a glance up at the window. Mr Parker looked at Lord Peter, nodded, and made a slight sign with his hand. At once the man in the check cap removed his cigarette from his mouth, extinguished it, and, tucking the stub behind his ear, moved off without a second glance.

'Very interesting,' said Lord Peter, when both were out of sight. 'Hark!'

There was a sound of running feet overhead – a cry – and a general commotion. The two men dashed to the door as the bride, rushing frantically downstairs with her bevy of bridesmaids after her, proclaimed in a hysterical shriek: 'The diamonds! They're stolen! They're gone!'

Instantly the house was in an uproar. The servants and the caterers' men crowded into the hall; the bride's father burst out from his room in a magnificent white waistcoat and no coat; the Duchess of Medway descended upon Mr Parker, demanding that something should be done; while the butler, who never to the day of his death got over the disgrace, ran out of the pantry with a corkscrew in one hand and a priceless bottle of crusted port in the other, which he shook with all the vehemence of a town-crier ringing a bell. The only dignified entry was made by the dowager duchess, who came down like a ship in sail, dragging Célestine with her, and admonishing her not to be so silly.

'Be quiet, girl,' said the dowager. 'Anyone would think you were going to be murdered.'

'Allow me, your grace,' said Mr Bunter, appearing suddenly from nowhere in his usual unperturbed manner, and taking the agitated Célestine firmly by the arm. 'Young woman, calm yourself.'

'But what is to be *done*?' cried the bride's mother. 'How did it happen?'

It was at this moment that Detective-Inspector Parker took the floor. It was the most impressive and dramatic moment in his whole career. His magnificent calm rebuked the clamorous nobility surrounding him.

'Your grace,' he said, 'there is no cause for alarm. Our measures have been taken. We have the criminals and the gems, thanks to Lord Peter Wimsey, from whom we received inf—'

'Charles!' said Lord Peter in an awful voice.

'Warning of the attempt. One of our men is just bringing in the male criminal at the front door, taken red handed with your grace's diamonds in his possession.'(All gazed round, and perceived indeed the check-capped lounger and a uniformed constable entering with the flower-seller between them.) 'The female criminal, who picked the lock of your grace's safe, is – here! No you don't,' he added, as Célestine, amid a torrent of apache language which nobody, fortunately, had French enough to understand, attempted to whip out a revolver from the bosom of her demure black dress. 'Célestine Berger,' he continued, pocketing the weapon. 'I arrest you in the name of the law, and I warn you that anything you say will be taken down and used as evidence against you.'

'Heaven help us,' said Lord Peter; 'the roof would fly off the court. And you've got the name wrong, Charles. Ladies and gentlemen, allow me to introduce to you Jacques Lerouge, known as Sans-culotte – the youngest and cleverest thief, safe-breaker, and female impersonator that ever occupied a dossier in the Palais de Justice.'

There was a gasp. Jacques Sans-culotte gave vent to a low oath and cocked a *gamin* grimace at Peter.

'C'est parfait,' said he; 'toutes mes félicitations, mi lord, what you call a fair cop, hein? And now I know him,' he added, grinning at Bunter, 'the so-patient Englishman who stand behind us in the queue at St Lazare. But tell me, please, how you know me, that I may correct it, *next time*.'

'I have mentioned to you before, Charles,' said Lord Peter, 'the unwisdom of falling into habits of speech: They give you away. Now, in France, every male child is brought up to use masculine adjectives about himself. He says: Que *je suis* beau. But a little girl has it rammed home to her that she is female; she must say: Que je suis belle! It must make it beastly hard to be a female impersonator. When I am at a station and I hear an excited young woman say to her companion, "Me prends-tu pour *un* imbécile" – the masculine article arouses curiosity. And that's that!' he concluded briskly. 'The rest was merely a matter of getting Bunter to take a photograph and communicating with our friends of the Sûreté and Scotland Yard.'

Jacques Sans-culotte bowed again.

'Once more I congratulate milord. He is the only Englishman I have ever met who is capable of appreciating our beautiful language. I will pay great attention in future to the article in question.'

With an awful look, the Dowager Duchess of Medway advanced upon Lord Peter.

'Peter,' she said, 'do you mean to say you *knew* about this, and that for the last three weeks you have allowed me to be dressed and undressed and put to bed by a *young man*?'

His lordship had the grace to blush.

'Duchess,' he said humbly, 'on my honour I didn't know absolutely for certain till this morning. And the police were so anxious to have these people caught red handed. What can I do to show my penitence? Shall I cut the privileged beast to pieces?'

The grim old mouth relaxed a little.

'After all,' said the dowager duchess, with the delightful consciousness that she was going to shock her daughter-in-law, 'there are very few women of my age who could make the same boast. It seems that we die as we have lived, my dear.'

For indeed the Dowager Duchess of Medway had been notable in her day.

THE INCREDIBLE ELOPEMENT OF
LORD PETER WIMSEY

'That house, señor?' said the landlord of the little *posada*. 'That is the house of the American physician, whose wife, may the blessed saints preserve us, is bewitched.' He crossed himself, and so did his wife and daughter.

'Bewitched, is she?' said Langley sympathetically. He was a professor of ethnology, and this was not his first visit to the Pyrenees. He had, however, never before penetrated to any place quite so remote as this tiny hamlet, clinging, like a rock-plant, high up the scarred granite shoulders of the mountain. He scented material here for his book on Basque folk-lore. With tact, he might persuade the old man to tell his story.

'And in what manner,' he asked, 'is the lady bespelled?'

'Who knows?' replied the landlord, shrugging his shoulders. '"The man that asked questions on Friday was buried on Saturday". Will your honour consent to take his supper?'

Langley took the hint. To press the question would be to encounter obstinate silence. Later, when they knew him better, perhaps—

His dinner was served to him at the family table – the oily, pepper-flavoured stew to which he was so well accustomed, and the harsh red wine of the country. His hosts chattered to him freely enough in that strange Basque language which has no fellow in the world, and is said by some to be the very speech of our first fathers in Paradise. They spoke of the bad winter, and young Esteban Arramandy, so strong and swift at the pelota, who had been lamed by a falling rock and now halted on two sticks; of three valuable goats carried off by a bear; of the torrential rains that, after a dry summer, had scoured the bare ribs of the mountains. It was raining now, and the wind was howling unpleasantly. This did not trouble Langley; he knew and loved this haunted and impenetrable country at all times and seasons. Sitting in that rude peasant inn, he thought of the oak-panelled hall of his Cambridge college and smiled, and his eyes gleamed happily behind his scholarly pince-nez. He was a young man, in spite of his professorship and the string of letters after his name. To his university colleagues it seemed strange that this man, so trim, so prim, so early old, should spend his vacations eating garlic, and scrambling on mule-back along precipitous mountain-tracks. You would never think it, they said, to look at him.

There was a knock at the door. 'That is Martha,' said the wife.

She drew back the latch, letting in a rush of wind and rain which made the candle gutter. A small, aged woman was blown in out of the night, her grey hair straggling in wisps from beneath her shawl.

'Come in, Martha, and rest yourself. It is a bad night. The parcel is ready – oh, yes. Dominique brought it from the town this morning. You must take a cup of wine or milk before you go back.'

The old woman thanked her and sat down, panting.

'And how goes all at the house? The doctor is well?'

'He is well.'

'And *she*?'

The daughter put the question in a whisper, and the landlord shook his head at her with a frown.

'As always at this time of the year. It is but a month now to the Day of the Dead. Jesu-Maria! it is a grievous affliction for the poor gentleman, but he is patient, patient.'

'He is a good man,' said Dominique, 'and a skilful doctor, but an evil like that is beyond his power to cure. You are not afraid, Martha?'

'Why should I be afraid? The Evil One cannot harm *me*. I have no beauty, no wits, no strength for him to envy. And the Holy Relic will protect me.'

Her wrinkled fingers touched something in the bosom of her dress.

'You come from the house yonder?' asked Langley.

She eyed him suspiciously.

'The señor is not of our country?'

'The gentleman is a guest, Martha,' said the landlord hurriedly. 'A learned English gentleman. He knows our country and speaks our language as you hear. He is a great traveller, like the American doctor, your master.'

'What is your master's name?' asked Langley. It occurred to him that an American doctor who had buried himself in this remote corner of Europe must have something unusual about him. Perhaps he also was an ethnologist. If so, they might find something in common.

'He is called Wetherall.' She pronounced the name several times before he was sure of it.

'Wetherall? Not Standish Wetherall?'

He was filled with extraordinary excitement.

The landlord came to his assistance.

'This parcel is for him,' he said. 'No doubt the name will be written there.'

It was a small package, neatly sealed, bearing the label of a firm of London chemists and addressed to 'Standish Wetherall, Esq., M.D.'

'Good Heavens!' exclaimed Langley. 'But this is strange. Almost a miracle. I know this man. I knew his wife, too—'

He stopped. Again the company made the sign of the cross.

'Tell me,' he said in great agitation, and forgetting his caution, 'you say his wife is bewitched – afflicted – how is this? Is she the same woman I know? Describe her. She was tall, beautiful, with gold hair and blue eyes like the Madonna. Is this she?'

There was a silence. The old woman shook her head and muttered something inaudible, but the daughter whispered:

'True – it is true. Once we saw her thus, as the gentleman says—'

'Be quiet,' said her father.

'Sir,' said Martha, 'we are in the hand of God.'

She rose, and wrapped her shawl about her.

'One moment,' said Langley. He pulled out his note-book and scribbled a few lines. 'Will you take this letter to your master the doctor? It is to say that I am here, his friend whom he once knew, and to ask if I may come and visit him. That is all.'

'You would not go to that house, excellence?' whispered the old man fearfully.

'If he will not have me, maybe he will come to me here.' He added a word or two and drew a piece of money from his pocket. 'You will carry my note for me?'

'Willingly, willingly. But the señor will be careful? Perhaps, though a foreigner, you are of the Faith?'

'I am a Christian,' said Langley.

This seemed to satisfy her. She took the letter and the money, and secured them, together with the parcel, in a remote pocket. Then she walked to the door, strongly and rapidly for all her bent shoulders and appearance of great age.

Langley remained lost in thought. Nothing could have astonished him more than to meet the name of Standish Wetherall in this place. He had thought that episode finished and done with over three years ago. Of all people! The brilliant surgeon in the prime of life and reputation, and Alice Wetherall, that delicate piece of golden womanhood – exiled in this forlorn corner of the world! His heart beat a little faster at the thought of seeing her again. Three years ago, he had decided that it would be wiser if he did not see too much of that porcelain loveliness. That folly was past now – but still he could not visualise her except against the background of the great white house in Riverside Drive, with the peacocks and the swimming-pool and the gilded tower with the roof-garden. Wetherall was a rich man, the son of old Hiram Wetherall the automobile magnate. What was Wetherall doing here?

He tried to remember. Hiram Wetherall, he knew, was dead, and all the money belonged to Standish, for there were no other children. There had been trouble when the only son had married a girl without parents or history. He had brought her from 'somewhere out west'. There had been some story of his having found her, years before, as a neglected orphan, and saved her from something or cured her of something and paid for her education, when he was still scarcely more than a student. Then, when he was a man over forty and she a girl of seventeen, he had brought her home and married her.

And now he had left his house and his money and one of the finest specialist practices in New York to come to live in the Basque country – in a spot so out of the way that men still believed in Black Magic, and could barely splutter more than a few words of bastard French or Spanish – a spot that was uncivilised even by comparison with the primitive civilisation surrounding it. Langley began to be sorry that he had written to Wetherall. It might be resented.

The landlord and his wife had gone out to see to their cattle. The daughter sat close to the fire, mending a garment. She did not look at him, but he had the feeling that she would be glad to speak.

'Tell me, child,' he said gently, 'what is the trouble which afflicts these people who may be friends of mine?'

'Oh!' she glanced up quickly and leaned across to him, her arms stretched out over the sewing in her lap. 'Sir, be advised. Do not go up there. No one will stay in that house at this time of the year, except Tomaso, who has not all his wits, and old Martha, who is—'

'What?'

'A saint – or something else,' she said hurriedly.

'Child,' said Langley again, 'this lady when I knew—'

'I will tell you,' she said, 'but my father must not know. The good doctor brought her here three years ago last June, and then she was as you say. She was beautiful. She laughed and talked in her own speech – for she knew no Spanish or Basque. But on the Night of the Dead—'

She crossed herself.

'All-Hallows Eve,' said Langley softly.

'Indeed, I do not know what happened. But she fell into the power of the darkness. She changed. There were terrible cries – I cannot tell. But little by little she became what she is now. Nobody sees her but Martha and she will not talk. But the people say it is not a woman at all that lives there now.'

'Mad?' said Langley.

'It is not madness. It is – enchantment. Listen. Two years since on Easter Day – is that my father?'

'No, no.'

'The sun had shone and the wind came up from the valley. We heard the blessed church bells all day long. That night there came a knock at the door. My father opened and one stood there like Our Blessed Lady herself, very pale like the image in the church and with a blue cloak over her head. She spoke, but we could not tell what she said. She wept and wrung her hands and pointed down the valley path, and my father went to the stable and saddled the mule. I thought of the flight from bad King Herod. But then – the American doctor came. He had run fast and was out of breath. And she shrieked at sight of him.'

A great wave of indignation swept over Langley. If the man was brutal to his wife, something must be done quickly. The girl hurried on.

'He said – Jesu-Maria – he said that his wife was bewitched. At Easter-tide the power of the Evil One was broken and she would try to flee. But as soon as the Holy Season was over, the spell would fall on her again, and therefore it was not safe to let her go. My parents were afraid to have touched the evil thing. They brought out the Holy Water and sprinkled the mule, but the wickedness had entered into the poor beast and she kicked my father so that he was lame for a month. The American took his wife away with him and we never saw her again. Even old Martha does not always see her. But every year the power waxes and wanes – heaviest at

Hallow-tide and lifted again at Easter. Do not go to that house, señor, if you value your soul! Hush! they are coming back.'

Langley would have liked to ask more, but his host glanced quickly and suspiciously at the girl. Taking up his candle, Langley went to bed. He dreamed of wolves, long, lean and black, running on the scent of blood.

Next day brought an answer to his letter:

> '*DEAR LANGLEY*, – *Yes, this is myself, and of course I remember you well. Only too delighted to have you come and cheer our exile. You will find Alice somewhat changed, I fear, but I will explain our misfortunes when we meet. Our house-hold is limited, owing to some kind of superstitious avoidance of the afflicted, but if you will came along about half-past seven, we can give you a meal of sorts. Martha will show you the way.*
>
> '*Cordially,*
> *STANDISH WETHERALL.*'

The doctor's house was small and old, stuck halfway up the mountain-side on a kind of ledge in the rock-wall. A stream, unseen but clamorous, fell echoing down close at hand. Langley followed his guide into a dim, square room with a great hearth at one end, and drawn close before the fire, an armchair with wide, sheltering ears. Martha, muttering some sort of apology, hobbled away and left him standing there in the half-light. The flames of the wood fire, leaping and falling, made here a gleam and there a gleam, and, as his eyes grew familiar with the room, he saw that in the centre was a table laid for a meal, and that there were pictures on the walls. One of these struck a familiar note. He went close to it and recognised a portrait of Alice Wetherall that he had last seen in New York. It was painted by Sargent in his happiest mood, and the lovely wild-flower face seemed to lean down to him with the sparkling smile of life.

A log suddenly broke and fell into the hearth, flaring. As though the little noise and light had disturbed something, he heard, or thought he heard, a movement from the big chair before the fire. He stepped forward, and then stopped. There was nothing to be seen, but a noise had begun; a kind of low, animal muttering, extremely disagreeable to listen to. It was not made by a dog or a cat, he felt sure. It was a sucking, slobbering sound that affected him in a curiously sickening way. It ended in a series of little grunts or squeals, and then there was silence.

Langley stepped backwards towards the door. He was positive that something was in the room with him that he did not care about meeting. An absurd impulse seized him to run away. He was prevented by the arrival of Martha, carrying a big, old-fashioned lamp, and behind her, Wetherall, who greeted him cheerfully.

The familiar American accents dispelled the atmosphere of discomfort that had been gathering about Langley. He held out a cordial hand.

'Fancy meeting *you* here,' said he.

'The world is very small,' replied Wetherall. 'I am afraid that is a hardy bromide, but I certainly am pleased to see you,' he added, with some emphasis.

The old woman had put the lamp on the table, and now asked if she could bring in the dinner. Wetherall replied in the affirmative, using a mixture of Spanish and Basque which she seemed to understand well enough.

'I didn't know you were a Basque scholar,' said Langley.

'Oh, one picks it up. These people speak nothing else. But of course Basque is your speciality, isn't it?'

'Oh, yes.'

'I daresay they have told you some queer things about us. But we'll go into that later. I've managed to make the place reasonably comfortable, though I could do with a few more modern conveniences. However, it suits us.'

Langley took the opportunity to mumble some sort of inquiry about Mrs Wetherall.

'Alice? Ah, yes, I forgot – you have not seen her yet.' Wetherall looked hard at him with a kind of half-smile. 'I should have warned you. You were – rather an admirer of my wife in the old days.'

'Like everyone else,' said Langley.

'No doubt. Nothing specially surprising about it, was there? Here comes dinner. Put it down, Martha, and we will ring when we are ready.'

The old woman set down a dish upon the table, which was handsomely furnished with glass and silver, and went out. Wetherall moved over to the fireplace, stepping sideways and keeping his eyes oddly fixed on Langley. Then he addressed the armchair.

'Alice! Get up, my dear, and welcome an old admirer of yours. Come along. You will both enjoy it. Get up.'

Something shuffled and whimpered among the cushions. Wetherall stooped, with an air of almost exaggerated courtesy, and lifted it to its feet. A moment, and it faced Langley in the lamplight.

It was dressed in a rich gown of gold satin and lace, that hung rucked and crumpled upon the thick and slouching body. The face was white and puffy, the eyes vacant, the mouth drooled open, with little trickles of saliva running from the loose corners. A dry fringe of rusty hair clung to the half-bald scalp, like the dead wisps on the head of a mummy.

'Come, my love,' said Wetherall. 'Say how do you do to Mr Langley.'

The creature blinked and mouthed out some inhuman sounds. Wetherall put his hand under its forearm, and it slowly extended a lifeless paw.

'There, she recognises you all right. I thought she would. Shake hands with him, my dear.'

With a sensation of nausea, Langley took the inert hand. It was clammy and coarse to the touch and made no attempt to return his pressure. He let it go; it pawed vaguely in the air for a moment and then dropped.

'I was afraid you might be upset,' said Wetherall, watching him. 'I have grown used to it, of course, and it doesn't affect me as it would an outsider. Not that you are an outsider – anything but that – eh? Premature senility is the lay name for it, I suppose. Shocking, of course, if you haven't met it before. You needn't mind, by the way, what you say. She understands nothing.'

'How did it happen?'

'I don't quite know. Came on gradually. I took the best advice, naturally, but there was nothing to be done. So we came here. I didn't care about facing things at home where everybody knew us. And I didn't like the idea of a sanatorium. Alice is my wife, you know – sickness or health, for better, for worse, and all that. Come along; dinner's getting cold.'

He advanced to the table, leading his wife, whose dim eyes seemed to brighten a little at the sight of food.

'Sit down, my dear, and eat your nice dinner. (She understands that, you see.) You'll excuse her table-

manners, won't you? They're not pretty, but you'll get
used to them.'

He tied a napkin round the neck of the creature and
placed food before her in a deep bowl. She snatched
at it hungrily, slavering and gobbling as she scooped
it up in her fingers and smeared face and hands with
the gravy.

Wetherall drew out a chair for his guest opposite to
where his wife sat. The sight of her held Langley with a
kind of disgusted fascination.

The food – a sort of salmis – was deliciously cooked,
but Langley had no appetite. The whole thing was an
outrage, to the pitiful woman and to himself. Her seat
was directly beneath the Sargent portrait, and his eyes
went helplessly from the one to the other.

'Yes,' said Wetherall, following his glance. 'There is a
difference, isn't there?' He himself was eating heartily
and apparently enjoying his dinner. 'Nature plays sad
tricks upon us.'

'Is it always like this?'

'No; this is one of her bad days. At times she will
be – almost human. Of course these people here don't
know what to think of it all. They have their own
explanation of a very simple medical phenomenon.'

'Is there any hope of recovery?'

'I'm afraid not – not of a permanent cure. You are
not eating anything.'

'I – well, Wetherall, this has been a shock to me.'

'Of course. Try a glass of burgundy. I ought not to
have asked you to come, but the idea of talking to an
educated fellow-creature once again tempted me, I
must confess.'

'It must be terrible for you.'

'I have become resigned. Ah, naughty, naughty!' The idiot had flung half the contents of her bowl upon the table. Wetherall patiently remedied the disaster, and went on:

'I can bear it better here, in this wild place where everything seems possible and nothing unnatural. My people are all dead, so there was nothing to prevent me from doing as I liked about it.'

'No. What about your property in the States?'

'Oh, I run over from time to time to keep an eye on things. In fact, I am due to sail next month. I'm glad you caught me. Nobody over there knows how we're fixed, of course. They just know we're living in Europe.'

'Did you consult no American doctor?'

'No. We were in Paris when the first symptoms declared themselves. That was shortly after that visit you paid to us.' A flash of some emotion to which Langley could not put a name made the doctor's eyes for a moment sinister. 'The best men on this side confirmed my own diagnosis. So we came here.'

He rang for Martha, who removed the salmis and put on a kind of sweet pudding.

'Martha is my right hand,' observed Wetherall. 'I don't know what we shall do without her. When I am away, she looks after Alice like a mother. Not that there's much one can do for her, except to keep her fed and warm and clean – and the last is something of a task.'

There was a note in his voice which jarred on Langley. Wetherall noticed his recoil and said:

'I won't disguise from you that it gets on my nerves sometimes. But it can't be helped. Tell me about yourself. What have you been doing lately?'

Langley replied with as much vivacity as he could assume, and they talked of indifferent subjects till the deplorable being which had once been Alice Wetherall began to mumble and whine fretfully and scramble down from her chair.

'She's cold,' said Wetherall. 'Go back to the fire, my dear.'

He propelled her briskly towards the hearth, and she sank back into the armchair, crouching and complaining and thrusting out her hands towards the blaze. Wetherall brought out brandy and a box of cigars.

'I contrive just to keep in touch with the world, you see,' he said. 'They send me these from London. And I get the latest medical journals and reports. I'm writing a book, you know, on my own subject; so I don't vegetate. I can experiment, too – plenty of room for a laboratory, and no Vivisection Acts to bother one. It's a good country to work in. Are you staying here long?'

'I think not very.'

'Oh! If you had thought of stopping on, I would have offered you the use of this house while I was away. You would find it more comfortable than the *posada,* and I should have no qualms, you know, about leaving you alone in the place with my wife – under the peculiar circumstances.'

He stressed the last words and laughed. Langley hardly knew what to say.

'Really, Wetherall—'

'Though, in the old days, *you* might have liked the prospect more and *I* might have liked it less. There was a time, I think, Langley, when you would have jumped at the idea of living alone with – *my wife.*'

Langley jumped up.

'What the devil are you insinuating, Wetherall?'

'Nothing, nothing. I was just thinking of the afternoon when you and she wandered away at a picnic and got lost. You remember? Yes, I thought you would.'

'This is monstrous,' retorted Langley. 'How dare you say such things – with that poor soul sitting there—?'

'Yes, poor soul. You're a poor thing to look at now aren't you, my kitten?'

He turned suddenly to the woman. Something in his abrupt gesture seemed to frighten her, and she shrank away from him.

'You devil!' cried Langley. 'She's afraid of you. What have you been doing to her? How did she get in this state? I will *know*!'

'Gently,' said Wetherall. 'I can allow for your natural agitation at finding her like this, but I can't have you coming between me and *my wife*. What a faithful fellow you are, Langley. I believe you still want her – just as you did before when you thought I was dumb and blind. Come now, have you got designs on *my wife*, Langley? Would you like to kiss her, caress her, take her to bed with you – my beautiful wife?'

A scarlet fury blinded Langley. He dashed an inexpert fist at the mocking face. Wetherall gripped his arm, but he broke away. Panic seized him. He fled stumbling against the furniture and rushed out. As he went he heard Wetherall very softly laughing.

The train to Paris was crowded. Langley, scrambling in at the last moment, found himself condemned to the corridor. He sat down on a suitcase and tried to think. He had not been able to collect his thoughts on his wild flight. Even now, he was not quite sure what he had fled from. He buried his head in his hands.

'Excuse me,' said a polite voice.

Langley looked up. A fair man in a grey suit was looking down at him through a monocle.

'Fearfully sorry to disturb you,' went on the fair man. 'I'm just tryin' to barge back to my jolly old kennel. Ghastly crowd, isn't it? Don't know when I've disliked my fellow-creatures more. I say, you don't look frightfully fit. Wouldn't you be better on something more comfortable?'

Langley explained that he had not been able to get a seat. The fair man eyed his haggard and unshaven countenance for a moment and then said:

'Well, look here, why not come and lay yourself down in my bin for a bit? Have you had any grub? No? That's a mistake. Toddle along with me and we'll get hold of a spot of soup and so on. You'll excuse my mentioning it, but you look as if you'd been backing a system that's come unstuck, or something. Not my business, of course, but do have something to eat.'

Langley was too faint and sick to protest. He stumbled obediently along the corridor till he was pushed into a first-class sleeper, where a rigidly correct man-servant was laying out a pair of mauve silk pyjamas and a set of silver-mounted brushes.

'This gentleman's feeling rotten, Bunter,' said the man with the monocle, 'so I've brought him in to rest his aching head upon thy breast. Get hold of the commissariat and tell 'em to buzz a plate of soup along and a bottle of something drinkable.'

'Very good, my lord.'

Langley dropped, exhausted, on the bed, but when the food appeared he ate and drank greedily. He could not remember when he had last made a meal.

'I say,' he said, 'I wanted that. It's awfully decent of you. I'm sorry to appear stupid. I've had a bit of a shock.'

'Tell me all,' said the stranger pleasantly.

The man did not look particularly intelligent, but he seemed friendly, and above all, normal. Langley wondered how the story would sound.

'I'm an absolute stranger to you,' he began.

'And I to you,' said the fair man. 'The chief use of strangers is to tell things to. Don't you agree?'

'I'd like –' said Langley. 'The fact is, I've run away from something. It's queer – it's – but what's the use of bothering you with it?'

The fair man sat down beside him and laid a slim hand on his arm.

'Just a moment,' he said. 'Don't tell me anything if you'd rather not. But my name is Wimsey – Lord Peter Wimsey – and I am interested in queer things.'

It was in the middle of November when the strange man came to the village. Thin, pale and silent, with his great black hood flapping about his face, he was surrounded with an atmosphere of mystery from the start. He settled down, not at the inn, but in a dilapidated cottage high up in the mountains, and he brought with him five mule loads of mysterious baggage and a servant. The servant was almost as uncanny as the master; he was a Spaniard and spoke Basque well enough to act as an interpreter for his employer when necessary; but his words were few, his aspect gloomy and stern, and such brief information as he vouchsafed, disquieting in the extreme. His master, he said, was a wise man; he spent all his time reading books; he ate no flesh; he was of no known country; he spoke the language of the

Apostles and had talked with blessed Lazarus after his return from the grave; and when he sat alone in his chamber by night, the angels of God came and conversed with him in celestial harmonies.

This was terrifying news. The few dozen villagers avoided the little cottage, especially at night-time; and when the pale stranger was seen coming down the mountain path, folded in his black robe and bearing one of his magic tomes beneath his arm, the women pushed their children within doors, and made the sign of the cross.

Nevertheless, it was a child that first made the personal acquaintance of the magician. The small son of the Widow Etcheverry, a child of bold and inquisitive disposition, went one evening adventuring into the unhallowed neighbourhood. He was missing for two hours, during which his mother, in a frenzy of anxiety, had called the neighbours about her and summoned the priest, who had unhappily been called away on business to the town. Suddenly, however, the child reappeared, well and cheerful, with a strange story to tell.

He had crept up close to the magician's house (the bold, wicked child, did ever you hear the like?) and climbed into a tree to spy upon the stranger (Jesu-Maria!) and he saw a light in the window, and strange shapes moving about and shadows going to and fro within the room. And then there came a strain of music so ravishing it drew the very heart out of his body, as though all the stars were singing together. (Oh, my precious treasure! The wizard has stolen the heart out of him, alas! alas!) Then the cottage door opened and the wizard came out and with him a great company of familiar spirits. One of them had wings like a seraph and talked in an unknown tongue, and another was like a wee man, no higher than your knee, with a black face and a white beard, and he sat on the wizard's shoulder and whispered in his ear. And the heavenly music played louder and louder. And the wizard had a pale flame all about his head, like the pictures of the saints. (Blessed St James of Compostela, be merciful to us all! And what then?) Why then he, the boy, had been very much frightened and wished he had not come, but the little dwarf spirit had seen him and jumped into the tree after him, climbing – oh! so fast! And he had tried to climb higher and had slipped and fallen to the ground. (Oh, the poor, wicked, brave, bad boy!)

Then the wizard had come and picked him up and spoken strange words to him and all the pain had gone away from the places where he had bumped himself (Marvellous! marvellous!), and he had carried him into the house. And inside, it was like the streets of Heaven all gold and glittering. And the familiar spirits had sat beside the fire, nine in number, and the music had stopped playing. But the wizard's servant had brought him marvellous fruits in a silver dish, like fruits of Paradise, very sweet and delicious, and he had eaten them, and drunk a strange, rich drink from a goblet covered with red and blue jewels. Oh, yes – and there had been a tall crucifix on the wall, big, big, with a lamp burning before it and a strange sweet perfume like the smell in church on Easter Day.

(A crucifix? That was strange. Perhaps the magician was not so wicked after all. And what next?)

Next, the wizard's servant had told him not to be afraid, and had asked his name and his age and whether he could repeat his Paternoster. So he had said the prayer and the Ave Maria and part of the Credo, but the Credo was long and he had forgotten what came after '*ascendit in caelum.*' So the wizard had prompted him and they had finished saying it together. And the wizard had pronounced the sacred names and words without flinching and in the right order, so far as he could tell. And then the servant had asked further about himself and his family, and he had told about the death of the black goat and about his sister's lover, who had left her because she had not so much money as the merchant's daughter. Then the wizard and his servant had spoken together and laughed, and the servant had said: 'My master gives this message to your sister: that where there is no love there is no wealth, but he that is bold shall have gold for the asking.' And with that, the wizard had put forth his hand into the air and taken from it – out of the empty air, yes, truly – one, two, three, four, five pieces of money and given them to him, And he was afraid to take them till he had made the sign of the cross upon them, and then, as they did not vanish or turn into fiery serpents, he had taken them, and here they were!

So the gold pieces were examined and admired in fear and trembling, and then, by grandfather's advice, placed under the feet of the image of Our Lady, after a sprinkling with Holy Water for their better purification. And on the next morning, as they were still there, they were shown to the priest, who arrived, tardy and flustered upon his last night's summons, and by him pronounced to be good Spanish coin, whereof one piece being devoted to the Church to put all right with Heaven, the rest might be put to secular uses without peril to the soul. After which, the good padre made his hasty way to the cottage, and returned, after an hour, filled with good reports of the wizard.

'For, my children,' said he, 'this is no evil sorcerer, but a Christian man, speaking the language of the Faith. He and I have conversed together with edification. Moreover, he keeps very good wine and is altogether a very worthy person. Nor did I perceive any familiar spirits or flaming apparitions; but it is true that there is a crucifix and also a very handsome Testament with pictures in gold and colour. *Benedicite*, my children. This is a good and learned man.'

And away he went back to his presbytery; and that winter the chapel of Our Lady had a new altar-cloth.

After that, each night saw a little group of people clustered at a safe distance to hear the music which poured out from the wizard's windows, and from time to time a few bold spirits would creep up close enough to peer through the chinks of the shutters and glimpse the marvels within.

The wizard had been in residence about a month, and sat one night after his evening meal in conversation with his servant. The black hood was pushed back from his head, disclosing a sleek poll of fair hair, and a pair of rather humorous grey eyes, with a cynical droop of the lids. A glass of Cockburn 1908 stood on the table at his elbow and from the arm of his chair a red-and-green parrot gazed unwinkingly at the fire.

'Time is getting on, Juan,' said the magician. 'This business is very good fun and all that – but is there anything doing with the old lady?'

'I think so, my lord. I have dropped a word or two here and there of marvellous cures and miracles. I think she will come. Perhaps even tonight.'

'Thank goodness! I want to get the thing over before Wetherall comes back, or we may find ourselves in Queer Street. It will take some weeks, you know, before we are ready to move, even if the scheme works at all. Damn it, what's that?'

Juan rose and went into the inner room, to return in a minute carrying the lemur.

'Mickey has been playing with your hair-brushes,' he said indulgently. 'Naughty one, be quiet! Are you ready for a little practice, my lord?'

'Oh, rather, yes! I'm getting quite a dab at this job. If all else fails, I shall try for an engagement with Maskelyne.'

Juan laughed, showing his white teeth. He brought out a set of billiard-balls, coins and other conjuring apparatus, palming and multiplying them negligently as he went. The other took them from him, and the lesson proceeded.

'Hush!' said the wizard, retrieving a ball which had tiresomely slipped from his fingers in the very act of vanishing. 'There's somebody coming up the path.'

He pulled his robe about his face and slipped silently into the inner room. Juan grinned, removed the decanter and glasses, and extinguished the lamp. In the firelight the great eyes of the lemur gleamed strongly as it hung on the back of the high chair. Juan pulled a large folio from the shelf, lit a scented pastille in a curiously shaped copper vase and pulled forward a heavy iron cauldron which stood on the hearth. As he piled the logs about it, there came a knock. He opened the door, the lemur running at his heels.

'Whom do you seek, mother?' he asked, in Basque.

'Is the Wise One at home?'

'His body is at home, mother; his spirit holds converse with the unseen. Enter. What would you with us?'

'I have come, as I said – ah, Mary! Is that a spirit?'

122

'God made spirits and bodies also. Enter and fear not.'

The old woman came tremblingly forward.

'Hast thou spoken with him of what I told thee?'

'I have. I have shown him the sickness of thy mistress – her husband's sufferings – all.'

'What said he?'

'Nothing; he read in his book.'

'Think you he can heal her?'

'I do not know; the enchantment is a strong one; but my master is mighty for good.'

'Will he see me?'

'I will ask him. Remain here, and beware thou show no fear, whatever befall.'

'I will be courageous,' said the old woman, fingering her beads.

Juan withdrew. There was a nerve-shattering interval. The lemur had climbed up to the back of the chair again and swung, teeth-chattering, among the leaping shadows. The parrot cocked his head and spoke a few gruff words from his corner. An aromatic steam began to rise from the cauldron. Then, slowly into the red light, three, four, seven white shapes came stealthily and sat down in a circle about the hearth. Then, a faint music, that seemed to roll in from leagues away. The flame flickered and dropped. There was a tall cabinet against the wall with gold figures on it that seemed to move with the moving firelight.

Then, out of the darkness, a strange voice chanted in an unearthly tongue that sobbed and thundered.

Martha's knees gave under her. She sank down. The seven white cats rose and stretched themselves, and came sidling slowly about her. She looked up and saw the wizard standing before her, a book in one hand and a silver wand in the other. The upper part of his face was hidden, but she saw his pale lips move and presently he spoke, in a deep, husky tone that vibrated solemnly in the dim room:

'ὦ πέπον, εἰ μὲν γὰρ, πόλεμον περὶ τόνδε φυγόντε,
αἰεὶ δὴ μέλλοιμεν ἀγήρω τ᾽ ἀθανάτω τε
ἔσσεθ᾽, οὔτε κεν αὐτὸς ἐνὶ πρώτοισι μαχοίμην,
οὔτε κέ σε στέλλοιμι μάχην ἐς κυδιάνειραν . . .'

The great syllables went rolling on. Then the wizard paused, and added, in a kinder tone:

'Great stuff, this Homer. "It goes so thunderingly as though it conjured devils". What do I do next?'

The servant had come back, and now whispered in Martha's ear.

'Speak now,' he said. 'The master is willing to help you.'

Thus encouraged, Martha stammered out her request. She had come to ask the Wise Man to help her mistress, who lay under an enchantment. She had brought an offering – the best she could find, for she had not liked to take anything of her master's during his absence. But here were a silver penny, an oat-cake, and a bottle of wine, very much at the wizard's service, if such small matters could please him.

The wizard, setting aside his book, gravely accepted the silver penny, turned it magically into six gold pieces and laid the offering on the table. Over the oat-cake and the wine he showed a little hesitation, but at length, murmuring:

'Ergo omnis longo solvit se Teucria luctu'

(a line notorious for its grave spondaic cadence), he metamorphosed the one into a pair of pigeons and the other into a curious little crystal tree in a metal pot, and set them beside the coins. Martha's eyes nearly started from her head, but Juan whispered encouragingly:

'The good intention gives value to the gift. The master is pleased. Hush!'

The music ceased on a loud chord. The wizard, speaking now with greater assurance, delivered himself with fair accuracy of a page or so from Homer's Catalogue of the Ships, and, drawing from the folds of his robe his long white hand laden with antique rings, produced from mid-air a small casket of shining metal, which he proffered to the suppliant.

'The master says,' prompted the servant, 'that you shall take this casket, and give to your lady of the wafers which it contains, one at every meal. When all have been consumed, seek this place again. And remember to say three Aves and two Paters morning and evening for the intention of the lady's health. Thus, by faith and diligence, the cure may be accomplished.'

Martha received the casket with trembling hands.

'Tendebantque manus ripae ulterioris amore,' said the wizard, with emphasis. 'Poluphloisboio thalasses. Ne plus ultra. Valete. Plaudite.'

He walked away into the darkness, and the audience was over.

'It is working, then?' said the wizard to Juan.

The time was five weeks later, and five more consignments of enchanted wafers had been ceremoniously dispatched to the grim house on the mountain.

'It is working,' agreed Juan. 'The intelligence is returning, the body is becoming livelier and the hair is growing again.'

'Thank the Lord! It was a shot in the dark, Juan, and even now I can hardly believe that anyone in the world could think of such a devilish trick. When does Wetherall return?'

'In three weeks' time.'

'Then we had better fix our grand finale for today fortnight. See that the mules are ready, and go down to the town and get a message off to the yacht.'

'Yes, my lord.'

'That will give you a week to get clear with the menagerie and the baggage. And – I say, how about Martha? Is it dangerous to leave her behind, do you think?'

'I will try to persuade her to come back with us.'

'Do. I should hate anything unpleasant to happen to her. The man's a criminal lunatic. Oh, lord! I'll be glad when this is over. I want to get into a proper suit of clothes again. What Bunter would say if he saw this—'

The wizard laughed, lit a cigar and turned on the gramophone.

The last act was duly staged a fortnight later.

It had taken some trouble to persuade Martha of the necessity of bringing her mistress to the wizard's house. Indeed, that supernatural personage had been obliged to make an alarming display of wrath and declaim two whole choruses from Euripides before gaining his point. The final touch was put to the terrors of the evening by a demonstration of the ghastly effects of a sodium flame – which lends a very corpse-like aspect to the human countenance, particularly in a lonely cottage on a dark night, and accompanied by incantations and the 'Danse Macabre' of Saint-Saëns.

Eventually the wizard was placated by a promise, and Martha departed, bearing with her a charm, engrossed upon parchment, which her mistress was to read and thereafter hang about her neck in a white silk bag.

Considered as a magical formula, the document was perhaps a little unimpressive in its language, but its meaning was such as a child could understand. It was in English, and ran:

> 'You have been ill and in trouble, but your friends are ready to cure you and help you. Don't be afraid, but do whatever Martha tells you, and you will soon be quite well and happy again.'

'And even if she can't understand it,' said the wizard to his man, 'it can't possibly do any harm.'

The events of that terrible night have become legend in the village. They tell by the fireside with bated breath how Martha brought the strange, foreign lady to the wizard's house, that she might be finally and for ever freed from the power of the Evil One. It was a dark night and a stormy, with the wind howling terribly through the mountains.

The lady had become much better and brighter through the wizard's magic – though this, perhaps, was only a fresh glamour and delusion – and she had followed Martha like a little child on that strange and secret journey. They had crept out very quietly to elude the vigilance of old Tomaso, who had strict orders from the doctor never to let the lady stir one step from the house. As for that, Tomaso swore that he had been cast into an enchanted sleep – but who knows? There may have been no more to it than over-much wine. Martha was a cunning woman, and, some said, little better than a witch herself.

Be that as it might, Martha and the lady had come to the cottage, and there the wizard had spoken likewise. Yes – she who for so long had only grunted like a beast, had talked with the wizard and answered him. Then the wizard had drawn strange signs upon the floor round about the lady and himself. And when the lamp was extinguished, the signs glowed awfully, with a pale light of their own. The wizard also drew a circle about Martha herself, and warned her to keep inside it. Presently they heard a rushing noise, like great wings beating, and all the familiars leaped about, and the little white man with the black face ran up the curtain and swung from the pole. Then a voice cried out: 'He comes! He comes!' and the wizard opened the door of the tall cabinet with gold images upon it, that stood in the centre of the circle, and he and the lady stepped inside it and shut the doors after them.

The rushing sound grew louder and the familiar spirits screamed and chattered – and then, all of a sudden, there was a thunder-clap and a great flash of light and the cabinet was shivered into pieces and fell down. And lo and behold! the wizard and the lady had vanished clean away and were never more seen or heard of.

This was Martha's story, told the next day to her neighbours. How she had escaped from the terrible house she could not remember. But when, some time after, a group of villagers summoned up courage to visit the place again, they found it bare and empty. Lady, wizard, servant, familiars, furniture, bags and baggage – all were gone, leaving not a trace behind them, except a few mysterious lines and figures traced on the floor of the cottage.

This was a wonder indeed. More awful still was the disappearance of Martha herself, which took place three nights afterwards.

Next day, the American doctor returned, to find an empty hearth and a legend.

'Yacht ahoy!'

Langley peered anxiously over the rail of the *Abracadabra* as the boat loomed out of the blackness. When the first passenger came aboard, he ran hastily to greet him.

'Is it all right, Wimsey?'

'Absolutely all right. She's a bit bewildered, of course – but you needn't be afraid. She's like a child, but she's getting better every day. Bear up, old man – there's nothing to shock you about her.'

Langley moved hesitatingly forward as a muffled female figure was hoisted gently on board.

'Speak to her,' said Wimsey. 'She may or may not recognise you. I can't say.'

Langley summoned up his courage. 'Good evening, Mrs Wetherall,' he said, and held out his hand.

The woman pushed the cloak from her face. Her blue eyes gazed shyly at him in the lamplight – then a smile broke out upon her lips.

'Why, I know you – of course I know you. You're Mr Langley. I'm so glad to see you.'

She clasped his hand in hers.

'Well, Langley,' said Lord Peter, as he manipulated the syphon, 'a more abominable crime it has never been my fortune to discover. My religious beliefs are a little ill-defined, but I hope something really beastly happens to Wetherall in the next world. Say when!

'You know, there were one or two very queer points about that story you told me. They gave me a line on the thing from the start.

'To begin with, there was this extraordinary kind of decay or imbecility settlin' in on a girl in her twenties – so conveniently, too, just after you'd been hangin' round the Wetherall home and showin' perhaps a trifle too much sensibility, don't you see? And then there was this tale of the conditions clearin' up regularly once a year or so – not like any ordinary brain-trouble. Looked as if it was being controlled by somebody.

'Then there was the fact that Mrs Wetherall had been under her husband's medical eye from the beginning, with no family or friends who knew anything about her to keep a check on the fellow. Then there was the determined isolation of her in a place where no doctor could see her and where, even if she had a lucid interval, there wasn't a soul who could understand or be understood by her. Queer, too, that it should be a part of the world where you, with your interests, might reasonably be expected to turn up some day and be treated to a sight of what she had turned into. Then there were Wetherall's well-known researches, and the fact that he kept in touch with a chemist in London.

'All that gave me a theory, but I had to test it before I could be sure I was right. Wetherall was going to America, and that gave me a chance; but of course he left strict orders that nobody should get into or out of his house during his absence. I had, somehow, to establish an authority greater than his over old Martha, who is a faithful soul, God bless her! Hence, exit Lord Peter Wimsey and enter the magician. The treatment was tried and proved successful – hence the elopement and the rescue.

'Well, now, listen – and don't go off the deep end. It's all over now. Alice Wetherall is one of those unfortunate people who suffer from congenital thyroid deficiency. You know the thyroid gland in your throat – the one that stokes the engine and keeps the old brain going. In some people the thing doesn't work properly, and they turn out cretinous imbeciles. Their bodies don't grow and their minds don't work. But feed 'em the stuff, and they come absolutely all right – cheery and handsome and intelligent and lively as crickets. Only, don't you see, you have to *keep* feeding it to 'em, otherwise they just go back to an imbecile condition.

'Wetherall found this girl when he was a bright young student just learning about the thyroid. Twenty years ago, very few experiments had been made in this kind of treatment, but he was a bit of a pioneer. He gets hold of the kid, works a miraculous cure, and, bein' naturally bucked with himself, adopts her, gets her educated, likes the look of her, and finally marries her. You understand, don't you, that there's nothing fundamentally unsound about those thyroid deficients. Keep 'em going on the little daily dose, and they're normal in every way, fit to live an ordinary life and have ordinary healthy children.

'Nobody, naturally, knew anything about this thyroid business except the girl herself and her husband. All goes well till *you* come along. Then Wetherall gets jealous—'

'He had no cause.'

Wimsey shrugged his shoulders.

'Possibly, my lad, the lady displayed a preference – we needn't go into that. Anyhow, Wetherall did get jealous and saw a perfectly marvellous revenge in his power. He carried his wife off to the Pyrenees, isolated her from all help, and then simply sat back and starved her of her thyroid extract. No doubt he told her what he was going to do, and why. It would please him to hear her desperate appeals – to let her feel herself slipping back day by day, hour by hour, into something less than a beast—'

'Oh, God!'

'As you say. Of course, after a time, a few months, she would cease to know what was happening to her. He would still have the satisfaction of watching her – seeing her skin thicken, her body coarsen, her hair fall out, her eyes grow vacant, her speech die away into mere animal noises, her brain go to mush; her habits—'

'Stop it, Wimsey.'

'Well, you saw it all yourself. But that wouldn't be enough for him. So, every so often, he would feed her the thyroid again and bring her back sufficiently to realise her own degradation—'

'If only I had the brute here!'

'Just as well you haven't. Well then, one day – by a stroke of luck – Mr Langley, the amorous Mr Langley, actually turns up. What a triumph to let him see—'

Langley stopped him again.

'Right-ho! but it was ingenious, wasn't it? So simple. The more I think of it, the more it fascinates me. But it was just that extra refinement of cruelty that defeated him. Because, when you told me the story, I couldn't help recognising the symptoms of thyroid deficiency, and I thought, "Just supposing" – so I hunted up the chemist whose name you saw on the parcel, and, after unwinding a lot of red tape, got him to admit that he had several times sent Wetherall consignments of thyroid extract. So then I was almost sure, don't you see.

'I got a doctor's advice and a supply of gland extract, hired a tame Spanish conjurer and some performing cats and things, and barged off complete with disguise and a trick cabinet devised by the ingenious Mr Devant. I'm a bit of a conjurer myself, and between us we didn't do so badly. The local superstitions helped, of course, and so did the gramophone records. Schubert's "Unfinished" is first class for producing an atmosphere of gloom and mystery, so are luminous paint and the remnants of a classical education.'

'Look here, Wimsey, will she get all right again?'

'Right as ninepence, and I imagine that any American court would give her a divorce on the grounds of persistent cruelty. After that – it's up to you!'

Lord Peter's friends greeted his reappearance in London with mild surprise.

'And what have *you* been doing with yourself?' demanded the Hon. Freddy Arbuthnot.

'Eloping with another man's wife,' replied his lordship. 'But only,' he hastened to add, 'in a purely Pickwickian sense. Nothing in it for yours truly. Oh, well! Let's toddle round to the Holborn Empire, and see what George Robey can do for us.'

THE FASCINATING PROBLEM OF
UNCLE MELEAGER'S WILL

'You look a little worried, Bunter,' said his lordship kindly to his manservant. 'Is there anything I can do?'

The valet's face brightened as he released his employer's grey trousers from the press.

'Perhaps your lordship could be so good as to think,' he said hopefully, 'of a word in seven letters with S in the middle, meaning two.'

'Also,' suggested Lord Peter thoughtlessly.

'I beg your lordship's pardon. T-w-o. And seven letters.'

'Nonsense!' said Lord Peter. 'How about that bath?'

'It should be just about ready, my lord.'

Lord Peter Wimsey swung his mauve silk legs lightly over the edge of the bed and stretched appreciatively. It was a beautiful June that year. Through the open door he saw the delicate coils of steam wreathing across a shaft of yellow sunlight. Every step he took into the bathroom was a conscious act of enjoyment. In the husky light tenor he carolled a few bars of '*Maman, dites-moi*.' Then a thought struck him, and he turned back.

'Bunter!'

'My lord?'

'No bacon this morning. Quite the wrong smell.'

'I was thinking of buttered eggs, my lord.'

'Excellent. Like primroses. The Beaconsfield touch,' said his lordship approvingly.

His song died into a rapturous crooning a she settled into the verbena-scented water, His eyes roamed vaguely over the pale blue-and-white tiles of the bathroom walls.

Mr Bunter had retired to the kitchen to put the coffee on the stove when the bell rang. Surprised, he hastened back to the bedroom. It was empty. With increased surprise, he realised that it must have been the bathroom bell. The words 'heart-attack' formed swiftly in his mind, to be displaced by the still more alarming thought, 'No soap.' He opened the door almost nervously.

'Did you ring, my lord?' he demanded of Lord Peter's head, alone visible.

'Yes,' said his lordship abruptly; 'Ambsace.'

'I beg your lordship's pardon?'

'Ambsace. Word of seven letters. Meaning two. With S in the middle. Two aces. Ambsace.'

Bunter's expression became beatified.

'Undoubtedly correct,' he said, pulling a small sheet of paper from his pocket, and entering the word upon it in pencil. 'I am extremely obliged to your lordship. In that case the "indifferent cook in six letters ending with *red*" must be Alfred.'

Lord Peter waved a dismissive hand.

On re-entering his bedroom, Lord Peter was astonished to see his sister Mary seated in his own particular chair and consuming his buttered eggs. He greeted her with a friendly acerbity, demanding why she look him up at that unearthly hour.

'I'm riding with Freddy Arbuthnot,' said her ladyship, 'as you might see by my legs, if you were really as big a Sherlock as you make out.'

'Riding,' replied her brother, 'I had already deduced though I admit that Freddy's name was not writ large to my before-breakfast eye, upon the knees of your breeches. But why this visit?'

'Well, because you were on the way,' said Lady Mary 'and I'm booked up all day, and I want you to come and dine at the Soviet Club with me tonight.'

'Good God, Mary, why? You know I hate the place Cooking's beastly, the men don't shave, and the conversation gets my goat. Besides, last time I went there, your friend Goyles plugged me in the shoulder I thought you'd chucked the Soviet Club.'

'It isn't me. It's Hannah Marryat.'

'What, the intense young woman with the badly bobbed hair and the brogues?'

'Well, she's never been able to afford a good hair dresser. That's just what I want your help about.'

'My dear child, I can't cut her hair for her. Bunter might. He can do most things.'

'Silly. No. But she's got – that is, she used to have – an uncle, the very rich, curmudgeony sort, you know who never gave anyone a penny. Well, he's dead, and they can't find his will.'

'Perhaps he didn't make one.'

'Oh, yes, he did. He wrote and told her so. But the nasty old thing hid it, and it can't be found.'

'Is the will in her favour?'

'Yes.'

'Who's the next of kin?'

'She and her mother are the only members of the family left.'

'Well, then, she's only got to sit tight and she'll get the goods.'

'No – because the horrid old man left two wills, and, if she can't find the latest one, they'll prove the first one. He explained that to her carefully.'

'Oh. I see. H'm. By the way I thought the young woman was a Socialist.'

'Oh, she is. Terrifically so. One really can't help admiring her. She has done some wonderful work—'

'Yes, I dare say. But in that case I don't see why she need be so keen on getting uncle's dollars.'

Mary began to chuckle.

'Ah! but that's where Uncle Meleager—'

'Uncle *what*?'

'Meleager. That's his name. Meleager Finch.'

'Oh!'

'Yes – well, that's where he's been so clever. Unless she finds the new will, the old will comes into force and hands over every penny of the money to the funds of the Primrose League.'

Lord Peter gave a little yelp of joy.

'Good for Uncle Meleager! But, look here, Mary, I'm a Tory, if anything. I'm certainly not a Red. Why should I help to snatch the good gold from the Primrose Leaguers and hand it over to the Third International? Uncle Meleager's a sport. I take to Uncle Meleager.'

'Oh, but Peter, I really don't think she'll do that with it. Not at present, anyway. They're awfully poor, and her mother ought to have some frightfully difficult operation or something, and go and live abroad, so it really is ever so important they should get the money. And perhaps Hannah wouldn't be quite so Red if she'd ever had a bean of her own. Besides, you could make it a condition of helping her that she should go and get properly shingled at Bresil's.'

'You are a very cynically-minded person,' said his lordship. 'However, it would be fun to have a go at Uncle M. Was he obliging enough to give any clues for finding the will?'

'He wrote a funny sort of letter, which we can't make head or tail of. Come to the club tonight and she'll show it to you.'

'Right-ho! Seven o'clock do? And we could go on and see a show afterwards. Do you mind clearing out now? I'm going to get dressed.'

Amid a deafening babble of voices in a low-pitched cellar, the Soviet Club meets and dines. Ethics and sociology, the latest vortices of the Whirligig school of verse combine with the smoke of countless cigarettes to produce an inspissated atmosphere, through which flat, angular mural paintings dimly lour upon the revellers. There is painfully little room for the elbows, or indeed for any part of one's body. Lord Peter – his feet curled under his chair to avoid the stray kicks of the heavy brogues opposite him – was acutely conscious of an unbecoming attitude and an overheated feeling about the head. He found it difficult to get any response from Hannah Marryat. Under her heavy ill-cut fringe her dark eyes gloomed sombrely at him. At the same time he received a strong impression of something enormously vital. He had a sudden fancy that if she were set free from self-defensiveness and the importance of being earnest, she would exhibit unexpected powers of enjoyment. He was interested, but oppressed. Mary, to his great relief, suggested that they should have their coffee upstairs.

They found a quiet corner with comfortable chairs.

'Well, now,' said Mary encouragingly.

'Of course you understand,' said Miss Marryat mournfully, 'that if it were not for the monstrous injustice of Uncle Meleager's other will, and mother being so ill; I shouldn't take any steps. But when there is £250,000, and the prospect of doing real good with it—'

'Naturally,' said Lord Peter, 'it isn't the money you care about, as the dear old bromide says, it's the principle of the thing. Right you are! Now supposin' we have a look at Uncle Meleager's letter.'

Miss Marryat rummaged in a very large handbag and passed the paper over.

This was Uncle Meleager's letter, dated from Sienna twelve months previously:

'MY DEAR HANNAH, – When I die – which I propose to do at my own convenience and not at that of my family – you will at last discover my monetary worth. It is, of course, considerably less than you had hoped, and quite fails, I assure you, adequately to represent my actual worth in the eyes of the discerning. I made my will yesterday, leaving the entire sum, such as it is, to the Primrose League – a body quite as fatuous as any other in our preposterous state, but which has the advantage of being peculiarly obnoxious to yourself. This will will be found in the safe in the library.

'I am not, however, unmindful of the fact that your mother is my sister, and you and she my only surviving relatives. I shall accordingly amuse myself by drawing up today a second will, superseding the other and leaving the money to you.

'I have always held that woman is a frivolous animal. A woman who pretends to be serious is wasting her time and spoiling her appearance. I consider that

you have wasted your time to a really shocking extent.
Accordingly, I intend to conceal this will, and that in
such a manner that you will certainly never find it
unless by the exercise of a sustained frivolity.

'*I hope you will contrive to be frivolous enough to*
become the heiress of your affectionate
'*UNCLE MELEAGER*'

'Couldn't we use that letter as proof of the testator's
intention, and fight the will?' asked Mary anxiously.

''Fraid not,' said Lord Peter. 'You see, there's no evidence here that the will was ever actually drawn up.
Though I suppose we could find the witnesses.'

'We've tried,' said Miss Marryat, 'but, as you see,
Uncle Meleager was travelling abroad at the time, and
he probably got some obscure people in some obscure
Italian town to witness it for him. We advertised, but
got no answer.'

'H'm. Uncle Meleager doesn't seem to have left
things to chance. And, anyhow, wills are queer things,
and so are the probate and divorce wallahs. Obviously
the thing to do is to find the other will. Did the clues
he speaks of turn up among his papers?'

'We hunted through everything. And, of course, we
had the whole house searched from top to bottom for
the will. But it was quite useless.'

'You've not destroyed anything, of course. Who were
the executors of the Primrose League will?'

'Mother and Mr Sands, Uncle Meleager's solicitor.
The will left mother a silver teapot for her trouble.'

'I like Uncle Meleager more and more. Anyhow,
he did the sporting thing. I'm beginnin' to enjoy this
case like anything. Where did Uncle Meleager hang
out?'

'It's an old house down at Dorking. It's rather quaint. Somebody had a fancy to build a little Roman villa sort of thing there, with a verandah behind, with columns and a pond in the front hall, and statues. It's very decent there just now, though it's awfully cold in the winter, with all those stone floors and stone stairs and the skylight over the hall! Mother said perhaps you would be very kind and come down and have a look at it.'

'I'd simply love to. Can we start tomorrow? I promise you we'll be frivolous enough to please even Uncle Meleager, if you'll do your bit, Miss Marryat. Won't we, Mary?'

'Rather! And, I say, hadn't we better be moving if we're going to the Pallambra?'

'I never go to music halls,' said Miss Marryat ungraciously.

'Oh, but you must come tonight,' said his lordship persuasively. 'It's so frivolous. Just think how it would please Uncle Meleager.'

Accordingly, the next day found the party, including the indispensable Mr Bunter, assembled at Uncle Meleager's house. Pending the settlement of the will question, there had seemed every reason why Mr Finch's executrix and next-of-kin should live in the house, thus providing every facility for what Lord Peter called the 'Treasure-hunt'. After being introduced to Mrs Marryat, who was an invalid and remained in her room, Lady Mary and her brother were shown over the house by Miss Marryat, who explained to them how carefully the search had been conducted. Every paper had been examined, every book in the library scrutinised page by page, the walls and chimneys tapped for hiding-places, the boards taken up, and so forth, but with no result.

'Y'know,' said his lordship, 'I'm sure you've been going the wrong way to work. My idea is, old Uncle Meleager was a man of his word. If he said frivolous, he meant really frivolous. Something beastly silly. I wonder what it was.'

He was still wondering when he went up to dress. Bunter was putting studs in his shirt. Lord Peter gazed thoughtfully at him, and then enquired:

'Are any of Mr Finch's old staff still here?'

'Yes, my lord. The cook and the housekeeper. Wonderful old gentleman they say he was, too. Eighty-three, but as up-to-date as you please. Had his wireless in his bedroom, and enjoyed the Savoy bands every night of his life. Followed his politics, and was always ready with the details of the latest big law-cases. If a young lady came to see him, he'd like to see she had her hair shingled and the latest style in fashions. They say he took up cross-words as soon as they came in, and was remarkably quick at solving them, my lord, and inventing them. Took a £10 prize in the *Daily Yell* for one, and was wonderfully pleased to get it, they say, my lord, rich as he was.'

'Indeed.'

'Yes, my lord. He was a great man for acrostics before that, I understood them to say, but, when cross-words came in, he threw away his acrostics and said he liked the new game better. Wonderfully adaptable, if I may say so, he seems to have been for an old gentleman.'

'Was he, by Jove?' said his lordship absently, and then, with sudden energy:

'Bunter, I'd like to double your salary, but I suppose you'd take it as an insult.'

The conversation bore fruit at dinner.

'What,' enquired his lordship, 'happened to Uncle Meleager's cross-words?'

'Cross-words?' said Hannah Marryat, knitting her heavy brows. 'Oh, those puzzle things! Poor old man, he went mad over them. He had every newspaper sent him, and in his last illness he'd be trying to fill the wretched things in. It was worse than his acrostics and his jig-saw puzzles. Poor old creature, he must have been senile, I'm afraid. Of course, we looked through them, but there wasn't anything there. We put them all in the attic.'

'The attic for me,' said Lord Peter.

'And for me,' said Mary. 'I don't believe there was anything senile about Uncle Meleager.'

The evening was warm, and they had dined in the little viridarium at the back of the house, with its tall vases and hanging baskets of flowers and little marble statues.

'Is there an attic here?' said Peter. 'It seems such a – well, such an un-attic thing to have in a house like this.'

'It's just a horrid, poky little hole over the porch,' said Miss Marryat, rising and leading the way. 'Don't tumble into the pond, will you? It's a great nuisance having it there, especially at night. I always tell them to leave a light on.'

Lord Peter glanced into the miniature impluvium, with its tiling of red, white, and black marble.

'That's not a very classic design,' he observed.

'No. Uncle Meleager used to complain about it and say he must have it altered. There was a proper one once, I believe, but it got damaged, and the man before Uncle Meleager had it replaced by some local

143

idiot. He built three bay windows out of the dining-room at the same time, which made it very much lighter and pleasanter, of course, but it looks awful. Now, this tiling is all right; uncle put that in himself.'

She pointed to a mosaic dog at the threshold, with the motto, 'Cave canem,' and Lord Peter recognised it as a copy of a Pompeian original.

A narrow stair brought them to the 'attic', where the Wimseys flung themselves with enthusiasm upon a huge heap of dusty old newspapers and manuscripts. The latter seemed the likelier field, so they started with them. They consisted of a quantity of cross-words in manuscript – presumably the children of Uncle Melager's own brain. The square, the list of definitions, and the solution were in every case neatly pinned together. Some (early efforts, no doubt) were childishly simple, but others were difficult, with allusive or punning clues, some of the ordinary newspaper type, others in the form of rhymed distichs. They scrutinised the solutions closely, and searched the definitions for acrostics or hidden words, unsuccessfully for a long time.

'This one's a funny one,' said Mary, 'nothing seems to fit. Oh! it's two pinned together. No, it isn't – yes, it is – it's only been pinned up wrong. Peter, have you seen the puzzle belonging to these clues anywhere?'

'What one's that?'

'Well, it's numbered rather funnily, with Roman and Arabic numerals, and it starts off with a thing that hasn't got any numbers at all:

'Truth, poor girl, was nobody's daughter;
She took off her clothes and jumped into the water.'

'Frivolous old wretch!' said Miss Marryat.

'Friv – here, gimme that!' cried Lord Peter. 'Look here, I say, Miss Marryat, you oughtn't to have over-looked this.'

'I thought it just belonged to that other square.'

'Not it. It's different. I believe it's our thing. Listen:

> 'Your expectation to be rich
> Here will reach its highest pitch.

That's one for you, Miss Marryat. Mary, hunt about. We *must* find the square that belongs to this.'

But, though they turned everything upside-down, they could find no square with Roman and Arabic numerals.

'Hang it all!' said Peter, 'it must be made to fit one of these others. Look! I know what he's done. He's just taken a fifteen-letter square, and numbered it with Roman figures one way and Arabic the other. I bet its fits into that one it was pinned up with.'

But the one it was pinned up with turned out to have only thirteen squares.

'Dash it all,' said his lordship, 'we'll have to carry the whole lot down, and work away at it till we find the one it *does* fit.'

He snatched up a great bundle of newspapers, and led the way out. The others followed, each with an armful. The search had taken some time, and the atrium was in semi-darkness.

'Where shall I take them?' asked Lord Peter, calling back over his shoulder.

'Hi!' cried Mary; and, 'Look where you're going!' cried her friend.

They were too late. A splash and a flounder proclaimed that Lord Peter had walked, like Johnny Head-in-Air, over the edge of the impluvium, papers and all.

'You ass!' said Mary.

His lordship scrambled out, spluttering, and Hannah Marryat suddenly burst out into the first laugh Peter had ever heard her give.

'Truth, they say, was nobody's daughter,
  She took off her clothes and fell into the water'

she proclaimed.

'Well, I couldn't take my clothes off with you here, could I?' grumbled Lord Peter. 'We'll have to fish out the papers. I'm afraid they've got a bit damp.'

Miss Marryat turned on the lights, and they started to clear the basin.

'Truth, poor girl –' began Lord Peter, and suddenly, with a little shriek, began to dance on the marble edge of the impluvium.

'One, two, three, four, five, six—'

'Quite, quite demented,' said Mary. 'How shall I break it to mother?'

'Thirteen, fourteen, *fifteen*!' cried his lordship, and sat down, suddenly and damply, exhausted by his own excitement.

'Feeling better?' asked his sister acidly.

'I'm well. I'm all right. Everything's all right. I *love* Uncle Meleager. Fifteen squares each way. Look at it. *Look* at it. The truth's in the water. Didn't he say so. Oh, frabjous day! Calloo! callay! I chortle. Mary, what became of those definitions?'

'They're in your pocket, all damp,' said Mary. Lord Peter snatched them out hurriedly.

'It's all right, they haven't run,' he said. 'Oh, *darling* Uncle Meleager. Can you drain the impluvium, Miss Marryat, and find a bit of charcoal. Then I'll get some dry clothes on and we'll get down to it. Don't you see?

146

There's your missing cross-word square – on the floor of the impluvium!'

It took, however, some time to get the basin emptied, and it was not till next morning that the party, armed with sticks of charcoal, squatted down in the empty impluvium to fill in Uncle Meleager's cross-word on the marble tiles. Their first difficulty was to decide whether the red squares counted as stops or had to be filled in, but, after a few definitions had been solved, the construction of the puzzle grew apace. The investigators grew steadily hotter and more thickly covered with charcoal, while the attentive Mr Bunter hurried to and fro between the atrium and the library, and the dictionaries piled up on the edge of the impluvium.

'Truth, poor girl, was nobody's daughter;
  She took off her clothes and jumped into the water.'

ACROSS.

I.1.   Foolish or wise, yet one remains alone,
     'Twixt Strength and Justice on a heavenly
     throne.

XI.1.   O to what ears the chink of gold was sweet!
     The greed for treasure brought him but defeat.

'That's a hint to us,' said Lord Peter.

I.2.   One drop of vinegar to two of oil
     Dresses this curly head sprung from the soil.

X.2.   Nothing itself, it needs but little more
     To be that nothingness the Preacher saw.

I.3.   Dusty though my fellows be,
     We are a kingly company.

IV.3.   Have your own will, though here, I hold,
      The new is *not* a patch upon the old.

XIV.3. Any loud cry would do as well,
Or so the poet's verses tell.

I.4. This is the most unkindest cut of all,
Except your skill be mathematical.

X.4. Little and hid from mortal sight.
I darkly work to make all light.

I.5. The need for this (like that it's cut off short)
The building of a tower to humans taught.

XI.5. 'More than mind discloses and more than men
believe'
(A definition by man whom Pussyfoot doth
grieve).

The Fascinating Problem

II.6.   Backward observe her turn her way,
         The way of wisdom, wise men say.

VII 6.   Grew long ago by river's edge
         Where grows to-day the common sedge.

XII.6.   One of three by which, they say,
         You'll know the Cornishmen alway.

VI.7.   Blow upon blow; five more the vanquished
         Roman shows;
         And if the foot slip one, on crippled feet one
         goes.

I.8.   By this Jew's work the whole we find,
         In a glass clearly, darkly in the mind.

IX.8.   Little by little see it grow
         Till cut off short by hammer-blow.

VI.9.   Watch him go, heel and toe,
         Across the wide Karroo!

II.10.   In expectation to be rich
         Here you reach the highest pitch.

VII.10. Of this, concerning nothing, much—
         Too often do we hear of such!

XII.10. O'er land and sea, passing on deadly
         wings,
         Pain to the strong, to weaklings death it brings.

I.11.   Requests like these, however long they be,
         Stop just too soon for common courtesy.

XI.11.   Caesar, the living dead salute thee here,
         Facing for thy delight tooth, claw, and spear.

I.12.   One word had served, but he in ranting vein
         'Lend me your ears' must mouth o'er Caesar
         slain.

X.12.   Helical circumvolution
         Adumbrates correct solution.

I.13.   One that works for Irish men
         Both by word and deed and pen.

DOROTHY L. SAYERS

'That's an easy one,' said Miss Marryat.

IV.13. Seven out of twelve this number makes complete
As the sun journeys on from seat to seat.

XIV.13. My brothers play with planets; Cicero,
Master of words, my master is below.

I.14. Free of her jesses let the falcon fly,
With sight undimmed into the azure sky.

X.14. And so you dine with Borgia? Let me lend
You this as a precaution, my poor friend.

I.15. Friendship carried to excess
Got him in a horrid mess.

XI.15. Smooth and elastic and, I guess,
The dearest treasure you possess.

Down

I.I. If step by step the Steppes you wander through
Many of those in this, of these in those you'll view.

'Bunter,' said Lord Peter, 'bring me a whisky-and-soda!'

II.I. If me without my head you do,
Then generously my head renew,
Or put it to my hinder end—
Your cheer it shall nor may nor mend.

I.II. Quietly, quietly, 'twixt edge and edge,
Do this unto the thin end of the wedge.

10.II. 'Something that hath a reference to my state?'
Just as you like, it shall be written straight.

I.III. When all is read, then give the world its due,
And never need the world read this of you.

'That's a comfort,' said Lady Mary. 'It shows we're on the right lines.'

4.III. Sing Nunc Dimittis and Magnificat—
       But look a little farther back than that.

14.III. Here in brief epitome
       Attribute of royalty.

1.IV. Lo! at a glance
       The Spanish gipsy and her dance.

10.IV. Bring me skin and a needle or a stick—
       A needle does it slowly, a stick does it quick.

1.V. It was a brazen business when
       King Phalaris made these for men.

11.V. This king (of whom not much is known),
       By Heaven's mercy was o'erthrown.

2.VI. 'Bid 'ον και μη 'ον farewell?' Nay, in this
       The sterner Roman stands by that which is.

7.VI. This the termination is
       Of many minds' activities.

12.VI. I mingle on Norwegian shore,
       With ebbing water's backward roar.

6.VII. I stand, a ladder to renown,
       Set 'twixt the stars and Milan town.

1.VIII. Highest and lowliest both to me lay claim,
       The little hyssop and the king of fame.

'That makes that point about the squares clear,' said Mary.

'I think it's even more significant,' said her brother.

9.VIII. This sensible old man refused to tread
       The path to Hades in a youngster's stead.

6.IX. Long since, at Nature's call, they let it drop,
       Thoughtlessly thoughtful for our next year's
       crop.

2.X.   To smallest words great speakers greatness give;
        Here Rome propounded her alternative.

7.X.   We heap up many with toil and trouble,
        And find that the whole of our gain is a
        bubble.

12.X.   Add it among the hidden things—
        A fishy tale to light it brings.

1.XI.   'Lions,' said a Gallic critic, 'are not these.'
        Benevolent souls – they'd make your heart's
        blood freeze.

11.XI. An epithet for husky fellows.
        That stand, all robed in greens and yellows.

1.XII. Whole without holes behold me here,
        My meaning should be wholly clear.

10.XII. Running all around, never setting foot to floor,
        If there isn't one in this room, there may be
        one next door.

1.XIII. Ye gods! think also of that goddess' name
        Whose might two hours on end the mob
        proclaim.

4.XIII. The Priest uplifts his voice on high,
        The choristers make their reply.

14.XIII. When you've guessed it, with one voice
        You'll say it was a golden choice.

1.XIV. Shall learning die amid a war's alarms?
        I, at my birth, was clasped in iron arms.

10.XIV. At sunset see the labourer now
        Loose all his oxen from the plough.

1.XV.   Without a miracle it cannot be—
        At this point, Solver, bid him pray for thee!

11.XV. Two thousand years ago and more
        (Just as we do to-day),
        The Romans saw these distant lights—
        But, oh? How hard the way!

The most remarkable part of the search – or so Lord Peter thought – was its effect on Miss Marryat. At first she hovered disconsolately on the margin, aching with wounded dignity, yet ashamed to dissociate herself from people who were toiling so hard and so cheerfully in her cause.

'I think that's so-and-so,' Mary would say hopefully.

And her brother would reply enthusiastically, 'Holed it in one, old lady. Good for you! We've got it this time, Miss Marryat' – and explain it.

And Hannah Marryat would say with a snort:

'That's just the childish kind of joke Uncle Meleager *would* make.'

Gradually, however, the fascination of seeing the squares fit together caught her, and, when the first word appeared which showed that the searchers were definitely on the right track, she lay down flat on the floor and peered over Lord Peter's shoulder as he grovelled below, writing letters in charcoal, rubbing them out with his handkerchief and mopping his heated face, till the Moor of Venice had nothing on him in the matter of blackness. Once, half scornfully, half timidly, she made a suggestion; twice, she made a suggestion; the third time she had an inspiration. The next minute she was down in the melee, crawling over the tiles flushed and excited, wiping important letters out with her knees as fast as Peter could write them in, poring over the pages of Roget, her eyes gleaming under her tumbled black fringe.

Hurried meals of cold meat and tea sustained the exhausted party, and towards sunset Peter, with a shout of triumph, added the last letter to the square.

They crawled out and looked at it.

'All the words can't be clues,' said Mary. 'I think it must be just those four.'

'Yes, undoubtedly. It's quite clear. We've only got to look it up. Where's a Bible?'

Miss Marryat hunted it out from the pile of reference books. 'But that isn't the name of a Bible book,' she said. 'It's those things they have at evening service.'

'That's all you know,' said Lord Peter. 'I was brought up religious, I was. It's Vulgate, that's what that is. You're quite right, of course, but, as Uncle Meleager says, we must "look a little further back than that". Here you are. Now, then.'

'But it doesn't say what chapter.'

'So it doesn't. I mean, nor it does.'

'And, anyhow, all the chapters are too short.'

'Damn! Oh! Here, suppose we just count right on from the beginning – one, two, three—'

'Seventeen in chapter one, eighteen, nineteen – this must be it.'

Two fair heads and one dark one peered excitedly at the small print, Bunter hovering decorously on the outskirts.

'O my dove, that art in the clefts of the rock, in the covert of the steep place.'

'Oh, dear!' said Mary, disappointed, 'that does sound rather hopeless. Are you sure you've counted right? It might mean *anything*.'

Lord Peter scratched his head.

'This is a bit of a blow,' he said. 'I don't like Uncle Meleager half as much as I did. Old beast!'

'After all our work!' moaned Mary.

'It must be right,' cried Miss Marryat. 'Perhaps there's some kind of an anagram in it. We can't give up now!'

'Bravo!' said Lord Peter. 'That's the spirit. 'Fraid we're in for another outburst of frivolity, Miss Marryat.'

'Well, it's been great fun,' said Hannah Marryat.

'If you will excuse me,' began the deferential voice of Bunter.

'I'd forgotten you, Bunter,' said his lordship. 'Of course you can put us right – you always can. Where have we gone wrong?'

'I was about to observe, my lord, that the words you mention do not appear to agree with my recollection of the passage in question. In my mother's Bible, my lord, it ran, I fancy, somewhat differently.'

Lord Peter closed the volume and looked at the back of it.

'Naturally,' he said, 'you are right again, of course. This is a Revised Version. It's your fault, Miss Marryat. You *would* have a Revised Version. But can we imagine Uncle Meleager with one? No. Bring me Uncle Meleager's Bible.'

'Come and look in the library,' cried Miss Marryat, snatching him by the hand and running. 'Don't be so dreadfully calm.'

On the centre of the library table lay a huge and venerable Bible – reverend in age and tooled leather binding. Lord Peter's hands caressed it, for a noble old book was like a song to his soul. Sobered by its beauty, they turned the yellow pages over.

'In the clefts of the rocks, in the secret places of the stairs.'

'Miss Marryat,' said his lordship, 'if your Uncle's will is not concealed in the staircase, then – well, all I can say is, he's played a rotten trick on us,' he concluded lamely.

'Shall we try the main staircase, or the little one up to the porch?'

'Oh, the main one, I think. I hope it won't mean pulling it down. No. Somebody would have noticed if Uncle Meleager had done anything drastic in that way. It's probably quite a simple hiding-place. Wait a minute. Let's ask the housekeeper.'

Mrs Meakers was called, and perfectly remembered that about nine months previously Mr Finch had pointed out to her a 'kind of a crack like' on the under surface of the staircase, and had had a man in to fill it up. Certainly, she could point out the exact place. There was the mark of the plaster filling quite clear.

'Hurray!' cried Lord Peter. 'Bunter – a chisel or something. Uncle Meleager, Uncle Meleager, we've *got* you! Miss Marryat, I think yours should be the hand to strike the blow. It's your staircase, you know – at least, if we find the will, so if any destruction has to be done it's up to you.'

Breathless they stood round, while with a few blows the new plaster flaked off, disclosing a wide chink in the stonework. Hannah Marryat flung down hammer and chisel and groped in the gap.

'There's something,' she gasped. 'Lift me up; I can't reach. Oh, it is! it is; it *is* it!' And she withdrew her hand, grasping along, sealed envelope, bearing the superscription:

POSITIVELY THE LAST WILL AND TESTAMENT of
MELEAGER FINCH

Miss Marryat gave a yodel of joy and flung her arms round Lord Peter's neck.

Mary executed a joy-dance. 'I'll tell the world,' she proclaimed.

'Come and tell mother!' cried Miss Marryat.

Mr Bunter interposed.

'Your lordship will excuse me,' he said firmly, 'but your lordship's face is all over charcoal.'

'Black but comely,' said Lord Peter, 'but I submit to your reproof. How clever we've all been. How topping everything is. How rich you are going to be. How late it is and how hungry I am. Yes, Bunter, I will wash my face. Is there anything else I can do for anybody while I feel in the mood?'

'If your lordship would be so kind,' said Mr Bunter, producing a small paper from his pocket, 'I should be grateful if you could favour me with a South African quadruped in six letters, beginning with Q.'

NOTE: *The solution of the cross-word will be found at the end of the book.*

The Unprincipled Affair of
the Practical Joker

The *Zambesi*, they said, was expected to dock at six in the morning. Mrs Ruyslaender booked a bedroom at the Magnifical, with despair in her heart. A bare nine hours and she would be greeting her husband. After that would begin the sickening period of waiting – it might be days, it might be weeks, possibly even months – for the inevitable discovery.

The reception-clerk twirled the register towards her. Mechanically, as she signed it, she glanced at the preceding entry:

'Lord Peter Wimsey and valet – London – Suite 24.'

Mrs Ruyslaender's heart seemed to stop for a second. Was it possible that, even now, God had left a loophole? She expected little from Him – all her life He had shown Himself a sufficiently stern creditor. It was fantastic to base the frailest hope on this signature of a man she had never even seen.

Yet the name remained in her mind while she dined in her own room. She dismissed her maid presently, and sat for a long time looking at her own haggard reflection in the mirror. Twice she rose and went to the door – then turned back, calling herself a fool. The third time she turned the handle quickly and hurried down the corridor, without giving herself time to think.

A large golden arrow at the corner directed her to Suite 24. It was 11 o'clock, and nobody was within view. Mrs Ruyslaender gave a sharp knock on Lord Peter

Wimsey's door and stood back, waiting, with the sort of desperate relief one experiences after hearing a dangerous letter thump the bottom of the pillar-box. Whatever the adventure, she was committed to it.

The manservant was of the imperturbable sort. He neither invited nor rejected, but stood respectfully upon the threshold.

'Lord Peter Wimsey?' murmured Mrs Ruyslaender.

'Yes, madam.'

'Could I speak to him for a moment?'

'His lordship has just retired, madam. If you will step in, I will enquire.'

Mrs Ruyslaender followed him into one of those palatial sitting-rooms which the Magnifical provides for the wealthy pilgrim.

'Will you take a seat, madam?'

The man stepped noiselessly to the bedroom door and passed in, shutting it behind him. The lock, however, failed to catch, and Mrs Ruyslaender caught the conversation.

'Pardon me, my lord, a lady has called. She mentioned no appointment, so I considered it better to acquaint your lordship.'

'Excellent discretion,' said a voice. It had a slow, sarcastic intonation, which brought a painful flush to Mrs Ruyslaender's cheek. 'I never make appointments. Do I know the lady?'

'No, my lord. But – hem – I know her by sight, my lord. It is Mrs Ruyslaender.'

'Oh, the diamond merchant's wife. Well, find out tactfully what it's all about, and, unless it's urgent, ask her to call tomorrow.'

The valet's next remark was inaudible, but the reply was:

'Don't be coarse, Bunter.'

The valet returned.

'His lordship desires me to ask you, madam, in what way he can be of service to you.'

'Will you say to him that I have heard of him in connection with the Attenbury diamond case, and am anxious to ask his advice.'

'Certainly, madam. May I suggest that, as his lordship is greatly fatigued, he would be better able to assist you after he has slept.'

'If tomorrow would have done, I would not have thought of disturbing him tonight. Tell him, I am aware of the trouble I am giving—'

'Excuse me one moment, madam.'

This time the door shut properly. After a short interval Bunter returned to say, 'His lordship will be with you immediately, madam,' and to place a decanter of wine and a box of Sobranies beside her.

Mrs Ruyslaender lit a cigarette, but had barely sampled its flavour when she was aware of a soft step beside her. Looking round, she perceived a young man, attired in a mauve dressing-gown of great splendour, from beneath the hem of which peeped coyly a pair of primrose silk pyjamas.

'You must think it very strange of me, thrusting myself on you at this hour,' she said, with a nervous laugh.

Lord Peter put his head to one side.

'Don't know the answer to that,' he said. 'If I say, "Not at all," it sounds abandoned. If I say, "Yes, very," it's rude. Supposin' we give it a miss, what? and you tell me what I can do for you.'

Mrs Ruyslaender hesitated. Lord Peter was not what she had expected. She noted the sleek, straw-coloured hair, brushed flat back from a rather sloping forehead, the ugly, lean, arched nose, and the faintly foolish smile, and her heart sank within her.

'I'm – I'm afraid it's ridiculous of me to suppose you can help me,' she began.

'Always my unfortunate appearance,' moaned Lord Peter, with such alarming acumen as to double her discomfort. 'Would it invite confidence more, d'you suppose, if I dyed my hair black an' grew a Newgate fringe? It's very tryin', you can't think, always to look as if one's name was Algy.'

'I only meant,' said Mrs Ruyslaender, 'that I don't think *anybody* could possibly help. But I saw your name in the hotel book, and it seemed just a chance.'

Lord Peter filled the glasses and sat down.

'Carry on,' he said cheerfully; 'it sounds interestin'.'

Mrs Ruyslaender took the plunge.

'My husband,' she explained, 'is Henry Ruyslaender, the diamond merchant. We came over from Kimberley ten years ago, and settled in England. He spends several months in Africa every year on business, and I am expecting him back on the *Zambesi* tomorrow morning. Now, this is the trouble. Last year he gave me a magnificent diamond necklace of a hundred and fifteen stones—'

'The Light of Africa – I know,' said Wimsey.

She looked a little surprised, but assented. 'The neck lace has been stolen from me, and I can't hope to conceal the loss from him. No duplicate would deceive him for an instant.'

She paused and Lord Peter prompted gently:

'You have come to me, I presume, because it is not to be a police matter. Will you tell me quite frankly why?'

'The police would be useless. I know who took it.'

'Yes?'

'There is a man we both know slightly – a man called Paul Melville.'

Lord Peter's eyes narrowed. 'M'm, yes, I fancy I've seen him about the clubs. New Army, but transferred himself into the Regulars. Dark. Showy. Bit of an ampelopsis, what?'

'Ampelopsis?'

'Suburban plant that climbs by suction. *You* know – first year, tender little shoots – second year, fine show – next year, all over the shop. Now tell me I am rude.'

Mrs Ruyslaender giggled. 'Now you mention it, he is *exactly* like an ampelopsis. What a relief to be able to think of him as that . . . Well, he is some sort of distant relation of my husband's. He called one evening when I was alone. We talked about jewels, and I brought down my jewel-box and showed him the Light of Africa. He knows a good deal about stones. I was in and out of the room two or three times, but didn't think to lock up the box. After he left, I was putting the things away, and I opened the jeweller's case the diamonds were in – and they had gone!'

'H'm – pretty barefaced. Look here, Mrs Ruyslaender, you agree he's an ampelopsis, but you won't call in the police. Honestly, now – forgive me; you're askin' my advice, you know – is he worth botherin' about?'

'It's not that,' said the woman, in a low tone. 'Oh, no! But he took something else as well. He took – a portrait – a small painting set with diamonds.'

'Oh!'

'Yes. It was in a secret drawer in the jewel-box. I can't imagine how he knew it was there, but the box was an old casket, belonging to my husband's family, and I fancy he must have known about the drawer and – well, thought that investigation might prove profitable. Any way, the evening the diamonds went, the portrait went too, and he knows I daren't try to get the necklace back because they'd both be found together.'

'Was there something more than just the portrait, then? A portrait in itself isn't necessarily hopeless of explanation. It was given – you to take care of, say.'

'The names were on it – and – and an inscription which nothing, *nothing* could ever explain away. A – a passage from Petronius.'

'Oh, dear!' said Lord Peter, 'dear me, yes. Rather a lively author.'

'I was married very young,' said Mrs Ruyslaender, 'and my husband and I have never got on well. Then one year, when he was in Africa, it all happened. We were wonderful – and shameless. It came to an end. I was bitter. I wish I had not been. He left me, you see, and I couldn't forgive it. I prayed day and night for revenge. Only now – I don't want it to be through me!'

'Wait a moment,' said Wimsey, 'you mean that, if the diamonds are found and the portrait is found too, all this story is bound to come out.'

'My husband would get a divorce. He would never forgive me – or him. It is not so much that I mind paying the price myself, but—'

She clenched her hands.

'I have cursed him again and again, and the clever girl who married him. She played her cards so well. This would ruin them both.'

'But if *you* were the instrument of vengeance,' said Wimsey gently, 'you would hate yourself. And it would be terrible to you because he would hate you. A woman like you couldn't stoop to get your own back. I see that. If God makes a thunderbolt, how awful and satisfying – if you help to make a beastly row, what a rotten business it would be.'

'You seem to understand,' said Mrs Ruyslaender. 'How unusual.'

'I understand perfectly. Though let me tell you,' said Wimsey, with a wry little twist of the lips, 'that it's sheer foolishness for a woman to have a sense of honour in such matters. It only gives her excruciating pain, and nobody expects it, anyway. Look here, don't let's get all worked up. You certainly shan't have your vengeance thrust on you by an ampelopsis. Why should you? Nasty fellow. We'll have him up – root, branch, and little suckers. Don't worry. Let's see. My business here will only take a day. Then I've got to get to know Melville – say a week. Then I've got to get the doings – say another week, provided he hasn't sold them yet, which isn't likely. Can you hold your husband off 'em for a fortnight, d'you think?'

'Oh, yes. I'll say they're in the country, or being cleaned, or something. But do you really think you can –?'

'I'll have a jolly good try, anyhow, Mrs Ruyslaender. Is the fellow hard up, to start stealing diamonds?'

'I fancy he has got into debt over horses lately. And possibly poker.'

'Oh! Poker player, is he? That makes an excellent excuse for gettin' to know him. Well, cheer up – we'll get the goods, even if we have to buy 'em. But we won't, if we can help it. Bunter!'

'My lord?' the valet appeared from the inner room.

'Just go an' give the "All Clear", will you?'

Mr Bunter accordingly stepped into the passage, and, having seen an old gentleman safely away to the bathroom and a young lady in a pink kimono pop her head out of an adjacent door and hurriedly pop it back on beholding him, blew his nose with a loud, trumpeting sound.

'Good night,' said Mrs Ruyslaender, 'and thank you.'

She slipped back to her room unobserved.

'Whatever has induced you, my dear boy,' said Colonel Marchbanks, 'to take up with that very objectionable fellow Melville?'

'Diamonds,' said Lord Peter. 'Do you find him so, really?'

'Perfectly dreadful man,' said the Hon. Frederick Arbuthnot. 'Hearts. What did you want to go and get him a room here for? This used to be a quite decent club.'

'Two clubs?' said Sir Impey Biggs, who had been ordering a whisky, and had only caught the last word.

'No, no, one heart.'

'I beg your pardon. Well, partner, how about spades? Perfectly good suit.'

'Pass,' said the Colonel. 'I don't know what the Army's coming to nowadays.'

'No trumps,' said Wimsey. 'It's all right, children. Trust your Uncle Pete. Come on, Freddy, how many of those hearts are you going to shout for?'

'None, the Colonel havin' let me down so 'orrid,' said the Hon. Freddy.

'Cautious blighter. All content? Righty-ho! Bring out your dead, partner. Oh, very pretty indeed. We'll make it a slam this time. I'm rather glad to hear that expression of opinion from you, Colonel, because I particularly want you and Biggy to hang on this evening and take a hand with Melville and me.'

'What happens to me?' enquired the Hon. Freddy.

'You have an engagement and go home early, dear old thing. I've specially invited friend Melville to meet the redoubtable Colonel Marchbanks and our greatest criminal lawyer. Which hand am I supposed to be playin' this from? Oh, yes. Come on, Colonel – you've got to hike that old king out some time, why not now?'

'It's a plot,' said Mr Arbuthnot, with an exaggerated expression of mystery. 'Carry on, don't mind me.'

'I take it you have your own reasons for cultivating the man,' said Sir Impey.

'The rest are mine, I fancy. Well, yes, I have. You and the Colonel would really do me a favour by letting Melville cut in tonight.'

'If you wish it,' growled the Colonel, 'but I hope the impudent young beggar won't presume on the acquaintance.'

'I'll see to that,' said his lordship. 'Your cards, Freddy. Who had the ace of hearts? Oh! I had it myself, of course. Our honours . . . Hullo! Evenin', Melville.'

The ampelopsis was rather a good-looking creature in his own way. Tall and bronzed, with a fine row of very persuasive teeth. He greeted Wimsey and Arbuthnot heartily, the Colonel with a shade too much familiarity, and expressed himself delighted to be introduced to Sir Impey Biggs.

'You're just in time to hold Freddy's hand,' said Wimsey; 'he's got a date. Not his littly paddy-paw, I don't mean – but the dam' rotten hand he generally gets dealt him. Joke.'

'Oh, well,' said the obedient Freddy, rising, 'I s'pose I'd better make a noise like a hoop and roll away. Night, night, everybody.'

Melville took his place, and the game continued with varying fortunes for two hours, at the end of which time Colonel Marchbanks, who had suffered much under his partner's eloquent theory of the game, was beginning to wilt visibly.

Wimsey yawned.

'Gettin' a bit bored, Colonel? Wish they'd invent somethin' to liven this game up a bit.'

'Oh, Bridge is a one-horse show, anyway,' said Melville. 'Why not have a little flutter at poker, Colonel? Do you all the good in the world, What d'you say, Biggs?'

Sir Impey turned on Wimsey a thoughtful eye, accustomed to sizing-up the witnesses. Then he replied:

'I'm quite willing, if the others are.'

'Damn good idea,' said Lord Peter.' Come now, Colonel, be a sport. You'll find the chips in that drawer, I think. I always lose money at poker, but what's the odds so long as you're happy. Let's have a new pack.'

'Any limit?'

'What do *you* say, Colonel?'

The Colonel proposed a twenty-shilling limit. Melville, with a grimace, amended this to one-tenth of the pool. The amendment was carried and the cards cut, the deal falling to the Colonel.

Contrary to his own prophecy, Wimsey began by winning considerably, and grew so garrously imbecile in the process that even the experienced Melville began to wonder whether this indescribable fatuity was the cloak of ignorance or the mask of the hardened poker-player. Soon, however, he was reassured. The luck came over to his side, and he found himself winning hands down steadily from Sir Impey and the Colonel, who played cautiously and took little risk – heavily from

Wimsey, who appeared reckless and slightly drunk, and was staking foolishly on quite impossible cards.

'I never knew such luck as yours, Melville,' said Sir Impey, when that young man had scooped in the proceeds from a handsome straight-flush.

'My turn tonight, yours tomorrow,' said Melville, pushing the cards across to Biggs, whose deal it was.

Colonel Marchbanks required one card. Wimsey laughed vacantly and demanded an entirely fresh hand. Briggs asked for three; and Melville, after a pause for consideration, took one.

It seemed as though everybody had something respectable this time – though Wimsey was not to be depended upon, frequently going the limit upon a pair of jacks in order, as he expressed it, to keep the pot a-boiling. He became particularly obstinate now, throwing his chips in with a flushed face, in spite of Melville's confident air.

The Colonel got out, and after a short time Biggs followed his example. Melville held on till the pool mounted to something under a hundred pounds, when Wimsey suddenly turned restive and demanded to see him.

'Four kings,' said Melville.

'Blast you!' said Lord Peter, laying down four queens. 'No holdin' this feller tonight, is there? Here, take the ruddy cards, Meville, and give somebody else a look in, will you.'

He shuffled them as he spoke, and handed them over. Melville dealt, satisfied the demands of the other three players, and was in the act of taking three new cards for himself, when Wimsey gave a sudden exclamation, and shot a swift hand across the table.

'Hullo! Melville,' he said, in a chill tone which bore no resemblance to his ordinary speech, 'what exactly does this mean?'

He lifted Melville's left arm clear of the table and, with a sharp gesture, shook it. From the sleeve something fluttered to the table and glided away to the floor. Colonel Marchbanks picked it up, and in a dreadful silence laid the joker on the table.

'Good God!' said Sir Impey.

'You young blackguard!' gasped the Colonel, recovering speech.

'What the hell do you mean by this?' gasped Melville, with a face like chalk. 'How dare you! This is a trick – a plant –' A horrible fury gripped him. 'You dare to say that I have been cheating. You liar! You filthy sharper! You put it there. I tell you, gentlemen,' he cried, looking desperately round the table, 'he must have put it there.'

'Come, come,' said Colonel Marchbanks, 'no good carryin' on that way, Melville. Dear me, no good at all. Only makes matters worse. We all saw it, you know. Dear, dear, I don't know what the Army's coming to.'

'Do you mean you believe it?' shrieked Melville. 'For God's sake, Wimsey, is this a joke or what? Biggs – you've got a head on your shoulders – are you going to believe this half-drunk fool and this doddering old idiot who ought to be in his grave?'

'That language won't do you any good, Melville,' said Sir Impey. 'I'm afraid we all saw it clearly enough.'

'I've been suspectin' this some time, y'know,' said Wimsey. 'That's why I asked you two to stay tonight. We don't want to make a public row, but—'

'Gentlemen,' said Melville more soberly, 'I swear to you that I am absolutely innocent of this ghastly thing. Can't you believe me?'

'I can believe the evidence of my own eyes, sir,' said the Colonel, with some heat.

'For the good of the club,' said Wimsey, 'this couldn't go on, but – also for the good of the club – I think we should all prefer the matter to be quietly arranged. In the face of what Sir Impey and the Colonel can witness, Melville, I'm afraid your protestations are not likely to be credited.'

Melville looked from the soldier's face to that of the great criminal lawyer.

'I don't know what your game is,' he said sullenly to Wimsey, 'but I can see you've laid a trap and pulled it off – all right.'

'I think, gentlemen,' said Wimsey, 'that, if I might have a word in private with Melville in his own room, I could get the thing settled satisfactorily, without undue fuss.'

'He'll have to resign his commission,' growled the Colonel.

'I'll put it to him in that light,' said Peter. 'May we go to your room for a minute, Melville?'

With a louring brow, the young soldier led the way. Once alone with Wimsey, he turned furiously on him.

'What do you want? What do you mean by making this monstrous charge? I'll take action for libel!'

'Do,' said Wimsey coolly, 'if you think anybody is likely to believe your story.'

He lit a cigarette, and smiled lazily at the angry young man.

'Well, what's the meaning of it, anyway?'

'The meaning,' said Wimsey, 'is simply that you, an officer and a member of this club, have been caught red-handed cheating at cards while playing for money, the witnesses being Sir Impey Biggs, Colonel Marchbanks, and myself. Now, I suggest to you, Captain Melville, that your best plan is to let me take charge of Mrs Ruyslaender's diamond necklace and portrait, and then just to trickle away quiet-like from these halls of dazzlin' light – without any questions asked.'

Melville leapt to his feet.

'My God!' he cried. 'I can see it now. It's blackmail.'

'You may certainly call it blackmail, and theft too,' said Lord Peter, with a shrug. 'But why use ugly names? I hold five aces, you see. Better chuck in your hand.'

'Suppose I say I never heard of the diamonds?'

'It's a bit late now, isn't it?' said Wimsey affably. 'But, in that case, I'm beastly sorry and all that, of course, but we shall have to make tonight's business public.'

'Damn you!' muttered Melville, 'you sneering devil.'

He showed all his white teeth, half springing, with crouched shoulders. Wimsey waited quietly, his hands in his pockets.

The rush did not come. With a furious gesture, Melville pulled out his keys and unlocked his dressing-case.

'Take them,' he growled, flinging a small parcel on the table; 'you've got me. Take 'em and go to hell.'

'Eventually – why not now?' murmured his lordship. 'Thanks frightfully. Man of peace myself, you know – hate unpleasantness and all that.' He scrutinised his booty carefully, running the stones expertly between his fingers. Over the portrait he pursed up his lips. 'Yes,' he murmured, 'that *would* have made a row.' He replaced the wrapping and slipped the parcel into his pocket.

'Well, good night, Melville – and thanks for a pleasant game.'

★

'I say, Biggs,' said Wimsey, when he had returned to the card-room. 'You've had a lot of experience. What tactics d'you think one's justified in usin' with a blackmailer?'

'Ah!' said the KC. 'There you've put your fingers on Society's sore place, where the Law is helpless. Speaking as a man, I'd say nothing could be too bad for the brute. It's a crime crueller and infinitely worse in its results than murder. As a lawyer, I can only say that I have consistently refused to defend a blackmailer or to prosecute any poor devil who does away with his tormentor.'

'H'm,' replied Wimsey. 'What do you say, Colonel?'

'A man like that's a filthy pest,' said the little warrior stoutly. 'Shootin's too good for him. I knew a man – close personal friend, in fact – hounded to death – blew his brains out – one of the best. Don't like to talk about it.'

'I want to show you something,' said Wimsey.

He picked up the pack which still lay scattered on the table, and shuffled it together.

'Catch hold of these, Colonel, and lay 'em face downwards. That's right. First of all you cut 'em at the twentieth card – you'll see the seven of diamonds at the bottom. Correct? Now I'll call 'em. Ten of hearts, ace of spades, three of clubs, five of clubs, king of diamonds, nine, jack, two of hearts. Right? I could pick 'em all out, you see, except the ace of hearts, and that's here.'

He leaned forward and produced it dexterously from Sir Impey's breast-pocket.

'I learnt it from a man who shared my dug-out near Ypres,' he said. 'You needn't mention tonight's business, you two. There are crimes which the Law cannot reach.'

The Undignified Melodrama of the Bone of Contention

'I am afraid you have brought shocking weather with you, Lord Peter,' said Mrs Frobisher-Pym, with playful reproof. 'If it goes on like this they will have a bad day for the funeral.'

Lord Peter Wimsey glanced out of the morning-room window to the soaked green lawn and the shrubbery, where the rain streamed down remorselessly over the laurel leaves, stiff and shiny like mackintoshes.

'Nasty exposed business, standing round at funerals,' he agreed.

'Yes, I always think it's such a shame for the old people. In a tiny village like this it's about the only pleasure they get during the winter. It makes something for them to talk about for weeks.'

'Is it anybody's funeral in particular?'

'My dear Wimsey,' said his host, 'it is plain that you, coming from your little village of London, are quite out of the swim. There has never been a funeral like it in Little Doddering before. It's an event.'

'Really?'

'Oh dear, yes. You may possibly remember old Burdock?'

'Burdock? Let me see. Isn't he a sort of local squire, or something?'

'He was,' corrected Mr Frobisher-Pym. 'He's dead – died in New York about three weeks ago, and they're sending him over to be buried. The Burdocks have lived

173

in the big house for hundreds of years, and they're all buried in the churchyard, except, of course, the one who was killed in the War. Burdock's secretary cabled the news of his death across, and said the body was following as soon as the embalmers had finished with it. The boat gets in to Southampton this morning, I believe. At any rate, the body will arrive here by the 6.30 from town.'

'Are you going down to meet it, Tom?'

'No, my dear. I don't think that is called for. There will be a grand turn-out of the village, of course. Joliffe's people are having the time of their lives; they borrowed an extra pair of horses from young Mortimer for the occasion. I only hope they don't kick over the traces and upset the hearse. Mortimer's horseflesh is generally on the spirited side.'

'But, Tom, we must show some respect to the Burdocks.'

'We're attending the funeral tomorrow, and that's quite enough. We must do that, I suppose, out of consideration for the family, though, as far as the old man himself goes, respect is the very last thing anybody would think of paying him.'

'Oh, Tom, he's dead.'

'And quite time too. No, Agatha, it's no use pretending that old Burdock was anything but a spiteful, bad-tempered, dirty-living old blackguard that the world's well rid of. The last scandal he stirred up made the place too hot to hold him. He had to leave the country and go to the States, and, even so, if he hadn't the money to pay the people off, he'd probably have been put in gaol. That's why I'm so annoyed with Hancock. I don't mind his calling himself a priest, though clergyman was always good enough for dear old

Weeks – who, after all, was a canon – and I don't mind his vestments. He can wrap himself up in a Union Jack if he likes – it doesn't worry *me*. But when it comes to having old Burdock put on trestles in the south aisle, with candles round him, and Hubbard from the "Red Cow" and Duggins's boy praying over him half the night, I think it's time to draw the line. The people don't like it, you know – at least, the older generation don't. It's all right for the young ones, I dare say; they must have their amusement; but it gives offence to a lot of the farmers. After all, they knew Burdock a bit too well. Simpson – he's people's warden, you know – came up quite in distress to speak to me about it last night. You couldn't have a sounder man than Simpson. I said I would speak to Hancock. I did speak to him this morning, as a matter of fact, but you might as well talk to the west door of the church.'

'Mr Hancock is one of those young men who fancy they know everything,' said his wife. 'A sensible man would have listened to you, Tom. You're a magistrate and have lived here all your life, and it stands to reason you know considerably more about the parish than he does.'

'He took up the ridiculous position,' said Mr Frobisher-Pym, 'that the more sinful the old man had been the more he needed praying for. I said, "I think it would need more praying than you or I could do to help old Burdock out of the place he's in now." Ha, ha! So he said, "I agree with you, Mr Frobisher-Pym; that is why I am having eight watchers to pray all through the night for him." I admit he had me there.'

'Eight people?' exclaimed Mrs Frobisher-Pym.

'Not all at once, I understand; in relays, two at a time. "Well," I said, "I think you ought to consider that

you will be giving a handle to the Noncomformists." O
course, he couldn't deny that.'

Wimsey helped himself to marmalade. Nonconformists, it seemed, were always searching for handles
Though what kind – whether door-handles, tea-po
handles, pump-handles, or starting-handles – was neve
explained, nor what the handles were to be used fo
when found. However, having been brought up in the
odour of the Establishment, he was familiar with thi
odd dissenting peculiarity, and merely said:

'Pity to be extreme in a small parish like this. Dis-
turbs the ideas of the simple fathers of the hamle
and the village blacksmith, with his daughter singin
in the choir and the Old Hundredth and all the res
of it. Don't Burdock's family have anything to say to it
There are some sons, aren't there?'

'Only the two, now. Aldine was the one that wa
killed, of course, and Martin is somewhere abroad. He
went off after that row with his father, and I don't think
he has been back in England since.'

'What was the row about?'

'Oh that was a disgraceful business. Martin got a gir
into trouble – a film actress or a typist or somebody o
that sort – and insisted on marrying her.'

'Oh?'

'Yes, so dreadful of him,' said the lady, taking up the
tale, 'when he was practically engaged to the Delaprime
girl – the one with glasses, you know. It made a terrible
scandal. Some horribly vulgar people came down and
pushed their way into the house and insisted on seeing
old Mr Burdock. I will say for him he stood up to
them – he wasn't the sort of person you could intimi-
date. He told them the girl had only herself to blame
and they could sue Martin if they liked – he wouldn'

176

be blackmailed on his son's account. The butler was listening at the door, naturally, and told the whole village about it. And then Martin Burdock came home and had a quarrel with his father you could have heard for miles. He said that the whole thing was a lie, and that he meant to marry the girl, anyway. I cannot understand how anybody could marry into a blackmailing family like that.'

'My dear,' said Mr Frobisher-Pym gently, 'I don't think you're being quite fair to Martin, or his wife's parents, either. From what Martin told me, they were quite decent people, only not his class, of course, and they came in a well-meaning way to find out what Martin's "intentions" were. You would want to do the same yourself, if it were a daughter of ours. Old Burdock naturally, thought they meant blackmail. He was the kind of man who thinks everything can be paid for; and he considered a son of his had a perfect right to seduce a young woman who worked for a living. I don't say Martin was altogether in the right—'

'Martin is a chip off the old block, I'm afraid,' retorted the lady. 'He married the girl, anyway, and why should he do that, unless he had to?'

'Well, they've never had any children, you know,' said Mr Frobisher-Pym.

'That's as may be. I've no doubt the girl was in league with her parents. And you know the Martin Burdocks have lived in Paris ever since.'

'That's true,' admitted her husband. 'It was an unfortunate affair altogether. They've had some difficulty in tracing Martin's address, too, but no doubt he'll be coming back shortly. He is engaged in producing some film play, they tell me, so possibly he can't get away in time for the funeral.'

'If he had any natural feeling, he would not let a film play stand in his way,' said Mrs Frobisher-Pym.

'My dear, there are such things as contracts, with very heavy monetary penalties for breaking them. And I don't suppose Martin could afford to lose a big sum of money. It's not likely that his father will have left him anything.'

'Martin is the younger son, then?' asked Wimsey, politely showing more interest than he felt in the rather well-worn plot of this village melodrama.

'No, he is the eldest of the lot. The house is entailed, of course, and so is the estate, such as it is. But there's no money in the land. Old Burdock made his fortune in rubber shares during the boom, and the money will go as he leaves it – wherever that may be, for they haven't found any will yet. He's probably left it all to Haviland.'

'The younger son?'

'Yes. He's something in the City – a director of a company – connected with silk stockings, I believe. Nobody has seen very much of him. He came down as soon as he heard of his father's death. He's staying with the Hancocks. The big house has been shut up since old Burdock went to the States four years ago. I suppose Haviland thought it wasn't worth while opening it up till they knew what Martin was going to do about it. That's why the body is being taken to the church.'

'Much less trouble, certainly,' said Wimsey.

'Oh, yes – though, mind you, I think Haviland ought to take a more neighbourly view of it. Considering the position the Burdocks have always held in the place, the people had a right to expect a proper reception after the funeral. It's usual. But these business people think less of tradition than we do down here. And, naturally, since the Hancocks are putting Haviland up, he can't raise much objection to the candles and the prayers and things.'

'Perhaps not,' said Mrs Frobisher-Pym, 'but it would have been more suitable if Haviland had come to us, rather than to the Hancocks, whom he doesn't even know.'

'My dear, you forget the very unpleasant dispute I had with Haviland Burdock about shooting over my land. After the correspondence that passed between us, last time he was down here, I could scarcely offer him hospitality. His father took a perfectly proper view of it, I will say that for him, but Haviland was exceedingly discourteous to me, and things were said which I could not possibly overlook. However, we mustn't bore you, Lord Peter, with our local small-talk. If you've finished your breakfast, what do you say to a walk round the place? It's a pity it's raining so hard – and you don't see the garden at its best this time of year, of course – but I've got some cocker spaniels you might like to have a look at.'

Lord Peter expressed eager anxiety to see the spaniels, and in a few minutes time found himself squelching down the gravel path which led to the kennels.

'Nothing like a healthy country life,' said Mr Frobisher-Pym. 'I always think London is so depressing in the winter. Nothing to do with one's self. All right to run up for a day or two and see a theatre now and again, but how you people stick it week in and week out beats me. I must speak to Plunkett about this archway,' he added. 'It's getting out of trim.'

He broke off a dangling branch of ivy as he spoke. The plant shuddered revengefully, tipping a small shower of water down Wimsey's neck.

The cocker spaniel and her family occupied a comfortable and airy stall in the stable buildings. A youngish man in breeches and leggings emerged to greet the visitors, and produced the little bundles of puppyhood for their inspection. Wimsey sat down on an upturned bucket and examined them gravely one by one. The bitch, after cautiously reviewing his boots and grumbling a little, decided that he was trustworthy and slobbered genially over his knees.

'Let me see,' said Mr Frobisher-Pym, 'how old are they?'

'Thirteen days, sir.'

'Is she feeding them all right?'

'Fine, sir. She's having some of the malt food. Seems to suit her very well, sir.'

'Ah, yes. Plunkett was a little doubtful about it, but I heard it spoken very well of. Plunkett doesn't care for experiments, and, in a general way, I agree with him. Where is Plunkett, by the way?'

'He's not very well this morning, sir.'

'Sorry to hear that, Merridew. The rheumatics again?'

'No, sir. From what Mrs Plunkett tells me, he's had a bit of a shock.'

'A shock? What sort of a shock? Nothing wrong with Alf or Elsie, I hope?'

'No, sir. The fact is – I understand he's seen something, sir.'

'What do you mean, seen something?'

'Well, sir – something in the nature of a warning, from what he says.'

'A warning? Good heavens, Merridew, he mustn't get those sort of ideas in his head. I'm surprised at Plunkett; I always thought he was a very level-headed man. What sort of warning did he say it was?'

'I couldn't say, sir.'

'Surely he mentioned what he thought he'd seen.'

Merridew's face took on a slightly obstinate look.

'I can't say, I'm sure, sir.'

'This will never do. I must go and see Plunkett. Is he at the cottage?'

'Yes, sir.'

'We'll go down there at once. You don't mind, do you, Wimsey? I can't allow Plunkett to make himself ill. If he's had a shock he'd better see a doctor. Well, carry on, Merridew, and be sure you keep her warm and comfortable. The damp is apt to come up through these brick floors. I'm thinking of having the whole place re-set with concrete, but it takes money, of course. I can't imagine,' he went on, as he led the way past the greenhouse towards a trim cottage set in its own square of kitchen-garden, 'what can have happened to have upset Plunkett. I hope it's nothing serious. He's getting elderly, of course, but he ought to be above believing in warnings. You wouldn't believe the extraordinary ideas these people get hold of. Fact is, I expect he's been round at the "Weary Traveller", and caught sight of somebody's washing out on the way home.'

'Not washing,' corrected Wimsey mechanically. He had a deductive turn of mind which exposed the folly of the suggestion even while irritably admitting that the matter was of no importance. 'It poured with rain last night, and, besides, it's Thursday. But Tuesday and Wednesday were fine, so the drying would have been done then. No washing.'

'Well, well – something else then – a post, or old Mrs Gidden's white donkey. Plunkett does occasionally take a drop too much, I'm sorry to say, but he's a very good kennel-man, so one overlooks it. They're superstitious round about these parts, and they can tell some queer tales if once you get into their confidence. You'd be surprised how far off the main track we are as regards civilisation. Why, not here, but at Abbotts Bolton, fifteen miles off, it's as much as one's life is worth to shoot a hare. Witches, you know, and that sort of thing.'

'I shouldn't be a bit surprised. They'll still tell you about werewolves in some parts of Germany.'

'Yes, I dare say. Well, here we are.' Mr Frobisher-Pym rapped loudly with his walking-stick on the door of the cottage and turned the handle without waiting for permission.

'You there, Mrs Plunkett? May we come in? Ah! Good morning. Hope we're not disturbing you, but Merridew told me Plunkett was not so well. This is Lord Peter Wimsey – a very old friend of mine; that is to say, I'm a very old friend of *his*; ha, ha!'

'Good morning, sir; good morning, your lordship. I'm sure Plunkett will be very pleased to see you. Please step in. Plunkett, here's Mr Pym to see you.'

The elderly man who sat crouching over the fire turned a mournful face towards them, and half rose, touching his forehead.

'Well, now, Plunkett, what's the trouble?' enquired Mr Frobisher-Pym, with the hearty bedside manner adopted by country gentlefolk visiting their dependants. 'Sorry not to see you out and about. Touch of the old complaint, eh?'

'No, sir; no, sir. Thank you, sir. I'm well enough in myself. But I've had a warning, and I'm not long for this world.'

'Not long for this world? Oh, nonsense, Plunkett. You mustn't talk like that. A touch of indigestion, that's what you've got, I expect. Gives one the blues, I know. I'm sure I often feel like nothing on earth when I've got one of my bilious attacks. Try a dose of castor-oil, or a good old fashioned blue pill and black draught. Nothing like it. Then you won't talk about warnings and dying.'

'No medicine won't do no good to *my* complaint, sir. Nobody as see what I've seed ever got the better of it. But as you and the gentleman are here, sir, I'm wondering if you'll do me a favour.'

'Of course, Plunkett, anything you like. What is it?'

'Why, just to draw up my will, sir. Old Parson, he used to do it. But I don't fancy this new young man, with his candles and bits of things. It don't seem as if he'd make it good and legal, sir, and I wouldn't like it if there was any dispute after I was gone. So as there ain't much time left me, I'd be grateful if you'd put it down clear for me in pen and ink that I wants my little bit to go to Sarah here, and after her to Alf and Elsie, divided up equal.'

Of course I'll do that for you, Plunkett, any time you like. But it's nonsense to be talking about wills. Bless my soul, I shouldn't be surprised if you were to see us all underground.'

'No, sir. I've been a hale and hearty man, I'm not denying. But I've been called, sir, and I've got to go. It must come to all of us, I know that. But it's a fearful thing to see the death-coach come for one, and know that the dead are in it, that cannot rest in the grave.'

'Come now, Plunkett, you don't mean to tell me you believe in that old foolishness about the death-coach. I thought you were an educated man. What would Alf say if he heard you talking such nonsense?'

'Ah, sir, young people don't know everything, and there's many more things in God's creation than what you'll find in the printed books.'

'Oh, well,' said Mr Frobisher-Pym, finding this opening irresistible, 'we know there are more things in heaven and earth, Horatio, than are dreamt of in your philosophy. Quite so. But that doesn't apply nowadays,' he added contradictorily. 'There are no ghosts in the twentieth century. Just you think the matter out quietly, and you'll find you've made a mistake. There's probably some quite simple explanation. Dear me! I remember Mrs Frobisher-Pym waking up one night and having a terrible fright, because she thought somebody'd been and hanged himself on our bedroom door. Such a silly idea, because I was safe in bed beside her – snoring, *she* said, ha, ha! – and, if anybody was feeling like hanging himself, he wouldn't come into our bedroom to do it. Well, she clutched my arm in a great state of mind, and when I went to see what had alarmed her, what do you think it was? My trousers, which I'd hung up by the braces, with the socks still in the legs! My word! and didn't I get a wigging for not having put my things away tidy!'

Mr Frobisher-Pym laughed, and Mrs Plunkett said dutifully, 'There now!' Her husband shook his head.

'That may be, sir, but I see the death-coach last night with my own eyes. Just striking midnight it was, by the church clock, and I see it come up the lane by the old priory wall.'

'And what were you doing out of bed at midnight, eh?'

'Well, sir, I'd been round to my sister's, that's got her boy home on leaf off of his ship.'

'And you'd been drinking his health, I dare say, Plunkett.' Mr Frobisher-Pym wagged an admonitory forefinger.

'No, sir, I don't deny I'd had a glass or two of ale, but not to fuddle me. My wife can tell you I was sober enough when I got home.'

'That's right, sir. Plunkett hadn't taken too much last night, that I'll swear to.'

'Well, what was it you saw, Plunkett?'

'I see the death-coach, same as I'm telling you, sir. It come up the lane, all ghostly white, sir, and never making no more sound than the dead – which it were, sir.'

'A waggon or something going through to Lymptree or Herriotting.'

'No, sir –'tweren't a waggon. I counted the horses – four white horses, and they went by with never a sound of hoof or bridle. And that weren't—'

'Four horses! Come, Plunkett, you must have been seeing double. There's nobody about here would be driving four horses, unless it was Mr Mortimer from Abbotts Bolton, and he wouldn't be taking his horse-flesh out at midnight.'

'Four horses they was, sir. I see them plain. And it weren't Mr Mortimer, neither, for he drives a drag, and this were a big, heavy coach, with no lights on it, but shinin' all of itself, with a colour like moonshine.'

'Oh, nonsense, man! You couldn't see the moon last night. It was pitch-dark.'

'No, sir, but the coach shone all moony-like, all the same.'

'And no lights? I wonder what the police would say to that.'

'No mortal police could stop that coach,' said Plunkett contemptuously, 'nor no mortal man could abide the sight on it. I tell you, sir, that ain't the worst of it. The horses—'

'Was it going slowly?'

'No, sir. It were going at a gallop, only the hoofs didn't touch the ground. There weren't no sound, and I see the black road and the white hoofs half a foot off of it. And the horses had no heads.'

'No heads?'

'No, sir.'

Mr Frobisher-Pym laughed.

'Come, come, Plunkett, you don't expect us to swallow that. No heads? How could even a ghost drive horses with no heads? How about the reins, eh?'

'You may laugh, sir, but we know that with God all things are possible. Four white horses they was. I see them clearly, but there was neither head nor neck beyond the collar, sir. I see the reins, shining like silver, and they ran up to the rings of the hames, and they didn't go no further. If I was to drop dead this minute, sir, that's what I see.'

'Was there a driver to this wonderful turn-out?'

'Yes, sir, there was a driver.'

'Headless too, I suppose?'

'Yes, sir, headless too. At least, I couldn't see nothing of him beyond his coat, which had them old-fashioned capes at the shoulders.'

'Well, I must say, Plunkett, you're very circumstantial. How far off was this – er – apparition when you saw it?'

'I was passing by the War Memorial, sir, when I see it come up the lane. It wouldn't be above twenty or thirty yards from where I stood. It went by at a gallop, and turned off to the left round the churchyard wall.'

'Well, well, it sounds odd, certainly, but it was a dark night, and at that distance your eyes may have deceived you. Now, if you'll take my advice you'll think no more about it.'

'Ah, sir, it's all very well saying that, but everybody knows the man who sees the death-coach of the Burdocks is doomed to die within the week. There's no use rebelling against it, sir; it is so. And if you'll be so good as to oblige me over that matter of a will, I'd die happier for knowing as Sarah and the children was sure of their bit of money.'

Mr Frobisher-Pym obliged over the will, though much against the grain, exhorting and scolding as he wrote. Wimsey added his own signature as one of the witnesses, and contributed his own bit of comfort.

'I shouldn't worry too much about the coach, if I were you,' he said. 'Depend upon it, if it's the Burdock coach it'll just have come for the soul of the old squire. It couldn't be expected to go to New York for him, don't you see? It's just gettin' ready for the funeral tomorrow.'

'That's likely enough,' agreed Plunkett. 'Often and often it's been seen in these parts when one of the Burdocks was taken. But it's terrible unlucky to see it.'

The thought of the funeral seemed, however, to cheer him a little. The visitors again begged him not to think about it, and took their departure.

'Isn't it wonderful,' said Mr Frobisher-Pym, 'what imagination will do with these people? And they're obstinate. You could argue with them till you were black in the face.'

'Yes. I say, let's go down to the church and have a look at the place. I'd like to know how much he could really have seen from where he was standing.'

The parish church of Little Doddering stands, like so many country churches, at some distance from the houses. The main road from Herriotting, Abbotts Bolton, and Frimpton runs past the west gate of the

churchyard – a wide God's acre, crowded with ancient stones. On the south side is a narrow and gloomy lane, heavily overhung with old elm-trees, dividing the church from the still more ancient ruins of Doddering Priory. On the main road, a little beyond the point where Old Priory Lane enters, stands the War Memorial, and from here the road runs straight on into Little Doddering. Round the remaining two sides of the churchyard winds another lane, known to the village simply as the Back Lane. This branches out from the Herriotting road about a hundred yards north of the church, connects with the far end of Priory Lane, and thence proceeds deviously to Shootering Underwood, Hamsey, Thripsey, and Wyck.

'Whatever it was Plunkett thinks he saw,' said Mr Frobisher-Pym, 'it must have came from Shootering. The Back Lane only leads round by some fields and a cottage or two, and it stands to reason anybody coming from Frimpton would have taken the main road, going and coming. The lane is in a very bad state with all this rain. I'm afraid even your detective ability, my dear Wimsey, would not avail to find wheel-marks on this modern tarmac.'

'Hardly,' said Wimsey, 'especially in the case of a ghostly chariot which gets along without touching the ground. But your reasoning seems perfectly sound, sir.'

'It was probably a couple of belated waggons going to market,' pursued Mr Frobisher-Pym, 'and the rest of it is superstition and, I am afraid, the local beer. Plunkett couldn't have seen all those details about drivers and harness and so on at this distance. And, if it was making no noise how did he come to notice it at all, since he'd got past he turn and was walking in the other direction? Depend upon it, he heard the wheels and imagined the rest.'

'Probably,' said Wimsey.

'Of course,' went on his host, 'if the waggons really were going about without lights, it ought to be looked into. It is a very dangerous thing, with all these motor vehicles about, and I've had to speak severely about it before now. I fined a man only the other day for the very same thing. Do you care to see the church while we're here?'

Knowing that in country places it is always considered proper to see the church, Lord Peter expressed his eagerness to do so.

'It's always open nowadays,' said the magistrate, leading the way to the west entrance. 'The vicar has a idea that churches should be always open for private prayer. He comes from a town living, of course. Round about here the people are always out on the land, and you can't expect them to come into church in their working clothes and muddy boots. They wouldn't think it respectful, and they've other things to do. Besides, I said to him, consider the opportunity it gives for undesirable conduct. But he's a young man, and he'll have to learn by experience.'

He pushed the door open. A curious, stuffy waft of stale incense, damp, and stoves rushed out at them as they entered – a kind of concentrated extract of Church of England. The two altars, bright with flowers and gilding, and showing as garish splashes among the heavy shadows and oppressive architecture of the little Norman building, sounded the same note of contradiction; it was the warm and human that seemed exotic and unfamiliar; the cold and unwelcoming that seemed native to the place and people.

'This Lady-chapel, as Hancock calls it, in the south aisle, is new, of course,' said Mr Frobisher-Pym. 'It aroused a good deal of opposition, but the Bishop is lenient with the High Church party – too lenient, some people think – but, after all, what does it matter? I'm sure I can say my prayers just as well with two communion tables as with one. And, I will say for Hancock, he is very good with the young men and the girls. In these days of motor-cycles, it's something to get them interested in religion at all. Those trestles in the chapel are for old Burdock's coffin, I suppose. Ah! Here is the vicar.'

A thin man in a cassock emerged from a door beside the high altar and came down towards them, carrying a tall, oaken candlestick in his hand. He greeted them with a slightly professional smile of welcome. Wimsey diagnosed him promptly as earnest, nervous, and not highly intellectual.

'The candlesticks have only just come,' he observed after the usual introductions had been made. 'I was afraid they would not be here in time. However, all is now well.'

He set the candlestick beside the coffin-trestles, and proceeded to decorate its brass spike with a long candle of unbleached wax, which he took from a parcel in a neighbouring pew.

Mr Frobisher-Pym said nothing. Wimsey felt it incumbent on him to express his interest, and did so.

'It is very gratifying,' said Mr Hancock, thus encouraged, 'to see the people beginning to take a real interest in their church. I have really had very little difficulty in finding watchers for tonight. We are having eight watchers, two by two, from 10 o'clock this evening – till which time I shall be myself on duty – till six in the morning, when I come in to say Mass. The men will carry on till 2 o'clock, then my wife and daughter will relieve them, and Mr Hubbard and young Rawlinson have kindly consented to take the hours from four till six.'

'What Rawlinson is that?' demanded Mr Frobisher-Pym.

'Mr Graham's clerk from Herriotting. It is true he is not a member of the parish, but he was born here, and was good enough to wish to take his turn in watching. He is coming over on his motor-cycle. After all, Mr Graham has had charge of Burdock's family affairs for very many years, and no doubt they wish to show their respect in some way.'

'Well, I only hope he'll be awake enough to do his work in the morning, after gadding about all night,' said Mr Frobisher-Pym gruffly. 'As for Hubbard, that's his own look-out, though I must say it seems an odd occupation for a publican. Still, if he's pleased and you're pleased, there's no more to be said about it.'

You've got a very beautiful old church here, Mr Hancock,' said Wimsey, seeing that controversy seemed imminent.

'Very beautiful indeed,' said the vicar. 'Have you noticed that apse? It is rare for a village church to possess such a perfect Norman apse. Perhaps you would like to come and look at it.' He genuflected as they passed a hanging lamp which burned before a niche. 'You see, we are permitted Reservation. The Bishop –' He prattled cheerfully as they wandered up the chancel, digressing from time to time to draw attention to the handsome miserere seats ('Of course, this was the original Priory Church'), and a beautifully carved piscina and aumbry ('It is rare to find them so well preserved').

Wimsey assisted him to carry down the remaining candlesticks from the vestry, and, when these had been put in position, joined Mr Frobisher-Pym at the door.

'I think you said you were dining with the Lumsdens tonight,' said the magistrate, as they sat smoking after lunch. 'How are you going? Will you have the car?'

'I'd rather you'd lend me one of the saddle-horses,' said Wimsey. 'I get few opportunities of riding in town.'

'Certainly, my dear boy, certainly. Only I'm afraid you'll have rather a wet ride. Take Polly Flinders; it will do her good to get some exercise. You are quite sure you would prefer it? Have you got your kit with you?'

'Yes – I brought an old pair of bags down with me, and, with this raincoat, I shan't come to any harm. They won't expect me to dress. How far is it to Frimpton, by the way?'

'Nine miles by the main road, and tarmac all the way, I'm afraid, but there's a good wide piece of grass each side. And, of course, you can cut off a mile or so by going across the common. What time will you want to start?'

'Oh, about seven o'clock, I should think. And, I say, sir – will Mrs Frobisher-Pym think it very rude if I'm rather late back? Old Lumsden and I went through the war together, and if we get yarning over old times we may go on into the small hours. I don't want to feel I'm treating your house like a hotel, but—'

'Of course not, of course not! That's absolutely all right. My wife won't mind in the very least. We want you to enjoy your visit and do exactly what you like. I'll give you the key, and I'll remember not to put the chain up. Perhaps you wouldn't mind doing that yourself when you come in?'

'Rather not. And how about the mare?'

'I'll tell Merridew to look out for you; he sleeps over the stables. I only wish it were going to be a better night for you. I'm afraid the glass is going back. Yes. Dear, dear! It's a bad lookout for tomorrow. By the way, you'll probably pass the funeral procession at the church. It should be along by about then, if the train is punctual.'

The train, presumably, was punctual, for as Lord Peter cantered up to the west gate of the church he saw a hearse of great funereal pomp drawn up before it, surrounded by a little crowd of people. Two mourning coaches were in attendance; the driver of the second seemed to be having some difficulty with the horses, and Wimsey rightly inferred that this was the pair which had been borrowed from Mr Mortimer. Restraining Polly Flinders as best he might, he sidled into a respectful position on the edge of the crowd, and watched the coffin taken from the hearse and carried through the gate, where it was met by Mr Hancock, in full pontificals, attended by a thurifer and two torch-bearers. The effect was a little marred by the rain, which had extinguished the candles, but the village seemed to look upon it as an excellent show nevertheless. A massive man, dressed with great correctness in a black frock coat and tall hat, and accompanied by a woman in handsome mourning and furs, was sympathetically commented on. This was Haviland Burdock of silk-stocking fame, the younger son of the deceased. A vast number of white wreaths were then handed out, and greeted with murmurs of admiration and approval. The choir struck up a hymn, rather raggedly, and the procession filed away into the church. Polly Flinders shook her head vigorously, and Wimsey, taking this as a signal to be gone, replaced his hat and ambled gently away towards Frimpton.

He followed the main road for about four miles, winding up through finely wooded country to the edge of Frimpton Common. Here the road made a wide sweep, skirting the common and curving gently down into Frimpton village. Wimsey hesitated for a moment, considering that it was growing dark and that both the way and the animal he rode were strange to him. There seemed, however, to be a well-defined bridle-path across the common, and eventually he decided to take it. Polly Flinders seemed to know it well enough, and cantered along without hesitation. A ride of about a mile and a half brought them without adventure into the main road again. Here a fork in the road presented itself confusingly; an electric torch, however, and a signpost solved the problem; after which ten minutes' ride brought the traveller to his goal.

Major Lumsden was a large, cheerful man – none the less cheerful for having lost a leg in the War. He had a large, cheerful wife, a large, cheerful house, and a large, cheerful family. Wimsey soon found himself seated before a fire as large and cheerful as the rest of the establishment, exchanging gossip with his hosts over a whisky-and-soda. He described the Burdock funeral with irreverent gusto, and went on to tell the story of the phantom coach. Major Lumsden laughed.

'It's a quaint part of the country,' he said. 'The policeman is just as bad as the rest of them. Do you remember, dear, the time I had to go out and lay a ghost, down at Pogson's farm?'

'I do, indeed,' said his wife emphatically. 'The maids had a wonderful time. Trivett – that's our local constable – came rushing in here and fainted in the kitchen, and they all sat round howling and sustaining him with our best brandy, while Dan went down and investigated.'

'Did you find the ghost?'

'Well, not the ghost, exactly, but we found a pair of boots and half a pork-pie in the empty house, so we put it all down to a tramp. Still, I must say odd things do happen about here. There were those fires on the common last year. They were never explained.'

'Gipsies, Dan.'

'Maybe; but nobody ever saw them, and the fires would start in the most unexpected way, sometimes in the pouring rain; and, before you could get near one, it would be out, and only a sodden wet black mark left behind it. And there's another bit of the common that animals don't like – near what they call the Dead Man's Post. My dogs won't go near it. Funny brutes. I've never seen anything there, but even in broad daylight they don't seem to fancy it. The common's not got a good reputation. It used to be a great place for highwaymen.'

'Is the Burdock coach anything to do with highwaymen?'

'No. I fancy it was some rakehelly dead-and-gone Burdock. Belonged to the Hell-fire Club or something. The usual sort of story. All the people round here believe in it, of course. It's rather a good thing. Keeps the servants indoors at night. Well, let's go and have some grub, shall we?'

'Do you remember,' said Major Lumsden, 'that damned old mill, and the three elms by the pig-sty?'

'Good Lord, yes! You very obligingly blew them out of the landscape for us, I remember. They made us a damned sight too conspicuous.'

'We rather missed them when they were gone.'

'Thank heaven you didn't miss them when they were there. I'll tell you what you did miss, though.'

'What's that?'

'The old sow.'

'By Jove, yes. Do you remember old Piper fetching her in?'

'I'll say I do. That reminds me. You knew Bunthorne . . .'

'I'll say good night,' said Mrs Lumsden, 'and leave you people to it.'

'Do you remember,' said Lord Peter Wimsey, 'that awkward moment when Popham went off his rocker?'

'No. I'd been sent back with a batch of prisoners. I heard about it, though. I never knew what became of him.'

'I got him sent home. He's married now and living in Lincolnshire.'

'Is he? Well, he couldn't help himself, I suppose. He was only a kid. What's happened to Philpotts?'

'Oh, Philpotts . . .'

'Where's your glass, old man?'

'Oh, rot, old man. The night is still young . . .'

'Really? Well but look here, why not stay the night? My wife will be delighted. I can fix you up in no time.'

'No, thanks most awfully. I must be rolling off home. I said I'd be back; and I'm booked to put the chain on the door.'

'As you like, of course, but it's still raining. Not a good night for a ride on an open horse.'

'I'll bring a saloon next time. We shan't hurt. Rain's good for the complexion – makes the roses grow. Don't wake your man up. I can saddle her myself.'

'My dear man, it's no trouble.'

'No, really, old man.'

'Well, I'll come along and lend you a hand.'

A gust of rain and wind blew in through the hall door as they struggled out into the night. It was past one in the morning and pitch-dark. Major Lumsden again pressed Wimsey to stay.

'No, thanks, really. The old lady's feelings might be hurt. It's not so bad, really – wet, but not cold. Come up, Polly, stand over, old lady.'

He put the saddle on and girthed it, while Lumsden held the lantern. The mare, fed and rested, came delicately dancing out of the warm loose-box, head well stretched forward, and nostrils snuffing at the rain.

'Well, so long, old lad. Come and look us up again. It's been great.'

'Rather! By Jove, yes. Best respects to madame. Is the gate open?'

'Yes.'

Well, cheerio!'

'Cheerio!'

Polly Flinders, with her nose turned homewards settled down to make short work of the nine miles of high-road. Once outside the gates, the night seemed lighter, though the rain poured heavily. Somewhere buried behind the thronging clouds there was a moon, which now and again showed as a pale stain on the sky, a paler reflection on the black road. Wimsey, with a mind full of memories and a skin full of whisky, hummed to himself as he rode.

As he passed the fork, he hesitated for a moment. Should he take the path over the common or stick to the road? On consideration, he decided to give the common a miss – not because of its sinister reputation, but because of ruts and rabbit-holes. He shook the reins, bestowed a word of encouragement on his mount, and continued by the road, having the common on his right hand, and, on the left, fields bounded by high hedges, which gave some shelter from the driving rain.

He had topped the rise, and passed the spot where the bridle-path again joined the high-road, when a slight start and stumble drew his attention unpleasantly to Polly Flinders.

'Hold up, mare,' he said disapprovingly.

Polly shook her head, moved forward, tried to pick up her easy pace again. 'Hullo!' said Wimsey, alarmed. He pulled her to a standstill.

'Lame in the near fore,' he said, dismounting. 'If you've been and gone and strained anything, my girl, four miles from home, father *will* be pleased.' It occurred to him for the first time how curiously lonely the road was. He had not seen a single car. They might have been in the wilds of Africa.

He ran an exploratory hand down the near foreleg. The mare stood quietly enough, without shrinking or wincing. Wimsey was puzzled.

'If these had been the good old days,' he said, 'I'd have thought she'd picked up a stone. But what—'

He lifted the mare's foot, and explored it carefully with fingers and pocket-torch. His diagnosis had been right, after all. A steel nut, evidently dropped from a passing car, had wedged itself firmly between the shoe and the frog. He grunted and felt for his knife. Happily, it was one of that excellent old-fashioned kind which includes, besides blades and corkscrews, an ingenious apparatus for removing foreign bodies from horses' feet.

The mare nuzzled him gently as he stooped over his task. It was a little awkward getting to work; he had to wedge the torch under his arm, so as to leave one hand free for the tool and the other to hold the hoof. He was swearing gently at these difficulties when, happening to glance down the road ahead, he fancied he caught the gleam of something moving. It was not easy to see, for at this point the tall trees stood up on both sides of the road, which dipped abruptly from the edge of the common. It was not a car, the light was too faint. A waggon, probably, with a dim lantern. Yet it seemed to move fast. He puzzled for a moment; then bent to work again.

The nut resisted his efforts, and the mare, touched in a tender spot, pulled away, trying to get her foot down. He soothed her with his voice and patted her neck. The torch slipped from his arm. He cursed it impatiently, set down the hoof, and picked up the torch from the edge of the grass, into which it had rolled. As he straightened himself again, he looked along the road and saw.

Up from under the dripping dark of the trees it came, shining with a thin, moony radiance. There was no clatter of hoofs, no rumble of wheels, no ringing of bit or bridle. He saw the white, sleek, shining shoulders with the collar that lay on each, like a faint fiery ring, enclosing nothing. He saw the gleaming reins, their cut ends slipping back and forward unsupported through the ring of the hames. The feet, that never touched the earth, ran swiftly – four times four noiseless hoofs bearing the pale bodies by like smoke. The driver leaned forward, brandishing his whip. He was faceless and headless, but his whole attitude bespoke desperate haste. The coach was barely visible through the driving rain, but Wimsey saw the dimly spinning wheels and a faint whiteness, still and stiff, at the window. It went past at a gallop – headless driver and headless horses and silent coach. Its passing left a stir, a sound that was less a sound than a vibration – and the wind roared suddenly after it, with a great sheet of water blown up out of the south.

'Good God!' said Wimsey. And then: 'How many whiskies did we have?'

He turned and looked back along the road, straining his eyes. Then suddenly he remembered the mare, and, without troubling further about the torch, picked up her foot and went to work by touch. The nut gave no more trouble, but dropped out into his hand almost immediately. Polly Flinders sighed gratefully and blew into his ear.

Wimsey led her forward a few steps. She put her feet down firmly and strongly. The nut, removed without delay, had left no tenderness. Wimsey mounted, let her go – then pulled her head round suddenly.

'I'm going to see,' he said resolutely. 'Come up, mare! We won't let any headless horses get the better of *us*. Perfectly indecent, goin' about without heads. Get on, old lady. Over the common with you. We'll catch 'em at the cross-roads.'

Without the slightest consideration for his host or his host's property, he put the mare to the bridle-path again, and urged her into a gallop.

At first he thought he could make out a pale, fluttering whiteness, moving away ahead of him on the road. Presently, as high-road and bridle-path diverged, he lost it altogether. But he knew there was no side-road. Bar any accident to his mount, he was bound to catch it before it came to the fork. Polly Flinders, answering easily to the touch of his heel, skimmed over the rough track with the indifference born of familiarity. In less than ten minutes her feet rang out again on the tarmac. He pulled her up, faced round in the direction of Little Doddering, and stared down the road. He could see nothing yet. Either he was well ahead of the coach, or it had already passed at unbelievable speed, or else—

He waited. Nothing. The violent rain had ceased, and the moon was struggling out again. The road appeared completely deserted. He glanced over his shoulder. A small beam of light near the ground moved, turned, flashed green, and red, and white again, and came towards him. Presently he made out that it was a policeman wheeling a bicycle.

'A bad night, sir,' said the man civilly, but with a faint note of enquiry in his voice.

'Rotten,' said Wimsey.

'Just had to mend a puncture, to make it all the pleasanter,' added the policeman.

Wimsey expressed sympathy. 'Have you been here long?' he added.

'Best part o' twenty minutes.'

'Did you see anything pass along this way from Little Doddering?'

'Ain't been nothing along while I've been here. What sort of thing did you mean, sir?'

'I thought I saw –' Wimsey hesitated. He did not care about the idea of making a fool of himself. 'A carriage with four horses,' he said hesitatingly. 'It passed me on this road not a quarter of an hour ago – down at the other end of the common. I – I came back to see. It seemed unusual –' He became aware that his story sounded very lame.

The policeman spoke rather sharply and rapidly.

'There ain't been nothing past here.'

'You're sure?'

'Yes, sir; and, if you don't mind me sayin' so, you'd best be getting home. It's a lonesome bit o' road.'

'Yes, isn't it?' said Wimsey. 'Well, good night, sergeant.'

He turned the mare's head back along the Little Doddering road, going very quietly. He saw nothing, heard nothing, and passed nothing. The night was brighter now, and, as he rode back, he verified the entire absence of side roads. Whatever the thing was which he had seen, it had vanished somewhere along the edge of the common; it had not gone by the main road, nor by any other.

Wimsey came down rather late for breakfast in the morning, to find his hosts in a state of some excitement. 'The most extraordinary thing has happened,' said Mrs Frobisher-Pym.

'Outrageous!' added her husband. 'I warned Hancock – he can't say I didn't warn him. Still, however much one may disapprove of his goings-on, there is no excuse whatever for such abominable conduct. Once let me get hold of the beggars, whoever they are—'

What's up?' said Wimsey, helping himself to broiled kidneys at the sideboard.

'A most scandalous thing,' said Mrs Frobisher-Pym. 'The vicar came up to Tom at once – I hope we didn't disturb you, by the way, with all the excitement. It appears that when Mr Hancock got to the church this morning at 6 o'clock to take the early service—'

'No, no, my dear, you've got it wrong. Let *me* tell it. When Joe Grinch – that's the sexton, you know, and he has to get there first to ring the bell – when he arrived, he found the south door wide open and nobody in the

chapel, where they should have been, beside the coffin.
He was very much perplexed, of course, but he supposed that Hubbard and young Rawlinson had got sick
of it and gone off home. So he went on to the vestry to
get the vestments and things ready, and to his amaze-
ment he heard women's voices, calling out to him from
inside. He was so astonished, didn't know where he
was, but he went on and unlocked the door—'

'With his own key?' put in Wimsey.

'The key was in the door. As a rule it's kept hanging up on a nail under a curtain near the organ, but it
was in the lock – where it ought not to have been. And
inside the vestry he found Mrs Hancock and her
daughter, nearly dead with fright and annoyance.'

'Great Scott!'

'Yes, indeed. They had a most extraordinary story to
tell. They'd taken over at 2 o'clock from the other pair
of watchers, and had knelt down by the coffin in the
Lady-chapel, according to plan, to say the proper sort
of prayers, whatever they are. They'd been there, to the
best of their calculation, about ten minutes, when they
heard a noise up by the High Altar, as though somebody was creeping stealthily about. Miss Hancock is a
very plucky girl, and she got up and walked up the aisle
in the dark, with Mrs Hancock following on behind
because, as she said, she didn't want to be left alone.
When they'd got as far as the rood-screen, Miss
Hancock called out aloud, 'Who's there?' At which
they heard a sort of rustling sound, and a noise like
something being knocked over. Miss Hancock most
courageously snatched up one of the churchwarden's
staffs, which was clipped on to the choir-stalls, and ran
forward, thinking, she says, that somebody was trying

to steal the ornaments off the altar. There's a very fine fifteenth-century cross—'

'Never mind the cross, Tom. That hasn't been taken, at any rate.'

'No, it hasn't, but she thought it might be. Anyhow, just as she got up to the sanctuary steps, with Mrs Hancock coming close after her and begging her to be careful, somebody seemed to rush out of the choir-stalls, and caught her by the arms and frog's-marched her – that's her expression – into the vestry. And before she could get breath even to shriek, Mrs Hancock was pushed in beside her, and the door locked on them.'

'By jove! You do have exciting times in your village.'

'Well,' said Mr Frobisher-Pym, 'of course they were dreadfully frightened, because they didn't know but what these wretches would come back and murder them and, in any case, they thought the church was being robbed. But the vestry windows are very narrow and barred, and they couldn't do anything except wait. They tried to listen, but they couldn't hear much. Their only hope was that the four-o'clock watchers might come early and catch the thieves at work. But they waited and waited, and they heard four strike, and five, and nobody came.'

'What happened to what's-his-name and Rawlinson then?'

'They couldn't make out, and nor could Grinch. However, they had a good look round the church, and nothing seemed to be taken or disturbed in any way. Just then the vicar came along, and they told him all about it. He was very much shocked, naturally, and his first thought – when he found the ornaments were safe and the poor-box all right – was that some Kensitite people had been stealing the wafers from the what d'you call it.'

'The tabernacle,' suggested Wimsey.

'Yes, that's his name for it. That worried him very much, and he unlocked it and had a look, but the wafers were all there all right, and, as there's only one key, and that was on his own watch-chain, it wasn't a case of anyone substituting unconsecrated wafers for consecrated ones, or any practical joke of that kind. So he sent Mrs and Miss Hancock home, and had a look round the church outside, and the first thing he saw, lying in the bushes near the south door, was young Rawlinson's motor-cycle.'

'Oho!'

'So his next idea was to hunt for Rawlinson and Hubbard. However, he didn't have to look far. He'd got round the church as far as the furnace-house on the north side, when he heard a terrific hullabaloo going on, and people shouting and thumping on the door. So he called Grinch, and they looked through the little window, and there, if you please, were Hubbard and young Rawlinson, bawling and going on and using the most shocking language. It seems they were set upon in exactly the same way, only before they got inside the church. Rawlinson had been passing the evening with Hubbard, I understand, and they had a bit of a sleep downstairs in the back bar, to avoid disturbing the house early – or so they say, though I dare say if the truth was known they were having drinks; and if that's Hancock's idea of a suitable preparation for going to church and saying prayers, all I can say is, it isn't mine. Anyway, they started off just before four, Hubbard going down on the carrier of Rawlinson's bicycle. They had to get off at the south gate, which was pushed to, and while Rawlinson was wheeling the machine up the path two or three men – they couldn't see exactly –

umped out from the trees. There was a bit of a scuffle, but what with the bicycle, and it's being so unexpected, they couldn't put up a very good fight, and the men dropped blankets over their heads, or something. I don't know all the details. At any rate, they were bundled into the furnace-house and left there. They may be here still, for all I know, if they haven't found the key. There should be a spare key, but I don't know what's become of it. They sent up for it this morning, but I haven't seen it about for a long time.'

'It wasn't left in the lock this time, then?'

'No, it wasn't. They've had to send for the locksmith. I'm going down now to see what's to be done about it. Like to come, if you're ready?'

Wimsey said he would. Anything in the nature of a problem always fascinated him.

'You were back pretty late, by the way,' said Mr Frobisher-Pym jovially, as they left the house. 'Yarning over old times, I suppose.'

'We were, indeed,' said Wimsey.

'Hope the old girl carried you all right. Lonely bit of road, isn't it? I don't suppose you saw anybody worse than yourself, as the saying goes?'

'Only a policeman,' said Wimsey untruthfully. He had not yet decided about the phantom coach. No doubt Plunkett would be relieved to know that he was not the only person to whom the 'warning' had come. But, then, had it really been the phantom coach, or merely a delusion, begotten by whisky upon reminiscence? Wimsey, in the cold light of day, was none too certain.

On arriving at the church, the magistrate and his guest found a little crowd collected, conspicuous among whom were the vicar, in cassock and biretta, gesticulating freely, and the local policeman, his tunic buttoned awry and his dignity much impaired by the small fry of the village, who clustered round his legs. He had just finished taking down the statements of the two men who had been released from the stoke-hole. The younger of these, a fresh-faced, impudent-looking fellow of twenty-five or so, was in the act of starting up his motor-cycle. He greeted Mr Frobisher-Pym pleasantly. 'Afraid they've made us look a bit small, sir. You'll excuse me, won't you? I'll have to be getting back to Herriotting. Mr Graham won't be any too pleased if I'm late for the office. I think some of the bright lads have been having a joke with us.' He grinned as he pushed the throttle-lever over and departed in a smother of unnecessary smoke that made Mr Frobisher-Pym sneeze. His fellow-victim, a large, fat man, who looked the sporting publican that he was, grinned shamefacedly at the magistrate.

'Well, Hubbard,' said the latter, 'I hope you've enjoyed your experience. I must say I'm surprised at a man of your size letting himself be shut up in a coalhole like a naughty urchin.'

'Yes, sir, I was surprised myself at the time,' retorted the publican, good-humouredly enough. 'When that there blanket came down on my head, I was the most surprised man in this here county. I gave 'em a hack or two on the shins, though, to remember me by,' he added, with a reminiscent chuckle.

'How many of them were there?' asked Wimsey.

'Three or four, I should say, sir. But not 'avin' seen 'em, I can only tell from 'earin' 'em talk. There was two laid 'old of me, I'm pretty sure, and young Rawlinson thinks there was only one 'ad 'old of 'im, but 'e was a wonderful strong 'un.'

'We must leave no stone unturned to find out who these people were,' said the vicar excitedly. 'Ah, Mr Frobisher-Pym, come and see what they have done in the church. It is as I thought – an anti-Catholic protest. We must be most thankful that they have done no more than they have.'

He led the way in. Somebody had lit two or three hanging lamps in the gloomy little chancel. By their light Wimsey was able to see that the neck of the eagle lectern was decorated with an enormous red-white-and-blue bow, and bore a large placard – obviously pinched from the local newspaper offices – 'VATICAN BANS IMMODEST DRESS.' In each of the choir-stalls a teddy-bear sat, lumpishly amiable, apparently absorbed in reading the choir-books upside-down, while on the ledge before them copies of the *Pink 'Un* were obtrusively displayed. In the pulpit, a waggish hand had set up a pantomime ass's head, elegantly arrayed in a nightgown, and crowned with a handsome nimbus, cut from gold paper.

'Disgraceful, isn't it?' said the vicar.

'Well Hancock,' replied Mr Frobisher-Pym, 'I must say I think you have brought it upon yourself – though I quite agree, of course, that this sort of thing cannot possibly be allowed, and the offenders must be discovered and severely punished. But you must see that many of your practices appear to these people to be papistical nonsense at best, and while that is no excuse . . .'

His reprimanding voice barked on.

'. . . what I really can only look upon as this sacrilegious business with old Burdock – a man whose life . . .'

The policeman had by this time shoved away the attendant villagers and was standing beside Lord Peter at the entrance of the rood-screen.

'Was that you was out on the road this morning, sir. Ah! I thought I reckernised your voice. Did you get home all right, sir? Didn't meet nothing?'

There seemed to be a shade more than idle questioning in the tone of his voice. Wimsey turned quickly.

'No, I met nothing – more. Who is it drives a coach with four white horses about this village of a night, sergeant?'

'Not sergeant, sir – I ain't due for promotion yet awhile. Well, sir, as to white horses, I don't altogether like to say. Mr Mortimer over at Abbotts Bolton has some nice greys, and he's the biggest horse-breeder about these parts – but, well, there, sir, he wouldn't be driving out in all that rain, sir, would he?'

'It doesn't seem a sensible thing to do, certainly.'

'No, sir. And' – the constable leaned close to Wimsey and spoke into his ear – 'and Mr Mortimer is a man that's got a head on his shoulders – *and, what's more, so have his horses.*'

'Why,' said Wimsey, a little startled by the aptness of this remark, 'did you ever know a horse that hadn't?'

'No, sir,' said the policeman, with emphasis, 'I never knew no *livin'* horse that hadn't. But that's neether here nor there, as the sayin' goes. But as to this church business, that's just a bit of a lark got up among the boys, that's what that is. They don't mean no harm, you know, sir; they likes to be up to their tricks. It's all very well for the vicar to talk, sir, but this ain't no Kensitite nor anythink of that, as you can see with half an eye. Just a bit of fun, that's all it is.'

'I'd come to the same conclusion myself,' said Wimsey, interested, 'but I'd rather like to know what makes you think so.'

'Lord bless you, sir, ain't it plain as the nose on your face? If it had a-bin these Kensitites, wouldn't they have gone for the crosses and the images and the lights and – that there?' He extended a horny finger in the direction of the tabernacle. 'No, sir, these lads what did this ain't laid a finger on the things what you might call sacred images – and they ain't done no harm neether to the communion-table. So I says as it ain't a case of controversy, but more a bit of fun, like. And they've treated Mr Burdock's corpse respectful, sir, you see, too. That shows they wasn't meaning anything wrong at heart, don't you see?'

'I agree absolutely,' said Wimsey. 'In fact, they've taken particular care not to touch anything that a churchman holds really sacred. How long have you been on this job, officer?'

'Three years, sir, come February.'

'Ever had any idea of going to town or taking up the detective side of the business?'

'Well, sir – I have – but it isn't ask and have, as you might say.'

Wimsey took a card from his note-case.

'If ever you think seriously about it,' he said, 'give this card to Chief Inspector Parker, and have a chat with him. Tell him I think you haven't got opportunities enough down here. He's a great friend of mine, and he'll give you a good chance, I know.'

'I've heard of you, my lord,' said the constable, gratified, 'and I'm sure it's very kind of your lordship. Well, I suppose I'd best be getting along now. You leave it to me, Mr Frobisher-Pym, sir; we'll soon get at the bottom of this here.'

'I hope you do,' said the magistrate. 'Meanwhile, Mr Hancock, I trust you will realise the inadvisability of leaving the church doors open at night. Well, come along, Wimsey; we'll leave them to get the church straight for the funeral. What have you found there?'

'Nothing,' said Wimsey, who had been peering at the floor of the Lady-chapel. 'I was afraid you'd got the worm in here, but I see it's only sawdust.' He dusted his fingers as he spoke, and followed Mr Frobisher Pym out of the building.

When you are staying in a village, you are expected to take part in the interests and amusements of the community. Accordingly, Lord Peter duly attended the funeral of Squire Burdock, and beheld the coffin safely committed to the ground, in a drizzle, certainly, but not without the attendance of a large and reverent congregation. After this ceremony, he was formally introduced to Mr and Mrs Haviland Burdock, and was able to confirm his previous impression that the lady was well, not to say too well, dressed, as might be expected from one whose wardrobe was based upon silk stockings. She was a handsome woman, in a large, bold style, and the hand that clasped Wimsey's was quite painfully encrusted with diamonds. Haviland was disposed to be friendly – and, indeed, silk manufacturers have no reason to be otherwise to rich men of noble birth. He seemed to be aware of Wimsey's reputation as an antiquarian and book-collector, and extended a hearty invitation to him to come and see the old house.

'My brother Martin is still abroad,' he said, 'but I'm sure he would be delighted to have you come and look at the place. I'm told there are some very fine old books in the library. We shall be staying here till Monday – Mrs Hancock will be good enough to have us. Suppose you come along tomorrow afternoon.'

Wimsey said he would be delighted.

Mrs Hancock interposed and said, wouldn't Lord Peter come to tea at the vicarage first.

Wimsey said it was very good of her.

'Then that's settled,' said Mrs Burdock. 'You and Mr Pym come to tea, and then we'll all go over the house together. I've hardly seen it myself yet.'

'It's very well worth seeing,' said Mr Frobisher-Pym. 'Fine old place, but takes some money to keep up. Has nothing been seen of the will yet, Mr Burdock?'

'Nothing whatever,' said Haviland. 'It's curious, because Mr Graham – the solicitor, you know, Lord Peter – certainly drew one up, just after poor Martin's unfortunate difference with our father. He remembers it perfectly.'

'Can't he remember what's in it?'

'He could, of course, but he doesn't think it etiquette to say. He's one of the crusted old type. Poor Martin always called him an old scoundrel – but then, of course, he never approved of Martin, so Martin was not altogether unprejudiced. Besides, as Mr Graham says, all that was some years ago, and it's quite possible that the governor destroyed the will later, or made a new one in America.'

'"Poor Martin" doesn't seem to have been popular hereabouts,' said Wimsey to Mr Frobisher-Pym, as they parted from the Burdocks and turned homewards.

'N-no,' said the magistrate. 'Not with Graham, anyway. Personally, I rather liked the lad, though he was a bit harum-scarum. I dare say he's sobered up with time – and marriage. It's odd that they can't find the will. But, if it was made at the time of the rumpus, it's bound to be in Haviland's favour.'

'I think Haviland thinks so,' said Wimsey. 'His manner seemed to convey a chastened satisfaction. I expect the discreet Graham made it fairly clear that the advantage was not with the unspeakable Martin.'

The following morning turned out fine, and Wimsey, who was supposed to be enjoying a rest-and-fresh-air cure in Little Doddering, petitioned for a further loan of Polly Flinders. His host consented with pleasure, and only regretted that he could not accompany his guest, being booked to attend a Board of Guardians meeting in connection with the workhouse.

'But you could go up and get a good blow on the common,' he suggested. 'Why not go round by Petering Friars, turn off across the common till you get to Dead Man's Post, and come back by the Frimpton road? It makes a very pleasant round – about nineteen miles. You'll be back in nice time for lunch if you take it easy.'

Wimsey fell in with the plan – the more readily that it exactly coincided with his own inward purpose. He had a reason for wishing to ride over the Frimpton road by daylight.

'You'll be careful about Dead Man's Post,' said Mrs Frobisher-Pym a little anxiously. 'The horses have a way of shying at it. I don't know why. People say, of course—'

'All nonsense,' said her husband. 'The villagers dislike the place and that makes the horses nervous. It's remarkable how a rider's feelings communicate themselves to his mount. *I've* never had any trouble at Dead Man's Post.'

It was a quiet and pretty road, even on a November day, that led to Petering Friars. Jogging down the winding Essex lanes in the wintry sunshine, Wimsey felt soothed and happy. A good burst across the common raised his spirits to exhilaration pitch. He had entirely forgotten Dead Man's Post and its uncanny reputation, when a violent start and swerve, so sudden that it nearly unseated him, recalled him to what he was doing. With some difficulty, he controlled Polly Flinders, and brought her to a standstill.

He was at the highest point of the common, following a bridle-path which was bordered on each side by gorse and dead bracken. A little way ahead of him another bridle-path seemed to run into it, and at the junction of the two was something which he had vaguely imagined to be a decayed sign-post. Certainly it was short and thick for a sign-post, and had no arms. It appeared, however, to bear some sort of inscription on the face that was turned towards him.

He soothed the mare, and urged her gently towards the post. She took a few hesitating steps, and plunged sideways, snorting and shivering.

'Queer!' said Wimsey. 'If this is my state of mind communicating itself to my mount, I'd better see a doctor. My nerves must be in a rotten state. Come up, old lady? What's the matter with you?'

Polly Flinders, apologetic but determined, refused to budge. He urged gently with his heel. She sidled away, with ears laid back, and he saw the white of a protesting eye. He slipped from the saddle, and, putting his hand through the bridle, endeavoured to lead her forward. After a little persuasion, the mare followed him, with stretched neck and treading as though on egg-shells. After a dozen hesitating paces, she stopped again, trembling in all her limbs. He put his hand on her neck and found it wet with sweat.

'Damn it all!' said Wimsey. 'Look here, I'm jolly well going to read what's on that post. If you won't come, will you stand still?'

He dropped the bridle. The mare stood quietly, with hanging head. He left her and went forward, glancing back from time to time to see that she showed no disposition to bolt. She stood quietly enough, however, only shifting her feet uneasily.

Wimsey walked up to the post. It was a stout pillar of ancient oak, newly painted white. The inscription, too, had been recently blacked in. It read:

ON THIS SPOT

GEORGE WINTER

WAS FOULLY MURTHERED

IN DEFENSE OF

HIS MASTER'S GOODS

BY BLACK RALPH

OF HERRIOTTING

WHO WAS AFTERWARD

HANGED IN CHAINS

ON THE PLACE OF HIS CRIME

9 NOVEMBER 1674

FEAR JUSTICE

'And very nice too,' said Wimsey. 'Dead Man's Post without a doubt. Polly Flinders seems to share the local feeling about the place. Well, Polly; if them's your sentiments, I won't do violence to them. But may I ask why, if you're so sensitive about a mere post, you should swallow a death-coach and four headless horses with such hardened equanimity?'

The mare took the shoulder of his jacket gently between her lips and mumbled at it.

'Just so,' said Wimsey. 'I perfectly understand. You would if you could, but you really can't. But those horses, Polly – did they bring with them no brimstone blast from the nethermost pit? Can it be that they really exuded nothing but an honest and familiar smell of stables?'

He mounted, and, turning Polly's head to the right; guided her in a circle, so as to give Dead Man's Post a wide berth before striking the path again.

'The supernatural explanation is, I think, excluded. Not on *a priori* grounds, which would be unsound but on the evidence of Polly's senses. There remain the alternatives of whisky and jiggery-pokery. Further investigation seems called for.'

He continued to muse as the mare moved quietly forward.

'Supposing I wanted, for some reason, to scare the neighbourhood with the apparition of a coach and headless horses, I should choose a dark, rainy night. Good! It was that kind of night. Now, if I took black horses and painted their bodies white – poor devils! what a state they'd be in. No. How do they do these Maskelyne-and-Devant stunts where they cut off people's heads? White horses, of course – and black felt clothing over their heads. Right! And luminous paint on the harness, with a touch here and there on their bodies, to make good contrast and ensure that the whole show wasn't invisible. No difficulty about that. But they must go silently. Well, why not? Four stout black cloth bags filled with bran, drawn well up and tied round the fetlocks would make any horse go quietly enough, especially if there was a bit of a wind going. Rags round the bridle-rings to prevent clinking, and round the ends of the traces to keep 'em from squeaking. Give 'em a coachman in a white coat and black mask, hitch 'em to a rubber-tyred fly, picked out with phosphorus and well-oiled at the joints – and I swear I'd make something quite ghostly enough to startle a rather well-irrigated gentleman on a lonely road at half past two in the morning.'

He was pleased with this thought, and tapped his boot cheerfully with his whip.

'But damn it all! They never passed me again. Where did they go? A coach-and-horses can't vanish into thin air, you know. There must be a side-road after all – or else, Polly Flinders, you've been pulling my leg all the time.'

The bridle-path eventually debouched upon the high way at the now familiar fork where Wimsey had met the policeman. As he slowly ambled homewards, his lord ship scanned the left-hand hedgerow, looking for the lane which surely must exist. But nothing rewarded his search. Enclosed fields with padlocked gates presented the only breaks in the hedge, till he again found himself looking down the avenue of trees up which the death-coach had come galloping two nights before.

'Damn!' said Wimsey.

It occurred to him for the first time that the coach might perhaps have turned round and gone back through Little Doddering. Certainly it had been seen by Little Doddering Church on Wednesday. But on that occasion, also, it had galloped off in the direction of Frimpton. In fact, thinking it over, Wimsey concluded that it had approached from Frimpton, gone round the church – widdershins, naturally – by the Back Lane, and returned by the high-road whence it came. But in that case—

'Turn again, Whittington,' said Wimsey, and Polly Flinders rotated obediently in the road. 'Through one of those fields it went, or I'm a Dutchman.'

He pulled Polly into a slow walk, and passed along the strip of grass at the right-hand side, staring at the ground as though he were an Aberdonian who had lost a sixpence.

The first gate led into a ploughed field, harrowed smooth and sown with autumn wheat. It was clear that no wheeled thing had been across it for many weeks. The second gate looked more promising. It gave upon fallow ground, and the entrance was seamed with innumerable wheel-ruts. On further examination, however, it was clear that this was the one and only gate. It seemed unlikely that the mysterious coach should have been taken into a field from which there was no way out. Wimsey decided to seek further.

The third gate was in bad repair. It sagged heavily from its hinges; the hasp was gone, and the gate and post had been secured with elaborate twists of wire. Wimsey dismounted and examined these, convincing himself that their rusty surface had not been recently disturbed.

There remained only two more gates before he came to the cross-roads. One led into plough again, where the dark ridge-and-furrow showed no sign of disturbance, but at sight of the last Wimsey's heart gave a leap.

There was plough-land here also, but round the edge of the field ran a wide, beaten path, rutted and water-logged. The gate was not locked, but opened simply with a spring catch. Wimsey examined the approach. Among the wide ruts made by farm-waggons was the track of four narrow wheels – the unmistakable prints of rubber tyres. He pushed the gate open and passed through.

The path skirted two sides of the plough; then came another gate and another field, containing a long barrow of mangold wurzels and a couple of barns. At the sound of Polly's hoofs, a man emerged from the nearest barn, with a paint-brush in his hand, and stood watching Wimsey's approach.

''Morning!' said the latter genially.

''Morning, sir.'

'Fine day after the rain?'

'Yes, it is, sir.'

'I hope I'm not trespassing?'

'Where was you wanting to go, sir?'

'I thought, as a matter of fact – hullo!'

'Anything wrong sir?'

Wimsey shifted in the saddle.

'I fancy this girth's slipped a bit. It's a new one.' (This was a fact.) 'Better have a look.'

The man advanced to investigate, but Wimsey had dismounted and was tugging at the strap, with his head under the mare's belly.

'Yes, it wants taking up a trifle. Oh! Thanks most awfully. Is this a short cut to Abbotts Bolton, by the way?'

'Not to the village, sir, though you can get through this way. It comes out by Mr Mortimer's stables.'

'Ah, yes. This his land?'

'No, sir it's Mr Topham's land, but Mr Mortimer rents this field and the next for fodder.'

'Oh, yes.' Wimsey peered across the hedge. 'Lucerne, I suppose. Or clover.'

'Clover, sir. And the mangolds is for the cattle.'

'Oh – Mr Mortimer keeps cattle as well as horses?'

'Yes, sir.'

'Very jolly. Have a gasper?' Wimsey had sidled across to the barn in his interest, and was gazing absently into its dark interior. It contained a number of farm implements and a black fly of antique construction, which seemed to be undergoing renovation with black varnish. Wimsey pulled some vestas from his pocket. The box was apparently damp, for, after one or two vain attempts he abandoned it, and struck a match on the wall of the barn. The flame, lighting up the ancient fly, showed it to be incongruously fitted with rubber tyres.

'Very fine stud, Mr Mortimer's, I understand,' said Wimsey carelessly.

'Yes, sir, very fine indeed.'

'I suppose he hasn't any greys, by any chance. My mother – queenly woman, Victorian ideas, and all that – is rather keen on greys. Sports a carriage and pay-ah, don't you know.'

'Yes, sir? Well, Mr Mortimer would be able to suit the lady, I think, sir. He has several greys.'

'No? Has he though? I must really go over and see him. Is it far?'

'Matter of five or six miles by the fields, sir.'

Wimsey looked at his watch.

'Oh, dear! I'm really afraid it's too far for this morning. I absolutely promised to get back to lunch. I must come over another day. Thanks *so* much. Is that girth right now? Oh, really, I'm immensely obliged. Get yourself a drink, won't you and tell Mr Mortimer not to sell his greys till I've seen them. Well, *good* morning, and many thanks.'

He set Polly Flinders on the homeward path and trotted gently away. Not till he was out of sight of the barn did he pull up and, stooping from the saddle, thoughtfully examine his boots. They were liberally plastered with bran.

'I must have picked it up in the barn,' said Wimsey. 'Curious, if true. Why should Mr Mortimer be lashing the stuffing out of his greys in an old fly at the dead of night – and with muffled hoofs and no heads, to boot? It's not a kind thing to do. It frightened Plunkett very much. It made me think I was drunk – a thought I hate to think. Ought I to tell the police? Are Mr Mortimer's jokes any business of mine? What do *you* think, Polly?'

The mare, hearing her name, energetically shook her head.

'You think not? Perhaps you are right. Let us say that Mr Mortimer did it for a wager. Who am I to interfere with his amusements? All the same,' added his lordship, 'I'm glad to know it wasn't Lumsden's whisky.'

'This is the library,' said Haviland, ushering in his guests. 'A fine room – and a fine collection of books, I'm told, though literature isn't much in my line. It wasn't much in the governor's line, either, I'm afraid. The place wants doing up, as you see. I don't know whether Martin will take it in hand. It's a job that'll cost money, of course.'

Wimsey shivered a little as he gazed round, more from sympathy than from cold, though a white November fog lay curled against the tall windows, and filtered damply through the frames.

A long, mouldering room, in the frigid neo-classical style, the library was melancholy enough in the sunless grey afternoon, even without the signs of neglect which wrung the book-collector's heart. The walls, panelled to half their height with book-cases, ran up in plaster to the moulded ceiling. Damp had blotched them into grotesque shapes, and here and there were ugly cracks and squamous patches, from which the plaster had fallen in yellowish flake. A wet chill seemed to ooze from the books, from the calf bindings peeling and perishing, from the stains of greenish mildew which spread horridly from volume to volume. The curious musty odour of decayed leather and damp paper added to the general cheerlessness of the atmosphere.

'Oh, dear, dear!' said Wimsey, peering dismally into this sepulchre of forgotten learning. With his shoulders hunched like the neck-feathers of a chilly bird, with his long nose and half-shut eyes, he resembled a dilapidated heron, brooding over the stagnation of a wintry pool.

'What a freezing-cold place,' exclaimed Mrs Hancock. 'You really ought to scold Mrs Lovall, Mr Burdock. When she was put in here as caretaker, I said to my husband – didn't I, Philip? – that your father had chosen the laziest woman in Little Doddering. She ought to have kept up big fires here, *at least* twice a week! It's really shameful, the way she has let things go.'

'Yes, isn't it?' agreed Haviland.

Wimsey said nothing. He was nosing along the shelves, every now and then taking a volume down and glancing at it.

'It was always rather a depressing room,' went on Haviland. 'I remember, when I was a kid, it used to overawe me rather. Martin and I used to browse about among the books, you know, but I think we were always afraid that something or somebody would stalk out upon us from the dark corners. What's that you've got there, Lord Peter? Oh, *Foxe's Book of Martyrs*. Dear me! How those pictures did terrify me in the old days! And there was a *Pilgrim's Progress*, with a most alarming picture of Apollyon straddling over the whole breadth of the way, which gave me many nightmares. Let me see. It used to live over in this bay, I think. Yes, here it is. How it does bring it all back, to be sure! Is it valuable, by the way?'

'No, not really. But this first edition of Burton is worth money; badly spotted, though – you'd better send it to be cleaned. And this is an extremely fine Boccaccio; take care of it.'

'John Boccace – *The Dance of Machabree*. It's a good title, anyhow. Is that the same Boccaccio that wrote the naughty stories?'

'Yes,' said Wimsey, a little shortly. He resented this attitude towards Boccaccio.

'Never read them,' said Haviland, with a wink at his wife, 'but I've seen 'em in the windows of those surgical shops – so I suppose they're naughty, eh? The vicar's looking shocked.'

'Oh, not at all,' said Mr Hancock, with a conscientious assumption of broad-mindedness. *'Et ego in Arcadia* – that is to say, one doesn't enter the Church without undergoing a classical education, and making the acquaintance of much more worldly authors even than Boccaccio. Those woodcuts are very fine, to my uninstructed eye.'

'Very fine indeed,' said Wimsey.

'There's another old book I remember, with jolly pictures,' said Haviland. 'A chronicle of some sort – what's 'is name – place in Germany – *you* know – where that hangman came from. They published his diary the other day. I read it, but it wasn't very exciting; not half as gruesome as old Harrison Ainsworth. What's the name of the place?'

'Nüremberg?' suggested Wimsey.

'That's it, of course – the *Nüremberg Chronicle*. I wonder if that's still in its old place. It was over here by the window, if I remember rightly.'

He led the way to the end of the bays, which ran up close against a window. Here the damp seemed to have done its worst. A pane of glass was broken, and rain had blown in.

'Now where has it gone to? A big book, it was, with a stamped leather binding. I'd like to see the old *Chronicle* again. I haven't set eyes on it for donkey's years.'

His glance roamed vaguely over the shelves. Wimsey, with the book-lover's instinct, was the first to spot the *Chronicle*, wedged at the extreme end of the shelf, against the outer wall. He hitched his finger into the top edge of the spine, but finding that the rotting leather was ready to crumble at a touch, he dislodged a neighbouring book and drew the *Chronicle* gently out, using his whole hand.

'Here he is – in pretty bad condition, I'm afraid. Hullo!'

As he drew the book away from the wall, a piece of folded parchment came away with it and fell at his feet. He stooped and picked it up.

'I say, Burdock – isn't this what you've been looking for?'

Haviland Burdock, who had been rooting about on one of the lower shelves, straightened himself quickly, his face red from stooping.

'By jove!' he said, turning first redder and then pale with excitement. 'Look at this, Winnie. It's the governor's will. What an extraordinary thing! Whoever would have thought of looking for it here, of all places?'

'Is it really the will?' cried Mrs Hancock.

'No doubt about it, I should say,' observed Wimsey coolly. 'Last Will and Testament of Simon Burdock.' He stood, turning the grimy document over and over in his hands, looking from the endorsement to the plain side of the folded parchment.

'Well, well!' said Mr Hancock. 'How strange! It seems almost providential that you should have taken that book down.'

'What does the will say?' demanded Mrs Burdock, in some excitement.

'I beg your pardon,' said Wimsey, handing it over to her. 'Yes, as you say, Mr Hancook, it does almost seem as if I was meant to find it.' He glanced down again at the *Chronicle,* mournfully tracing with his finger the outline of a damp stain which had rotted the cover and spread to the inner pages, almost obliterating the colophon.

Haviland Burdock meanwhile had spread the will out on the nearest table. His wife leaned over his shoulder. The Hancocks, barely controlling their curiosity, stood near, awaiting the result. Wimsey, with an elaborate pretence of non-interference in this family matter, examined the wall against which the *Chronicle* had stood, feeling its moist surface and examining the damp-stains. They had assumed the appearance of a grinning face. He compared them with the corresponding mark on the book, and shook his head desolately over the damage.

Mr Frobisher-Pym, who had wandered away some time before and was absorbed in an ancient book of farriery, now approached, and enquired what the excitement was about.

'Listen to this!' cried Haviland. His voice was quiet, but a suppressed triumph throbbed in it and glittered from his eyes.

'"I bequeath everything of which I die possessed" – there's a lot of enumeration of properties here, which doesn't matter – "to my eldest son, Martin"—'

Mr Frobisher-Pym whistled.

'Listen! "To my eldest son Martin, for so long as my body shall remain above ground. But so soon as I am buried, I direct that the whole of this property shall revert to my younger son Haviland absolutely"—'

'Good God!' said Mr Frobisher-Pym.

'There's a lot more,' said Haviland, 'but that's the gist of it.'

'Let me see,' said the magistrate.

He took the will from Haviland, and read it through with a frowning face.

'That's right,' he said. 'No possible doubt about it. Martin has had his property and lost it again. How very curious. Up till yesterday everything belonged to him, though nobody knew it. Now it is all yours, Burdock. This certainly is the strangest will I ever saw. Just fancy that. Martin the heir, up to the time of the funeral. And now – well, Burdock, I must congratulate you.'

'Thank you,' said Haviland. 'It is very unexpected.' He laughed unsteadily.

'But what a queer idea!' cried Mrs Burdock. 'Suppose Martin had been at home. It almost seems a mercy that he wasn't, doesn't it? I mean, it would all have been so awkward. What would have happened if he had tried to stop the funeral, for instance?'

'Yes,' said Mrs Hancock. 'Could he have done anything? Who decides about funerals?'

'The executors, as a rule,' said Mr Frobisher-Pym.

'Who are the executors in this case?' enquired Wimsey.

'I don't know. Let me see.' Mr Frobisher-Pym examined the document again. 'Ah yes! Here we are: "I appoint my two sons, Martin and Haviland, joint executors of this my will." What an extraordinary arrangement.'

'I call it a wicked, un-Christian arrangement,' cried Mrs Hancock. 'It might have caused dreadful mischief if the will hadn't been – quite providentially – lost!'

'Hush, my dear!' said her husband.

'I'm afraid,' said Haviland grimly, 'that that was my father's idea. It's no use my pretending he wasn't spiteful; he was, and I believe he hated both Martin and me like poison.'

'Don't say that,' pleaded the vicar.

'I do say it. He made our lives a burden to us, and he obviously wanted to go on making them a burden after he was dead. If he'd seen us cutting each other's throats, he'd only have been too pleased. Come, vicar, it's no use pretending. He hated our mother and was jealous of us. Everybody knows that. It probably pleased his unpleasant sense of humour to think of us squabbling over his body. Fortunately, he over-reached himself when he hid the will here. He's buried now, and the problem settles itself.'

'Are you quite sure of that?' said Wimsey.

'Why, of course,' said the magistrate. 'The property goes to Mr Haviland Burdock as soon as his father's body is underground. Well, his father was buried yesterday.'

'But are you sure of *that*?' repeated Wimsey. He looked from one to the other, quizzically, his long lips curling into something like a grin.

'Sure of that?' exclaimed the vicar. 'My dear Lord Peter, you were present at the funeral. You saw him buried yourself.'

'I saw his coffin buried,' said Wimsey mildly. 'That the body was in it is merely an unverified inference.'

'I think,' said Mr Frobisher-Pym, 'this is rather an unseemly kind of jest, There is no reason to imagine that the body was not in the coffin.'

'I saw it in the coffin,' said Haviland, 'and so did my wife.'

'And so did I,' said the vicar. 'I was present when it was transferred from the temporary shell in which it crossed over from the States to a permanent lead-and-oak coffin provided by Joliffe. And, if further witnesses are necessary, you can easily get Joliffe himself and his men, who put the body in and screwed it down.'

'Just so,' said Wimsey. 'I'm not denying that the body was in the coffin when the coffin was placed in the chapel. I only doubt whether it was there when it was put in the ground.'

'That is a most unheard-of suggestion to make, Lord Peter,' said Mr Frobisher-Pym, with severity. 'May I ask if you have anything to go upon? And, if the body is not in the grave, perhaps you wouldn't mind telling us where you imagine it to be?'

'Not at all,' said Wimsey. He perched himself on the edge of the table and sat, swinging his legs and looking down at his own hands, as he ticked his points off on his fingers.

'I think,' he said, 'that this story begins with young Rawlinson. He is a clerk in the office of Mr Graham, who drew up his will, and I fancy he knows something about its conditions. So, of course, does Mr Graham, but I don't somehow suspect *him* of being mixed up in this. From what I can hear, he is not a man to take sides – or not Mr Martin's side, at any rate.

'When the news of Mr Burdock's death was cabled over from the States, I think young Rawlinson remembered the terms of the will, and considered that Mr Martin – being abroad and all that – would be rather at a disadvantage. Rawlinson must be rather attached to your brother, by the way—'

'Martin always had a way of picking up good-for-nothing youths and wasting his time with them,' agreed Haviland sulkily.

The vicar seemed to feel that this statement needed some amendment, and murmured that he had always heard how good Martin was with the village lads.

'Quite so,' said Wimsey. 'Well, I think young Rawlinson wanted to give Martin an equal chance of securing the legacy, don't you see. He didn't like to say anything about the will – which might or might not turn up – and possibly he thought that even if it did turn up there might be difficulties. Well, anyway, he decided that the best thing to do was to steal the body and keep it above ground till Martin came home to see to things himself.'

'This is an extraordinary accusation,' began Mr Frobisher-Pym.

'I dare say I'm mistaken,' said Wimsey, 'but it's just my idea. It makes a damn good story, anyhow – you see! Well, then, young Rawlinson saw that this was too big a job to carry out alone, so he looked round for somebody to help him. And he pitched on Mr Mortimer.'

'Mortimer?'

'I don't know Mr Mortimer personally, but he seems to be a sportin' sort of customer from what I can hear with certain facilities which everybody hasn't got. Young Rawlinson and Mortimer put their heads together and worked out a plan of action. Of course, Mr Hancock, you helped them enormously with this lying-in-state idea of yours. Without that, I don't know if they could have worked it.'

Mr Hancock made an embarrassed clucking sound.

'The idea was this. Mortimer was to provide an antique fly and four white horses, made up with luminous paint and black cloth to represent the Burdock death-coach. The advantage of that idea was that nobody would feel inclined to inspect the turn-out too closely if they saw it hangin' round the churchyard at unearthly hours. Meanwhile, young Rawlinson had to get himself accepted as a watcher for the chapel, and to find a sporting companion to watch with him and take a hand in the game. He fixed things up with the publican fellow, and spun a tale for Mr Hancock, so as to get the vigil from four to six. Didn't it strike you as odd, Mr Hancock, that he should be so keen to come all the way from Herriotting?'

'I am accustomed to find keenness in my congregation,' said Mr Hancock stiffly.

'Yes, but Rawlinson didn't belong to your congregation. Anyway it was all worked out, and there was a dress-rehearsal on the Wednesday night, which frightened your man Plunkett into fits, sir.'

'If I thought this was true –' said Mr Frobisher-Pym.

'On Thursday night,' pursued Wimsey, 'the conspirators were ready, hidden in the chancel at two in the morning. They waited till Mrs and Miss Hancock had taken their places, and then made a row to attract their attention. When the ladies courageously advanced to find out what was up, they popped out and bundled 'em into the vestry.'

'Good gracious!' said Mrs Hancock.

'That was when the death-coach affair was timed to drive up to the south door. It came round the Back Lane, I fancy, though I can't be sure. Then Mortimer and the other two took the embalmed body out of the coffin and filled its place up with bags of sawdust. I know it was sawdust, because I found the remains of it on the Lady-chapel floor in the morning. They put the body in the fly, and Mortimer drove off with it. They passed me on the Herriotting road at half-past two, so they can't have wasted much time over the job. Mortimer may have been alone, or possibly he had someone with him to see to the body while he himself did the headless coachman business in a black mask. I'm not certain about that. They drove through the last gate before you come to the fork at Frimpton, and went across the fields to Mortimer's barn. They left the fly there – I know that, because I saw it, and I saw the bran they used to muffle the horses' hoofs, too. I expect they took it on from there in a car, and fetched the horses up next day – but that's a detail. I don't know, either, where they took the body to, but I expect, if you went and asked Mortimer about it, he would be able to assure you that it was still above ground.'

Wimsey paused. Mr Frobisher-Pym and the Hancocks were looking only puzzled and angry, but Haviland's face was green. Mrs Haviland showed a red, painted spot on each cheek, and her mouth was haggard. Wimsey picked up the *Nüremberg Chronicle* and caressed its covers thoughtfully as he went on.

'Meanwhile, of course, young Rawlinson and his companion were doing the camouflage in the church to give the idea of a Protestant outrage. Having fixed everything up neat and pretty, all they had to do was to lock themselves up in the furnace-house and chuck the key through the window. You'll probably find it there, Mr Hancock, if you care to look. Didn't you think that story of an assault by two or three men was a bit thin? Hubbard is a hefty great fellow, and Rawlinson's a sturdy lad – and yet, on their own showing, they were bundled into a coal-hole like helpless infants, without a scratch on either of 'em. Look for the men in buckram, my dear sir, look for the men in buckram!'

'Look here, Wimsey, are you sure you're not romancing?' said Mr Frobisher-Pym. 'One would need some very clear proof before—'

'Certainly,' said Wimsey. 'Get a Home Office order. Open the grave. You'll soon see whether it's true or whether it's just my diseased imagination.'

'I think this whole conversation is disgusting,' cried Mrs Burdock. 'Don't listen to it, Haviland. Anything more heartless on the day after father's funeral than sitting here and inventing such a revolting story I simply can't imagine. It is not worth paying a moment's attention to. You will certainly not permit your father's body to be disturbed. It's horrible. It's a desecration.'

'It is very unpleasant indeed,' said Mr Frobisher-Pym gravely, 'but if Lord Peter is seriously putting forward this astonishing theory, which I can scarcely credit—'

Wimsey shrugged his shoulders.

'– then I feel bound to remind you, Mr Burdock, that your brother, when he returns, may insist on having the matter investigated.'

'But he can't, can he?' said Mrs Burdock.

'Of course he can, Winnie,' snapped her husband savagely. 'He's an executor. He has as much right to have the governor dug up as I have to forbid it. Don't be a fool.'

'If Martin had any decency, he would forbid it, too,' said Mrs Burdock.

'Oh, well!' said Mrs Hancock, 'shocking as it may seem, there's the money to be considered. Mr Martin might think it a duty to his wife, and his family, if he should ever have any—'

'The whole thing is preposterous,' said Haviland decidedly. 'I don't believe a word of it. If I did, naturally I should be the first person to take action in the matter – not only in justice to Martin, but on my own account. But if you ask me to believe that a responsible man like Mortimer would purloin a corpse and desecrate a church – the thing only has to be put into plain words to show how absurd and unthinkable it is. I suppose Lord Peter Wimsey, who consorts, as I understand, with criminals and police officers, finds the idea conceivable. I can only say that I do not. I am sorry that his mind should have become so blunted to all decent feeling. That's all. Good afternoon.'

Mr Frobisher-Pym jumped up.

'Come, come, Burdock, don't take that attitude. I am sure Lord Peter intended no discourtesy. I must say I think he's all wrong, but, 'pon my soul, things have been so disturbed in the village these last few days, I'm not surprised anybody should think there was something behind it. Now, let's forget about it – and hadn't we better be moving out of this terribly cold room? It's nearly dinner-time. Bless me, what will Agatha think of us?'

Wimsey held out his hand to Burdock, who took it reluctantly.

'I'm sorry,' said Wimsey. 'I suffer from hypertrophy of the imagination, y'know. Over-stimulation of the thyroid probably. Don't mind me. I apologise, and all that.'

'I don't think, Lord Peter,' said Mrs Burdock acidly, 'you ought to exercise your imagination at the expense of good taste.'

Wimsey followed her from the room in some confusion. Indeed, he was so disturbed that he carried away the *Nüremberg Chronicle* beneath his arm, which was an odd thing for him to do under the circumstances.

'I am gravely distressed,' said Mr Hancock.

He had come over, after Sunday evening service, to call upon the Frobisher-Pyms. He sat upright on his chair, his thin face flushed with anxiety.

'I could never have believed such a thing of Hubbard. It has been a grievous shock to me. It is not only the great wickedness of stealing a dead body from the very precincts of the church, though that is grave enough. It is the sad hypocrisy of his behaviour – the mockery of sacred things – the making use of the holy services of his religion to further worldly ends. He actually attended the funeral, Mr Frobisher-Pym, and exhibited every sign of grief and respect. Even now he hardly seems to realise the sinfulness of his conduct. I feel it very much, as a priest and as a pastor – very much indeed.'

'Oh, well, Hancock,' said Mr Frobisher-Pym, 'you must make allowances, you know. Hubbard's not a bad fellow, but you can't expect refinement of feeling from a man of his class. The point is, what are we to do about it? Mr Burdock must be told, of course. It's a most awkward situation. Dear me! Hubbard confessed the whole conspiracy, you say? How did he come to do that?'

'I taxed him with it,' said the parson. 'When I came to think over Lord Peter Wimsey's remarks, I was troubled in my mind. It seemed to me – I cannot say why – that there might be some truth in the story, wild as it appeared. I was so worried about it that I swept the floor of the Lady-chapel myself last night, and I found quite a quantity of sawdust among the sweepings. That led me to search for the key of the furnace-house, and I discovered it in some bushes at a little distance – in fact, within a stone's throw – of the furnace-house window. I sought guidance in prayer – and from my wife, whose judgement I greatly respect – and I made up my mind to speak to Hubbard after Mass. It was a great relief to me that he did not present himself at Early Celebration. Feeling as I did, I should have had scruples.'

'Just so, just so,' said the magistrate, a little impatiently. 'Well, you taxed him with it, and he confessed?'

'He did. I am sorry to say he showed no remorse at all. He even laughed. It was a most painful interview.'

'I am sure it must have been,' said Mrs Frobisher-Pym sympathetically.

'We must go and see Mr Burdock,' said the magistrate, rising. 'Whatever old Burdock may or may not have intended by that iniquitous will of his, it's quite evident that Hubbard and Mortimer and Rawlinson were entirely in the wrong. Upon my word, I've no idea whether it's an indictable offence to steal a body. I must look it up. But I should say it was. If there is any property in a corpse, it must belong to the family or the executors. And in any case, it's sacrilege, to say nothing of the scandal in the parish. I must say, Hancock, it won't do us any good in the eyes of the Nonconformists. However, no doubt you realise that. Well, it's an unpleasant job, and the sooner we tackle it the better. I'll run over to the vicarage with you and help you to break it to the Burdocks. How about you, Wimsey? You were right, after all, and I think Burdock owes you an apology.'

'Oh, I'll keep out of it,' said Wimsey. 'I shan't be exactly *persona grata*, don't you know. It's going to mean a deuce of a big financial loss to the Haviland Burdocks.'

'So it is. Most unpleasant. Well, perhaps you're right Come along, vicar.'

Wimsey and his hostess sat discussing the matter by the fire for half an hour or so, when Mr Frobisher-Pym suddenly put his head in and said:

'I say, Wimsey – we're all going over to Mortimer's. I wish you'd come and drive the car. Merridew always has the day off on Sunday, and I don't care about driving at night, particularly in this fog.'

'Right you are,' said Wimsey. He ran upstairs, and came down in a few moments wearing a heavy leather flying-coat, and with a parcel under his arm. He greeted the Burdocks briefly, climbed into the driving-seat, and was soon steering cautiously through the mist along the Herriotting Road.

He smiled a little grimly to himself as they came up under the trees to the spot where the phantom coach had passed him. As they passed the gate through which the ingenious apparition had vanished, he indulged himself by pointing it out, and was rewarded by hearing a snarl from Haviland. At the well-remembered fork, he took the right-hand turning into Frimpton and drove steadily for six miles or so, till a warning shout from Mr Frobisher-Pym summoned him to look out for the turning up to Mortimer's.

Mr Mortimer's house, with its extensive stabling and farm buildings, stood about two miles back from the

main road. In the darkness Wimsey could see little of it;
but he noticed that the ground-floor windows were all
lit up, and, when the door opened to the magistrate's
imperative ring, a loud burst of laughter from the interior gave evidence that Mr Mortimer was not taking his
misdoings too seriously.

'Is Mr Mortimer at home?' demanded Mr Frobisher-
Pym, in the tone of a man not to be trifled with.

'Yes, sir. Will you come in, please?'

They stepped into a large, old-fashioned hall, bril-
liantly lit, and made cosy with a heavy oak screen across
the door. As Wimsey advanced, blinking, from the,
darkness, he saw a large, thick-set man, with a ruddy
face, advancing with hand outstretched in welcome.

'Frobisher-Pym! By Jove! how decent of you to come
over! We've got some old friends of yours here. Oh!' (in
a slightly altered tone) 'Burdock! Well, well—'

'Damn you!' said Haviland Burdock, thrusting furiously past the magistrate, who was trying to hold him
back, 'Damn you, you swine! Chuck this bloody farce.
What have you done with the body?'

'The body, eh?' said Mr Mortimer, retreating in
some confusion.

'Yes, curse you! Your friend Hubbard's split. It's good
denying it. What the devil do you mean by it? You've got
the body here somewhere. Where is it? Hand it over!'

He strode threateningly round the screen into the
lamplight. A tall, thin man rose up unexpectedly from
the depths of an armchair and confronted him.

'Hold hard, old man!'

'Good God! said Haviland, stepping heavily back on
Wimsey's toes. 'Martin!'

'Sure,' said the other. 'Here I am. Come back like a
bad halfpenny. How are you?'

'So *you're* at the bottom of this!' stormed Haviland. 'I might have known it. You damned, dirty hound! I suppose you think it's decent to drag your father out of his coffin and tote him about the country like a circus. It's degrading. It's disgusting. It's abominable. You must be perfectly dead to all decent feeling. You don't deny it, I suppose?'

'I say, Burdock!' expostulated Mortimer.

'Shut up, curse you!' said Haviland. 'I'll deal with you in a minute. Now, look here, Martin, I'm not going to stand any more of this disgraceful behaviour. You'll give up that body, and—'

'Just a moment, just a moment,' said Martin. He stood, smiling a little, his hands thrust into the pockets of his dinner-jacket. 'This *éclaircissement* seems to be rather public. Who are all these people? Oh, it's the vicar, I see. I'm afraid we owe you a little explanation, vicar. And, er—'

'This is Lord Peter Wimsey,' put in Mr Frobisher-Pym, 'who discovered your – I'm afraid, Burdock, I must agree with your brother in calling it your disgraceful plot.'

'Oh, Lord!' said Martin. 'I say, Mortimer, you didn't know you were up against Lord Peter Wimsey, did you? No wonder the cat got out of the bag. The man's known to be a perfect Sherlock. However, I seem to have got home at the crucial moment, so there's no harm done. Diana, this is Lord Peter Wimsey – my wife.'

A young and pretty woman in a black evening dress greeted Wimsey with a shy smile, and turned deprecatingly to her brother-in-law.

'Haviland, we want to explain—'

He paid no attention to her.

'Now then, Martin, the game's up.'

'I think it is, Haviland. But why make all this racket?'

'Racket! I like that. You take your own father's body out of its coffin—'

'No, no, Haviland. I knew nothing about it. I swear that. I only got the news of his death a few days ago. We were right out in the wilds, filming a show in the Pyrenees, and I came straight back as soon as I could get away. Mortimer here, with Rawlinson and Hubbard, staged the whole show by themselves. I never heard a word about it till yesterday morning in Paris, when I found his letter waiting at my old digs. Honestly, Haviland, I had nothing to do with it. Why should I? I didn't need to.'

'What do you mean?'

'Well, if I'd been here, I should only have had to speak to stop the funeral altogether. Why on earth should I have gone to the trouble of stealing the body? Quite apart from the irreverence and all that. As it is, when Mortimer told me about it, I must say I was a bit revolted at the idea, though I appreciated the kindness and the trouble they'd been to on my account. I think Mr Hancock has most cause for wrath, really. But Mortimer has been as careful as possible, sir – really he has. He has placed the old governor quite reverently and decently in what used to be the chapel, and put flowers round him and so on. You will be quite satisfied, I'm sure.'

'Yes, yes,' said Mortimer. 'No disrespect intended, don't you know. Come and see him.'

'This is dreadful,' said the vicar helplessly.

'They had to do the best they could, don't you see, in my absence,' said Mortimer. 'As soon as I can, I'll make proper arrangements for a suitable tomb – above ground, of course. Or possibly cremation would fit the case.'

'What!' gasped Haviland. 'Do you mean to say you imagine I'm going to let my father stay unburied, simply because of your disgusting greed about money?'

'My dear chap, do you think I'm going to let you put him underground, simply to enable you to grab my property?'

'I'm the executor of his will, and I say he shall be buried whether you like it or not!'

'And *I'm* an executor too – and I say he shan't be buried. He can be kept absolutely decently above ground, and he shall be.'

'But hear me,' said the vicar, distracted between these two disagreeable and angry young men.

'I'll see what Graham says about you,' bawled Haviland.

'Oh, yes – the honest lawyer, Graham,' sneered Martin. '*He* knew what was in the will, didn't he? I suppose he didn't mention it to *you*, by any chance?'

'He did not,' retorted Haviland. 'He knew too well the sort of skunk *you* were to say anything about it. Not content with disgracing us with your miserable, black-mailing marriage—'

'Mr Burdock, Mr Burdock—'

'Take care, Haviland!'

'You have no more decency——'

'Stop it!'

'Than to steal your father's body and my money so that you and your damned wife can carry on your loose living, beastly ways with a parcel of film-actors and chorus-girls—'

'Now then, Haviland. Keep your tongue off my wife and my friends. How about your own? Somebody told me Winnie'd been going the pace pretty well – next door to bankruptcy, aren't you, with the gees and the tables and God knows what! No wonder you want to do your brother out of his money. I never thought much of you, Haviland, but by God—'

'One moment!'

Mr Frobisher-Pym at last succeeded in asserting himself, partly through the habit of authority, and partly because the brothers had shouted themselves breathless.

'One moment, Martin. I will call you so, because I have known you a long time, and your father too. I understand your anger at the things Haviland has said. They were unpardonable, as I am sure he will realise when he comes to his right mind. But you must remember that he has been greatly shocked and upset – as we all have been – by this very very painful business. And it is not fair to say that Haviland has tried to "do you out" of anything. He knew nothing about this iniquitous will, and he naturally saw to it that the funeral arrangements were carried out in the usual way. You must settle the future amicably between you, just as you would have done had the will not been accidentally mislaid. Now, Martin – and Haviland too – think it over. My dear boys, this scene is simply appalling. It really must not happen. Surely the estate can be divided up in a friendly manner between you. It is horrible that an old man's body should be a bone of contention between his own sons, just over a matter of money.'

'I'm sorry,' said Martin. 'I forgot myself. You're quite right, sir. Look here, Haviland, forget it. I'll let you have half the money—'

'Half the money! But it's all mine. *You'll* let me have half? How damned generous! My own money!'

'No, old man. It's mine at the moment. The governor's not buried yet, you know. That's right, isn't it, Mr Frobisher-Pym?'

'Yes; the money is yours, legally, at this moment. You must see that, Haviland. But your brother offers you half, and—'

'Half! I'm damned if I'll take half. The man's tried to swindle me out of it. I'll send for the police, and have him put in gaol for robbing the Church. You see if I don't. Give me the telephone.'

'Excuse me,' said Wimsey. 'I don't want to butt in on your family affairs any more than I have already, but I really don't advise you to send for the police.'

'*You* don't, eh? What the hell's it got to do with you?'

'Well,' said Wimsey deprecatingly, 'if this will business comes into court, I shall probably have to give evidence, because I was the bird who found the thing, don't you see?'

'Well, then?'

'Well, then. They might ask how long the will was supposed to have been where I found it.'

Haviland appeared to swallow something which obstructed his speech.

'What about it, curse you!'

'Yes. Well, you see, it's rather odd when you come to think of it. I mean, your late father must have hidden that will in the bookcase before he went abroad. That was – how long ago? Three years? Five years?'

'About four years.'

'Quite. And since then your bright caretaker has let the damp get into the library, hasn't she? No fires, and the window getting broken and so on. Ruinous to the books. Very distressin' to anybody like myself, you know. Yes. Well, supposin' they asked that question

243

about the will and you said it had been there in the damp for four years. Wouldn't they think it a bit funny if I told 'em that there was a big damp stain like a grinning face on the end of the bookshelf, and a big, damp, grinning face on the jolly old *Nüremberg Chronicle* to correspond with it, and no stain on the will which had been sittin' for four years between the two?'

Mrs Haviland screamed suddenly. 'Haviland! You fool! You utter fool!'

'Shut up!'

Haviland snapped round at his wife with a cry of rage, and she collapsed into a chair, with her hand snatched to her mouth.

'Thank you, Winnie,' said Martin. 'No, Haviland – don't trouble to explain. Winnie's given the show away. So you knew – you *knew* about the will, and you deliberately hid it away and let the funeral go on. I'm immensely obliged to you – nearly as obliged as I am to the discreet Graham. Is it fraud or conspiracy or what, to conceal wills? Mr Frobisher-Pym will know.'

'Dear, dear!' said the magistrate. 'Are you certain of your facts, Wimsey?'

'Positive,' said Wimsey, producing the *Nüremberg Chronicle* from under his arm. 'Here's the stain – you can see it yourself. Forgive me for having borrowed your property, Mr Burdock. I was rather afraid Mr Haviland might think this little discrepancy over in the still watches of the night, and decide to sell the *Chronicle,* or give it away, or even think it looked better without its back pages and cover. Allow me to return it to you, Mr Martin – intact. You will perhaps excuse my saying that I don't very much admire any of the roles in this melodrama. It throws, as Mr Pecksniff would say, a sad light on human nature. But I resent extremely

he way in which I was wangled up to that bookshelf
and made to be the bright little independent witness
who found the will. I may be an ass, Mr Haviland Burdock, but I'm not a bloody ass. Good night. I will wait
in the car till you are all ready.'

Wimsey stalked out with some dignity.

Presently he was followed by the vicar and by Mr
Frobisher-Pym.

'Mortimer's taking Haviland and his wife to the station,' said the magistrate. 'They're going back to town
at once. You can send their traps off in the morning,
Hancock. We'd better make ourselves scarce.'

Wimsey pressed the self-starter.

As he did so, a man ran hastily down the steps and
came up to him. It was Martin.

'I say,' he muttered. 'You've done me a good turn –
more than I deserve, I'm afraid. You must think I'm a
damned swine. But I'll see the old man decently put
away, and I'll share with Haviland. You mustn't judge
him too hardly, either. That wife of his is an awful
woman. Run him over head and ears in debt. Bust up
his business. I'll see it's all squared up. See? Don't want
you to think us too awful.'

'Oh, right-ho!' said Wimsey.

He slipped in the clutch, and faded away into the
wet, white fog.

THE UNSOLVED PUZZLE OF THE MAN WITH NO FACE

'And what would *you* say, sir,' said the stout man, 'to this here business of the bloke what's been found down on the beach at East Felpham?'

The rush of travellers after the Bank Holiday had caused an overflow of third-class passengers into the firsts, and the stout man was anxious to seem at ease in his surroundings. The youngish gentleman whom he addressed had obviously paid full fare for a seclusion which he was fated to forgo. He took the matter amiably enough, however, and replied in a courteous tone

'I'm afraid I haven't read more than the headlines Murdered, I suppose, wasn't he?'

'It's murder, right enough,' said the stout man, with relish. 'Cut about he was, something shocking.'

'More like as if a wild beast had done it,' chimed in the thin, elderly man opposite. 'No face at all he hadn' got, by what my paper says. It'll be one of these maniacs, I shouldn't be surprised, what goes about killing children.'

'I wish you wouldn't talk about such things,' said his wife, with a shudder. 'I lays awake at nights thinking what might 'appen to Lizzie's girls, till my head feels regular in a fever, and I has such a sinking in my inside I has to get up and eat biscuits. They didn't ought to put such dreadful things in the papers.'

'It's better they should, ma'am,' said the stout man 'then we're warned, so to speak, and can take our measures accordingly. Now, from what I can make out, this unfortunate gentleman had gone bathing all by himself n a lonely spot. Now, quite apart from cramps, as is a thing that might 'appen to the best of us, that's a very foolish thing to do.'

'Just what I'm always telling my husband,' said the young wife. The young husband frowned and fidgeted. 'Well, dear, it really isn't safe, and you with your heart not strong—' Her hand sought his under the newspaper. He drew away, self-consciously, saying, 'That'll do, Kitty.'

'The way I look at it is this,' pursued the stout man. 'Here we've been and had a war, what has left 'undreds o' men in what you might call a state of unstable ekilibrium. They've seen all their friends blown up or shot to pieces. They've been through five years of 'orrors and bloodshed, and it's given 'em what you might call a twist in the mind towards 'orrors. They may seem to forget it and go along as peaceable as anybody to all outward appearance, but it's all artificial, if you get my meaning. Then, one day something 'appens to upset them – they 'as words with the wife, or the weather's extra hot, as it is today – and something goes pop inside their brains and makes raving monsters of them. It's all in the books. I do a good bit of reading myself of an evening, being a bachelor without encumbrances.'

'That's all very true,' said a prim little man, looking up from his magazine, 'very true indeed – too true. But do you think it applies in the present case? I've studied the literature of crime a good deal – I may say I make it my hobby – and it's my opinion there's more in this than meets the eye. If you will compare this murder with some of the most mysterious crimes of late years – crimes which, mind you, have never been solved, and, in my opinion, never will be – what do you find?' He paused and looked round. 'You will find many features in common with this case. But especially you will find that the face – and the face only, mark you – has been disfigured, as though to prevent recognition. As though to blot out the victim's personality from the world. And you will find that, in spite of the most thorough investigation, the criminal is never discovered. Now what does all that point to? To organisation. Organisation. To an immensely powerful influence at work behind the scenes. In this very magazine that I'm reading now' – he tapped the page impressively – 'there's an account – not a faked-up story, but an account extracted from the annals of the police – of the organisation of one of these secret societies, which mark down men against whom they bear a grudge, and destroy them. And, when they do this, they disfigure their faces with the mark of the Secret Society, and they cover up the track of the assassin so completely – having money and resources at their disposal – that nobody is ever able to get at them.'

'I've read of such things, of course,' admitted the stout man, 'but I thought as they mostly belonged to the medieval days. They had a thing like that in Italy once. What did they call it now? A Gomorrah, was it? Are there any Gomorrahs nowadays?'

'You spoke a true word, sir, when you said Italy,' replied the prim man. 'The Italian mind is made for intrigue. There's the Fascisti. That's come to the surface now, of course, but it started by being a secret society. And, if you were to look below the surface, you would be amazed at the way in which that country is honeycombed with hidden organisations of all sorts. Don't you agree with me, sir?' he added, addressing the first-class passenger.

'Ah!' said the stout man, 'no doubt this gentleman has been in Italy and knows all about it. Should you say this murder was the work of a Gomorrah, sir?'

'I hope not, I'm sure,' said the first-class passenger. 'I mean, it rather destroys the interest, don't you think? I like a nice, quiet, domestic, murder myself, with the millionaire found dead in the library. The minute I open a detective story and find a Camorra in it, my interest seems to dry up and turn to dust and ashes – a sort of Sodom and Camorra, as you might say.'

'I agree with you there,' said the young husband, 'from what you might call the artistic standpoint. But in this particular case I think there may be something to be said for this gentleman's point of view.'

'Well,' admitted the first-class passenger, 'not having read the details—'

'The details are clear enough,' said the prim man. 'This poor creature was found lying dead on the beach at East Felpham early this morning, with his face cut about in the most dreadful manner. He had nothing on him but his bathing-dress—'

'Stop a minute. Who was he, to begin with?'

'They haven't identified him yet. His clothes had been taken—'

'That looks more like robbery, doesn't it?' suggested Kitty.

'If it was just robbery,' retorted the prim man, 'why should his face have been cut up in that way? No – the clothes were taken away, as I said, to prevent identification. That's what these societies always try to do.'

'Was he stabbed?' demanded the first-class passenger.

'No,' said the stout man. 'He wasn't. He was strangled.'

'Not a characteristically Italian method of killing,' observed the first-class passenger.

'No more it is,' said the stout man. The prim man seemed a little disconcerted.

'And if he went down there to bathe,' said the thin, elderly man, 'how did he get there? Surely somebody must have missed him before now, if he was staying at Felpham. It's a busy spot for visitors in the holiday season.'

'No,' said the stout man, 'not East Felpham. You're thinking of West Felpham, where the yacht-club is. East Felpham is one of the loneliest spots on the coast. There's no house near except a little pub all by itself at the end of a long road, and after that you have to go through three fields to get to the sea. There's no real road, only a cart track, but you can take a car through. I've been there.'

'He came in a car,' said the prim man. 'They found the track of the wheels. But it had been driven away again.'

'It looks as though the two men had come there together,' suggested Kitty.

'I think they did,' said the prim man. 'The victim was probably gagged and bound and taken along in the car to the place, and then he was taken out and strangled and—'

'But why should they have troubled to put on his bathing-dress?' said the first-class passenger.

'Because,' said the prim man, 'as I said, they didn't want to leave any clothes to reveal his identity.'

'Quite; but why not leave him naked? A bathing-dress seems to indicate an almost excessive regard for decorum, under the circumstances.'

'Yes, yes,' said the stout man impatiently, 'but you 'aven't read the paper carefully. The two men couldn't have come there in company, and for why? There was only one set of footprints found, and they belonged to the murdered man.'

'Only one set of footprints, eh?' said the first-class passenger quickly. 'This looks interesting. Are you sure?'

'It says so in the paper. A single set of footprints, it says, made by bare feet, which by a careful comparison 'ave been shown to be those of the murdered man, lead from the position occupied by the car to the place where the body was found. What do you make of that?'

'Why,' said the first-class passenger, 'that tells one quite a lot, don't you know. It gives one a sort of a bird's eye view of the place, and it tells one the time of the murder, besides castin' quite a good bit of light on the character and circumstances of the murderer – or murderers.'

'How do you make that out, sir?' demanded the elderly man.

'Well, to begin with – though I've never been near the place, there is obviously a sandy beach from which one can bathe.'

'That's right,' said the stout man.

'There is also, I fancy, in the neighbourhood, a spur of rock running out into the sea, quite possibly with a handy diving-pool. It must run out pretty far; at any rate, one can bathe there before it is high water on the beach.'

'I don't know how you know that, sir, but it's a fact. There's rocks and a bathing-pool, exactly as you describe, about a hundred yards farther along. Many's the time I've had a dip off the end of them.'

'And the rocks run right back inland, where they are covered with short grass.'

'That's right.'

'The murder took place shortly before high tide, I fancy, and the body lay just about at high-tide mark.'

'Why so?'

'Well, you say there were footsteps leading right up to the body. That means that the water hadn't been up beyond the body. But there no other marks. Therefore the murderer's footprints must have been washed away by the tide. The only explanation is that the two men were standing together just below the tide-mark. The murderer came up out of the sea. He attacked the other man – maybe he forced him back a little on his own tracks – and there he killed him. Then the water came up and washed out any marks the murderer may have left. One can imagine him squatting there, wondering if the sea was going to come up high enough?'

'Ow!' said Kitty, 'you make me creep all over.'

'Now, as to these marks on the face,' pursued the first-class passenger. 'The murderer, according to the idea I get of the thing, was already in the sea when the victim came along. You see the idea?'

'I get you,' said the stout man. 'You think as he went in, off them rocks what we was speaking of, and came up through the water, and that's why there weren't no footprints.'

'Exactly. And since the water is deep round those rocks, as you say, he was presumably in a bathing-dress too.'

'Looks like it.'

'Quite so. Well, now – what was the face-slashing done with? People don't usually take knives out with them when they go for a morning dip.'

'That's a puzzle,' said the stout man.

'Not altogether. Let's say, either the murderer had a knife with him or he had not. If he had—'

'If he had,' put in the prim man eagerly, 'he must have laid wait for the deceased on purpose. And, to my mind, that bears out my idea of a deep and cunning plot.'

'Yes. But, if he was waiting there with the knife, why didn't he stab the man and have done with it? Why strangle him, when he had a perfectly good weapon there to hand? No – I think he came unprovided, and, when he saw his enemy there, he made for him with his hands in the characteristic British way.'

'But the slashing?'

'Well, I think that when he had got his man down, dead before him, he was filled with a pretty grim sort of fury and wanted to do more damage. He caught up something that was lying near him on the sand – it might be a bit of old iron, or even one of those sharp shells you sometimes see about, or a bit of glass – and he went for him with that in a desperate rage of jealousy or hatred.'

'Dreadful, dreadful!' said the elderly woman.

'Of course, one can only guess in the dark, not having seen the wounds. It's quite possible that the murderer dropped his knife in the struggle and had to do the actual killing with his hands, picking the knife up afterwards. If the wounds were clean knife-wounds; that is probably what happened, and the murder was premeditated. But if they were rough, jagged gashes, made by an impromptu weapon, then I should say it was a chance encounter, and that the murderer was either mad or—'

'Or?'

'Or had suddenly come upon somebody whom he hated very much.'

What do you think happened afterwards?'

'That's pretty clear. The murderer, having waited, as I said, to see that all his footprints were cleaned up by the tide, waded or swam back to the rock where he had left his clothes, taking the weapon with him. The sea would wash away any blood from his bathing-dress or body. He then climbed out upon the rocks, walked with bare feet, so as to leave no tracks on any seaweed or anything, to the short grass of the shore, dressed, went along to the murdered man's car, and drove it away.'

'Why did he do that?'

'Yes, why? He may have wanted to get somewhere in a hurry. Or he may have been afraid that if the murdered man were identified too soon it would cast suspicion on him. Or it may have been a mixture of motives. The point is where did he come from? How did he come to be bathing at that remote spot, early in the morning? He didn't get there by car, or there would be a second car to be accounted for. He may have been camping near the spot; but it would have taken him a long time to strike camp and pack all his belongings into the car, and he might have been seen. I am rather inclined to think he had bicycled there, and that he hoisted the bicycle into the back of the car and took it away with him.'

'But, in that case, why take the car?'

'Because he had been down at East Felpham longer than he expected, and he was afraid of being late. Either he had to get back to breakfast at some house, where his absence would be noticed, or else he lived some distance off, and had only just time enough for the journey home. I think, though, he had to be back to breakfast.'

'Why?'

'Because, if it was merely a question of making up time on the road, all he had to do was to put himself and his bicycle on the train for part of the way. No; I fancy he was staying in a smallish hotel somewhere. Not a large hotel, because there nobody would notice whether he came in or not. And not, I think, in lodgings, or somebody would have mentioned before now that they had a lodger who went bathing at East Felpham. Either he lives in the neighbourhood, in which case he should be easy to trace, or was staying with friends who have an interest in concealing his movements. Or else – which I think is more likely – he was in a smallish hotel, where he would be missed from the breakfast-table, but where his favourite bathing-place was not a matter of common knowledge.'

'That seems feasible,' said the stout man.

'In any case,' went on the first-class passenger,' he must have been staying within easy bicycling distance of East Felpham, so it shouldn't be too hard to trace him. And then there is the car.'

'Yes. Where is the car, on your theory?' demanded the prim man, who obviously still had hankerings after the Camorra theory.

'In a garage, waiting to be called for,' said the first-class passenger promptly.

'Where?' persisted the prim man.

'Oh! somewhere on the other side of wherever it was the murderer was staying. If you have a particular reason for not wanting it to be known that you were in a certain place at a specified time, it's not a bad idea to come back from the opposite direction. I rather think I should look for the car at West Felpham, and the hotel in the nearest town on the main road beyond where the two roads to East and West Felpham join. When you've found the car, you've found the name of the victim, naturally. As for the murderer, you will have to look for an active man, a good swimmer and ardent bicyclist – probably not very well off, since he cannot afford to have a car – who has been taking a holiday in the neighbourhood of the Felphams, and who has a good reason for disliking the victim, whoever he may be.'

'Well, I never,' said the elderly woman admiringly. 'How beautiful you do put it all together. Like Sherlock Holmes, I do declare.'

'It's a very pretty theory,' said the prim man, 'but all the same, you'll find it's a secret society. Mark my words. Dear me! We're just running in. Only twenty minutes late. I call that very good for holiday-time. Will you excuse me? My bag is just under your feet.'

There was an eighth passenger in the compartment, who had remained throughout the conversation apparently buried in a newspaper. As the passengers decanted themselves upon the platform, this man touched the first-class passenger upon the arm.

'Excuse me, sir,' he said. 'That was a very interesting suggestion of yours. My name is Winterbottom, and I am investigating this case. Do you mind giving me your name? I might wish to communicate with you later on.'

'Certainly,' said the first-class passenger. 'Always delighted to have a finger in any pie, don't you know. Here is my card. Look me up any time you like.'

Detective-Inspector Winterbottom took the card and read the name:

The Unsolved Puzzle

LORD PETER WIMSEY,
110A Piccadilly.

The *Evening Views* vendor outside Piccadilly Tube Station arranged his placard with some care. It looked very well, he thought.

MAN WITH
NO FACE
IDENTIFIED

It was, in his opinion, considerably more striking than that displayed by a rival organ, which announced, unimaginatively:

BEACH MURDER
VICTIM
IDENTIFIED

A youngish gentleman in a grey suit who emerged at that moment from the Criterion Bar appeared to think so too, for he exchanged a copper for the *Evening Views*, and at once plunged into its perusal with such concentrated interest that he bumped into a hurried man outside the station and had to apologise.

The *Evening Views*, grateful to murderer and victim alike for providing so useful a sensation in the dead days after the Bank Holiday, had torn Messrs Negretti & Zambra's rocketing thermometrical statistics from the 'banner' position which they had occupied in the lunch edition, and substituted:

FACELESS VICTIM OF
BEACH OUTRAGE IDENTIFIED
MURDER OF PROMINENT
PUBLICITY ARTIST
POLICE CLUES

The body of a middle-aged man who was discovered, attired only in a bathing-costume and with his face horribly disfigured by some jagged instrument, on the beach at East Felpham last Monday morning, has been identified as that of Mr Coraggio Plant, studio manager of Messrs Crichton Ltd, the well-known publicity experts of Holborn.

Mr Plant, who was forty-five years of age and a bachelor, was spending his annual holiday in making a motoring tour along the West Coast. He had no companion with him and had left no address for the forwarding of letters, so that, without the smart work of Detective-Inspector Winterbottom of the Westshire police, his disappearance might not in the ordinary way have been noticed until he became due to return to his place of business in three weeks' time. The murderer had no doubt counted on this, and had removed the motor car, containing the belongings of his victim, in the hope of covering up all traces of this dastardly outrage so as to gain time for escape.

A rigorous search for the missing car, however, eventuated in its discovery in a garage at West Felpham, where it had been left for decarbonisation and repairs to the magneto. Mr Spiller, the garage proprietor, himself saw the man who left the car, and has furnished a description of him to the police. He is said to be a small, dark man of foreign appearance. The police hold a clue to his identity, and an arrest is confidently expected in the near future.

Mr Plant was for fifteen years in the employment of Messrs Crichton, being appointed Studio Manager in the latter years of the war. He was greatly liked by all his colleagues, and his skill in the lay-out and designing of advertisements did much to justify the truth of Messrs Crichton's well-known slogan: "Crichton's for Admirable Advertising."

The funeral of the victim will take place tomorrow at Golders Green Cemetery.

(Pictures on Back Page.)

Lord Peter Wimsey turned to the back page. The portrait of the victim did not detain him long; it was one of the characterless studio photographs which establish nothing except that the sitter has a tolerable set of features. He noted that Mr Plant had been thin rather than fat, commercial in appearance rather than artistic, and that the photographer had chosen to show him serious rather than smiling. A picture of East Felpham beach, marked with a cross where the body was found, seemed to arouse in him rather more than a casual interest. He studied it intently for some time, making little surprised noises. There was no obvious reason why he should have been surprised, for the photograph bore out in every detail the deductions he had made in the train. There was the curved line of sand, with a long spur of rock stretching out behind it into deep water, and running back it mingled with the short, dry turf. Nevertheless, he looked at it for several minutes with close attention, before folding the newspaper and hailing a taxi; and when he was in the taxi he unfolded the paper and looked at it again.

'Your lordship having been kind enough,' said Inspector Winterbottom, emptying his glass rather too rapidly for true connoisseurship, 'to suggest I should look you up in Town, I made bold to give you a call in passing.

Thank you, I won't say no. Well, as you've seen in the papers by now, we found that car all right.'

Wimsey expressed his gratification at this result.

'And very much obliged I was to your lordship for the hint,' went on the Inspector generously, 'not but what I wouldn't say but what I should have come to the same conclusion myself, given a little more time. And, what's more, we're on the track of the man.'

'I see he's supposed to be foreign-looking. Don't say he's going to turn out to be a Camorrist after all!'

'No, my lord.' The Inspector winked. 'Our friend in the corner had got his magazine stories a bit on the brain, if you ask me. And *you* were a bit out too, my lord, with your bicyclist idea.'

'Was I? That's a blow.'

'Well, my lord, these here theories *sound* all right, but half the time they're too fine-spun altogether. Go for the facts – that's our motto in the Force – facts and motive, and you won't go far wrong.'

'Oh! you've discovered the motive, then?'

The Inspector winked again.

'There's not many motives for doing a man in,' said he. 'Women or money – or women *and* money – it mostly comes down to one or the other. This fellow Plant went in for being a bit of a lad, you see. He kept a little cottage down Felpham way, with a nice little skirt to furnish it and keep the love-nest warm for him – see?'

'Oh! I thought he was doing a motor-tour.'

'Motor-tour your foot!' said the Inspector, with more energy than politeness. 'That's what the old [epithet] told 'em at the office. Handy reason, don't you see, for leaving no address behind him. No, no. There was a lady in it all right. I've seen her. A very taking piece too, if you like 'em skinny, which I don't. I prefer 'em better upholstered myself.'

'That chair is really more comfortable with a cushion,' put in Wimsey, with anxious solicitude. 'Allow me.'

'Thanks, my lord, thanks. I'm doing very well. It seems that this woman – by the way, we're speaking in confidence, you understand. I don't want this to go further till I've got my man under lock and key.'

Wimsey promised discretion.

'That's all right, my lord, that's all right. I know I can rely on you. Well, the long and the short is, this young woman had another fancy man – a sort of an Italiano, whom she'd chucked for Plant, and this same dago got wind of the business and came down to East Felpham on the Sunday night, looking for her. He's one of these professional partners in a Palais de Danse up Cricklewood way, and that's where the girl comes from, too. I suppose she thought Plant was a cut above him. Anyway, down he comes, and busts in upon them Sunday night when they were having a bit of supper – and that's when the row started.'

'Didn't you know about this cottage and the goings-on there?'

'Well, you know, there's such a lot of these week-enders nowadays. We can't keep tabs on all of them, so long as they behave themselves and don't make a disturbance. The woman's been there – so they tell me – since last June, with him coming down Saturday to Monday; but it's a lonely spot, and the constable didn't take much notice. He came in the evenings, so there wasn't anybody much to recognise him, except the old girl who did the slops and things, and she's half-blind. And of course, when they found him, he hadn't any face to recognise. It'd be thought he'd just gone off in the ordinary way. I dare say the dago fellow reckoned on that. As I was saying, there was a big row, and the dago was kicked out. He must have lain in wait for Plant down by the bathing-place, and done him in.'

'By strangling?'

'Well, he *was* strangled.'

'Was his face cut up with a knife, then?'

'Well, no – I don't think it was a knife. More like a broken bottle, I should say, if you ask me. There's plenty of them come in with the tide.'

'But then we're brought back to our old problem. If this Italian was lying in wait to murder Plant, why didn't he take a weapon with him, instead of trusting to the chance of his hands and a broken bottle?'

The Inspector shook his head.

'Flighty,' he said. 'All these foreigners are flighty. No headpiece. But there's our man and there's our motive, plain as a pikestaff. You don't want more.'

'And where is the Italian fellow now?'

'Run away. That's pretty good proof of guilt in itself. But we'll have him before long. That's what I've come to Town about. He can't get out of the country. I've had an all-stations call sent out to stop him. The dance-hall people were able to supply us with a photo and a good description. I'm expecting a report in now any minute. In fact, I'd best be getting along. Thank you very much for your hospitality, my lord.'

'The pleasure is mine,' said Wimsey, ringing the bell to have the visitor shown out. 'I have enjoyed our little chat immensely.'

Sauntering into the Falstaff at twelve o'clock the following morning, Wimsey, as he had expected, found Salcombe Hardy supporting his rather plump contours against the bar. The reporter greeted his arrival with a heartiness amounting almost to enthusiasm, and called for two large Scotches immediately. When the usual skirmish as to who should pay had been honourably settled by the prompt disposal of the drinks and the standing of two more, Wimsey pulled from his pocket the copy of last night's *Evening Views*.

'I wish you'd ask the people over at your place to get hold of a decent print of this for me,' he said, indicating the picture of East Felpham beach.

Salcombe Hardy gazed limpid enquiry at him from eyes like drowned violets.

'See here, you old sleuth,' he said, 'does this mean you've got a theory about the thing? I'm wanting a story badly. Must keep up the excitement, you know. The police don't seem to have got any further since last night.'

'No; I'm interested in this from another point of view altogether. I did have a theory – of sorts – but it seems it's all wrong. Bally old Homer nodding, I suppose. But I'd like a copy of the thing.'

'I'll get Warren to get you one when we come back. I'm just taking him down with me to Crichton's. We're going to have a look at a picture. I say, I wish you'd come too. Tell me what to say about the damned thing.'

'Good God! I don't know anything about commercial art.'

''Tisn't commercial art. It's supposed to be a portrait of this blighter Plant. Done by one of the chaps in his studio or something. Kid who told me about it says it's clever. I don't know. Don't suppose she knows, either. You go in for being artistic, don't you?'

'I wish you wouldn't use such filthy expressions, Sally. Artistic! Who is this girl?'

'Typist in the copy department.'

'Oh, Sally!'

'Nothing of that sort. I've never met her. Name's Gladys Twitterton. I'm sure that's beastly enough to put anybody off. Rang us up last night and told us there was a bloke there who'd done old Plant in oils and was it any use to us? Drummer thought it might be worth looking into. Make a change from that everlasting syndicated photograph.'

'I see. If you haven't got an exclusive story, an exclusive picture's better than nothing. The girl seems to have her wits about her. Friend of the artist's?'

'No – said he'd probably be frightfully annoyed at her having told me. But I can wangle that. Only I wish you'd come and have a look at it. Tell me whether I ought to say it's an unknown masterpiece or merely a striking likeness.'

'How the devil can I say if it's a striking likeness of a bloke I've never seen?'

'I'll say it's that, in any case. But I want to know if it's well painted.'

'Curse it, Sally, what's it matter whether it is or not? I've got other things to do. Who's the artist, by the way? Anybody one's ever heard of?'

'Dunno. I've got the name here somewhere.' Sally rooted in his hip-pocket and produced a mass of dirty correspondence, its angles blunted by constant attrition. 'Some comic name like Buggie or Snagtooth – wait a bit – here it is. Crowder. Thomas Crowder. I knew it was something out of the way.'

'Singularly like Buggie or Snagtooth. All right, Sally. I'll make a martyr of myself. Lead me to it.'

'We'll have another quick one. Here's Warren. This is Lord Peter Wimsey. This is on me.'

'On me,' corrected the photographer, a jaded young man with a disillusioned manner. 'Three large White Labels, please. Well, here's all the best. Are you fit, Sally? Because we'd better make tracks. I've got to be up at Golders Green by two for the funeral.'

Mr Crowder of Crichton's appeared to have had the news broken to him already by Miss Twitterton, for he received the embassy in a spirit of gloomy acquiescence.

'The directors won't like it,' he said, 'but they've had to put up with such a lot that I suppose one irregularity more or less won't give 'em apoplexy.' He had a small, anxious, yellow face like a monkey. Wimsey put him down as being in his late thirties. He noticed his fine, capable hands, one of which was disfigured by a strip of sticking-plaster.

'Damaged yourself?' said Wimsey pleasantly, as they made their way upstairs to the studio. 'Mustn't make a practice of that, what? An artist's hands are his livelihood – except, of course, for Armless Wonders and people of that kind! Awkward job, painting with your toes.'

'Oh, it's nothing much,' said Crowder, 'but it's best to keep the paint out of surface scratches. There's such a thing as lead-poisoning. Well, here's this dud portrait, such as it is. I don't mind telling you that it didn't please the sitter. In fact, he wouldn't have it at any price.'

'Not flattering enough?' asked Hardy.

'As you say.' The painter pulled out a four by three canvas from its hiding-place behind a stack of poster cartoons, and heaved it up on to the easel.

'Oh!' said Hardy, a little surprised. Not that there was any reason for surprise as far as the painting itself was concerned. It was a straightforward handling enough; the skill and originality of the brushwork being of the kind that interests the painter without shocking the ignorant.

'Oh!' said Hardy. 'Was he really like that?'

He moved closer to the canvas, peering into it as he might have peered into the face of the living man, hoping to get something out of him. Under this microscopic scrutiny, the portrait, as is the way of portraits, dislimned, and became no more than a conglomeration of painted spots and streaks. He made the discovery that, to the painter's eye, the human face is full of green and purple patches.

He moved back again, and altered the form of his question:

'So that's what he was like, was he?'

He pulled out the photograph of Plant from his pocket, and compared it with the portrait. The portrait seemed to sneer at his surprise.

'Of course, they touch these things up at these fashionable photographers,' he said. 'Anyway, that's not my business. This thing will make a jolly good eye-catcher, don't you think so, Wimsey? Wonder if they'd give us a two-column spread on the front page? Well, Warren, you'd better get down to it.'

The photographer, bleakly unmoved by artistic or journalistic considerations, took silent charge of the canvas, mentally resolving it into a question of panchromatic plates and coloured screens. Crowder gave him a hand in shifting the easel into a better light. Two or three people from other departments, passing through the studio on their lawful occasions, stopped, and lingered in the neighbourhood of the disturbance, as though it were a street accident. A melancholy, grey-haired man, temporary head of the studio, vice

Coreggio Plant, deceased, took Crowder aside, with a muttered apology, to give him some instructions about adapting a whole quad to an eleven-inch treble. Hardy turned to Lord Peter.

'It's damned ugly,' he said. 'Is it good?'

'Brilliant,' said Wimsey. 'You can go all out. Say what you like about it.'

'Oh, splendid! Could we discover one of our neglected British masters?'

'Yes; why not? You'll probably make the man the fashion and ruin him as an artist, but that's his pigeon.'

'But, I say – do you think it's a good likeness? He's made him look a most sinister sort of fellow. After all, Plant thought it was so bad he wouldn't have it.'

'The more fool he. Ever heard of the portrait of a certain statesman that was so revealing of his inner emptiness that he hurriedly bought it up and hid it to prevent people like you from getting hold of it?'

Crowder came back.

'I say,' said Wimsey, 'whom does that picture belong to? You? Or the heirs of the deceased, or what?'

'I suppose it's back on my hands,' said the painter. 'Plant – well, he more or less commissioned it, you see, but—'

'How more or less?'

'Well, he kept on hinting, don't you know, that he would like me to do him, and, as he was my boss, I thought I'd better. No price actually mentioned. When he saw it, he didn't like it, and told me to alter it.'

'But you didn't.'

'Oh – well, I put it aside and said I'd see what I could do with it. I thought he'd perhaps forget about it.'

'I see. Then presumably it's yours to dispose of.'

'I should think so. Why?'

'You have a very individual technique, haven't you?' pursued Wimsey. 'Do you exhibit much?'

'Here and there. I've never had a show in London.'

'I fancy I once saw a couple of small seascapes of yours somewhere. Manchester, was it? or Liverpool? I wasn't sure of your name, but I recognised the technique immediately.'

'I dare say. I did send a few things to Manchester about two years ago.'

'Yes – I felt sure I couldn't be mistaken. I want to buy the portrait. Here's my card, by the way. I'm not a journalist; I collect things.'

Crowder looked from the card to Wimsey and from Wimsey to the card, a little reluctantly.

'If you want to exhibit it, of course,' said Lord Peter, 'I should be delighted to leave it with you as long as you liked.'

'Oh, it's not that,' said Crowder. 'The fact is, I'm not altogether keen on the thing. I should like to – that is to say, it's not really finished.'

'My dear man, it's a bally masterpiece.'

'Oh, the painting's all right. But it's not altogether satisfactory as a likeness.'

'What the devil does the likeness matter? I don't know what the late Plant looked like and I don't care. As I look at the thing it's a damn fine bit of brush-work, and if you tinker about with it you'll spoil it. You know that as well as I do. What's biting you? It isn't the price, is it? You know I shan't boggle about that. I can afford my modest pleasures, even in these thin and piping times. You don't want me to have it? Come now – what's the real reason?'

'There's no reason at all why you shouldn't have it if you really want it, I suppose,' said the painter, still a little sullenly. 'If it's really the painting that interests you.'

'What do you suppose it is? The notoriety? I can have all I want of *that* commodity, you know, for the asking even without asking. Well, anyhow, think it over, and when you've decided, send me a line and name your price.'

Crowder nodded without speaking, and the photographer having by this time finished his job, the party took their leave.

As they left the building, they became involved in the stream of Crichton's staff going out to lunch. A girl, who seemed to have been loitering in a semi-intentional way in the lower hall, caught them as the lift descended.

'Are you the *Evening Views* people? Did you get your picture all right?'

'Miss Twitterton?' said Hardy interrogatively. 'Yes, rather – thank you so much for giving us the tip. You'll see it on the front page this evening.'

'Oh! that's splendid! I'm frightfully thrilled. It has made an excitement here – all this business. Do they know anything yet about who murdered Mr Plant? Or am I being horribly indiscreet?'

'We're expecting news of an arrest any minute now,' said Hardy. 'As a matter of fact, I shall have to buzz back to the office as fast as I can, to sit with one ear glued to the telephone. You will excuse me, won't you? And, look here – will you let me come round another day, when things aren't so busy, and take you out to lunch?'

'Of course. I should love to.' Miss Twitterton giggled. 'I do so want to hear about all the murder cases.'

'Then here's the man to tell you about them, Miss Twitterton,' said Hardy, with mischief in his eye. 'Allow me to introduce Lord Peter Wimsey.'

Miss Twitterton offered her hand in an ecstasy of excitement which almost robbed her of speech.

'How do you do?' said Wimsey. 'As this blighter is in such a hurry to get back to his gossip-shop, what do you say to having a spot of lunch with me?'

'Well, really—' began Miss Twitterton.

'He's all right,' said Hardy; 'he won't lure you into any gilded dens of infamy. If you look at him, you will see he has a kind, innocent face.'

'I'm sure I never thought of such a thing,' said Miss Twitterton. 'But you know – really – I've only got my old things on. It's no good wearing anything decent in this dusty old place.'

'Oh, nonsense!' said Wimsey. 'You couldn't possibly look nicer. It isn't the frock that matters – it's the person who wears it. *That's* all right, then. See you later, Sally! Taxi! Where shall we go? What time do you have to be back, by the way?'

'Two o'clock,' said Miss Twitterton regretfully.

'Then we'll make the Savoy do,' said Wimsey; 'it's reasonably handy.'

Miss Twitterton hopped into the waiting taxi with a little squeak of agitation.

'Did you see Mr Crichton?' she said. 'He went by just as we were talking. However, I dare say he doesn't really know me by sight. I hope not – or he'll think I'm getting too grand to need a salary.' She rooted in her hand-bag. 'I'm sure my face is getting all shiny with excitement. What a silly taxi. It hasn't got a mirror – and I've bust mine.'

Wimsey solemnly produced a small looking-glass from his pocket.

'How wonderfully competent of you!' exclaimed

Miss Twitterton. 'I'm afraid, Lord Peter, you are used to taking girls about.'

'Moderately so,' said Wimsey. He did not think it necessary to mention that the last time he had used that mirror it had been to examine the back teeth of a murdered man.

'Of course,' said Miss Twitterton, 'they had to say he was popular with his colleagues. Haven't you noticed that murdered people are always well dressed and popular?'

'They have to be,' said Wimsey. 'It makes it more mysterious and pathetic. Just as girls who disappear are always bright and home-loving and have no men friends.'

'Silly, isn't it?' said Miss Twitterton, with her mouth full of roast duck and green peas. 'I should think everybody was only too glad to get rid of Plant – nasty, rude creature. So mean, too, always taking credit for other people's work. All those poor things in the studio, with all the spirit squashed out of them. I always say, Lord Peter, you can tell if a head of a department's fitted for his job by noticing the atmosphere of the place as you go into it. Take the copy-room, now. We're all as cheerful and friendly as you like, though I must say the language that goes on there is something awful, but these writing fellows are like that, and they don't mean anything by it. But then, Mr Ormerod is a real gentleman – that's our copy-chief, you know – and he makes them all take an interest in the work, for all they grumble about the cheese-bills and the department-store bilge they have to turn out. But it's quite different in the studio. A sort of dead-and-alive feeling about it, if you understand what I mean. We girls notice things like that more than some of the high-up people think. Of course, I'm very sensitive to these feelings – almost psychic, I've been told.'

Lord Peter said there was nobody like a woman for sizing up character at a glance. Women, he thought, were remarkably intuitive.

'That's a fact,' said Miss Twitterton. 'I've often said, if I could have a few frank words with Mr Crichton, I could tell him a thing or two. There are wheels within wheels beneath the surface of a place like this that these brass hats have no idea of.'

Lord Peter said he felt sure of it.

'The way Mr Plant treated people he thought were beneath him,' went on Miss Twitterton, 'I'm sure it was enough to make your blood boil. I'm sure, if Mr Ormerod sent me with a message to him, I was glad to get out of the room again. Humiliating, it was, the way he'd speak to you. I don't care if he's dead or not; being dead doesn't make a person's past behaviour any better, Lord Peter. It wasn't so much the rude things he said. There's Mr Birkett, for example; *he's* rude enough, but nobody minds him. He's just like a big, blundering puppy – rather a lamb, really. It was Mr Plant's nasty sneering way we all hated so. And he was always running people down.'

'How about this portrait?' asked Wimsey. 'Was it like him at all?'

'It was a lot too like him,' said Miss Twitterton emphatically. 'That's why he hated it so. He didn't like Crowder, either. But, of course, he knew he could paint, and he made him do it, because he thought he'd be getting a valuable thing cheap. And Crowder couldn't very well refuse, or Plant would have got him sacked.'

The Unsolved Puzzle

'I shouldn't have thought that would have mattered much to a man of Crowder's ability.'

'Poor Mr Crowder! I don't think he's ever had much luck. Good artists don't always seem able to sell their pictures. And I know he wanted to get married – otherwise he'd never have taken up this commercial work. He's told me a good bit about himself. I don't know why – but I'm one of the people men seem to tell things to.'

Lord Peter filled Miss Twitterton's glass.

'Oh, please! No, really! Not a drop more! I'm talking a lot too much as it is. I don't know what Mr Ormerod will say when I go in to take his letters. I shall be writing down all kinds of funny things. Ooh! I really must be getting back. Just look at the time!'

'It's not really late. Have a black coffee – just as a corrective.' Wimsey smiled. 'You haven't been talking at all too much. I've enjoyed your picture of office life enormously. You have a very vivid way of putting things, you know. I see now why Mr Plant was not altogether a popular character.'

'Not in the office, anyway – whatever he may have been elsewhere,' said Miss Twitterton darkly.

'Oh?'

'Oh! he was a one,' said Miss Twitterton. 'He certainly was a one. Some friends of mine met him one evening up in the West End, and they came back with some nice stories. It was quite a joke in the office – old Plant and his rosebuds, you know. Mr Cowley – he's *the* Cowley, you know, who rides in the motor-cycle races – he always said he knew what to think of Mr Plant and his motor tours. That time Mr Plant pretended he'd gone touring in Wales, Mr Cowley was asking him about the roads, and he didn't know a thing about

273

them. Because Mr Cowley really had been touring there, and he knew quite well Mr Plant hadn't been where he said he had; and, as a matter of fact, Mr Cowley knew he'd been staying the whole time in a hotel at Aberystwyth, in very attractive company.'

Miss Twitterton finished her coffee and slapped the cup down defiantly.

'And now I really *must* run away, or I shall be most dreadfully late. And thank you ever so much.'

'Hullo!' said Inspector Winterbottom, 'you've bought that portrait, then?'

'Yes,' said Wimsey. 'It's a fine bit of work.' He gazed thoughtfully at the canvas. 'Sit down, Inspector; I want to tell you a story.'

'And I want to tell *you* a story,' replied the Inspector.

'Let's have yours first,' said Wimsey, with an air of flattering eagerness.

'No, no, my lord. You take precedence. Go ahead.'

He snuggled down with a chuckle into his arm-chair.

'Well!' said Wimsey. 'Mine's a sort of a fairy-story. And, mind you, I haven't verified it.'

'Go ahead, my lord, go ahead.'

'Once upon a time—' said Wimsey, sighing.

'That's the good old-fashioned way to begin a fairy-story,' said Inspector Winterbottom.

'Once upon a time,' repeated Wimsey, 'there was a painter. He was a good painter, but the bad fairy of Financial Success had not been asked to his christening – what?'

'That's often the way with painters,' agreed the Inspector.

'So he had to take up a job as a commercial artist, because nobody would buy his pictures and, like so many people in fairy-tales, he wanted to marry a goose-girl.'

'There's many people want to do the same,' said the Inspector.

'The head of his department,' went on Wimsey, 'was a man with a mean, sneering soul. He wasn't even really good at his job, but he had been pushed into authority during the war, when better men went to the Front. Mind you, I'm rather sorry for the man. He suffered from an inferiority complex' – the Inspector snorted – 'and he thought the only way to keep his end up was to keep other people's end down. So he became a little tin tyrant and a bully. He took all the credit for the work of the men under his charge, and he sneered and harassed them till they got inferiority complexes even worse than his own.'

'I've known that sort,' said the Inspector, 'and the marvel to me is how they get away with it.'

'Just so,' said Wimsey. 'Well, I dare say this man would have gone on getting away with it all right, if he hadn't thought of getting this painter to paint his portrait.'

'Damn silly thing to do,' said the Inspector. 'It was only making the painter-fellow conceited with himself.'

'True. But, you see, this tin tyrant person had a fascinating female in tow, and he wanted the portrait for the lady. He thought that, by making the painter do it, he would get a good portrait at starvation price. But unhappily he'd forgotten that, however much an artist will put up with in the ordinary way, he is bound to be sincere with his art. That's the one thing a genuine artist won't muck about with.'

'I dare say,' said the Inspector. 'I don't know much about artists.'

'Well, you can take it from me. So the painter painted the portrait as he saw it, and he put the man's whole creeping, sneering, paltry soul on the canvas for everybody to see.'

Inspector Winterbottom stared at the portrait, and the portrait sneered back at him.

'It's not what you'd call a flattering picture, certainly,' he admitted.

'Now, when a painter paints a portrait of anybody,' went on Wimsey, 'that person's face is never the same to him again. It's like – what shall I say? Well, it's like the way a gunner, say, looks at a landscape where he happens to be posted. He doesn't see it as a landscape. He doesn't see it as a thing of magic beauty, full of sweeping lines and lovely colour. He sees it as so much cover, so many landmarks to aim by, so many gun emplacements. And when the war is over and he goes back to it, he will still see it as cover and landmarks and gun-emplacements. It isn't a landscape any more. It's a war map.'

'I know that,' said Inspector Winterbottom. 'I was a gunner myself.'

'A painter gets just the same feeling of deadly familiarity with every line of a face he's once painted,' pursued Wimsey. 'And, if it's a face he hates, he hates it with a new and more irritable hatred. It's like a defective barrel-organ, everlastingly grinding out the same old maddening tune, and making the same damned awful wrong note every time the barrel goes round.'

'Lord! how you can talk!' ejaculated the Inspector.

'That was the way the painter felt about this man's hateful face. All day and every day he had to see it. He couldn't get away because he was tied to his job, you see.'

'He ought to have cut loose,' said the Inspector. 'It's no good going on like that, trying to work with uncongenial people.'

'Well, anyway, he said to himself, he could escape for a bit during his holidays. There was a beautiful little quiet spot he knew on the West Coast, where nobody ever came. He'd been there before and painted it. Oh! by the way, that reminds me – I've got another picture to show you.'

He went to a bureau and extracted a small panel in oils from a drawer.

'I saw that two years ago at a show in Manchester, and I happened to remember the name of the dealer who bought it.'

Inspector Winterbottom gaped at the panel. 'But that's East Felpham!' he exclaimed.

'Yes. It's only signed T.C., but the technique is rather unmistakable, don't you think?'

The Inspector knew little about technique, but initials he understood. He looked from the portrait to the panel and back at Lord Peter.

'The painter—'

'Crowder?'

'If it's all the same to you, I'd rather go on calling him the painter. He packed up his traps on his push-bike carrier, and took his tormented nerves down to this beloved and secret spot for a quiet weekend. He stayed at a quiet little hotel in the neighbourhood, and each morning he cycled off to this lovely little beach to bathe. He never told anybody at the hotel where he went, because it was *his* place, and he didn't want other people to find it out.'

Inspector Winterbottom set the panel down on the table, and helped himself to whisky.

DOROTHY L. SAYERS

'One morning – it happened to be the Monday
morning' – Wimsey's voice became slower and more
reluctant – 'he went down as usual. The tide was not
yet fully in, but he ran out over the rocks to where he
knew there was a deep bathing-pool. He plunged in and
swam about, and let the small noise of his jangling
troubles be swallowed up in the innumerable laughter
of the sea.'

'Eh?'

'κυμάτων ἀνήριθμον γέλασμα – quotation from the
classics. So people say it means the dimpled surface of
the waves in the sunlight – but how could Prometheus,
bound upon his rock, have seen it? Surely it was the
chuckle of the incoming tide among the stones that
came up to his ears on the lonely peak where the vul-
ture fretted at his heart. I remember arguing about it
with old Philpotts in class, and getting rapped over the
knuckles for contradicting him. I didn't know at the
time that he was engaged in producing a translation on
his own account, or doubtless I should have contra-
dicted him more rudely and been told to take my
trousers down. Dear old Philpotts!'

'I don't know anything about that,' said the Inspector.

'I beg your pardon. Shocking way I have of wandering. The painter – well! he swam round the end of
the rocks, for the tide was nearly in by that time; and,
as he came up from the sea, he saw a man standing on
the beach – that beloved beach, remember, which he
thought was his own sacred haven of peace. He came
wading towards it, cursing the Bank Holiday rab-
ble who must needs swarm about everywhere with
their cigarette-packets and their kodaks and their
gramophones – and then he saw that it was a face he
knew. He knew every hated line in it, on that clear

278

sunny morning. And, early as it was, the heat was coming up over the sea like a haze?'

'It was a hot weekend,' said the Inspector.

'And then the man hailed him, in his smug, mincing voice. "Hullo!" he said, "you here? How did you find my little bathing-place?" And that was too much for the painter. He felt as if his last sanctuary had been invaded. He leapt at the lean throat – it's rather a stringy one, you may notice, with a prominent Adam's apple – an irritating throat. The water chuckled round their feet as they swayed to and fro. He felt his thumbs sink into the flesh he had painted. He saw, and laughed to see, the hateful familiarity of the features change and swell into an unrecognisable purple. He watched the sunken eyes bulge out and the thin mouth distort itself as the blackened tongue thrust through it – I am not unnerving you, I hope?'

The Inspector laughed.

'Not a bit. It's wonderful, the way you describe things. You ought to write a book.'

'I sing but as the throstle sings,
    Amid the branches dwelling,'

replied his lordship negligently, and went on without further comment.

'The painter throttled him. He flung him back on the sand. He looked at him, and his heart crowed within him. He stretched out his hand, and found a broken bottle, with a good jagged edge. He went to work with a will, stamping and tearing away every trace of the face he knew and loathed. He blotted it out and destroyed it utterly.

'He sat beside the thing he had made. He began to be frightened. They had staggered back beyond the edge of the water, and there were the marks of his feet on the sand. He had blood on his face and on his bathing-suit, and he had cut his hand with the bottle. But the blessed sea was still coming in. He watched it pass over the bloodstains and the footprints and wipe the story of his madness away. He remembered that this man had gone from his place, leaving no address behind him. He went back, step by step, into the water, and as it came up to his breast, he saw the red stains smoke away like a faint mist in the brown-blueness of the tide. He went – wading and swimming and plunging his face and arms deep in the water, looking back from time to time to see what he had left behind him. I think that when he got back to the point and drew himself out, clean and cool, upon the rocks, he remembered that he ought to have taken the body back with him and let the tide carry it away, but it was too late. He was clean, and could not bear to go back for the thing. Besides, he was late, and they would wonder at the hotel if he was not back in time for breakfast. He ran lightly over the bare rocks and the grass that showed no footprint. He dressed himself, taking care to leave no trace of his presence. He took the car, which would have told a story. He put his bicycle in the back seat, under the rugs, and he went – but you know as well as I do where he went.'

Lord Peter got up with an impatient movement, and went over to the picture, rubbing his thumb meditatively over the texture of the painting.

'You may say, if he hated the face so much, why didn't he destroy the picture? He couldn't. It was the best thing he'd ever done. He took a hundred guineas for it. It was cheap at a hundred guineas. But then – I think he was afraid to refuse me. My name is rather well known. It was a sort of blackmail, I suppose. But I wanted that picture.'

Inspector Winterbottom laughed again.

'Did you take any steps, my lord, to find out if Crowder has really been staying at East Felpham?'

'No.' Wimsey swung round abruptly. 'I have taken no steps at all. That's your business. I have told you the story, and, on my soul, I'd rather have stood by and said nothing.'

'You needn't worry.' The Inspector laughed for the third time. 'It's a good story, my lord, and you told it well. But you're right when you say it's a fairy-story. We've found this Italian fellow – Francesco, he called himself, and he's the man all right.'

'How do you know? Has he confessed?'

'Practically. He's dead. Killed himself. He left a letter to the woman, begging for forgiveness, and saying that when he saw her with Plant he felt murder come into his heart. "I have revenged myself," he says, "on him who dared to love you." I suppose he got the wind up when he saw we were after him – I wish these newspapers wouldn't be always putting these criminals on their guard – so he did away with himself to cheat the gallows. I may say it's been a disappointment to me.'

'It must have been,' said Wimsey. 'Very unsatisfactory, of course. But I'm glad my story turned out to be only a fairy-tale after all. You're not going?'

'Got to get back to my duty,' said the Inspector, heaving himself to his feet. 'Very pleased to have met you, my lord. And I mean what I say – you ought to take to literature.'

Wimsey remained after he had gone, still looking at the portrait.

'"What is Truth?" said jesting Pilate. No wonder, since it is so completely unbelievable . . . I could prove it . . . if I liked . . . but the man had a villainous face, and there are few good painters in the world.'

THE VINDICTIVE STORY OF THE
FOOTSTEPS THAT RAN

Mr Bunter withdrew his head from beneath the focusing cloth.

'I fancy that will be quite adequate, sir,' he said deferentially, 'unless there are any further patients, if I may call them so, which you would wish put on record.'

'Not today,' replied the doctor. He took the last stricken rat gently from the table, and replaced it in its cage with an air of satisfaction. 'Perhaps on Wednesday, if Lord Peter can kindly spare your services once again—'

'What's that?' murmured his lordship, withdrawing his long nose from the investigation of a number of unattractive-looking glass jars. 'Nice old dog,' he added vaguely. 'Wags his tail when you mention his name, what? Are these monkey-glands, Hartman, or a southwest elevation of Cleopatra's duodenum?'

'You don't know anything, do you?' said the young physician, laughing. 'No use playing your bally-fool-with-an-eyeglass tricks on me, Wimsey. I'm up to them. I was saying to Bunter that I'd be no end grateful if you'd let him turn up again three days hence to register the progress of the specimens – always supposing they do progress, that is.'

'Why ask, dear old thing?' said his lordship. 'Always a pleasure to assist a fellow-sleuth, don't you know. Trackin' down murderers – all in the same way of business and all that. All finished? Good egg! By the way, if you don't have that cage mended you'll lose one of your patients – Number 5. The last wire but one is workin' loose – assisted by the intelligent occupant. Jolly little beasts, ain't they? No need of dentists – wish I was a rat – wire much better for the nerves than that fizzlin' drill.'

Dr Hartman uttered a little exclamation.

'How in the world did you notice that, Wimsey? I didn't think you'd even looked at the cage.'

'Built noticin' – improved by practice,' said Lord Peter, quietly. 'Anythin' wrong leaves a kind of impression on the eye; brain trots along afterwards with the warnin'. I saw that when we came in. Only just grasped it. Can't say my mind was glued on the matter. Shows the victim's improvin', anyhow. All serene, Bunter?'

'Everything perfectly satisfactory, I trust, my lord,' replied the manservant. He had packed up his camera and plates, and was quietly restoring order in the little laboratory, whose fittings – compact as those of an ocean liner – had been disarranged for the experiment.

'Well,' said the doctor, 'I am enormously obliged to you, Lord Peter, and to Bunter too. I am hoping for a great result from these experiments, and you cannot imagine how valuable an assistance it will be to me to have a really good series of photographs. I can't afford this sort of thing – yet,' he added, his rather haggard young face wistful as he looked at the great camera, 'and I can't do the work at the hospital. There's no time; I've got to be here. A struggling G.P. can't afford to let his practice go, even in Bloomsbury. There are times when even a half-crown visit makes all the difference between making both ends meet and having an ugly hiatus.'

'As Mr Micawber said,' replied Wimsey, '"Income twenty pounds, expenditure nineteen, nineteen, six – result: happiness; expenditure twenty pounds, ought, six – result: misery." Don't prostrate yourself in gratitude, old bean; nothin' Bunter loves like messin' round with pyro and hyposulphite. Keeps his hand in. All kinds of practice welcome. Finger-prints and process plates spell seventh what-you-may-call-it of bliss, but focal-plane work on scurvy-ridden rodents (good phrase!) acceptable if no crime forthcoming. Crimes have been rather short lately. Been eatin' our heads off, haven't we, Bunter? Don't know what's come over London. I've taken to prying into my neighbour's affairs to keep from goin' stale. Frightened the postman into a fit the other day by askin' him how his young lady at Croydon was. He's a married man, livin' in Great Ormond Street.'

'How did you know?'

'Well, I didn't really. But he lives just opposite to a friend of mine – Inspector Parker; and his wife – not Parker's; he's unmarried; the postman's, I mean – asked Parker the other day whether the flyin' shows at Croydon went on all night. Parker, bein' flummoxed, said. "No," without thinkin'. Bit of a giveaway, what? Thought I'd give the poor devil a word in season, don't you know. Uncommonly thoughtless of Parker.'

The doctor laughed. 'You'll stay to lunch, won't you?' he said. 'Only cold meat and salad, I'm afraid. My woman won't come Sundays. Have to answer my own door. Deuced unprofessional, I'm afraid, but it can't be helped.'

'Pleasure,' said Wimsey, as they emerged from the laboratory and entered the dark little flat by the back door. 'Did you build this place on?'

'No,' said Hartman; 'the last tenant did that. He was an artist. That's why I took the place. It comes in very useful, ramshackle as it is, though this glass roof is a bit sweltering on a hot day like this. Still, I had to have something on the ground floor, cheap, and it'll do till times get better.'

'Till your vitamin experiments make you famous, eh?' said Peter cheerfully. 'You're goin' to be the comin' man, you know. Feel it in my bones. Uncommonly neat little kitchen you've got, anyhow.'

'It does,' said the doctor. 'The lab makes it a bit gloomy, but the woman's only here in the daytime.'

He led the way into a narrow little dining-room, where the table was laid for a cold lunch. The one window at the end farthest from the kitchen looked out into Great James Street. The room was little more than a passage, and full of doors – the kitchen door, a door in the adjacent wall leading into the entrance-hall, and a third on the opposite side, through which his visitor caught a glimpse of a moderate-sized consulting-room.

Lord Peter Wimsey and his host sat down to table, and the doctor expressed a hope that Mr Bunter would sit down with them. That correct person, however, deprecated any such suggestion.

'If I might venture to indicate my own preference, sir,' he said, 'it would be to wait upon you and his lord-ship in the usual manner.'

'It's no use,' said Wimsey. 'Bunter likes me to know my place. Terrorisin' sort of man, Bunter. Can't call my soul my own. Carry on, Bunter; we wouldn't presume for the world.'

Mr Bunter handed the salad, and poured out the water with a grave decency appropriate to a crusted old tawny port.

It was a Sunday afternoon in that halcyon summer of 1921. The sordid little street was almost empty. The ice-cream man alone seemed thriving and active. He leaned luxuriously on the green post at the corner, in the intervals of driving a busy trade. Bloomsbury's swarm of able-bodied and able-voiced infants was still; presumably within-doors, eating steamy Sunday dinners inappropriate to the tropical weather. The only disturbing sounds came from the flat above, where heavy footsteps passed rapidly to and fro.

'Who's the merry-and-bright bloke above?' enquired Lord Peter presently. 'Not an early riser, I take it. Not that anybody is on a Sunday mornin'. Why an inscrutable Providence ever inflicted such a ghastly day on people livin' in town I can't imagine. I ought to be in the country, but I've got to meet a friend at Victoria this afternoon. Such a day to choose . . . Who's the lady? Wife or accomplished friend? Gather she takes a properly submissive view of woman's duties in the home either way. That's the bedroom overhead, I take it.'

Hartman looked at Lord Peter in some surprise.

''Scuse my beastly inquisitiveness, old thing,' said Wimsey. 'Bad habit. Not my business.'

'How did you –?'

'Guesswork,' said Lord Peter, with disarming frankness. 'I heard the squawk of an iron bedstead on the ceiling and a heavy fellow get out with a bump, but it may quite well be a couch or something. Anyway, he's been potterin' about in his stocking feet over these few feet of floor for the last half-hour, while the woman has been clatterin' to and fro, in and out of the kitchen and away into the sittin'-room, with her high heels on, ever since we've been here. Hence deduction as to domestic habits of the first-floor tenants.'

'I thought,' said the doctor, with an aggrieved expression, 'you'd been listening to my valuable exposition of the beneficial effects of Vitamin B, and Lind's treatment of scurvy with fresh lemons in 1755.'

'I was listenin',' agreed Lord Peter hastily, 'but I heard the footsteps as well. Fellow's toddled into the kitchen – only wanted the matches, though; he's gone off into the sittin'-room and left her to carry on the good work. What was I sayin'? Oh, yes! You see, as I was sayin' before, one hears a thing or sees it without knowin' or thinkin' about it. Then afterwards one starts meditatin', and it all comes back, and one sorts out one's impressions. Like those plates of Bunter's. Picture all there, l – la – what's the word I want, Bunter?'

'Latent, my lord.'

'That's it. My right-hand man, Bunter; couldn't do a thing without him. The picture's latent till you put the developer on. Same with the brain. No mystery. Little grey books all my respected grandmother! Little grey matter's all you want to remember things with. As a matter of curiosity, was I right about those people above?'

'Perfectly. The man's a gas-company's inspector. A bit surly, but devoted (after his own fashion) to his wife. I mean, he doesn't mind hulking in bed on a Sunday morning and letting her do the chores, but he spends all the money he can spare on giving her pretty hats and fur coats and what not. They've only been married about six months. I was called in to her when she had a touch of flu in the spring, and he was almost off his head with anxiety. She's a lovely little woman, I must say – Italian. He picked her up in some eating-place in Soho, I believe. Glorious dark hair and eyes: Venus sort of figure; proper contours in all the right places; good skin – all

288

that sort of thing. She was a bit of a draw to that restaurant while she was there, I fancy. Lively. She had an old admirer round here one day – awkward little Italian fellow, with a knife – active as a monkey. Might have been unpleasant, but I happened to be on the spot, and her husband came along. People are always laying one another out in these streets. Good for business, of course, but one gets tired of tying up broken heads and slits in the jugular. Still, I suppose the girl can't help being attractive, though I don't say she's what you might call stand-offish in her manner. She's sincerely fond of Brotherton, I think, though – that's his name.'

Wimsey nodded inattentively. 'I suppose life is a bit monotonous here,' he said.

'Professionally, yes. Births and drunks and wife-beatings are pretty common. And all the usual ailments, of course. Just at present, I'm living on infant diarrhoea chiefly – bound to, this hot weather, you know. With the autumn, flu and bronchitis set in. I may get an occasional pneumonia. Legs, of course, and varicose veins – God!' cried the doctor explosively, 'if only I could get away, and do my experiments!'

'Ah!' said Peter, 'where's that eccentric old millionaire with a mysterious disease, who always figures in the novels? A lightning diagnosis – a miraculous cure – "God bless you, doctor, here are five thousand pounds" – Harley Street—'

'That sort doesn't live in Bloomsbury,' said the doctor.

'It must be fascinatin', diagnosin' things,' said Peter thoughtfully. 'How d'you do it? I mean, is there a regular set of symptoms for each disease, like callin' a club to show you want your partner to go no trumps? You don't just say: "This fellow's got a pimple on his nose, therefore he has fatty degeneration of the heart—"'

'I hope not,' said the doctor dryly.

'Or is it more like gettin' a clue to a crime?' went on Peter. 'You see somethin' – a room, or a body, say, all knocked about anyhow, and there's a damn sight of symptoms of somethin' wrong, and you've got just to pick out the ones which tell the story?'

'That's more like it,' said Dr Hartman. 'Some symptoms are significant in themselves – like the condition of the gums in scurvy, let us say – others in conjunction with—'

He broke off, and both sprang to their feet as a shrill scream sounded suddenly from the flat above, followed by a heavy thud. A man's voice cried out lamentably; feet ran violently to and fro; then, as the doctor and his guests stood frozen in consternation, came the man himself – falling down the stairs in his haste, hammering at Hartman's door.

'Help! Help! Let me in! My wife! He's murdered her!'

They ran hastily to the door and let him in. He was a big, fair man, in his shirt-sleeves and stockings. His hair stood up, and his face was set in bewildered misery.

'She is dead – dead. He was her lover,' he groaned. 'Come and look – take her away – Doctor! I have lost my wife! My Maddalena –' He paused, looked wildly for a moment, and then said hoarsely, 'Someone's been in – somehow – stabbed her – murdered her. I'll have the law on him, doctor. Come quickly – she was cooking the chicken for my dinner – Ah-h-h!'

He gave a long, hysterical shriek, which ended in a hiccupping laugh. The doctor took him roughly by the arm and shook him. 'Pull yourself together, Mr Brotherton,' he said sharply. 'Perhaps she is only hurt. Stand out of the way!'

'Only hurt?' said the man, sitting heavily down on the nearest chair. 'No – no – she is dead – little Maddalena – Oh, my God!'

Dr Hartman had snatched a roll of bandages and a few surgical appliances from the consulting-room, and he ran upstairs, followed closely by Lord Peter. Bunter remained for a few moments to combat hysterics with cold water. Then he stepped across to the dining-room window and shouted.

'Well, wot is it?' cried a voice from the street. 'Would you be so kind as to step in here a minute, officer?' said Bunter. 'There's been murder done?'

When Brotherton and Bunter arrived upstairs with the constable, they found Dr Hartman and Lord Peter in the little kitchen. The doctor was kneeling beside the woman's body. At their entrance he looked up, and shook his head.

'Death instantaneous,' he said. 'Clean through the heart. Poor child. She cannot have suffered at all. Oh, constable, it is very fortunate you are here. Murder appears to have been done – though I'm afraid the man has escaped. Probably Mr Brotherton can give us some help. He was in the flat at the time.'

The man had sunk down on a chair, and was gazing at the body with a face from which all meaning seemed to have been struck out. The policeman produced a notebook.

'Now, sir,' he said, 'don't let's waste any time. Sooner we can get to work the more likely we are to catch our man. Now, you was 'ere at the time, was you?'

Brotherton stared a moment, then, making a violent effort, he answered steadily:

'I was in the sitting-room, smoking and reading the paper. My – *she* – was getting the dinner ready in here. I heard her give a scream, and I rushed in and found her lying on the floor. She didn't have time to say anything. When I found she was dead, I rushed to the window, and saw the fellow scrambling away over the glass roof there. I yelled at him, but he disappeared. Then I ran down—'

''Arf a mo',' said the policeman. 'Now, see 'ere, sir, didn't you think to go after 'im at once?'

'My first thought was for her,' said the man. 'I thought maybe she wasn't dead. I tried to bring her round—' His speech ended in a groan.

'You say he came in through the window,' said the policeman.

'I beg your pardon, officer,' interrupted Lord Peter, who had been apparently making a mental inventory of the contents of the kitchen. 'Mr Brotherton suggested that the man went *out* through the window. It's better to be accurate.'

'It's the same thing,' said the doctor. 'It's the only way he could have come in. These flats are all alike. The staircase door leads into the sitting-room, and Mr Brotherton was there, so the man couldn't have come that way.'

'And,' said Peter, 'he didn't get in through the bedroom window, or we should have seen him. We were in the room below. Unless, indeed, he let himself down from the roof. Was the door between the bedroom and the sitting-room open?' he asked suddenly, turning to Brotherton.

The man hesitated a moment. 'Yes,' he said finally. 'Yes, I'm sure it was.'

'Could you have seen the man if he had come through the bedroom window?'

'I couldn't have helped seeing him.'

'Come, come, sir,' said the policeman, with some irritation, 'better let *me* ask the questions. Stands to reason the fellow wouldn't get in through the bedroom window in full view of the street.'

'How clever of you to think of that,' said Wimsey. 'Of course not. Never occurred to me. Then it must have been this window, as you say.'

'And, what's more, here's his marks on the window sill,' said the constable triumphantly, pointing to some blurred traces among the London soot. 'That's right. Down he goes by that drain-pipe, over the glass roof down there – what's that the roof of?'

'My laboratory,' said the doctor. 'Heavens! to think that while we were there at dinner this murdering villain—'

'Quite so, sir,' agreed the constable. 'Well, he'd get away over the wall into the court be'ind. 'E'll 'ave been seen there, no fear; you needn't anticipate much trouble in layin' 'ands on 'im, sir. I'll go round there in arf a tick. Now then, sir' – turning to Brotherton – ''ave you any idea wot this party might have looked like?'

Brotherton lifted a wild face, and the doctor interposed.

'I think you ought to know, constable,' he said, 'that there was – well, not a murderous attack, but what might have been one, made on this woman before – about eight weeks ago – by a man named Marincetti – an Italian waiter – with a knife.'

'Ah!' The policeman licked his pencil eagerly. 'Do you know this party as 'as been mentioned?' he enquired of Brotherton.

'That's the man,' said Brotherton, with concentrated fury. 'Coming here after my wife – God curse him! I wish to God I had him dead here beside her!'

'Quite so,' said the policeman. 'Now, sir' – to the doctor – ''ave you got the weapon wot the crime was committed with?'

'No,' said Hartman, 'there was no weapon in the body when I arrived.'

'Did *you* take it out?' pursued the constable to Brotherton.

'No,' said Brotherton, 'he took it with him.'

'Took it with 'im,' the constable entered the fact in his notes. 'Phew! Wonderful 'ot it is in 'ere ain't it, sir?' he added, mopping his brow.

'It's the gas-oven, I think,' said Peter mildly. 'Uncommon hot thing, a gas-oven, in the middle of July. D'you mind if I turn it out? There's the chicken inside, but I don't suppose you want—'

Brotherton groaned, and the constable said: 'Quite right, sir. A man wouldn't 'ardly fancy 'is dinner after a thing like this. Thank you, sir. Well now, doctor, wot kind of weapon do you take this to 'ave been?'

'It was a long, narrow weapon – something like an Italian stiletto, I imagine,' said the doctor, 'about six inches long. It was thrust in with great force under the fifth rib, and I should say it had pierced the heart centrally. As you see, there has been practically no bleeding. Such a wound would cause instant death. Was she lying just as she is now when you first saw her, Mr Brotherton?'

'On her back, just as she is,' replied the husband.

'Well, that seems clear enough,' said the policeman.
'This 'ere Marinetti, or wotever 'is name is, 'as a
grudge against the poor young lady—'

'I believe he was an admirer,' put in the doctor. 'Quite
so,' agreed the constable. 'Of course, these foreigners
are like that – even the decentest of 'em. Stabbin' and
such-like seems to come nateral to them, as you might
say. Well, this 'ere Marinetti climbs in 'ere, sees the poor
young lady stendin' 'ere by the table all alone, gettin' the
dinner ready; 'e comes in be'ind, catches 'er round the
waist, stabs 'er – easy job, you see; no corsets nor
nothink – she shrieks out, 'e pulls 'is stiletty out of 'er
an' makes tracks. Well, now we've got to find 'im, and by
your leave, sir, I'll be gettin' along. We'll 'ave 'im by the
heels before long, sir, don't you worry. I'll 'ave to put a
man in charge 'ere, sir; to keep folks out, but that
needn't worry you. Good mornin', gentlemen.'

'May we move the poor girl now?' asked the doctor.

'Certainly. Like me to 'elp you, sir?'

'No. Don't lose any time. We can manage.' Dr Hartman turned to Peter as the constable clattered down
stairs. 'Will you help me, Lord Peter?'

'Bunter's better at that sort of thing,' said Wimsey,
with a hard mouth.

The doctor looked at him in some surprise, but said
nothing, and he and Bunter carried the still form away.
Brotherton did not follow them. He sat in a grief-
tricken heap, with his head buried in his hands. Lord
Peter walked about the little kitchen, turning over the
various knives and kitchen utensils, peering into the sink
bucket, and apparently taking an inventory of the bread,
butter, condiments, vegetables, and so forth which lay
about in preparation for the Sunday meal. There were
potatoes in the sink, half peeled, a pathetic witness to

the quiet domestic life which had been so horribly interrupted. The colander was filled with green peas. Lord
Peter turned these things over with an inquisitive finger
gazed into the smooth surface of a bowl of dripping as
though it were a divining-crystal, ran his hands several
times right through a bowl of flour – then drew his pipe
from his pocket and filled it slowly.

The doctor returned, and put his hand on Brotherton's shoulder.

'Come,' he said gently, 'we have laid her in the other
bedroom. She looks very peaceful. You must remember
that, except for that moment of terror when she saw the
knife, she suffered nothing. It is terrible for you, but you
must try not to give way. The police—'

'The police can't bring her back to life,' said the man
savagely. 'She's dead. Leave me alone, curse you! Leave
me alone, I say!'

He stood up, with a violent gesture.

'You must not sit here,' said Hartman firmly. 'I will
give you something to take, and you must try to keep
calm. Then we will leave you, but if you don't control
yourself—'

After some further persuasion, Brotherton allowed
himself to be led away.

'Bunter,' said Lord Peter, as the kitchen door closed
behind them, 'do you know why I am doubtful about
the success of those rat experiments?'

'Meaning Dr Hartman's, my lord?'

'Yes. Dr Hartman has a theory. In any investigation,
my Bunter, it is most damnably dangerous to have a
theory.'

'I have heard you say so, my lord.'

'Confound you – you know it as well as I do! What
is wrong with the doctor's theories, Bunter?'

'You wish me to reply, my lord, that he only sees the facts which fit into the theory.'

'Thought-reader!' exclaimed Lord Peter bitterly.

'And that he supplies them to the police, my lord.'

'Hush!' said Peter, as the doctor returned.

'I have got him to lie down,' said Dr Hartman, 'and I think the best thing we can do is to leave him to himself.'

'D'you know,' said Wimsey, 'I don't cotton to that idea, somehow.'

'Why? Do you think he's likely to destroy himself?'

'That's as good a reason to give as any other, I suppose,' said Wimsey, 'when you haven't got any reason which can be put into words. But my advice is, don't leave him for a moment.'

'But why? Frequently, with a deep grief like this, the presence of other people is merely an irritant. He begged me to leave him.'

'Then for God's sake go back to him,' said Peter.

'Really, Lord Peter,' said the doctor, 'I think I ought to know what is best for my patient.'

'Doctor,' said Wimsey, 'this is not a question of your patient. A crime has been committed.'

'But there is no mystery.'

'There are twenty mysteries. For one thing, when was the window-cleaner here last?'

'The window-cleaner?'

'Who shall fathom the ebony-black enigma of the window-cleaner?' pursued Peter lightly, putting a match to his pipe. 'You are quietly in your bath, in a state of more or less innocent nature, when an intrusive head appears at the window, like the ghost of Hamilton Tighe, and a gruff voice, suspended between earth and heaven, says, "Good morning, sir." Where do window-cleaners go between visits? Do they hibernate, like busy bees? Do they –?'

'Really, Lord Peter,' said the doctor, 'don't you think you're going a bit beyond the limit?'

'Sorry you feel like that,' said Peter, 'but I really want to know about the window-cleaner. Look how clear these panes are.'

'He came yesterday, if you want to know,' said Dr Hartman, rather stiffly.

'You are sure?'

'He did mine at the same time.'

'I thought as much,' said Lord Peter. 'In the words of the song:

> 'I thought as much,
> It was a little – window-cleaner.

'In that case,' he added, 'it is absolutely imperative that Brotherton should not be left alone for a moment. Bunter! Confound it all, where's that fellow got to?'

The door into the bedroom opened.

'My lord?' Mr Bunter unobtrusively appeared, as he had unobtrusively stolen out to keep an unobtrusive eye upon the patient.

'Good,' said Wimsey. 'Stay where you are.' His lackadaisical manner had gone, and he looked at the doctor as four years previously he might have looked at a refractory subaltern.

'Dr Hartman,' he said, 'something is wrong. Cast your mind back. We were talking about symptoms. Then came the scream. Then came the sound of feet running. *Which direction did they run in?*'

'I'm sure I don't know.'

'Don't you? Symptomatic, though, doctor. They have

been troubling me all the time, subconsciously. Now I know why. They ran *from the kitchen.*'

'Well?'

'Well! And now the window-cleaner—'

'What about him?'

'Could you swear that it wasn't the window-cleaner who made those marks on the sill?'

'And the man Brotherton saw—?'

'Have we examined your laboratory roof for his footsteps?'

'But the weapon? Wimsey, this is madness! Someone took the weapon.'

'I know. But did you think the edge of the wound was clean enough to have been made by a smooth stiletto? It looked ragged to me.'

'Wimsey, what are you driving at?'

'There's a clue here in the flat – and I'm damned if I can remember it. I've seen it – I know I've seen it. It'll come to me presently. Meanwhile, don't let Brotherton—'

'What?'

'Do whatever it is he's going to do.'

'But what is it?'

'If I could tell you that I could show you the clue. Why couldn't he make up his mind whether the bedroom door was open or shut? Very good story, but not quite thought out. Anyhow – I say, doctor, make some excuse and strip him, and bring me his clothes. And send Bunter to me.'

The doctor stared at him, puzzled. Then he made a gesture of acquiescence and passed into the bedroom. Lord Peter followed him, casting a ruminating glance at Brotherton as he went. Once in the sitting-room, Lord Peter sat down on a red velvet arm-chair, fixed his eyes on a gilt-framed oleograph, and became wrapped in contemplation.

Presently Bunter came in, with his arms full of clothing. Wimsey took it, and began to search it, methodically enough, but listlessly. Suddenly he dropped the garments, and turned to the manservant.

'No, he said, 'this is a precaution, Bunter mine, but I'm on the wrong tack. It wasn't here I saw – whatever I did see. It was in the kitchen. Now, what was it?'

'I could not say, my lord, but I entertain a conviction that I was also, in a manner of speaking, conscious – not consciously conscious, my lord, if you understand me, but still conscious of an incongruity.'

'Hurray!' said Wimsey suddenly. 'Cheer-oh! for the subconscious what's-his-name! Now let's remember the kitchen. I cleared out of it because I was gettin' obfuscated. Now then. Begin at the door. Fryin'-pans and saucepans on the wall. Gas-stove – oven goin' – chicken inside. Racks of wooden spoons on the wall, gas-lighter pan-lifter. Stop me when I'm gettin' hot. Mantelpiece Spice-boxes and stuff. Anything wrong with them? No. Dresser. Plates. Knives and forks – all clean; flour dredger – milk-jug – sieve on the wall – nutmeg-grater. Three-tier steamer. Looked inside – no grisly secrets in the steamer.'

'Did you look in all the dresser drawers, my lord?'

'No. That could be done. But the point is, I *did* notice somethin'. What did I notice? That's the point. Never mind. On with the dance – let joy be unconfined! Knife board. Knife-powder. Kitchen table. Did you speak?'

'No,' said Bunter, who had moved from his attitude of wooden deference.

'Table stirs a chord. Very good. On table. Choppin'

board. Remains of ham and herb stuffin'. Packet of suet. Another sieve. Several plates. Butter in a glass dish. Bowl of drippin'—'

'Ah!'

'Drippin' –! Yes, there was—'

'Something unsatisfactory, my lord—'

'About the drippin'! Oh, my head! What's that they say in *Dear Brutus*, Bunter? "Hold on to the workbox." That's right. Hold on to the drippin'. Beastly slimy stuff to hold on to – Wait!'

There was a pause.

'When I was a kid,' said Wimsey, 'I used to love to go down into the kitchen and talk to old cookie. Good old soul she was, too. I can see her now, gettin' chicken ready, with me danglin' my legs on the table. *She* used to pluck an' draw 'em herself. I revelled in it. Little beasts boys are, ain't they, Bunter? Pluck it, draw it, wash it, stuff it, tuck its little tail through its little what-you-may call-it, truss it, grease the dish – Bunter?'

'My lord!'

'Hold on to the dripping!'

'The bowl, my lord—'

'The bowl – visualise it – what was wrong?'

'It was full, my lord!—'

'Got it – got it – *got* it! The bowl was full – smooth surface. Golly! I knew there was something queer about it. Now why shouldn't it be full? Hold on to the—'

'The bird was in the oven.'

'Without dripping!'

'Very careless cookery my lord.'

'The bird – in the oven – no dripping. Bunter! Suppose it was never put in till after she was dead? Thrust in hurriedly by someone who had something to hide – horrible!'

'But with what object, my lord?'

'Yes, why? That's the point. One more mental association with the bird. It's just coming. Wait a moment. Pluck, draw, wash, stuff, tuck up, truss – By God!'

'My lord?'

'Come on, Bunter. Thank Heaven we turned off the gas!'

He dashed through the bedroom, disregarding the doctor and the patient, who sat up with a smothered shriek. He flung open the oven door and snatched out the baking-tin. The skin of the bird had just begun to discolour. With a little gasp of triumph, Wimsey caught the iron ring that protruded from the wing, and jerked out – the six-inch spiral skewer.

The doctor was struggling with the excited Brotherton in the doorway. Wimsey caught the man as he broke away, and shook him into the corner with a jiu-jitsu twist.

'Here is the weapon,' he said.

'Prove it, blast you!' said Brotherton savagely.

'I will,' said Wimsey. 'Bunter, call in the policeman whom you will find at the door. Doctor, we shall need your microscope.'

In the laboratory the doctor bent over the microscope. A thin layer of blood from the skewer had been spread upon the slide.

'Well?' said Wimsey impatiently.

'It's all right,' said Hartman. 'The roasting didn't get anywhere near the middle. My God, Wimsey, yes, you're right – round corpuscles, diameter $1/3621$ – mammalian blood – probably human—'

'Her blood,' said Wimsey.

*

'It was very clever, Bunter,' said Lord Peter, as the taxi trundled along on the way to his flat in Piccadilly. 'If that fowl had gone on roasting a bit longer the blood-corpuscles might easily have been destroyed beyond all hope of recognition. It all goes to show that the unpremeditated crime is usually the safest.'

'And what does your lordship take the man's motive to have been?'

'In my youth,' said Wimsey meditatively, 'they used to make me read the Bible. Trouble was, the only books I ever took to naturally were the ones they weren't over and above keen on. But I got to know the Song of Songs pretty well by heart. Look it up, Bunter; at your age it won't hurt you; it talks sense about jealousy.'

'I have perused the work in question, your lordship,' replied Mr Bunter, with a sallow blush. 'It says, if I remember rightly: "*Jealousy is cruel as the grave.*"'

ABSOLUTELY ELSEWHERE

Lord Peter Wimsey sat with Chief-Inspector Parker, of the C.I.D., and Inspector Henley, of the Baldock police, in the library at 'The Lilacs'.

'So you see,' said Parker, 'that all the obvious suspects were elsewhere at the time.'

'What do you mean by "elsewhere"?' demanded Wimsey, peevishly. Parker had hauled him down to Wapley, on the Great North Road, without his breakfast, and his temper had suffered. 'Do you mean that they couldn't have reached the scene of the murder without travelling at over 186,000 miles a second? Because, if you don't mean that, they weren't absolutely elsewhere. They were only relatively and apparently elsewhere.'

'For heaven's sake, don't go all Eddington. Humanly speaking, they were elsewhere, and if we're going to nail one of them we shall have to do it without going into their Fitzgerald contractions and coefficients of spherical curvature. I think, Inspector, we had better have them in one by one, so that I can hear all their stories again. You can check them up if they depart from their original statements at any point. Let's take the butler first.'

The Inspector put his head out into the hall and said: 'Hamworthy.'

The butler was a man of middle age, whose spherical curvature was certainly worthy of consideration. His large face was pale and puffy, and he looked unwell. However, he embarked on his story without hesitation.

'I have been in the late Mr Grimbold's service for twenty years, gentlemen, and I have always found him a good master. He was a strict gentleman, but very just. I know he was considered very hard in business matters, but I suppose he had to be that. He was a bachelor, but he brought up his two nephews, Mr Harcourt and Mr Neville, and was very good to them. In his private life I should call him a kind and considerate man. His profession? Yes, I suppose you would call him a moneylender.

'About the events of last night, sir, yes. I shut up the house at 7.30 as usual. Everything was done exactly to time, sir – Mr Grimbold was very regular in his habits. I locked all the windows on the ground floor, as was customary during the winter months. I am quite sure I didn't miss anything out. They all have burglar-proof bolts and I should have noticed if they had been out of order. I also locked and bolted the front door and put up the chain.'

'How about the conservatory door?'

'That, sir, is a Yale lock. I tried it, and saw that it was shut. No, I didn't fasten the catch. It was always left that way, sir, in case Mr Grimbold had business which kept him in Town late, so that he could get in without disturbing the household.'

'But he had no business in Town last night?'

'No, sir, but it was always left that way. Nobody could get in without the key, and Mr Grimbold had that on his ring.'

'Is there no other key in existence?'

'I believe' – the butler coughed – 'I believe, sir, though I do not know, that there is *one*, sir – in the possession of – of a lady, sir, who is at present in Paris.'

'I see. Mr Grimbold was about sixty years old, I believe. Just so. What is the name of this lady?'

'Mrs Winter, sir. She lives at Wapley, but since her husband died last month, sir, I understand she has been residing abroad.'

'I see. Better make a note of that, Inspector. Now, how about the upper rooms and the back door?'

'The upper-room windows were all fastened in the same way, sir, except Mr Grimbold's bedroom and the cook's room and mine, sir; but that couldn't be reached without a ladder, and the ladder is locked up in the tool-shed.'

'That's all right,' put in Inspector Henley. 'We went into that last night. The shed was locked and, what's more, there were unbroken cobwebs between the ladder and the wall.'

'I went through all the rooms at half-past seven, sir, and there was nothing out of order.'

'You may take it from me,' said the Inspector, again, 'that there was no interference with any of the locks. Carry on, Hamworthy.'

'Yes, sir. While I was seeing to the house, Mr Grimbold came down into the library for his glass of sherry. At 7.45 the soup was served and I called Mr Grimbold to dinner. He sat at the end of the table as usual, facing the serving-hatch.'

'With his back to the library door,' said Parker, making a mark on a rough plan of the room, which lay before him. 'Was that door shut?'

'Oh, yes, sir. All the doors and windows were shut.'

'It looks a dashed draughty room,' said Wimsey. 'Two doors and a serving-hatch and two french windows.'

'Yes, my lord; but they are all very well-fitting, and the curtains were drawn.'

His lordship moved across to the connecting door and opened it.

'Yes,' he said; 'good and heavy and moves in sinister silence. I like these thick carpets, but the pattern's a bit fierce.' He shut the door noiselessly, and returned to his seat.

'Mr Grimbold would take about five minutes over his soup, sir. When he had done, I removed it and put on the fish. I did not have to leave the room; everything comes through the serving-hatch. The wine – that is, the Chablis – was already on the table. That course was only a small portion of turbot, and would take Mr Grimbold about five minutes again. I removed that, and put on the roast pheasant. I was just about to serve Mr Grimbold with the vegetables, when the telephone-bell rang. Mr Grimbold said: "You'd better see who it is. I'll help myself." It was not the cook's business, of course, to answer the telephone.'

'Are there no other servants?'

'Only the woman who comes in to clean during the day, sir. I went out to the instrument, shutting the door behind me.'

'Was that this telephone or the one in the hall?'

'The one in the hall, sir. I always used that one, unless I happened to be actually in the library at the time. The call was from Mr Neville Grimbold in Town, sir. He and Mr Harcourt have a flat in Jermyn Street. Mr Neville spoke, and I recognised his voice. He said: "Is that you, Hamworthy? Wait a moment. Mr Harcourt wants you." He put the receiver down and then Mr Harcourt came on. He said: "Hamworthy, I want to run down tonight to see my uncle, if he's at home." I said: "Yes, sir, I'll tell him." The young gentlemen often come down for a night or two, sir. We keep their bedrooms ready for them. Mr Harcourt said he would be starting at once and expected to get down by about half-past nine. While he was speaking I heard the big grandfather-clock up in their flat chime the quarters and strike eight, and immediately after, our own hall-clock struck, and then I heard the Exchange say "Three minutes." So the call must have come through at three minutes to eight, sir.'

'Then there's no doubt about the time. That's a comfort. What next, Hamworthy?'

'Mr Harcourt asked for another call and said. "Mr Neville has got something to say," and then Mr Neville came back to the phone. He said he was going up to Scotland shortly, and he wanted me to send up a country suit and some stockings and shirts that he had left down here. He wanted the suit sent to the cleaner's first, and there were various other instructions, so that he asked for another three minutes. That would be at 8.3, sir, yes. And about a minute after that, while he was still speaking, the front-door bell rang. I couldn't very well leave the phone, so the caller had to wait, and at five past eight he rang the bell again. I was just going to ask Mr Neville to excuse me, when I saw Cook come out of the kitchen and go through the hall to the front door. Mr Neville asked me to repeat his instructions, and then the Exchange interrupted us again, so he rang off, and when I turned round I saw Cook just closing the library door. I went to meet her, and she said: "Here's that Mr Payne again, wanting Mr Grimbold. I've put him in the library, but I don't like the looks of him." So I said: "All right; I'll fix him," and Cook went back to the kitchen.'

'One moment,' said Parker. 'Who's Mr Payne?'

'He's one of Mr Grimbold's clients, sir. He lives about five minutes away, across the fields, and he's been here before, making trouble. I think he owes Mr Grimbold money, sir, and wanted more time to pay.'

'He's here, waiting in the hall,' added Henley.

'Oh?' said Wimsey. 'The unshaven party with the scowl and the ash-plant, and the blood-stained coat?'

'That's him, my lord,' said the butler. 'Well, sir' – he turned to Parker again, 'I started to go along to the library, when it come over me sudden – like that I'd never taken in the claret – Mr Grimbold would be getting very annoyed. So I went back to my pantry – you see where that is, sir – and fetched it from where it was warming before the fire. I had a little hunt then for the salver, sir, till I found I had put down my evening paper on top of it, but I wasn't more than a minute, sir, before I got back into the dining-room. And then, sir' – the butler's voice faltered – 'then I saw Mr Grimbold fallen forward on the table, sir, all across his plate, like. I thought he must have been took ill, and I hurried up to him and found – I found he was dead, sir, with a dreadful wound in his back.'

'No weapon anywhere?'

'Not that I could see, sir. There was a terrible lot of blood. It made me feel shockingly faint, sir, and for a minute I didn't hardly know what to do. As soon as I could think of anything, I rushed over to the serving hatch and called Cook. She came hurrying in and let out an awful scream when she saw the master. Then I remembered Mr Payne and opened the library door. He was standing there, and he began at once, asking how long he'd have to wait. So I said: "Here's an awful thing! Mr Grimbold has been murdered!" and he pushed past me into the dining-room, and the first thing he said was: "How about those windows?" He pulled back the curtain of the one nearest the library, and there was the window standing open. "This is the way he went," he said, and started to rush out. I said, "No, you don't" – thinking he meant to get away, and I hung on to him. He called me a lot of names, and then he said: "Look here, my man, be reasonable. The fellow's getting away all this time. We must have a look for him." So I said, "Not without I go with you." And he said, "All right." So I told Cook not to touch anything but to ring up the police, and Mr Payne and I went out after I'd fetched my torch from the pantry.'

'Did Payne go with you to fetch it?'

'Yes, sir. Well, him and me went out and we searched about in the garden, but we couldn't see any footprints or anything, because it's an asphalt path all round the house and down to the gate. And we couldn't see any weapon, either. So then he said: "We'd better go back and get the car and search the roads," but I said: "No, he'll be away by then," because it's only a quarter of a mile from our gate to the Great North Road, and it would take us five or ten minutes before we could start. So Mr Payne said: "Perhaps you're right," and came back to the house with me. Well, then, sir, the constable came from Wapley, and after a bit, the Inspector here and Dr Crofts from Baldock, and they made a search and asked a lot of questions, which I answered to the best of my ability, and I can't tell you no more sir.'

'Did you notice,' asked Parker, 'whether Mr Payne had any stains of blood about him?'

'No sir – I can't say that he had. When I first saw him, he was standing in here, right under the light, and I think I should have seen it if there was anything, sir. I can't say fairer than that.'

'Of course you've searched this room, Inspector, for bloodstains or a weapon or for anything such as gloves or a cloth, or anything that might have been used to protect the murderer from bloodstains?'

'Yes, Mr Parker. We searched very carefully.'

'Could anybody have come downstairs while you were in the dining-room with Mr Grimbold?'

'Well, sir, I suppose they might. But they'd have to have got into the house before half-past seven, sir, and hidden themselves somewhere. Still, there's no doubt it might have happened that way. They couldn't come down by the back stairs, of course, because they'd have had to pass the kitchen and Cook would have heard them, the passage being flagged, sir, but the front stairs – well, I don't know hardly what to say about that.'

'That's how the man got in, depend upon it,' said Parker. 'Don't look so distressed, Hamworthy. You can't be expected to search all the cupboards in the house every evening for concealed criminals. Now I think I had better see the two nephews. I suppose they and their uncle got on together all right?'

'Oh, yes, sir. Never had a word of any sort. It's been a great blow to them, sir. They were terribly upset when Mr Grimbold was ill in the summer—'

'He was ill, was he?'

'Yes sir, with his heart, last July. He took a very bad turn, sir, and we had to send for Mr Neville. But he pulled round wonderfully, sir – only he never seemed to be quite such a cheerful gentleman afterwards. I think it made me feel he wasn't getting younger, sir. But I'm sure nobody ever thought he'd be cut off like this.'

'How is his money left?' asked Parker.

'Well, sir, that I don't know. I believe it would be divided between the two gentlemen, sir – not but what they have plenty of their own. But Mr Harcourt would be able to tell you, sir. He's the executor.'

'Very well, we'll ask him. Are the brothers on good terms?'

'Oh, yes, indeed, sir. Most devoted. Mr Neville would do anything for Mr Harcourt – and Mr Harcourt for him, I'm sure. A very pleasant pair of gentlemen, sir. You couldn't have nicer.'

'Thanks, Hamworthy. That will do for the moment, unless anybody else has anything to ask?'

'How much of the pheasant was eaten, Hamworthy?'

'Well, my lord, not a great deal of it – I mean, nothing like all of what Mr Grimbold had on his plate. But he'd ate some of it. It might have taken three or four minutes or so to eat what he had done, my lord, judging by what I helped him to.'

'There was nothing to suggest that he had been interrupted, for example, by somebody coming to the windows, or of his having got up to let the person in?'

'Nothing at all, my lord, that I could see.'

'The chair was pushed in close to the table when I saw him,' put in the Inspector, 'and his napkin was on his knees and the knife and fork lying just under his hands, as though he had dropped them when the blow came. I understand that the body was not disturbed.'

'No sir, I never moved it – except, of course, to make sure that he was dead. But I never felt any doubt of that, sir, when I saw that dreadful wound in his back. I just lifted his head and let it fall forward again, same as before.'

'All right, then, Hamworthy. Ask Mr Harcourt to come in.'

Mr Harcourt Grimbold was a brisk-looking man of about thirty-five. He explained that he was a stock-broker and his brother Neville an official in the Ministry of Public Health, and that they had been brought up by their uncle from the ages of eleven and ten respectively. He was aware that his uncle had had many business enemies, but for his own part he had received nothing from him but kindness.

'I'm afraid I can't tell you much about this terrible business, as I didn't get here till 9.45 last night, when, of course, it was all over.'

'That was a little later than you hoped to be here?'

'Just a little. My tail-lamp went out between Welwyn Garden City and Welwyn, and I was stopped by a bobby. I went to a garage in Welwyn, where they found that the lead had come loose. They put it right, and that delayed me for a few minutes more.'

'It's about forty miles from here to London?'

'Just over. In the ordinary way, at that time of night, I should reckon an hour and a quarter from door to door. I'm not a speed merchant.'

'Did you drive yourself?'

'Yes. I have a chauffeur, but I don't always bring him down here with me.'

'When did you leave London?'

'About 8.20, I should think. Neville went round to the garage and fetched the car as soon as he'd finished telephoning, while I put my toothbrush and so on in my bag.'

'You didn't hear about the death of your uncle before you left?'

'No. They didn't think of ringing me up, I gather, till after I had started. The police tried to get Neville later on, but he'd gone round to the club, or something. I phoned him myself after I got here, and he came down this morning.'

'Well, now, Mr Grimbold, can you tell us anything about your late uncle's affairs?'

313

'You mean his will? Who profits, and that kind of thing? Well, I do, for one, and Neville, for another. And Mrs –. Have you heard of a Mrs Winter?'

'Something, yes.'

'Well, she does, for a third. And then, of course, old Hamworthy gets a nice little nest-egg, and the cook gets something, and there is a legacy of £500 to the clerk at my uncle's London office. But the bulk of it goes to us and to Mrs Winter. I know what you're going to ask – how much is it? I haven't the faintest idea, but I know it must be something pretty considerable. The old man never let on to a soul how much he really was worth, and we never bothered about it. I'm turning over a good bit, and Neville's salary is a heavy burden on a long-suffering public, so we only had a mild, academic kind of interest in the question.'

'Do you suppose Hamworthy knew he was down for a legacy?'

'Oh, yes – there was no secret about that. He was to get £100 and a life-interest in £200 a year, provided, of course, he was still in my uncle's service when he – my uncle, I mean – died.'

'And he wasn't under notice, or anything?'

'N-no. No. Not more than usual. My uncle gave everybody notice about once a month, to keep them up to the mark. But it never came to anything. He was like the Queen of Hearts in *Alice* – he never executed nobody, you know.'

'I see. We'd better ask Hamworthy about that, though. Now, this Mrs Winter. Do you know anything about her?'

'Oh, yes. She's a nice woman. Of course, she was Uncle William's mistress for donkey's years, but her husband was practically potty with drink, and you could scarcely blame her. I wired her this morning and here's her reply, just come.'

He handed Parker a telegram, despatched from Paris, which read: 'Terribly shocked and grieved. Returning immediately. Love and sympathy. Lucy.'

'You are on friendly terms with her, then?'

'Good Lord, yes. Why not? We were always damned sorry for her. Uncle William would have taken her away with him somewhere, only she wouldn't leave Winter. In fact, I think they had practically settled that they were to get married now that Winter has had the grace to peg out. She's only about thirty-eight, and it's time she had some sort of show in life, poor thing.'

'So, in spite of the money, she hadn't really very much to gain by your uncle's death?'

'Not a thing. Unless, of course, she wanted to marry somebody younger, and was afraid of losing the cash. But I believe she was honestly fond of the old boy. Anyhow, she couldn't have done the murder, because she's in Paris.'

'H'm!' said Parker. 'I suppose she is. We'd better make sure, though. I'll ring through to the Yard and have her looked out for at the ports. Is this phone through to the Exchange?'

'Yes,' said the Inspector. 'It doesn't have to go through the hall phone; they're connected in parallel.'

'All right. Well, I don't think we need trouble you further, at the moment, Mr Grimbold. I'll put my call through, and after that we'll send for the next witness . . . Give me Whitehall 1212, please . . . I suppose the time of Mr Harcourt's call from town has been checked, Inspector?'

'Yes, Mr Parker. It was put in at 7.57 and renewed at 8 o'clock and 8.3. Quite an expensive little item. And we've also checked up on the constable who spoke to him about his lights and the garage that put them right for him. He got into Welwyn at 9.5 and left again about 9.15. The number of the car is right, too.'

'Well, he's out of it in any case, but it's just as well to check all we can . . . Hullo, is that Scotland Yard? Put me through to Chief-Inspector Hardy. Chief-Inspector Parker speaking.'

As soon as he had finished with his call, Parker sent for Neville Grimbold. He was rather like his brother, only a little slimmer and a little more suave in speech, as befitted a Civil Servant. He had nothing to add, except to confirm his brother's story and to explain that he had gone to a cinema from 8.20 to about 10 o'clock, and then on to his club, so that he had heard nothing about the tragedy till later in the evening.

The cook was the next witness. She had a great deal to say, but nothing very convincing to tell. She had not happened to see Hamworthy go to the pantry for the claret, otherwise she confirmed his story. She scouted the idea that somebody had been concealed in one of the upper rooms, because the daily woman, Mrs Crabbe, had been in the house till nearly dinner-time, putting camphor-bags in all the wardrobes; and, anyhow, she had no doubt but what 'that Payne' had stabbed Mr Grimbold – 'a nasty, murdering beast'. After which, it only remained to interview the murderous Mr Payne.

Mr Payne was almost aggressively frank. He had been treated very harshly by Mr Grimbold. What with exorbitant usury and accumulated interest added to the principal, he had already paid back about five times the original loan, and now Mr Grimbold had refused him any more time to pay, and had announced his intention of foreclosing on the security, namely, Mr Payne's house and land. It was all the more brutal because Mr Payne had every prospect of being able to pay off the entire debt in six months' time, owing to some sort of interest or share in something or other which was confidently expected to turn up trumps. In his opinion, old Grimbold had refused to renew on purpose, so as to prevent him from paying – what *he* wanted was the property. Grimbold's death was the saving of the situation, because it would postpone settlement till after the confidently-expected trumps had turned up. Mr Payne would have murdered old Grimbold with pleasure, but he hadn't done so, and in any case he wasn't the sort of man to stab anybody in the back, though, if the money-lender had been a younger man, he, Payne, would have been happy to break all his bones for him. There it was, and they could take it or leave it. If that old fool, Hamworthy, hadn't got in his way, he'd have laid hands on the murderer all right – if Hamworthy was a fool, which he doubted. Blood? Yes, there was blood on his coat. He had got that in struggling with Hamworthy at the window. Hamworthy's hands had been all over blood when he made his appearance in the library. No doubt he had got it from the corpse. He, Payne, had taken care not to change his clothes, because, if he had done so, somebody would have tried to make out that he was hiding something. Actually, he had not been home, or asked to go home, since the murder. Mr Payne added that he objected strongly to the attitude taken up by the local police, who had treated him with undisguised hostility. To which Inspector Henley replied that Mr Payne was quite mistaken.

'Mr Payne,' said Lord Peter, 'will you tell me one

thing? When you heard the commotion in the dining-room, and the cook screaming, and so on, why didn't you go in at once to find out what was the matter?'

'Why?' retorted Mr Payne. 'Because I never heard anything of the sort, that's why. The first thing I knew about it was seeing the butler-fellow standing there in the doorway, waving his bloody hands about and gibbering.'

'Ah!' said Wimsey. 'I thought it was a good, solid door. Shall we ask the lady to go in and scream for us now, with the dining-room window open?'

The Inspector departed on this errand, while the rest of the company waited anxiously to count the screams. Nothing happened, however, till Henley put his head in and asked, what about it?

'Nothing,' said Parker.

'It's a well-built house,' said Wimsey. 'I suppose any sound coming through the window would be muffled by the conservatory. Well, Mr Payne, if you didn't hear the screams it's not surprising that you didn't hear the murderer. Are those all your witnesses, Charles? Because I've got to get back to London to see a man about a dog. But I'll leave you with two suggestions with my blessing. One is, that you should look for a car, which was parked within a quarter of a mile of this house last night, between 7.30 and 8.15; the second is, that you should all come and sit in the dining-room tonight, with the doors and windows shut, and watch the french windows. I'll give Mr Parker a ring about eight. Oh, and you might lend me the key of the conservatory door. I've got a theory about it.'

The Chief Inspector handed over the key, and his lordship departed.

*

The party assembled in the dining-room was in no very companionable mood. In fact, all the conversation was supplied by the police, who kept up a chatty exchange of fishing reminiscences, while Mr Payne glowered, the two Grimbolds smoked cigarette after cigarette, and the cook and the butler balanced themselves nervously on the extreme edges of their chairs. It was a relief when the telephone-bell rang.

Parker glanced at his watch as he got up to answer it. 'Seven-fifty-seven,' he observed, and saw the butler pass his handkerchief over his twitching lips. 'Keep your eye on the windows.' He went out into the hall.

'Hullo!' he said.

'Is that Chief-Inspector Parker?' asked a voice he knew well. 'This is Lord Peter Wimsey's man speaking from his lordship's rooms in London. Would you hold the line a moment? His lordship wishes to speak to you.'

Parker heard the receiver set down and lifted again. Then Wimsey's voice came through: 'Hullo, old man? Have you found that car yet?'

'We've heard of *a* car,' replied the Chief Inspector cautiously, 'at a Road-House on the Great North Road, about five minutes' walk from the house.'

'Was the number ABJ 28?'

'Yes. How did you know?'

'I thought it might be. It was hired from a London garage at five o'clock yesterday afternoon and brought back just before ten. Have you traced Mrs Winter?'

'Yes, I think so. She landed from the Calais boat this evening. So apparently she's O.K.'

'I thought she might be. Now listen. Do you know that Harcourt Grimbold's affairs are in a bit of a mess? He nearly had a crisis last July, but somebody came to

319

his rescue – possibly his Uncle, don't you think? All rather fishy, my informant saith. And I'm told, very confidentially, that he's got badly caught over the Biggars-Whitlow crash. But of course he'll have no difficulty in raising money now, on the strength of Uncle's will. But I imagine the July business gave Uncle William a jolt. I expect—'

He was interrupted by a little burst of tinkling music, followed by the eight silvery strokes of a bell.

'Hear that? Recognise it? That's the big French clock in my sitting-room . . . What? All right, Exchange, give me another three minutes. Bunter wants to speak to you again.'

The receiver rattled, and the servant's suave voice took up the tale.

'His lordship asks me to ask you, sir, to ring off at once and go straight into the dining-room.'

Parker obeyed. As he entered the room, he got an instantaneous impression of six people, sitting as he had left them, in an expectant semi-circle, their eyes strained towards the french windows. Then the library door opened noiselessly and Lord Peter Wimsey walked in.

'Good God!' exclaimed Parker, involuntarily. 'How did you get here?' The six heads jerked round suddenly.

'On the back of the light waves,' said Wimsey, smoothing back his hair. 'I have travelled eighty miles to be with you, at 186,000 miles a second.'

'It was rather obvious, really,' said Wimsey, when they had secured Harcourt Grimbold (who fought desperately) and his brother Neville (who collapsed and had to be revived with brandy). It had to be those two; they were so very much elsewhere – almost absolutely elsewhere. The murder could only have been committed between 7.57 and 8.6, and there had to be a reason for that prolonged phone-call about something that Harcourt could very well have explained when he came. And the murderer had to be in the library before 7.57, or he would have been seen in the hall – unless Grimbold had let him in by the french window, which didn't appear likely.

'Here's how it was worked. Harcourt set off from town in a hired car about six o'clock, driving himself. He parked the car at the Road-House, giving some explanation. I suppose he wasn't known there?'

'No; it's quite a new place; only opened last month.'

'Ah! Then he walked the last quarter-mile on foot, arriving here at 7.45. It was dark, and he probably wore goloshes, so as not to make a noise coming up the path. He let himself into the conservatory with a duplicate key.'

'How did he get that?'

'Pinched Uncle William's key off his ring last July, when the old boy was ill. It was probably the shock of hearing that his dear nephew was in trouble that caused the illness. Harcourt was here at the time – you remember it was only Neville that had to be "sent for" – and I suppose Uncle paid up then, on conditions. But I doubt if he'd have done as much again – especially as he was thinking of getting married. And I expect, too, Harcourt thought that Uncle might easily alter his will after marriage. He might even have founded a family, and what would poor Harcourt do then, poor thing? From every point of view, it was better that Uncle should depart this life. So the duplicate key was cut and the plot thought out, and Brother Neville who would "do anything for Mr Harcourt," was roped in to help.

I'm inclined to think that Harcourt must have done something rather worse than merely lose money, and Neville may have troubles of his own. But where was I?'

'Coming in at the conservatory door.'

'Oh, yes – that's the way I came tonight. He'd take cover in the garden and would know when Uncle William went into the dining-room, because he'd see the library light go out. Remember, he knew the household. He came in, in the dark, locking the outer door after him, and waited by the telephone until Neville's call came through from London. When the bell stopped ringing, he lifted the receiver in the library. As soon as Neville had spoken his little piece, Harcourt chipped in. Nobody could hear him through these sound-proof doors, and Hamworthy couldn't possibly tell that his voice wasn't coming from London. In fact, it *was* coming from London, because, as the phones are connected in parallel, it could only come by way of the Exchange. At eight o'clock, the grandfather clock in Jermyn Street struck – further proof that the London line was open. The minute Harcourt heard that, he called on Neville to speak again, and hung up under cover of the rattle of Neville's receiver. Then Neville detained Hamworthy with a lot of rot about a suit, while Harcourt walked into the dining-room, stabbed his uncle, and departed by the window. He had five good minutes in which to hurry back to his car and drive off – and Hamworthy and Payne actually gave him a few minutes more by suspecting and hampering one another.'

'Why didn't he go back through the library and conservatory?'

'He hoped everybody would think that the murderer had come in by the window. In the meantime, Neville left London at 8.20 in Harcourt's car, carefully drawing the attention of a policeman and a garage man to the licence number as he passed through Welwyn. At an appointed place outside Welwyn he met Harcourt, primed him with his little story about tail-lights, and changed cars with him. Neville returned to town with the hired bus; Harcourt came back here with his own car. But I'm afraid you'll have a little difficulty in finding the weapon and the duplicate key and Harcourt's blood-stained gloves and coat. Neville probably took them back, and they may be anywhere. There's a good, big river in London.'

STRIDING FOLLY

'Shall I expect you next Wednesday for our game as usual?' asked Mr Mellilow.

'Of course, of course,' replied Mr Creech. 'Very glad there's no ill feeling, Mellilow. Next Wednesday as usual. Unless . . .' his heavy face darkened for a moment, as though at some disagreeable recollection. 'There may be a man coming to see me. If I'm not here by nine, don't expect me. In that case, I'll come on Thursday.'

Mr Mellilow let his visitor out through the french window and watched him cross the lawn to the wicket gate leading to the Hall grounds. It was a clear October night, with a gibbous moon going down the sky. Mr Mellilow slipped on his goloshes (for he was careful of his health and the grass was wet) and himself went down past the sundial and the fish-pond and through the sunk garden till he came to the fence that bounded his tiny freehold on the southern side. He leaned his arms on the rail and gazed across the little valley at the tumbling river and the wide slope beyond, which was crowned, at a mile's distance, by the ridiculous stone tower known as the Folly. The valley, the slope and the tower all belonged to Striding Hall. They lay there, peaceful and lovely in the moonlight, as though nothing could ever disturb their fantastic solitude. But Mr Mellilow knew better.

He had bought the cottage to end his days in, thinking that here was a corner of England the same yesterday, today and for ever. It was strange that he, a chess-player, should not have been able to see three moves ahead. The first move had been the death of the old squire. The second had been the purchase by Creech of the whole Striding property. Even then, he had not been able to see why a rich business man – unmarried and with no rural interests – should have come to live in a spot so remote. True, there were three considerable towns at a few miles' distance, but the village itself was on the road to nowhere. Fool! he had forgotten the Grid! It had come, like a great, ugly chess-rook swooping from an unconsidered corner, marching over the country, straddling four, six, eight parishes at a time, planting hideous pylons to mark its progress, and squatting now at Mr Mellilow's very door. For Creech had just calmly announced that he was selling the valley to the Electrical Company; and there would be a huge power-plant on the river and workmen's bungalows on the slope, and then Development – which, to Mr Mellilow, was another name for the devil. It was ironical that Mr Mellilow, alone in the village, had received Creech with kindness, excusing his vulgar humour and insensitive manners, because he thought Creech was lonely and believed him to be well-meaning, and because he was glad to have a neighbour who could give him a weekly game of chess.

Mr Mellilow came in sorrowful and restored his goloshes to their usual resting-place on the verandah by the french window. He put the chessmen away and the cat out and locked up the cottage – for he lived quite alone, with a woman coming in by the day. Then he went up to bed with his mind full of the Folly, and presently he fell asleep and dreamed.

He was standing in a landscape whose style seemed very familiar to him. There was a wide plain, intersected with hedgerows, and crossed in the middle distance by a river, over which was a small stone bridge. Enormous blue-black thunderclouds hung heavy overhead, and the air had the electric stillness of something stretched to snapping point. Far off, beyond the river, a livid streak of sunlight pierced the clouds and lit up with theatrical brilliance a tall, solitary tower. The scene had a curious unreality, as though of painted canvas. It was a picture, and he had an odd conviction that he recognised the handling and could put a name to the artist. 'Smooth and tight,' were the words that occurred to him. And then: 'It's bound to break before long.' And then: 'I ought not to have come out without my goloshes.'

It was important, it was imperative that he should get to the bridge. But the faster he walked, the greater the distance grew, and without his goloshes the going was very difficult. Sometimes he was bogged to the knee, sometimes he floundered on steep banks of shifting shale; and the air was not merely oppressive – it was *hot* like the inside of an oven. He was running now, with the breath labouring in his throat, and when he looked up he was astonished to see how close he was to the tower. The bridge was fantastically small now, dwindled to a pin-point on the horizon, but the tower fronted him just across the river, and close on his right was a dark wood, which had not been there before. Something flickered on the wood's edge, out and in again, shy and swift as a rabbit; and now the wood was between him and the bridge and the tower behind it, still glowing in that unnatural streak of sunlight. He was at the river's brink, but the bridge was nowhere to be seen – and the tower, the tower was moving. It had crossed the river. It had taken the wood in one gigantic leap. It was no more than fifty yards off, immensely high, shining, and painted. Even as he ran, dodging and twisting, it took another field in its stride, and when he turned to flee it was there before him. It was a double tower – twin towers – a tower and its mirror image, advancing with a swift and awful stealth from either side to crush him. He was pinned now between them, panting. He saw their smooth, yellow sides tapering up to heaven, and about their feet went a monstrous stir, like the quiver of a crouching cat. Then the low sky burst like a sluice and through the drench of the rain he leapt at a doorway in the foot of the tower before him and found himself climbing the familiar stair of Striding Folly. 'My goloshes will be here,' he said, with a passionate sense of relief. The lightning stabbed suddenly through a loop-hole and he saw a black crow lying dead upon the stairs. Then thunder . . . like the rolling of drums.

The daily woman was hammering upon the door. 'You *have* slept in,' she said, 'and no mistake.'

Mr Mellilow, finishing his supper on the following Wednesday, rather hoped that Mr Creech would not come. He had thought a good deal during the week about the electric power scheme, and the more he thought about it, the less he liked it. He had discovered another thing which had increased his dislike. Sir Henry Hunter, who owned a good deal of land on the other side of the market town, had, it appeared, offered the Company a site more suitable than Striding in every way on extremely favourable terms. The choice of Striding seemed inexplicable, unless on the supposition that Creech had bribed the surveyor. Sir Henry voiced his suspicions without any mincing of words. He admitted, however, that he could prove nothing. 'But he's crooked,' he said;

'I have heard things about him in Town. Other things. Ugly rumours.' Mr Mellilow suggested that the deal might not, after all, go through. 'You're an optimist,' said Sir Henry. 'Nothing stops a fellow like Creech. Except death. He's a man with enemies . . .' He broke off, adding, darkly, 'Let's hope he breaks his damned neck one of these days – and the sooner the better.'

Mr Mellilow was uncomfortable. He did not like to hear about crooked transactions. Business men, he supposed, were like that; but if they were, he would rather not play games with them. It spoilt things, somehow. Better, perhaps, not to think too much about it. He took up the newspaper, determined to occupy his mind, while waiting for Creech, with that day's chess problem. White to play and mate in three.

He had just become pleasantly absorbed when a knock came at the door front. Creech? As early as eight o'clock? Surely not. And in any case, he would have come by the lawn and the french window. But who else would visit the cottage of an evening? Rather disconcerted, he rose to let the visitor in. But the man who stood on the threshold was a stranger.

'Mr Mellilow?'

'Yes, my name is Mellilow. What can I do for you?'

(A motorist, he supposed, inquiring his way or wanting to borrow something.)

'Ah! that is good. I have come to play chess with you.'

'To play chess?' repeated Mr Mellilow, astonished.

'Yes; I am a commercial traveller. My car has broken down in the village. I have to stay at the inn and I ask the good Potts if there is anyone who can give me a game of chess to pass the evening. He tells me Mr Mellilow lives here and plays well. Indeed, I recognise the name. Have I not read *Mellilow on Pawn-Play*? It is yours, no?'

Rather flattered, Mr Mellilow admitted the authorship of this little work.

'So. I congratulate you. And you will do me the favour to play with me, hey? Unless I intrude, or you have company.'

'No,' said Mr Mellilow. 'I am more or less expecting a friend, but he won't turn up till nine and perhaps he won't come at all.'

'If he come, I go,' said the stranger. 'It is very good of you.' He had somehow oozed his way into the house without any direct invitation and was removing his hat and overcoat. He was a big man with a short, thick curly beard and tinted spectacles, and he spoke in a deep voice with a slight foreign accent. 'My name,' he added, 'is Moses. I represent Messrs. Cohen & Gold of Farringdon Street, the manufacturers of electrical fittings.'

He grinned widely, and Mr Mellilow's heart contracted. Such haste seemed almost indecent. Before the site was even taken! He felt an unreasonable resentment against this harmless Jew. Then, he rebuked himself. It was not the man's fault. 'Come in,' he said, with more cordiality in his voice than he really felt, 'I shall be very glad to give you a game.'

'I am very grateful,' said Mr Moses, squeezing his great bulk through into the sitting-room. 'Ha! you are working out the *Record*'s two-mover. It is elegant but not profound. You will not take long to break his back. You permit that I disturb?'

Mr Mellilow nodded, and the stranger began to arrange the board for play.

'You have hurt your hand?' inquired Mr Mellilow.

'It is nothing,' replied Mr Moses, turning back the glove he wore and displaying a quantity of sticking plaster. 'I break my knuckles trying to start the dam' car. She kick me. Bah! a trifle. I wear a glove to protect him. So, we begin?'

'Won't you have something to drink first?'

'No, no, thank you very much. I have refreshed myself already at the inn. Too many drinks are not good. But do not let that prevent you.'

Mr Mellilow helped himself to a modest whisky and soda and sat down to the board. He won the draw and took the white pieces, playing his king's pawn to king's fourth.

'So!' said Mr Moses, as the next few moves and countermoves followed their prescribed course, 'the *gluco piano*, hey? Nothing spectacular. We try the strength. When we know what we have each to meet, then the surprises will begin.'

The first game proceeded cautiously. Whoever Mr Moses might be, he was a sound and intelligent player, not easily stampeded into indiscretions. Twice Mr Mellilow baited a delicate trap; twice, with a broad smile, Mr Moses stepped daintily out between the closing jaws. The third trap was set more carefully. Gradually, and fighting every step of the way, black was forced behind his last defences. Yet another five minutes and Mr Mellilow said gently, 'Check;' adding, 'and mate in four.' Mr Moses nodded. 'That was good.' He glanced at the clock. 'One hour. You give me my revenge, hey? Now we know one another. Now we shall see.'

Mr Mellilow agreed. Ten minutes past nine. Creech would not come now. The pieces were set up again. This time, Mr Moses took white, opening with the difficult and dangerous Steinitz gambit. Within a few minutes Mr Mellilow realised that, up till now, his opponent had been playing with him in a double sense. He experienced that eager and palpitating excitement which attends the process of biting off more than one can chew. By half-past nine, he was definitely on the defensive; at a quarter to ten, he thought he spied a way out; five minutes later, Mr Moses said suddenly: 'It grows late: we must begin to push a little,' and thrust forward a knight, leaving his queen *en prise*.

Mr Mellilow took prompt advantage of the oversight – and became aware, too late, that he was menaced by the advance of a white rook.

Stupid! How had he come to overlook that? There was an answer, of course ... but he wished the little room were not so hot and that the stranger's eyes were not so inscrutable behind the tinted glasses. If he could manoeuvre his king out of harm's way for the moment and force his pawn through, he had still a chance. The rook moved in upon him as he twisted and dodged; it came swooping and striding over the board, four, six, eight squares at a time; and now the second white rook had darted out from its corner; they were closing in upon him – a double castle, twin castles, a castle and its mirror-image: O God! it was his dream of striding towers, smooth and yellow and painted. Mr Mellilow wiped his forehead.

'Check!' said Mr Moses. And again, 'Check!' And then, 'Checkmate!'

Mr Mellilow pulled himself together. This would never do. His heart was thumping as though he had been running a race. It was ridiculous to be so much overwrought by a game of chess; and if there was one kind of man in the world that he despised, it was a bad loser. The stranger was uttering some polite common-place – he could not tell what – and replacing the pieces in their box.

'I must go now,' said Mr Moses. 'I thank you very much for the pleasure you have so kindly given me . . . Pardon me, you are a little unwell?'

'No, no,' said Mr Mellilow. 'It is the heat of the fire and the lamp. I have enjoyed our games very much. Won't you take anything before you go?'

'No, I thank you. I must be back before the good Potts locks me out. Again, my hearty thanks.'

He grasped Mr Mellilow's hand in his gloved grip and passed out quickly into the hall. In another moment he had seized hat and coat and was gone. His footsteps died away along the cobbled path.

Mr Mellilow returned to the sitting-room. A curious episode; he could scarcely believe that it had really happened. There lay the empty board, the pieces in their box, the *Record* on the old oak chest with a solitary tumbler beside it; he might have dozed off and dreamed the whole thing for all the trace the stranger's visit had left. Certainly the room was very hot. He threw the french window open. A lop-sided moon had risen, chequering the valley and the slope beyond with patches of black and white. High up and distant, the Folly made a pale streak upon the sky. Mr Mellilow thought he would walk down to the bridge to clear his head. He groped in the accustomed corner for his goloshes. They were not there. 'Where on earth has that woman put them?' muttered Mr Mellilow. And he answered himself, irrationally but with complete conviction: 'My goloshes are up at the Folly.'

His feet seemed to move of their own accord. He was through the garden now, walking quickly down the field to the little wooden foot-bridge. His goloshes were at the Folly. It was imperative that he should fetch them back; the smallest delay would be fatal. 'This is ridiculous,' thought Mr Mellilow to himself. 'It is that foolish dream running in my head. Mrs Gibbs must have taken them away to clean them. But while I am here, I may as well go on; the walk will do me good.'

The power of the dream was so strong upon him that he was almost surprised to find the bridge in its accustomed place. He put his hand on the rail and was comforted by the roughness of the untrimmed bark. Half a mile uphill now to the Folly. Its smooth sides shone in the moonlight, and he turned suddenly, expecting to see the double image striding the fields behind him. Nothing so sensational was to be seen, however. He breasted the slope with renewed courage. Now he stood close beneath the tower – and with a little shock he saw that the door at its base stood open.

He stepped inside, and immediately the darkness was all about him like a blanket. He felt with his foot for the stair and groped his way up between the newel and the wall. Now in gloom, now in the gleam of a loophole, the stair seemed to turn endlessly. Then, as his head rose into the pale glimmer of the fourth window, he saw a shapeless blackness sprawled upon the stair. With a sudden dreadful certainty that *this* was what he had come to see, he mounted further and stooped over it. Creech was lying there dead. Close beside the body lay a pair of goloshes. As Mr Mellilow moved to pick them up, something rolled beneath his foot. It was a white chess-rook.

The police surgeon said that Creech had been dead since about nine o'clock. It was proved that at eight fifty he had set out towards the wicket gate to play chess with Mr Mellilow. And in the morning light the prints of Mr Mellilow's goloshes were clear, leading down the gravelled path on the far side of the lawn, past the sundial and the fish-pond and through the sunk garden and so over the muddy field and the footbridge and up the slope to the Folly. Deep foot-prints they were and close together, such as a man might make who carried a monstrous burden. A good mile to the Folly and half of it uphill. The doctor looked inquiringly at Mr Mellilow's spare form.

'Oh, yes,' said Mr Mellilow. 'I could have carried him. It's a matter of knack, not strength. You see—' he blushed faintly, 'I'm not really a gentleman. My father was a miller and I spent my whole boyhood carrying sacks. Only I was always fond of my books, and so I managed to educate myself and earn a little money. It would be silly to pretend I couldn't have carried Creech. But I didn't do it, of course.'

'It's unfortunate,' said the superintendent, 'that we can't find no trace of this man Moses.' His voice was the most unpleasant Mr Mellilow had ever heard – a sceptical voice with an edge like a saw. 'He never come down to the Feathers, that's a certainty. Potts never set eyes on him, let alone sent him up here with a tale about chess. Nor nobody saw no car neither. An odd gentleman this Mr Moses seems to have been. No footmarks to the front door? Well, it's cobbles, so you wouldn't expect none. That his glass of whisky by any chance, sir? . . . Oh? he wouldn't have a drink, wouldn't he? Ah! And you played two games of chess in this very room? Ah! very absorbing pursoot, so I'm told. You didn't hear poor Mr Creech come up the garden?'

'The windows were shut,' said Mr Mellilow, 'and the

urtains drawn. And Mr Creech always walked straight
over the grass from the wicket gate.'

'H'm!' said the superintendent. 'So he come, or
somebody come, right up on to the verandah and
sneaks a pair of goloshes; and you and this Mr Moses
are so occupied you don't hear nothing.'

'Come, Superintendent,' said the Chief Constable,
who was sitting on Mr Mellilow's oak chest and looked
rather uncomfortable. 'I don't think that's impossible.
The man might have worn tennis-shoes or something.
How about fingerprints on the chessmen?'

'He wore a glove on his right hand,' said Mr Mellilow, unhappily. 'I can remember that he didn't use his
left hand at all – not even when taking a piece.'

'A very remarkable gentleman,' said the superintendent again. 'No fingerprints, no footprints, no drinks, no
eyes visible, no features to speak of, pops in and out
without leaving no trace – a kind of a vanishing gentleman.' Mr Mellilow made a helpless gesture. 'These the
chessmen you was using?' Mr Mellilow nodded, and
the superintendent turned the box upside-down upon
the board, carefully extending a vast enclosing paw to
keep the pieces from rolling away. 'Let's see. Two big
'uns with crosses on the top and two big 'uns with
spikes. Four chaps with split-open 'eads. Four 'orses.
Two black 'uns – what d'you call these? Rooks, eh?
Look more like churches to me. One white church –
rook if you like. What's gone with the other one? Or
don't these rook-affairs go in pairs like the rest?'

'They must both be there,' said Mr Mellilow. 'He was
using two white rooks in the end-game. He mated me
with them . . . I remember . . .'

He remembered only too well. The dream, and the
double castle moving to crush him. He watched the

superintendent feeling in his pocket and suddenly knew that name of the terror that had flickered in and out of the black wood.

The superintendent set down the white rook that had lain by the corpse at the Folly. Colour, height and weight matched with the rook on the board.

'Staunton men,' said the Chief Constable, 'all of a pattern.'

But the superintendent, with his back to the french window, was watching Mr Mellilow's grey face.

'He must have put it in his pocket,' said Mr Mellilow. 'He cleared the pieces away at the end of the game.'

'But he couldn't have taken it up to Striding Folly,' said the superintendent, 'nor he couldn't have done the murder, by your own account.'

'Is it possible that you carried it up to the Folly yourself,' asked the Chief Constable, 'and dropped it there when you found the body?'

'The gentleman has said that he saw this man Moses put it away,' said the superintendent.

They were watching him now, all of them. Mr Mellilow clasped his head in his hands. His forehead was drenched. 'Something must break soon,' he thought.

Like a thunderclap there came a blow on the window; the superintendent leapt nearly out of his skin.

'Lord, my lord!' he complained, opening the window and letting a gust of fresh air into the room, 'How you startled me!'

Mr Mellilow gaped. Who was this? His brain wasn't working properly. That friend of the Chief Constable's, of course, who had disappeared somehow during the conversation. Like the bridge in his dream. Disappeared. Gone out of the picture.

'Absorbin' game, detectin',' said the Chief Constable's friend. 'Very much like chess. People come creepin' right up on to the verandah and you never even notice them. In broad daylight, too. Tell me, Mr Mellilow – what made you go up last night to the Folly?'

Mr Mellilow hesitated. This was the point in his story that he had made no attempt to explain. Mr Moses had sounded unlikely enough; a dream about goloshes would sound more unlikely still.

'Come now,' said the Chief Constable's friend, polishing his monocle on his handkerchief and replacing it with an exaggerated lifting of the eyebrows. 'What was it? Woman, woman, lovely woman? Meet me by moonlight and all that kind of thing?'

'Certainly not,' said Mr Mellilow, indignantly. 'I wanted a breath of fresh—' He stopped, uncertainly. There was something in the other man's childish-foolish face that urged him to speak the reckless truth. 'I had a dream,' he said.

The superintendent shuffled his feet, and the Chief Constable crossed one leg awkwardly over the other.

'Warned of God in a dream,' said the man with the monocle, unexpectedly. 'What did you dream of?' He followed Mr Mellilow's glance at the board. 'Chess?'

'Of two moving castles,' said Mr Mellilow, 'and the dead body of a black crow.'

'A pretty piece of fused and inverted symbolism,' said the other. 'The dead body of a black crow become a dead man with a white rook.'

'But that came afterwards,' said the Chief Constable.

'So did the end-game with the two rooks,' said Mr Mellilow.

'Our friend's memory works both ways,' said the man with the monocle, 'like the White Queen's. She, by

337

the way, could believe as many as six impossible things before breakfast. So can I. Pharaoh tell your dream.'

'Time's getting on, Wimsey,' said the Chief Constable.

'Let time pass,' retorted the other, 'for, as a great chess-player observed, it helps more than reasoning.'

'What player was that?' demanded Mr Mellilow.

'A lady,' said Wimsey, 'who played with living men and mated kings, popes and emperors.'

'Oh,' said Mr Mellilow. 'Well—' he told his tale from the beginning, making no secret of his grudge against Creech and his nightmare fancy of the striding electric pylons. 'I think,' he said, 'that was what gave me the dream.' And he went on to his story of the goloshes, the bridge, the moving towers and death on the stairs at the Folly.

'A damned lucky dream for you,' said Wimsey. 'But I see now why they chose you. Look! it is all clear as daylight. If you had had no dream – if the murderer had been able to come back later and replace your goloshes – if someone else had found the body in the morning with the chess-rook beside it and your tracks leading back and home again, that might have been mate in one move. There are two men to look for, Superintendent. One of them belongs to Creech's household, for he knew that Creech came every Wednesday through the wicket gate to play chess with you; and he knew that Creech's chessmen and yours were twin sets. The other was a stranger – probably the man whom Creech half-expected to call upon him. One lay in wait for Creech and strangled him near the wicket gate as he arrived; fetched your goloshes from the verandah and carried the body down to the Folly. And the other came here in disguise to hold you in play and give you an alibi that no one could believe. The one man is strong in his hands and strong in the back – a sturdy, stocky man with feet no bigger than yours. The other is a big man, with noticeable eyes and probably clean-shaven, and he plays brilliant chess. Look among Creech's enemies for those two men and ask them where they were between eight o'clock and ten-thirty last night.'

'Why didn't the strangler bring back the goloshes?' asked the Chief Constable.

'Ah!' said Wimsey; 'that was where the plan went wrong. I think he waited up at the Folly to see the light go out in the cottage. He thought it would be too great a risk to come up twice on to the verandah while Mr Mellilow was there.'

'Do you mean,' asked Mr Mellilow, 'that he was there, *in* the Folly, watching me, when I was groping up those black stairs?'

'He may have been,' said Wimsey. 'But probably, when he saw you coming up the slope, he knew that things had gone wrong and fled away in the opposite direction, to the high road that runs behind the Folly. Mr Moses, of course, went, as he came, by the road that passes Mr Mellilow's door, removing his disguise in the nearest convenient place.'

'That's all very well, my lord,' said the superintendent, 'but where's the proof of it?'

'Everywhere,' said Wimsey. 'Go and look at the tracks again. There's one set going outwards in goloshes, deep and short, made when the body was carried down. One, made later, in walking shoes, which is Mr Mellilow's track going outwards towards the Folly. And the third is Mr Mellilow again, coming back, the track of a man running very fast. Two out and only one in. Where is the man who went out and never came back?'

'Yes,' said the superintendent, doggedly. 'But suppose Mr Mellilow made that second lot of tracks himself to put us off the scent, like? I'm not saying he did, mind you, but why couldn't he have?'

'Because,' said Wimsey, 'he had no time. The in-and-out tracks left by the shoes were made *after* the body was carried down. There is no other bridge for three miles on either side, and the river runs waist-deep. It can't be forded; so it must be crossed by the bridge. But at half-past ten, Mr Mellilow was in the Feathers, on *this* side of the river, ringing up the police. It couldn't be done, Super, unless he had wings. The bridge is there to prove it; for the bridge was crossed three times only.'

'The bridge,' said Mr Mellilow, with a great sigh. 'I knew in my dream there was something important about that. I knew I was safe if only I could get to the bridge.'

THE HAUNTED POLICEMAN

'Good god!' said his lordship. 'Did I do that?'

'All the evidence points that way,' replied his wife.

'Then I can only say that I never knew so convincing a body of evidence produce such an inadequate result.'

The nurse appeared to take this reflection personally. She said in a tone of rebuke:

'He's a *beautiful* boy.'

'H'm,' said Peter. He adjusted his eyeglass more carefully. 'Well, you're the expert witness. Hand him over.'

The nurse did so, with a dubious air. She was relieved to see that this disconcerting parent handled the child competently; as, in a man who was an experienced uncle, was not, after all, so very surprising. Lord Peter sat down gingerly on the edge of the bed.

'Do you feel it's up to standard?' he inquired with some anxiety. 'Of course, *your* workmanship's always sound – but you never know with these collaborate efforts.'

'I think it'll do,' said Harriet, drowsily.

'Good.' He turned abruptly to the nurse. 'All right; we'll keep it. Take it and put it away and tell 'em to invoice it to me. It's a very interesting addition to you, Harriet; but it would have been a hell of a rotten substitute.' His voice wavered a little, for the last twenty-four hours had been trying ones, and he had had the fright of his life.

The doctor, who had been doing something in the other room, entered in time to catch the last words.

'There was never any likelihood of that, you goop,' he said, cheerfully. 'Now, you've seen all there is to be seen, and you'd better run away and play.' He led his charge firmly to the door. 'Go to bed,' he advised him in kindly accents; 'you look all in.'

'I'm all right,' said Peter. 'I haven't been doing anything. And look here—' He stabbed a belligerent finger in the direction of the adjoining room. 'Tell those nurses of yours, if I want to pick my son up, I'll pick him up. If his mother wants to kiss him, she can damn well kiss him. I'll have none of your infernal hygiene in *my* house.'

'Very well,' said the doctor, 'just as you like. Anything for a quiet life. I rather believe in a few healthy germs myself. Builds up resistance. No, thanks, I won't have a drink. I've got to go on to another one, and an alcoholic breath impairs confidence.'

'Another one?' said Peter, aghast.

'One of my hospital mothers. You're not the only fish in the sea by a long chalk. One born every minute.'

'God! what a hell of a world.' They passed down the great curved stair. In the hall a sleepy footman clung, yawning, to his post of duty.

'All right, William,' said Peter. 'Buzz off now; I'll lock up.' He let the doctor out. 'Good-night – and thanks very much, old man. I'm sorry I swore at you.'

'They mostly do,' replied the doctor philosophically. 'Well, bung-ho, Flim. I'll look in again later, just to earn my fee, but I shan't be wanted. You've married into a good tough family, and I congratulate you.'

The car, spluttering and protesting a little after its long wait in the cold, drove off, leaving Peter alone on the doorstep. Now that it was all over and he could go to bed, he felt extraordinarily wakeful. He would have liked to go to a party. He leaned back against the wrought-iron railings and lit a cigarette, staring vaguely into the lamp-lit dusk of the square. It was thus that he saw the policeman.

The blue-uniformed figure came up from the direction of South Audley Street. He too was smoking and he walked, not with the firm tramp of a constable on his beat, but with the hesitating step of a man who has lost his bearings. When he came in sight, he had pushed back his helmet and was rubbing his head in a puzzled manner. Official habit made him look sharply at the bare-headed gentleman in evening dress, abandoned on a doorstep at three in the morning, but since the gentleman appeared to be sober and bore no signs of being about to commit a felony, he averted his gaze and prepared to pass on.

'Morning, officer,' said the gentleman, as he came abreast with him.

'Morning, sir,' said the policeman.

'You're off duty early,' pursued Peter, who wanted somebody to talk to. 'Come in and have a drink.'

This offer re-awakened all the official suspicion.

'Not just now, sir, thank you,' replied the policeman guardedly.

'Yes, now. That's the point.' Peter tossed away his cigarette-end. It described a fiery arc in the air and shot out a little train of sparks as it struck the pavement. 'I've got a son.'

'Oh, ah!' said the policeman, relieved by this innocent confidence. 'Your first, eh?'

'And last, if I know anything about it.'

'That's what my brother says, every time,' said the policeman. 'Never no more, he says. He's got eleven. Well, sir, good luck to it. I see how you're situated, and

I thank you kindly, but after what the sergeant said I dunno as I better. Though if I was to die this moment, not a drop 'as passed me lips since me supper beer.'

Peter put his head on one side and considered this.

'The sergeant said you were drunk?'

'He did, sir.'

'And you were not?'

'No, sir. I saw everything just the same as I told him, though what's become of it now is more than I can say. But drunk I was not, sir, no more than you are yourself.'

'Then,' said Peter, 'as Mr Joseph Surface remarked to Lady Teazle, what is troubling you is the consciousness of your own innocence. He insinuated that you had looked on the wine when it was red – you'd better come in and make it so. You'll feel better.'

The policeman hesitated.

'Well, sir, I dunno. Fact is, I've had a bit of a shock.'

'So've I,' said Peter. 'Come in for God's sake and keep me company.'

'Well, sir—' said the policeman again. He mounted the steps slowly.

The logs in the hall chimney were glowing a deep red through their ashes. Peter raked them apart, so that the young flame shot up between them. 'Sit down,' he said; 'I'll be back in a moment.'

The policeman sat down, removed his helmet, and stared about him, trying to remember who occupied the big house at the corner of the square. The engraved coat of arms upon the great silver bowl on the chimney-piece told him nothing, even though it was repeated in colour upon the backs of two tapestried chairs: three white mice skipping upon a black ground. Peter, returning quietly from the shadows beneath the

stair, caught him as he traced the outlines with a thick
finger.

'A student of heraldry?' he said. 'Seventeenth-
century work and not very graceful. You're new to this
beat, aren't you? My name's Wimsey.'

He put down a tray on the table.

'If you'd rather have beer or whisky, say so. These
bottles are only a concession to my mood.'

The policeman eyed the long necks and bulging
silver-wrapped corks with curiosity. 'Champagne?' he
said. 'Never tasted it, sir. But I'd like to try the stuff.'

'You'll find it thin,' said Peter, 'but if you drink
enough of it, you'll tell me the story of your life.' The
cork popped and the wine frothed out into the wide
glasses.

'Well!' said the policeman. 'Here's to your good lady,
sir, and the new young gentleman. Long life and all the
best. A bit in the nature of cider, ain't it, sir?'

'Just a trifle. Give me your opinion after the third
glass, if you can put up with it so long. And thanks for
your good wishes. You a married man?'

'Not yet, sir. Hoping to be when I get promotion. If
only the sergeant – but that's neither here nor there. You
been married long, sir, if I may ask.'

'Just over a year.'

'Ah! and do you find it comfortable, sir?'

Peter laughed.

'I've spent the last twenty-four hours wondering why,
when I'd had the blazing luck to get on to a perfectly
good thing, I should be fool enough to risk the whole
show on a damned silly experiment.'

The policeman nodded sympathetically.

'I see what you mean, sir. Seems to me, life's like
that. If you don't take risks, you get nowhere. If you do,

things may go wrong, and then where are you? And 'alf the time, when things happen, they happen first, before you can even think about 'em.'

'Quite right,' said Peter, and filled the glasses again. He found the policeman soothing. True to his class and training, he turned naturally in moments of emotion to the company of the common man. Indeed, when the recent domestic crisis had threatened to destroy his nerve, he had headed for the butler's pantry with the swift instinct of the homing pigeon. There, they had treated him with great humanity, and allowed him to clean the silver.

With a mind oddly clarified by champagne and lack of sleep, he watched the constable's reaction to Pol Roger 1926. The first glass had produced a philosophy of life; the second produced a name – Alfred Burt – and a further hint of some mysterious grievance against the station sergeant; the third glass, as prophesied, produced the story.

'You were right, sir' (said the policeman) 'when you spotted I was new to the beat. I only come on it at the beginning of the week, and that accounts for me not being acquainted with you, sir, nor with most of the residents about here. Jessop, now, he knows everybody and so did Pinker – but he's been took off to another division. You'd remember Pinker – big chap, make two o' me, with a sandy moustache. Yes, I thought you would.

'Well, sir, as I was saying, me knowing the district in a general way, but not, so to speak, like the palm o' me 'and, might account for me making a bit of a fool of myself, but it don't account for me seeing what I did see. See it I did, and not drunk nor nothing like it. And as for making a mistake in the number, well, that might happen to anybody. All the same, sir, 13 was the number I see, plain as the nose on your face.'

'You can't put it stronger than that,' said Peter, whose nose was of a kind difficult to overlook.

'You know Merriman's End, sir?'

'I think I do. Isn't it a long cul-de-sac running somewhere at the back of South Audley Street, with a row of houses on one side and a high wall on the other?'

'That's right, sir. Tall, narrow houses they are, all alike, with deep porches and pillars to them.'

'Yes. Like an escape from the worst square in Pimlico. Horrible. Fortunately, I believe the street was never finished, or we should have had another row of the monstrosities on the opposite side. This house is pure eighteenth century. How does it strike you?'

P.C. Burt contemplated the wide hall – the Adam fireplace and panelling with their graceful shallow mouldings, the pedimented doorways, the high round-headed window lighting hall and gallery, the noble proportions of the stair. He sought for a phrase.

'It's a gentleman's house,' he pronounced at length. 'Room to breathe, if you see what I mean. Seems like you couldn't act vulgar in it.' He shook his head. 'Mind you, I wouldn't call it cosy. It ain't the place I'd choose to sit down to a kipper in me shirtsleeves. But it's got class. I never thought about it before, but now you mention it I see what's wrong with them other houses in Merriman's End. They're sort of squeezed-like. I been into more'n one o' them tonight, and that's what they are; they're squeezed. But I was going to tell you about that.

'Just upon midnight it was' (pursued the policeman) 'when I turns into Merriman's End in the ordinary course of my dooties. I'd got pretty near down toward the far end, when I see a fellow lurking about in a suspicious way under the wall. There's back gates there, you know, sir, leading into some gardens, and this chap was hanging about inside one of the gateways. A rough-looking fellow, in a baggy old coat – might a' been a tramp off the Embankment. I turned my light on him – that street's not very well lit, and it's a dark night – but I couldn't see much of his face, because he had on a ragged old hat and a big scarf round his neck. I thought he was up to no good, and I was just about to ask him what he was doing there, when I hear a most awful yell come out o' one o' them houses opposite. Ghastly it was, sir. "Help!" it said. "Murder! help!", fit to freeze your marrow.'

'Man's voice or woman's?'

'Man's, sir. I think. More of a roaring kind of yell, if you take my meaning. I says, "Hullo! What's up there? Which house is it?" The chap says nothing, but he points, and him and me runs across together. Just as we gets to the house, there's a noise like as if someone was being strangled just inside, and a thump, as it might be something falling against the door.'

'Good God!' said Peter.

'I gives a shout and rings the bell. "Hoy!" I says. "What's up here?" and then I knocked on the door. There's no answer, so I rings and knocks again. Then the chap who was with me, he pushed open the letter-flap and squints through it.'

'Was there a light in the house?'

'It was all dark, sir, except the fanlight over the door. That was lit up bright, and when I looks up, I see the number of the house – number 13, painted plain as you like on the transom. Well, this chap peers in, and all of a sudden he gives a kind of gurgle and falls back.

"Here!" I says, "what's amiss? Let me have a look." So I puts me eye to the flap and I looks in.'

P.C. Burt paused and drew a long breath. Peter cut the wire of the second bottle.

'Now, sir,' said the policeman, 'believe me or believe me not, I was as sober at that moment as I am now. I can tell you everything I see in that house, same as if it was wrote up there on that wall. Not as it was a great lot, because the flap wasn't all that wide but by squinnying a bit, I could make shift to see right across the hall and a piece on both sides and part way up the stairs. And here's what I see, and you take notice of every word, on account of what come after.'

He took another gulp of the Pol Roger to loosen his tongue and continued:

'There was the floor of the hall. I could see that very plain. All black and white squares it was, like marble, and it stretched back a good long way. About half-way along, on the left, was the staircase, with a red carpet, and the figure of a white naked woman at the foot, carrying a big pot of blue and yellow flowers. In the wall next the stairs there was an open door, and a room all lit up. I could just see the end of a table, with a lot of glass and silver on it. Between that door and the front door there was a big black cabinet, shiny, with gold figures painted on it, like them things they had at the Exhibition. Right at the back of the hall there was a place like a conservatory, but I couldn't see what was in it, only it looked very gay. There was a door on the right, and that was open, too. A very pretty drawing-room, by what I could see of it, with pale blue paper and pictures on the walls. There were pictures in the hall, too, and a table on the right with a copper bowl, like as it might be for visitors' cards to be put in. Now,

I see all that, sir, and I put it to you, if it hadn't a' been there, how could I describe it so plain?'

'I have known people describe what wasn't there,' said Peter thoughtfully, 'but it was seldom anything of that kind. Rats, cats and snakes I have heard of, and occasionally naked female figures; but delirious lacquer cabinets and hall-tables are new to me.'

'As you say, sir,' agreed the policeman, 'and I see you believe me so far. But here's something else, what you mayn't find so easy. There was a man laying in that hall, sir, as sure as I sit here and he was dead. He was a big man and clean-shaven, and he wore evening dress. Somebody had stuck a knife into his throat. I could see the handle of it – it looked like a carving knife, and the blood had run out, all shiny, over the marble squares.'

The policeman looked at Peter, passed his handkerchief over his forehead, and finished the fourth glass of champagne.

'His head was up against the end of the hall table,' he went on, 'and his feet must have been up against the door, but I couldn't see anything quite close to me, because of the bottom of the letter-box. You understand, sir, I was looking through the wire cage of the box, and there was something inside – letters, I suppose that cut off my view downwards. But I see all the rest – in front and a bit of both sides; and it must have been regularly burnt in upon me brain, as they say, for I don't suppose I was looking more than a quarter of a minute or so. Then all the lights went out at once, same as if somebody has turned off the main switch. So I looks round, and I don't mind telling you I felt a bit queer. And *when* I looks round, lo and behold! my bloke in the muffler had hopped it.'

'The devil he had,' said Peter.

'Hopped it,' repeated the policeman, 'and there I was. And just there, sir, is where I made my big mistake, for I thought he couldn't a' got far, and I started off up the street after him. But I couldn't see him, and I couldn't see nobody. All the houses was dark, and it come over me what a sight of funny things may go on, and nobody take a mite o' notice. The way I'd shouted and banged on the door, you'd a' thought it'd a' brought out every soul in the street, not to mention that awful yelling. But there – you may have noticed it yourself, sir. A man may leave his ground-floor windows open, or have his chimney a' fire, and you may make noise enough to wake the dead, trying to draw his attention, and nobody give no heed. He's fast asleep, and the neighbours say, "Blast that row, but, it's no business of mine," and stick their 'eads under the bedclothes.'

'Yes,' said Peter. 'London's like that.'

'That's right, sir. A village is different. You can't pick up a pin there without somebody coming up to ask where you got it from – but London keeps itself to itself ... Well, something'll have to be done, I thinks to myself, and I blows me whistle. They heard that all right. Windows started to go up all along the street. That's London, too.'

Peter nodded. 'London will sleep through the last trump. Puddley-in-the-Rut and Doddering-in-the-Dumps will look down their noses and put on virtuous airs. But God, who is never surprised, will say to his angel, "Whistle up 'em, Michael, whistle 'em up; East and West will rise from the dead at the sound of the policeman's whistle".'

'Quite so, sir,' said P.C. Burt; and wondered for the first time whether there might not be something in this champagne stuff after all. He waited for a moment and then resumed:

'Well, it so happened that just when I sounded my whistle, Withers – that's the man on the other beat – was in Audley Square, coming to meet me. You know, sir, we has times for meeting one another, arranged different-like every night; and twelve o'clock in the square was our rendy-voos tonight. So up he comes in, you might say, no time at all, and finds me there, with everyone a' hollering at me from the windows to know what was up. Well, naturally, I didn't want the whole bunch of 'em running out into the street and our man getting away in the crowd, so I just tells 'em there's nothing, only a bit of an accident farther along. And then I see Withers and glad enough I was. We stands there at the top o' the street, and I tells him there's a dead man laying in the hall at Number 13, and it looks to me like murder. "Number 13," he says, "you can't mean Number 13. There ain't no Number 13 in Merriman's End, you fathead; it's all even numbers.' And so it is, sir, for the houses on the other side were never built, so there's no odd numbers at all barrin' Number 1, as is the big house on the corner.

'Well, that give me a bit of a jolt. I wasn't so much put out at not having remembered about the numbers, for as I tell you, I never was on the beat before this week. No; but I knew I'd seen that there number writ up plain as pie on the fanlight, and I didn't see how I could have been mistaken. But when Withers heard the rest of the story, he thought maybe I'd misread it for Number 12. It couldn't be 18, for there's only sixteen houses in the road; nor it couldn't be 16 neither, for I knew it wasn't the end house. But we thought it might be 12 or 10; so away we goes to look.

'We didn't have no difficulty about getting in at Number 12. There was a very pleasant old gentleman came down in his dressing-gown, asking what the disturbance was, and could he be of use. I apologised for disturbing him, and said I was afraid there'd been an accident in one of the houses, and had he heard anything. Of course, the minute he opened the door I could see it wasn't Number 12 we wanted; there was only a little hall with polished boards, and the walls plain panelled – all very bare and neat – and no black cabinet nor naked woman nor nothing. The old gentleman said, yes, his son had heard somebody shouting and knocking a few minutes earlier. He'd got up and put his head out of the window, but couldn't see nothing, but they both thought from the sound it was Number 14 forgotten his latch-key again. So we thanked him very much and went on to Number 14.

'We had a bit of a job to get Number 14 downstairs. A fiery sort of gentleman he was, something in the military way, I thought, but he turned out to be a retired Indian Civil Servant. A dark gentleman, with a big voice, and his servant was dark, too – some sort of a nigger. The gentleman wanted to know what the blazes all this row was about, why a decent citizen wasn't allowed to get his proper sleep. He supposed that young fool at Number 12 was drunk again. Withers had to speak a bit sharp to him; but at last the nigger came down and let us in. Well, we had to apologise once more. The hall was not a bit like – the staircase was on the wrong side, for one thing, and though there was a statue at the foot of it, it was some kind of a heathen idol with a lot of heads and arms, and the walls were covered with all sorts of brass stuff and native goods, you know the kind of thing. There was a black-and-white linoleum on the floor, and that was about all there was to it. The servant had a soft sort of way with him I didn't half like. He said he slept at the back and had heard nothing till his master rang for him. Then the gentleman came to the top of the stairs and shouted out it was no use disturbing him; the noise came from Number 12 as usual, and if that young man didn't stop his blanky Bohemian goings-on, he'd have the law on his father. I asked if he'd seen anything, and he said, no, he hadn't. Of course, sir, me and that other chap was inside the porch, and you can't see anything what goes on inside those porches from the other houses, because they're filled in at the sides with coloured glass – all the lot of them.'

Lord Peter Wimsey looked at the policeman and then looked at the bottle, as though estimating the alcoholic content of each. With deliberation, he filled both glasses again.

'Well, sir,' said P.C. Burt after refreshing himself, 'by this time Withers was looking at me in rather an old-fashioned manner. However, he said nothing, and we went back to Number 10, where there was two maiden ladies and a hall full of stuffed birds and wallpaper like a florists' catalogue. The one who slept in the front was deaf as a post, and the one who slept at the back hadn't heard nothing. But we got hold of their maids, and the cook said she'd heard the voice calling "Help!" and thought it was in Number 12, and she'd hid her head in the pillow and said her prayers. The housemaid was a sensible girl. She'd looked out when she heard me knocking. She couldn't see anything at first, owing to us being in the porch, but she thought something must be going on, so, not wishing to catch cold, she went back to put on her bedroom slippers. When she got back to the window, she was just in time to see a man running up the road. He went very quick and very silent, as if he had goloshes on, and she could see the ends of his muffler flying out behind him. She saw him run out of the street and turn to the right, and then she heard me coming along after him. Unfortunately, her eye being on the man, she didn't notice which porch I came out of. Well, that showed I wasn't inventing the whole story at any rate, because there was my bloke in the muffler. The girl didn't recognise him at all, but that wasn't surprising, because she'd only just entered the old ladies' service. Besides, it wasn't likely the man had anything to do with it, because he was outside with me when the yelling started. My belief is, he was the sort as doesn't care to have his pockets examined too close, and the minute my back was turned he thought he'd be better and more comfortable elsewhere.

'Now there ain't no need' (continued the policeman) 'for me to trouble you, sir, with all them houses what we went into. We made inquiries at the whole lot, from Number 2 to Number 16, and there wasn't one of them had a hall in any ways comfortable to what that chap and I saw through the letter-box. Nor there wasn't a soul in 'em could give us any help more than what we'd had already. You see, sir, though it took me a bit o' time telling, it all went very quick. There was the yells; they didn't last beyond a few seconds or so, and before they was finished, we was across the road and inside the porch. Then there was me shouting and knocking; but I hadn't been long at that afore the chap with me looks through the box. Then I has my look inside, for fifteen seconds it might be, and while I'm doing that, my chap's away up the street. Then I runs after him, and then I blows me whistle. The whole thing might take a minute or a minute and a half, maybe. Not more.

'Well, sir; by the time we'd been into every house in Merriman's End, I was feeling a bit queer again, I can tell you, and Withers, he was looking queerer. He says to me, "Burt," he says, "is this your idea of a joke? Because if so, the 'Olborn Empire's where you ought to be, not the police force." So I tells him over again, most solemn, what I seen – "and," I says, "if only we could lay hands on that chap in the muffler, he could tell you he seen it, too. And what's more," I says, "do you think I'd risk me job, playing a silly trick like that?" He says, "Well, it beats me," he says, "If I didn't know you was a sober kind of chap, I'd say you was seein' things." "Things?" I says to him, "I see that there corpse a-layin' there with the knife in' his neck, and that was enough for me. 'Orrible, he looked, and the blood all over the floor." "Well," he says, 'maybe he wasn't dead after all, and they've cleared him out of the way." "And cleared the house away, too, I suppose," I said to him. So Withers says, in an odd sort o' voice, "You're sure about the house? You wasn't letting your imagination run away with you over naked females and such?" That was a nice thing to say. I said. "No, I wasn't. There's been some monkey business going on in this street and I'm going to get to the bottom of it, if we has to comb-out London for that chap in the muffler." "Yes," says Withers, nasty-like, "it's a pity he cleared off so sudden." "Well," I says, "you can't say I imagined *him*, anyhow, because that there girl saw him, and a mercy she did," I said, "or you'd be saying next I ought to be in Colney Hatch." "Well," he says, "I dunno what you think you're going to do about it. You better ring up the station and ask for instructions."

'Which I did. And Sergeant Jones, he come down himself, and he listens attentive-like to what we both has to say. And then he walks along the street, slowlike, from end to end. And then he comes back and says to me, "Now, Burt," he says, "just you describe that hall to me again, careful." Which I does, same as I described it to your, sir. And he says, "You're sure there was the room on the left of the stairs with the glass and silver on the table; and the room on the right with the pictures in it?" And I says, "Yes, Sergeant, I'm quite sure of that." And Withers says, "Ah!" in a kind of got-you-now voice, if you take my meaning. And the sergeant says, "Now, Burt," he says, "pull yourself together and take a look at these here houses. Don't you see they're all single-fronted? There ain't one on 'em has rooms *both* sides o' the front hall. Look at the windows, you fool," he says.'

Lord Peter poured out the last of the champagne.

'I don't mind telling you, sir' (went on the policeman) 'that I was fair knocked silly to think of me never noticing that! Withers had noticed it all right, and that's what made him think I was drunk or barmy. But I stuck to what I'd seen. I said, there must be two of them houses knocked into one, somewhere, but that didn't work, because we'd been into all of them, and there wasn't no such thing – not without there was one o' them concealed doors like you read about in crook stories. "Well, anyhow," I says to the sergeant, "the yells was real all right, because other people heard 'em. Just you ask, and they'll tell you." So the sergeant says, "Well, Burt, I'll give you every chance." So he knocks up Number 12 again – not wishing to annoy Number 14 any more than he was already – and this time the son comes down. An agreeable gentleman he was, too; not a bit put out. He says, Oh, yes, he'd heard the yells and his father'd heard them too. "Number 14," he says, "that's where the trouble is. A very odd bloke, is Number 14, and I shouldn't be surprised if he beats that unfortunate servant of his. The Englishman abroad, you know! The outposts of Empire and all that kind of thing. They're rough and ready – and then the curry in them parts is bad for the liver." So I was for inquiring at Number 14 again; but the sergeant, he loses patience, and says, "You know quite well," he says, "it ain't Number 14, and in my opinion, Burt, you're either dotty or drunk. You best go home straight away," he says, "and sober up, and I'll see you again when you can give a better account of yourself." So I argues a bit, but it ain't no use, and away he goes, and Withers goes back to his beat. And I walks up and down a bit till Jessop comes to take over, and then I comes away, and that's when I sees you, sir.

'But I ain't drunk, sir – at least, I wasn't then, though there do seem to be a kind of a swimming in me head at this moment. Maybe that stuff's stronger than it tastes. But I wasn't drunk then, and I'm pretty sure I'm not dotty. I'm haunted, sir, that's what it is – haunted. It might be there was someone killed in one of them houses many years ago, and that's what I see tonight. Perhaps they changed the numbering of the street on account of it – I've heard tell of such things – and when the same night comes round the house goes back to what it was before. But there I am, with a black mark against me, and it ain't a fair trick for no ghost to go getting a plain man into trouble. And I'm sure, sir, you'll agree with me.'

The policeman's narrative had lasted some time, and the hands of the grandfather clock stood at a quarter to five. Peter Wimsey gazed benevolently at his companion, for whom he was beginning to feel a positive affection. He was, if anything, slightly more drunk than the policeman, for he had missed tea and had no appetite for his dinner; but the wine had not clouded his wits; it had only increased excitability and postponed sleep. He said:

'When you looked through the letter-box, could you see any part of the ceiling, or the lights?'

'No, sir; on account, you see, of the flap. I could see right and left and straight forward; but not upwards, and none of the near part of the floor.'

'When you looked at the house from outside, there was no light except through the fanlight. But when you looked through the flap, all the rooms were lit, right and left and at the back?'

'That's so, sir.'

'Are there back doors to the houses?'

'Yes, sir. Coming out of Merriman's End, you turn to the right, and there's an opening a little way along which takes you to the back doors.'

'You seem to have a very distinct visual memory. I wonder if your other kinds of memory are as good. Can you tell me, for instance, whether any of the houses you went into had any particular smell? Especially 10, 12 and 14?'

'Smell, sir?' The policeman closed his eyes to stimulate recollection. 'Why, yes, sir. Number 10, where the two ladies live, that had a sort of an old-fashioned smell. I can't put me tongue to it. Not lavender – but something as ladies keeps in bowls and such – rose-leaves and what not. Pot-pourri, that's the stuff. Pot-pourri. And Number 12 – well, no there was nothing particular there, except I remember thinking they must keep pretty good servants, though we didn't see anybody except the family. All that floor and panelling was polished beautiful – you could see your face in it. Beeswax and turpentine, I says to meself. And elbow-grease.

What you'd call a clean house with a good, clean smell. But Number 14 – that was different. I didn't like the smell of that. Stuffy, like as if the nigger had been burning some o' that there incense to his idols, maybe. I never could abide niggers.'

'Ah!' said Peter. 'What you say is very suggestive.' He placed his finger-tips together and shot his last question over them:

'Ever been inside the National Gallery?'

'No, sir,' said the policeman, astonished. 'I can't say as I ever was.'

'That's London again,' said Peter. 'We're the last people in the world to know anything of our great metropolitan institutions. Now, what is the best way to tackle this bunch of toughs, I wonder? It's a little early for a call. Still, there's nothing like doing one's good deed before breakfast, and the sooner you're set right with the sergeant, the better. Let me see. Yes – I think that may do it. Costume pieces are not as a rule in my line, but my routine has been so much upset already, one way and another, that an irregularity more or less will hardly matter. Wait there for me while I have a bath and change. I may be a little time; but it would hardly be decent to get there before six.'

The bath had been an attractive thought, but was perhaps ill-advised, for a curious languor stole over him with the touch of the hot water. The champagne was losing its effervescence. It was with an effort that he dragged himself out and re-awakened himself with a cold shower. The matter of dress required a little thought. A pair of grey flannel trousers was easily found, and though they were rather too well creased for the part he meant to play, he thought that with luck they would probably pass unnoticed. The shirt was a difficulty. His collection of shirts was a notable one, but they were mostly of an inconspicuous and gentlemanly sort. He hesitated for some time over a white shirt with an open sports collar, but decided at length upon a blue one, bought as an experiment and held to be not quite successful. A red tie, if he had possessed such a thing, would have been convincing. After some consideration, he remembered that he had seen his wife in a rather wide Liberty tie, whose prevailing colour was orange. That, he felt, would do if he could find it. On her it had looked rather well; on him, it would be completely abominable. He went through into the next room; it was queer to find it empty. A peculiar sensation came over him. Here *he* was, rifling his wife's drawers, and there *she* was, spirited out of reach at the top of the house with a couple of nurses and an entirely new baby, which might turn into goodness knew what. He sat down before the glass and stared at himself. He felt as though he ought to have changed somehow in the night; but he only looked unshaven and, he thought, a trifle intoxicated. Both were quite good things to look at the moment, though hardly suitable for the father of a family. He pulled out all the drawers in the dressing table; they emitted vaguely familiar smells of face-powder and handkerchief-sachet. He tried the big built-in wardrobe: frocks, costumes and trays full of underwear, which made him feel sentimental. At last he struck a promising vein of gloves and stockings. The next tray held ties, the orange of the desired Liberty creation gleaming in a friendly way among them. He put it on, and observed with pleasure that the effect was Bohemian beyond description. He wandered out again, leaving all the drawers open behind him as though a burglar had passed through the room. An ancient tweed jacket of his own, of a very countrified pattern, suitable only for fishing in Scotland, was next unearthed, together with a pair of brown canvas shoes. He secured his trousers by a belt, searched for and found an old soft-brimmed felt hat of no recognisable colour, and, after removing a few trout-flies from the hat-band and tucking his shirt-sleeves well up inside the coat-sleeve, decided that he would do. As an afterthought, he returned to his wife's room and selected a wide woollen scarf in a shade of greenish blue. Thus equipped, he came downstairs again, to find P.C. Burt fast asleep, with his mouth open and snoring.

Peter was hurt. Here he was, sacrificing himself in the interests of this stupid policeman, and the man hadn't the common decency to appreciate it. However, there was no point in waking him yet. He yawned horribly and sat down.

It was the footman who wakened the sleepers at half-past six. If he was surprised to see his master, very strangely attired, slumbering in the hall in company with a large policeman, he was too well-trained to admit the fact even to himself. He merely removed the tray. The faint chink of glass roused Peter, who slept like a cat at all times.

'Hullo, William,' he said. 'Have I overslept myself? What's the time?'

'Five and twenty to seven, my lord.'

'Just about right.' He remembered that the footman slept on the top floor. 'All quiet on the Western Front, William?'

'Not altogether quiet, my lord.' William permitted himself a slight smile. 'The young master was lively about five. But all is satisfactory, I gather from Nurse Jenkyn.'

'Nurse Jenkyn? Is that the young one? Don't let yourself be run away with, William. I say, just give P.C. Burt a light prod in the ribs, would you? He and I have business together.'

In Merriman's End, the activities of the morning were beginning. The milkman came jingling out of the cul-de-sac; lights were twinkling in upper rooms; hands were withdrawing curtains; in front of Number 10, the house maid was already scrubbing the steps. Peter posted his policeman at the top of the street.

'I don't want to make my first appearance with official accompaniment,' he said. 'Come along when I beckon. What by the way is the name of the agreeable gentleman in Number 12? I think he may be of some assistance to us.'

'Mr O'Halloran, sir.'

The policeman looked at Peter expectantly. He seemed to have abandoned all initiative and to place implicit confidence in this hospitable and eccentric gentleman. Peter slouched down the street with his hands in his trousers pocket and his shabby hat pulled rakishly over his eyes. At Number 12 he paused and examined the windows. Those on the ground floor were open; the house was awake. He marched up the steps, took a brief glance through the flap of the letter-box, and rang the bell. A maid in a neat blue dress and white cap and apron opened the door.

'Good morning,' said Peter, slightly raising the shabby hat; 'is Mr O'Halloran in?' He gave the *r* a soft continental roll. 'Not the old gentleman. I mean young Mr O'Halloran?'

'He's in,' said the maid, doubtfully, 'but he isn't up yet.'

'Oh!' said Peter. 'Well it is a little early for a visit. But I desire to see him urgently. I am – there is a little trouble where I live. Could you entreat him – would you be so kind? I have walked all the way,' he added, pathetically, and with perfect truth.

'Have you, sir?' said the maid. She added kindly, 'You do look tired, sir, and that's a fact.'

'It is nothing,' said Peter. 'It is only that I forgot to have any dinner. But if I can see Mr O'Halloran it will be all right.'

'You'd better come in, sir,' said the maid. 'I'll see if I can wake him.' She conducted the exhausted stranger in and offered him a chair. 'What name shall I say, sir?'

'Petrovinsky,' said his lordship, hardily. As he had rather expected, neither the unusual name nor the unusual clothes of this unusually early visitor seemed to cause very much surprise. The maid left him in the tidy little panelled hall and went upstairs without so much as a glance at the umbrella-stand.

Left to himself, Peter sat still, noticing that the hall was remarkably bare of furniture, and was lit by a single electric pendant almost immediately inside the front door. The letter-box was the usual wire cage the bottom of which had been carefully lined with brown paper. From the back of the house came a smell of frying bacon.

Presently there was the sound of somebody running downstairs. A young man appeared in a dressing-gown. He called out as he came: 'Is that you, Stefan? Your name came up as Mr Whisky. Has Marfa run away again, or – What the hell? Who the devil are you, sir?'

'Wimsey,' said Peter, mildly, 'not Whisky; Wimsey the policeman's friend. I just looked in to congratulate you on a mastery of the art of false perspective which I thought had perished with van Hoogstraten, or at least with Grace and Lambelet.'

'Oh!' said the young man. He had a pleasant countenance, with humorous eyes and ears pointed like a faun's. He laughed a little ruefully. 'I suppose my beautiful murder is out. It was too good to last. Those bobbies! I hope to God they gave Number 14 a bad night. May I ask how you come to be involved in the matter?'

'I,' said Peter, 'am the kind of person in whom distressed constables confide – I cannot imagine why. And when I had the picture of that sturdy blue-clad figure, led so persuasively by a Bohemian stranger and invited to peer through a hole, I was irresistibly transported in mind to the National Gallery. Many a time have I squinted sideways through those holes into the little black box, and admired that Dutch interior of many vistas painted so convincingly on the four flat sides of the box. How right you were to preserve your eloquent silence! Your Irish tongue would have given you away. The servants, I gather, were purposely kept out of sight.'

'Tell me,' said Mr O'Halloran, seating himself sideways upon the hall table, 'do you know by heart the occupation of every resident in this quarter of London? I do not paint under my own name.'

'No,' said Peter. 'Like the good Dr Watson, the constable could observe, though he could not reason from his observation; it was the smell of turpentine that betrayed you. I gather that at the time of his first call the apparatus was not very far off.'

'It was folded together and lying under the stairs,' replied the painter. 'It has since been removed to the studio. My father had only just had time to get it out of the way and hitch down the "13" from the fanlight before the police reinforcements arrived. He had not even time to put back this table I am sitting on; a brief search would have discovered it in the dining room. My father is a remarkable sportsman; I cannot too highly recommend the presence of mind he displayed while I was hareing around the houses and leaving him to hold the fort. It would have been so simple and so unenterprising to explain; but my father, being an Irishman, enjoys treading on the coat-tails of authority.'

'I should like to meet your father. The only thing I do not thoroughly understand is the reason of this elaborate plot. Were you by any chance executing a burglary round the corner, and keeping the police in play while you did it?'

'I never thought of that,' said the young man, with regret in his voice. 'No. The bobby was not the predestined victim. He happened to be present at a full-dress rehearsal, and the joke was too good to be lost. The fact is, my uncle is Sir Lucius Preston, the R.A.'

'Ah!' said Peter, 'the light begins to break.'

'My own style of draughtsmanship,' pursued Mr O'Halloran, 'is modern. My uncle has on several occasions informed me that I draw like that only because I do not know how to draw. The idea was that he should be invited to dinner tomorrow and regaled with a story of the mysterious "Number 13", said to appear from time to time in this street and to be haunted by strange noises. Having thus detained him till close upon midnight, I should have set out to see him to the top of the street. As we went along, the cries would have broken out. I should have led him back—'

'Nothing,' said Peter, 'could be more clear. After the preliminary shock, he would have been forced to confess that your draughtsmanship was a triumph of academic accuracy.'

'I hope,' said Mr O'Halloran, 'the performance may still go forward as originally intended.' He looked with some anxiety at Peter, who replied:

'I hope so, indeed. I also hope that your uncle's heart is a strong one. But may I, in the meantime, signal to my unfortunate policeman and relieve his mind? He is in danger of losing his promotion, through a suspicion that he was drunk on duty.'

'Good God!' said Mr O'Halloran. 'No – I don't want that to happen. Fetch him in.'

The difficulty was to make P.C. Burt recognise in the daylight what he had seen by night through the letter-flap. Of the framework of painted canvas, with its forms and figures oddly foreshortened and distorted, he could make little. Only when the thing was set up and lighted in the curtained studio was he at length reluctantly convinced.

'It's wonderful,' he said. 'It's like Maskelyne and Devant. I wish the sergeant could a' seen it.'

'Lure him down here tomorrow night,' said Mr O'Halloran. 'Let him come as my uncle's bodyguard. You—' he turned to Peter – 'you seem to have a way with policemen. Can't you inveigle the fellow along? Your impersonation of starving and disconsolate Bloomsbury is fully as convincing as mine. How about it?'

'I don't know,' said Peter. 'The costume gives me pain. Besides, is it kind to a p.b. policeman? I give you the R.A., but when it comes to the guardians of the law – Damn it all! I'm a family man, and I must have *some* sense of responsibility.'

TALBOYS

'Father!'

'Yes, my son.'

'You know those peaches of Mr Puffett's, the whacking great big ones you said I wasn't to take?'

'Well?'

'Well, I've tooken them.'

Lord Peter Wimsey rolled over on his back and stared at his offspring in consternation. His wife laid down her sewing.

'Oh, Bredon, how naughty! Poor Mr Puffett was going to exhibit them at the Flower-Show.'

'Well, Mummy, I didn't mean to. It was a dare.'

Having offered this explanation for what it was worth, Master Bredon Wimsey again turned candid eyes upon his father, who groaned and sat up.

'And *must* you come and tell me about it? I hope, Bredon, you are not developing into a prig.'

'Well, Father, Mr Puffett saw me. An' he's coming up to have a word with you when he's put on a clean collar.'

'Oh, I see,' said his lordship, relieved. 'And you thought you'd better come and get it over before my temper became further inflamed by hearing his version of the matter?'

'Yes, please, sir.'

'That is rational, at any rate. Very well, Bredon. Go up into my bedroom and prepare for execution. You will find the cane behind the dressing-table.'

'Yes, Father. You won't be long, will you, sir?'

'I shall allow precisely the right time for apprehension and remorse. Off with you!'

The culprit vanished hastily in the direction of the house; the executioner heaved himself to his feet and followed at a leisurely pace, rolling up his sleeves as he went with a certain grimness.

'My dear!' exclaimed Miss Quirk. She gazed in horror through her spectacles at Harriet, who had placidly returned to her patchwork. 'Surely, *surely* you don't allow him to cane that mite of a child.'

'Allow?' said Harriet, amused. 'That's hardly the right word, is it?'

'But Harriet, dear, he oughtn't to do it. You don't realise how dangerous it is. He may ruin the boy's character for life. One must reason with these little people, not break their spirits by brutality. When you inflict pain and humiliation on a child like that, you make him feel helpless and inferior, and all that suppressed resentment will break out later in the most extraordinary and shocking ways.'

'Oh, I don't think he resents it,' said Harriet. 'He's devoted to his father.'

'Well, if he is,' retorted Miss Quirk, 'it must be a sort of masochism, and it ought to be stopped – I mean, it ought to be led gently into some other direction. It's unnatural. How could anyone feel a *healthy* devotion for a person who beats him?'

'I can't think; but it often seems to happen. Peter's mother used to lay into him with a slipper, and they've always been the best of friends.'

'If I had a child belonging to me,' said Miss Quirk, 'I would never permit anybody to lay a hand on him. All my little nephews and nieces have been brought up on enlightened modern lines. They never even hear the word, Don't. Now, you see what happens. Just *because* your boy was told *not* to pick the peaches, he picked them. If he hadn't been forbidden to do it, he wouldn't have been disobedient.'

'No,' said Harriet. 'I suppose that's quite true. He would have picked the peaches just the same, but it wouldn't have been disobedience.'

'Exactly,' cried Miss Quirk, triumphantly. 'You see – you manufacture a crime and then punish the poor child for it. Besides, if it hadn't been for the prohibition, he'd have left the fruit alone.'

'You don't know Bredon. He never leaves anything alone.'

'Of course not,' said Miss Quirk, 'and, he never will, so long as you surround him with prohibitions. His meddling with what doesn't belong to him is just an act of defiance.'

'He's not defiant very often,' said Harriet, 'but of course it's very difficult to refuse a dare from a big boy like George Waggett. I expect it was George; it usually is.'

'No doubt,' observed Miss Quirk, 'the village children are all brought up in an atmosphere of fault-finding and defiance. That kind of thing is contagious. Democratic principles are all very well, but I should scarcely have thought it wise to expose your little boy to contamination.'

'Would you forbid him to play with George Waggett?'

'I should never *forbid* anything. I should endeavour to suggest some more suitable companion. Bredon could be encouraged to look after his little brother; that would give him a useful outlet for his energies and allow him to feel himself important.'

'Oh, but he's really very good with Roger,' said Harriet, equably. She looked up, to see chastiser and chastised emerging from the house, hand in hand. 'They seem to be quite good friends. Bredon was rather uplifted when he was promoted to a cane; he thinks it dignified and grown-up . . . Well, ruffian, how many did you get?'

'Three,' said Master Bredon, confidentially. 'Awful hard ones. One for being naughty, an' one for being young ass enough to be caught, and one for making a 'fernal nuisance of myself on a hot day.'

'Oh, dear,' said Miss Quick, appalled by the immorality of all this. 'And are you sorry for having taken poor Mr Puffett's peaches, so that he can't get a prize at the Show.'

Bredon looked at her in astonishment.

'We've done all that,' he said, with a touch of indignation. His father thought it well to intervene.

'It's a rule in this household,' he announced, 'that once we've been whacked, nothing more can be said. The topic is withdrawn from circulation.'

'Oh,' said Miss Quirk. She still felt that something ought to be done to compensate the victim of brutality and relieve his repressions. 'Well, as you're a good boy, would you like to come and sit on my knee?'

'No thank you,' said Bredon. Training, or natural politeness, prompted him to amplify the refusal. 'Thank you very much all the same.'

'A more tactless suggestion,' said Peter, 'I never heard.' He dropped into a deck-chair, picked up his son and heir by the waist-belt and slung him face downwards across his knees. 'You'll have to eat your tea on all-fours, like Nebuchadnezzar.'

'Who was Nebuchadnezzar?'

'Nebuchadnezzar, the King of the Jews—' began Peter. His version of that monarch's inquities was interrupted by the appearance, from behind the house, of a stout figure, unsuitably clad for the season in sweater, corduroy trousers and bowler hat. 'The curse is come upon me, cried the Lady of Shalott.'

'Who was the Lady of Shalott?'

'I'll tell you at bedtime. Here is Mr Puffett, breathing out threatenings and slaughter. We must now stand up and face the music. Afternoon, Puffett.'

'Arternoon, me lord and me lady,' said Mr Puffett. He removed his bowler and mopped his streaming brow. 'And miss,' he added, with a vague gesture in Miss Quirk's direction. 'I made bold, me lord, to come round—'

'That,' said Peter, 'was very kind of you. Otherwise, of course, we should have come to see you and say we were sorry. We were overcome by a sudden irresistible impulse, attributable, we think, to the beauty of the fruit and the exciting nature of the enterprise. We hope very much that we have left enough for the Flower-Show, and we will be careful not to do it again. We should like to mention that a measure of justice has already been done, in the shape of three of the juiciest, but if there is anything further coming to us, we shall try to receive it in a becoming spirit of penitence.'

'Well, there!' said Mr Puffett. 'If I didn't say to Jinny, "Jinny," I says, "I 'ope the young gentleman doesn't tell 'is lordship. He'll be main angry," I says, "and I wouldn't wonder if 'e didn't wallop 'im." "Oh Dad," she says, "run up quick, never mind your Sunday coat, and tell 'is lordship as 'e didn't take only two peaches and there's plenty left," she says. So I comes as quick as I can, only I 'ad ter wash, what with doin' out the

pigstyes, and jest to put on a clean collar; but not bein'
as young as I was, and gettin' stout-like, I don't get up
the 'ill as quick as I might. There wasn't no call to
thrash the young gentleman, me lord, me 'avin' caught
'im afore much 'arm was done. Boys will be boys – and
I'll lay what you like it was some of them other young
devils put 'im up to it, begging your pardon, me lady.'

'Well, Bredon,' said his father; 'it's very kind of Mr
Puffett to take that view of it. Suppose you go with him
up to the house and ask Bunter to draw him a glass of
beer. And on the way, you may say whatever your good
feeling may suggest.'

He waited till the oddly-assorted couple were half-
way across the lawn, and then called 'Puffett?'

'Me lord?' said Mr Puffett, returning alone.

'Was there really much damage done?'

'No, me lord. Only two peaches, like I said. I jest
popped out from be'ind the potting-shed in time, and
'e was off like one o'clock.'

'Thank heaven! From what he said, I was afraid he
had wolfed the lot. And, look here, Puffett. Don't ask
him who put him up to it. I shouldn't imagine he'd tell,
but he might fancy he was a bit of a hero for refusing.'

'I get you,' said Mr Puffett. ''E's a proper 'igh-
sperrited young gentleman, ain't 'e?' He winked, and
went ponderously to rejoin his penitent robber.

The episode was considered closed; and everybody
(except Miss Quirk) was surprised when Mr Puffett
arrived next morning at breakfast-time and announced
without preliminary:

'Beg pardon, me lord, but all my peaches 'as bin took
in the night, and I'd be glad to know 'oo done it.'

'All your peaches taken, Puffett?'

'Every blessed one on 'em, me lord, practically speakin'. And the Flower-Show ter-morrer.'

'Coo!' said Master Bredon. He looked up from his plate, and found Miss Quirk's eye fixed upon him.

'That's a dirty trick,' said his lordship. 'Have you any idea who it was? Or would you like me to come and look into the matter for you?'

Mr Puffett turned his bowler hat slowly over between his large hands.

'Not wishin' yer lordship ter put yourself out,' he said slowly. 'But it jest crossed me mind as summun at the 'ouse might be able ter throw light, as it were, upon the subjick.'

'I shouldn't think so,' said Peter, 'but it's easy to ask. Harriet, do you by any chance know anything about the disappearance of Puffett's peaches?'

Harriet shook her head.

'Not a thing. Roger, dear, please eat your egg not quite so splashily. You've given yourself a moustache like Mr Billing's.'

'Can you give us any help, Bredon?'

'No.'

'No, what?'

'No, sir. Please, Mummy, may I get down?'

'Just a minute, darling. You haven't folded up your napkin.'

'Oh, sorry.'

'Miss Quirk?'

Miss Quirk was so much aghast at hearing this flat denial, that she had remained staring at the eldest Master Wimsey, and started on hearing herself addressed.

'Do *I* know anything? Well!' She hesitated. 'Now, Bredon, am I to tell Daddy? Wouldn't you rather do it yourself?' Bredon shot a quick look at his father, but made no answer. That was only to be expected. Beat a child, and you make him a liar and a coward. 'Come now,' said Miss Quirk, coaxingly, 'it would be *ever* so much nicer and better and braver to own up, don't you think? It'll make Mummy and Daddy very very sad if you leave it to *me* to tell them.'

'To tell us what?' inquired Harriet.

'My dear Harriet,' said Miss Quirk, annoyed by this foolish question, 'if I tell you *what*, then I've told you, haven't I? And I'm quite *sure* Bredon would much rather tell you himself.'

'Bredon,' said his father, 'have you any idea what Miss Quirk thinks you ought to tell us? Because, if so, you could tell us and we could get on.'

'No, sir. I don't know anything about Mr Puffett's peaches. May I get down *now*, Mummy, please?'

'Oh, Bredon!' cried Miss Quirk, reproachfully. 'When I saw you, you know, with my own eyes! Ever so early – at five o'clock this morning. Now, won't you say what you were doing?'

'Oh, that!' said Bredon; and blushed. Mr Puffett scratched his head.

'What were you doing?' asked Harriet, gently. 'Not anything naughty, darling, were you? Or is it a secret?'

Bredon nodded. 'Yes, it's a secret. Something we were doing.' He sighed. 'I don't think it's naughty, Mum.'

'I expect it is though,' said Peter in a resigned tone. 'Your secrets so often are. Quite unintentionally, no doubt, but they do have a tendency that way. Be warned in time, Bredon, and undo it, or stop doing it, before I discover it. I understand it had nothing to do with Mr Puffett's peaches?'

'Oh, no, Father. Please, Mummy, may I—'

'Yes, dear, you may get down. But you must ask Miss Quirk to excuse you.'

'Please, Miss Quirk, will you excuse me?'

'Yes, certainly,' said Miss Quirk in a mournful tone. Bredon scrambled down hastily, said, 'I'm *very* sorry about your peaches, Mr Puffett,' and made his escape.

'I am sorry to have to say it,' said Miss Quirk, 'but I think, Mr Puffett, you will find your peaches in the woodshed. I woke up early this morning, and I saw Bredon and another little boy crossing the yard, carrying something between them in a bucket. I waved at them from the window, and they hurried off to the woodshed in what I *can* only call a furtive kind of way.'

'Well, Puffett,' said his lordship, 'I'm sorry about this. Shall I come up and take a look at the place? Or do you wish to search the woodshed? I am quite sure you will not find your peaches there, though I should hesitate to say what else you might not find.'

'I'd be grateful,' replied Mr Puffett, 'to 'ave yer advice, me lord, if so be as you could spare the time. What beats me, it's a wide bed, and yet there ain't no footprints, in a manner of speaking, except as it might be young master's, there. Which, footprints bein' in a manner your lordship's walk in life, I made bold to come. But, Master Bredon 'avin' said it weren't 'im, I reckon them marks'll be wot 'e left yesterday, though 'ow a man or a boy either could cross that there bed of damp earth and not leave no sign of 'imself, unless 'e wos a bird, is more than I can make out, nor Jinny neither.'

Mr Tom Puffett was proud of his walled garden. He had built the wall himself (for he was a builder by trade), and it was a handsome brick structure, ten feet high, and topped on all four sides with a noble parapet of broken bottle-glass. The garden lay on the opposite side of the road from the little house where its owner lived with his daughter and son-in-law, and possessed a solid wooden gate, locked at night with a padlock. On either side of it were flourishing orchards; at the back ran a deeply rutted lane, still muddy – for the summer, up to the last few days, had been a wet one.

'That there gate,' said Mr Puffett, 'was locked last night at nine o'clock as ever is, 'an it was still locked when I came in at seven this mornin'; so 'ooever done it 'ad to climb this yer wall.'

'So I see,' replied Lord Peter. 'My demon child is of tender years; still, I admit that he is capable of almost anything, when suitably inspired and assisted. But I don't think he would have done it after yesterday's little incident, and I am positive that if he had done it, he'd have said so.'

Reckon you're right,' agreed Mr Puffett, unlocking the door, 'though when I was a nipper like 'im, if I'd 'ad that old woman a-joring' at me, I'd a' said anythink.'

'So'd I,' said Peter. 'She's a friend of my sister-in-law's, said to need a country holiday. I feel we shall all shortly need a town holiday. Your plums seem to be doing well. H'm. A pebble path isn't the best medium for showing footprints.'

'That it's not,' admitted Mr Puffett. He led the way between the neat flower and vegetable beds to the far end of the garden. Here at the foot of the wall was a border about nine feet wide, the middle section of which was empty except for some rows of late-sown peas. At the back, trained against the wall, stood the peach-tree, on which one great, solitary fruit glowed rosily among the dark leafage. Across the bed ran a double line of small footprints.

'Did you hoe this bed over after my son's visit yesterday?'

'No, my lord.'

'Then he hasn't been here since. Those are his marks all right – I ought to know; I see enough of them on my own flower-beds.' Peter's mouth twitched a little. 'Look! He came very softly, trying most honorably not to tread on the peas. He pinched a peach and bolted it where he stood. I enquire, with a parent's natural anxiety, whether he ejected the stone, and observe, with relief, that he did. He moved on, he took a second peach, you popped out from the potting-shed, he started like a guilty thing and ran off in a hurry – this time, I am sorry to see, trampling on the peas. I hope he deposited the second peach-stone somewhere. Well, Puffett, you're right; there are no other footprints. Could the thief have put down a plank and walked on that, I wonder?'

'There's no planks here,' said Mr Puffett, 'except the little 'un I uses meself for bedding-out. That's three feet long or thereabouts. Would yer like ter look at it, me lord?'

'No good. A little reflection shows that one cannot cross a nine-foot bed on a three-foot plank without shifting the plank, and that one cannot at the same time stand on the plank and shift it. You're sure there's only one? Yes? Then that's washed out.'

'Could 'e a' brought one with 'im?'

'The orchard walls are high and hard, to climb even without the additional encumbrance of a nine-foot plank. Besides, I'm almost sure no plank has been used. I think, if it had, the edges would have left some mark. No, Puffett, nobody crossed this bed. By the way, doesn't it strike you as odd that the thief should have left just one big peach behind? It's pretty conspicuous.

Was that done merely to point the joke? Or – wait a minute, what's that?'

Something had caught his eye at the back of the box border, some dozen feet to the right of where they were standing. He picked it up. It was a peach; firm and red and not quite ripe. He stood weighing it thoughtfully in his hand.

'Having picked the peach, he found it wasn't ripe and chucked it away in a temper. Is that likely, Puffett, do you think? And unless I'm mistaken, there are quite a number of green leaves scattered about the foot of the tree. How often, when one picks a peach, does one break off the leaves as well?

He looked expectantly at Mr Puffett, who returned no answer.

'I think,' went on Peter, 'we will go and have a look in the lane.'

Immediately behind the wall ran a rough grass verge. Mr Puffett, leading the way to this, was peremptorily waved back, and was thereafter treated to a fine exposition of detective work in the traditional manner; his lordship, extended on his stomach, thrusting his long nose and long fingers delicately through each successive tuft of grass, Mr Puffett himself, stooping with legs well apart and hands on knees, peering anxiously at him from the edge of the lane. Presently the sleuth sat up on his heels and said:

'Here you are, Puffett. There were two men. They came up the lane from the direction of the village, wearing hob-nailed boots and carrying a ladder between them. They set up the ladder *here*; the grass, you see, is still a little bent, and there are two deepish dents in the soil. One man climbed to the top and took the peaches, while the other, I think, stood at the foot to keep guard and receive the fruit in a bag or basket or something. This isn't a case of larking youngsters, Puffett; from the length of the strides they were grown men. What enemies have you made in your harmless career? Or who are your chief rivals in the peach class?'

'Well, there,' said Mr Puffett, slowly. 'There's the Vicar shows peaches, and Dr Jellyband from Great Pagford, and Jack Baker – he's the policeman, you know, came when Joe Sellon went off to Canada. And there's old Critch; him and me had a dispute about a chimbley. And Maggs the blacksmith –'e didn't 'arf like it w'en I wiped 'is eye last year with me vegetable marrers. Oh, and Waggett the butcher, 'e shows peaches. But I dunno as any o' them 'ud do me a turn like this 'ere. But 'ere, me lord, 'ow did they *get* the peaches? They couldn't reach 'em from the top of the ladder, nor yet off the wall, let alone sitting on them there bottles. The top o' the tree's five foot below the top o' the wall.'

'That's simple,' said Peter. 'Think of the broken leaves and the peach in the box border, and consider how *you* would have done it. By the way, if you want proof that the robbing was done from this side, get a ladder and look over. I'll lay you anything you like, you'll find that the one peach that was left is hidden by the leaves from anybody looking *down* on it, though it's clearly enough seen from the garden. No, there's no difficulty about how it was done; the difficulty is to put one's hand on the culprits. Unfortunately, there's no footprints clear enough to show the complete pattern of the hob-nails.'

He considered a moment, while Mr Puffett watched him with the air of one confidently expecting a good conjuring trick.

'One could make a house-to-house visitation,' went on his lordship, 'and ask questions, or search. But it's surprising how things disappear, and how people dry up when asked direct questions. Children especially. Look here, Puffett, I'm not at all sure my prodigal son mightn't be able to throw some light on this, after all. But leave me to conduct the examination, it may need delicate handling.'

There is one drawback about retreating to a really small place in the country and leaving behind you the stately publicity of town life in a house with ten servants. When you have tucked in yourselves, and your three children, and your indispensable man and your one equally indispensable and devoted maid, both time and space become rather fully occupied. You may, by taking your husband into your own room and accommodating the two elder boys in his dressing-room, squeeze in an extra person who, like Miss Quirk, has been wished upon you; but it is scarcely possible to run after her all day to see that she is not getting into mischief. This is more particularly the case if you are a novelist by profession, and if, moreover, your idea of a happy holiday is to dispose as completely and briskly as possible of children, book, servants and visitor, so as to snatch all the available moments for playing the fool with a congenial, but admittedly distracting, husband. Harriet Wimsey, writing for dear life in the sitting-room, kept one eye on her paper and the other on Master Paul Wimsey, who was disembowelling his old stuffed rabbit in the window-seat. Her ears were open for a yell from young Roger, whose rough-and-tumble with the puppy on the lawn might at any moment end in disaster. Her consciousness was occupied with her plot, her subconsciousness with the fact that she was three months behind on her contract. If she gave an occasional vague thought to her first-born, it was only to wonder whether he was hindering Bunter at his work, or merely concocting, in his own quiet way, some more than usually hideous shock for his parents. Himself was the last person he ever damaged; he was a child with a singular talent for falling on his feet. She had no attention to spare for Miss Quirk.

Miss Quirk had tried the woodshed, but it was empty, and among its contents she could find nothing more suspicious than a hatchet, a saw, a rabbit hutch, a piece of old carpet and a wet ring among the sawdust. She was not surprised that the evidence had been removed; Bredon had been extraordinarily anxious to leave the breakfast-table, and his parents had shut their eyes and let him go. Nor had Peter troubled to examine the premises; he had walked straight out of the house with that man Puffett, who naturally could not insist upon a search. Both Peter and Harriet were obviously burking inquiry; they did not want to admit the consequences of their wickedly mistaken system of training.

'Mummy! come out an' play wiv' me an' Bom-bom!'

'Presently, darling. I've only got a little bit to finish.'

'When's presently, Mummy?'

'Very soon. In about ten minutes.'

'What's ten minutes, Mummy?'

Harriet laid down her pen. As a conscientious parent, she could not let this opportunity pass. Four years old was said to be too early, but children differed and you never knew.

'Look, darling. Here's the clock. When this long hand gets to *that*, that'll be ten minutes.'

'When *this* gets to *that*?'

'Yes, darling. Sit quiet just for a little bit and look after it and tell me when it gets there.'

An interval. Miss Quirk had by this time searched the garage, the greenhouse and the shed that housed the electric plant.

'It isn't moving, Mummy.'

'Yes, it is, really, only it goes very, *very* slowly. You'll have to keep a very sharp eye on it.'

Miss Quirk had reached the back parts of the house itself. She entered by the back door, and passed through the scullery into a passage, containing, among other things, the door of the boot-hole. In this retreat, she discovered a small village maiden, cleaning a pair of very youthful boots.

'Have you seen –?' began Miss Quirk. Then her eye fell on the boots. 'Are those Master Bredon's boots?'

'Yes, miss,' said the girl, with the startled look peculiar to young servants when suddenly questioned by strangers.

'They're very dirty,' said Miss Quirk. She remembered that Bredon had worn clean sandals when he came in to breakfast. 'Give those to me for a moment,' said Miss Quirk.

The small maid looked round with a gasp for advice and assistance, but both Bunter and the maid seemed to be occupied elsewhere, and one could not refuse a request from a lady staying in the house. Miss Quirk took charge of the boots. 'I'll bring them back presently,' she said, with a nod, and passed on. Fresh, damp earth on Bredon's boots, and something secret brought home in a pail – it scarcely needed a Peter Wimsey to put two and two together. But Peter Wimsey was refusing to detect in the right place. Miss Quirk would show him.

Miss Quirk went on along the passage and came to a door. As she approached it, it opened and Bredon's face, very dirty, appeared round the edge. At sight of her, it popped in again like a bolting rabbit.

'Ah!' said Miss Quirk. She pushed the door briskly. But even a child of six, if he can reach it and is determined, can make proper use of a bolt.

'Roger, darling, no! Shaking won't make it go any faster. It'll only give the poor clock tummyache. Oh, look, what a dreadful mess Paul's made with his rabbit. Help him pick up the bits, dear, and then you'll see, the ten minutes will be up.'

Peter, returning from Mr Puffett's garden, found his wife and two-thirds of his family rolling vigorously about the lawn with Bom-bom. Being invited to roll, he rolled, but with only half his attention.

'It's a curious thing,' he observed plaintively, 'that though my family makes a great deal of noise and always seems to be on top of me' (this was, at the moment, a fact), 'I never can lay hands on the bit of it I want at the moment. Where is the pest, Bredon?'

'I haven't dared to ask.'

Peter rose up, with his youngest son clinging, leech-like, to his shoulder, and went in search of Bunter, who knew everything without asking.

'Master Bredon, my lord, is engaged at present in an altercation with Miss Quirk through the furnace-room door.'

'Good God, Bunter! Which of them is inside?'

'Master Bredon, my lord.'

'I breathe again. I feared we might have to effect a rescue. Catch hold of this incubus, will you, and hand him back to her ladyship.'

All Miss Quirk's coaxing had been impotent to lure Bredon out of the furnace-room. At Peter's voice she turned quickly.

'Oh, Peter! Do get the child to come out. He's got those peaches in there, and I'm sure he'll make himself ill.'

Lord Peter raised his already sufficiently surprised eyebrows.

'If your expert efforts fail,' said he, 'will my brutal threats have any effect, do you suppose? Besides, even if he *were* eating peaches, ought we, in this peremptory way, to suppress that natural expression of his personality? And whatever makes you imagine that we keep peaches in the furnace-room?'

'I know he's got them there,' said Miss Quirk. 'And I don't blame the child. If you beat a boy for stealing, he'll steal again. Besides, look at these boots he went out in this morning – all covered with damp mould.'

Lord Peter took the boots and examined them with interest.

'Elementary, my dear Watson. But allow me to suggest that some training is necessary, even for the work of a practical domestic detective. This mould is not the same colour as the mould in Puffett's garden, and in fact is not garden mould at all. Further, if you take the trouble to look at the flower-beds, you will see that they are not wet enough to leave as much mud as this on a pair of boots. Thirdly, I can do all the detective work required in this family. And fourthly, you might realise that it is rather discourteous of you to insist that my son is a liar.'

'Very well,' said Miss Quirk, a little red in the face. 'Fetch him out of there, and you'll see.'

'But why should I fetch him out, and implant a horrible frustration-complex around the furnace-room?'

'As you like,' said Miss Quirk. 'It's no business of mine.'

'True,' said Peter. He watched her stride angrily away, and said:

'Bredon! You can come out. She's gone.'

There was a sound of the sliding of iron, and his son slithered out like an eel, pulling the door carefully to behind him.

'You're not very clean, are you?' said his father, dispassionately. 'It looks to me as though the furnace-room needed dusting. I'm not very clean myself, if it comes to that. I've been crawling in the lane behind Mr Puffett's garden, trying to find out who stole his peaches.'

'*She* says *I* did.'

'I'll tell you a secret, Bredon. Grown-up people don't always know everything, though they try to pretend they do. That is called "prestige" and is responsible for most of the wars that devastate the continent of Europe.'

'I think,' said Bredon, who was accustomed to his father's meaningless outbursts of speech, 'she's silly.'

'So do I; but don't say I said so.'

'And rude.'

'*And* rude. I, on the other hand, am silly, but seldom rude. Your mother is neither rude nor silly.'

'Which am I?'

'You are an egotistical extravert of the most irrepressible type. Why do you wear boots when you go mud-larking? It's much less trouble to clean your feet than your boots.'

'There's thistles and nettles.'

'True, O King! Yes, I know the place now. Down by

the stream, at the far end of the paddock . . . Is that the Secret you've got in the furnace-room?'

Bredon nodded, his mouth obstinately shut.

'Can't you let me in on it?'

Bredon shook his head.

'No, I don't think so,' he explained candidly. 'You see, you might feel you ought to stop it.'

'That's awkward. It's so often my duty to stop things. Miss Quirk thinks I oughtn't ever to stop anything, but I don't feel I can go quite as far as that. I wonder what the devil you've been up to. We've had newts and frogs and sticklebacks, and tadpoles are out of season. I hope it isn't adders, Bredon, or you'll swell up and turn purple. I can stand for most livestock, but not adders.'

'Tisn' *tadders*,' replied his son, with dawning hope. 'Only very nearly. An' I don't know what it lives on. I say, if you will let me keep it, d'you mind coming in quick, 'cos I 'spect it's creeped out of the bucket.'

'In that case,' said his lordship, 'I think we'd better conduct a search of the premises instantly. My nerves are fairly good; but if it were to go up the flue and come out in the kitchen—'

He followed his offspring hastily into the furnace-room.

'I wish,' said Harriet, a little irritably, for she strongly disliked being lectured about her duties and being thus prevented from attending to them, 'you wouldn't always talk about "a" child, as if all children were alike. Even my three are all quite different.'

'Mothers always think their own children are different,' said Miss Quirk. 'But the fundamental principles of child-psychology are the same in all, I have studied the subject. Take this question of punishment. When you punish a child—'

'*Which* child?'

'Any child – you harm the delicate mechanism of its reaction to life. Some become hardened, some become cowed, but in either case you set up a feeling of inferiority.'

'It's not so simple. Don't take any child – take mine. If you reason with Bredon, he gets obstinate. He knows perfectly well when he's been naughty, and sometimes he prefers to be naughty and take the consequences. Roger's another matter. I don't think we shall ever whip Roger, because he's sensitive and easily frightened and rather likes having his feelings appealed to. But he's already beginning to feel a little inferior to Bredon, because he isn't allowed to be whipped. I suppose we shall have to persuade him that whipping is part of the eldest son's prerogative. Which will be all right provided we don't have to whip Paul.'

There were so many dreadful errors in this speech, that Miss Quirk scarcely knew where to begin.

'I think it's such a mistake to let the younger ones fancy that there is anything superior in being the eldest. My little nephews and nieces—'

'Yes,' said Harriet. 'But one's got to prepare people for life, hasn't one? The day is bound to come when they realise that all Peter's real property is entailed.'

Miss Quirk said she so much preferred the French custom of dividing all property equally. 'It's *so* much better for the children.'

'Yes; but it's very bad for the property.'

'But Peter wouldn't put his property before his children!'

Harriet smiled.

'My dear Miss Quirk! Peter's fifty-two, and he's reverting to type.'

Peter at that moment was not looking or behaving like fifty-two, but he was rapidly reverting to a much more ancient and early type than the English landed gentleman. He had, with some difficulty, retrieved the serpent from the ash-hole, and now sat on a heap of clinker, watching it as it squirmed at the bottom of the bucket.

'Golly, what a whopper!' he said, reverently. 'How did you catch him, old man?'

'Well, we went to get minnows, and he came swimming along, and Joey Maggs caught him in his net. And he wanted to kill him along of biting, but I said he couldn't bite, 'cos you told us the difference between snakes. And Joe bet me I wouldn't let him bite me, an' I said I didn' mind and he said, is it a dare? an' I said, Yes, if I can have him afterwards, so I let him bite me, only of course he didn' bite an' George helped me bring him back in the bucket.'

'So Joey Maggs caught him in his net, did he?'

'Yes, but *I* knew he wasn't a nadder. And please, sir, will you give me a net, 'cos Joe's got a lovely big one, only he was awfully late this morning and we thought he wasn't coming, and he said somebody had hidden his net.'

'Did he? That's very interesting.'

'Yes. May I have a net, please?'

'You may.'

'Oh, thank-you, Father. May I keep him, please, and what does he live on?'

'Beetles, I think.' Peter plunged his hand into the bucket, and the snake wound itself about his wrist and slithered along his arm. 'Come on, Cuthbert. You

remind me of when I was at my prep. school, and we
put one the dead spit of you into—' He caught himself
up, too late.

'Where, Father?'

'Well, there was a master we all hated, and we put a
snake in his bed. It's rather frequently done. In fact, I
believe it's what grass-snakes are for.'

'Is it very naughty to put snakes in people you don't
like's beds?'

'Yes. Exceedingly naughty. No nice boy would ever
think of doing such a thing . . . I say, *Bredon*—'

Harriet Wimsey sometimes found her eldest son disconcerting. 'You know, Peter, he's a most unconvincing-
looking child. *I* know he's yours, because there is
nobody else's he could be. And the colour's more or
less right. But where on earth did he get that square,
stolid appearance, and that incredible snub nose?'

But at that instant, in the furnace-room, over the
body of the writhing Cuthbert, square-face and
hatchet-face stared at one another and grew into an
awful, impish likeness.

'Oh, Father!'

'I don't know what your mother will say. We shall get
into most frightful trouble. You'd better leave it to me.
Cut along now, and ask Bunter if he's got such a thing
as a strong flour-bag and a stout piece of string,
because you'll never make Cuthbert stay in this bucket.
And for God's sake, don't go about looking like Guy
Fawkes and Gunpowder Treason. When you've brought
the bag, go and wash yourself. I want you to run down
with a note to Mr Puffett.'

★

Mr Puffett made his final appearance just after dinner, explaining that he had not been able to come earlier, 'along of a job out Lopsley way.' He was both grateful and astonished.

'To think of it being old Billy Maggs and that brother of his, and all along o' them perishin' old vegetable marrers. You wouldn't think a chap cud 'arbour a grievance that way, would yer? 'Tain't even as though 'e wor a'showin' peaches of his own. It beat me. Said 'e did it for a joke. "Joke?" I says to 'im. "I'd like to 'ear wot the magistrate ud say to that there kinder joke." Owsumdever, I got me peaches back, and the Show being ter-morrer, mebbe they won't 'ave took no 'arm. Good thing 'im and they boys 'adn't 'ave ate the lot.'

The household congratulated Mr Puffett on this happy termination to the incident, Mr Puffett chuckled.

'Ter think o' Billy Maggs an' that good-fer-nothin' brother of 'is a-standin' on that there ladder a-fishin' for any peaches with young Joey's stickleback net. A proper silly sight they'd a-bin if anybody'd come that way. "Think yerselves clever," I says to Bill. "W'y, 'is lordship didn't only cast one eye over the place afore 'e says, 'W'y, Puffett,' e' says, ''ere's Billy Maggs an' that there brother of 'is been a-wallerin' all over your wall like a 'erd of elephants.'" Ah! An' a proper fool 'e looked. 'Course, I see now it couldn't only a'been a net, knockin' the leaves about that way. But that there unripe 'un got away from 'im all right. "Bill," I says, "you'll never make no fisherman, lettin' 'em get away from you like that." Pulled 'is leg proper, I did. But see 'ere, me lord, 'ow did you come ter know it was Billy Maggs's Joey's net? 'E ain't the only one.'

'A little judicious inquiry in the proper quarter,' replied his lordship. 'Billy Maggs's Joe gave the show away, unbeknownst. But see here, Puffett, don't blame Joe. He knew nothing about it, nor did my boy. Only from something Joe said to Bredon I put two and two together.'

'Ah!' said Mr Puffett, 'an' that reminds me. I've got more peaches back nor I wants for the Show, so I made bold to bring 'arf-a-dozen round for Master Bredon. I don't mind tellin' you, I did think for about 'arf a minute it might a' bin 'im. Only 'arf a minute, mind you – but knowin' wot boys is, I did jest think it might be.'

'It's very kind of you,' said Harriet. 'Bredon's in bed now, but we'll give them to him in the morning. He'll enjoy them so much and be so pleased to know you've quite forgiven him for those other two.'

'Oh, *them!*' replied Mr Puffett. 'Don't you say nothing more about them. Jest a bit o' fun, that wos. Well, goodnight all, and many thanks to your lordship. Coo!' said Mr Puffett, as Peter escorted him to the door, 'ter think o' Billy Maggs and that there spindle-shanked brother of 'is a-fishin' for peaches with a kid's net a-top o' my wall. I didden 'arf make 'em all laugh round at the Crown.'

Miss Quirk had said nothing, Peter slipped upstairs by the back way, through Harriet's bedroom into his own. In the big four-poster, one boy was asleep, but the other sat up at his cautious approach.

'Have you done the deed, Mr Scatterblood?'

'No, Cap'n Teach, but your orders shall be carried out in one twirl of a marlin spike. In the meantime, the bold Mr Puffett has recovered his lost treasure and has haled the criminals up before him and had them hanged at the yardarm after a drum-head court-martial. He has sent you a share of the loot.'

'Oh, good egg! what did *she* say?'

'Nothing. Mind you, Bredon, if she apologises, we'll have to call Cuthbert off. A guest is a guest, so long as she behaves like a gentleman.'

'Yes, I see. Oh, I do hope she won't apologise!'

'That's a very immoral thing to hope. If you bounce like that, you'll wake your brother.'

'Father! Do you think she'll fall down in a fit an' foam at the mouth?'

'I sincerely hope not. As it is, I'm taking my life in my hands. If I perish in the attempt, remember I was true to the Jolly Roger. Good night, Cap'n Teach.'

'Good-night, Mr Scatterblood. I *do* love you.'

Lord Peter Wimsey embraced his son, assumed the personality of Mr Scatterblood and crept softly down the back way to the furnace-room. Cuthbert, safe in his bag, was drowsing upon a hot-water bottle, and made no demonstration as he was borne upstairs.

Miss Quirk did not apologise, and the subject of peaches was not mentioned again. But she may have sensed a certain constraint in the atmosphere, for she rose rather earlier than usual, saying she was tired and thought she would go to bed.

'Peter,' said Harriet, when they were alone: 'what *are* you and Bredon up to? You have both been so unnaturally quiet since lunch. You must be in some sort of mischief.'

'To a Teach or a Scatterblood,' said Peter with dignity, 'There is no such word as mischief. We call it piracy on the high seas.'

'I knew it,' replied Harriet, resignedly. 'If I'd realised the disastrous effect sons would have on your character, I'd never have trusted you with any. Oh, dear! I'm thankful that woman's gone to bed; she's *so* in the way.'

'Isn't she? I think she must have picked up her infant psychology from the Woman's page in the *Morning Mercury*. Harriet, absolve me now from all my sins of the future, so that I may enjoy them without remorse.'

His wife was not unmoved by this appeal, only observing after an interval, 'There's something deplorably frivolous about making love to one's wife after seven years of marriage. Is it my lord's pleasure to come to bed?'

'It is your lord's very great pleasure.'

My lord, who in the uncanonical process of obtaining absolution without confession or penitence, had almost lost sight of the sin, was recalled to himself by his wife's exclamation as they passed through the outer bedroom:

'Peter! Where is Bredon?'

He was saved from having to reply by a succession of long and blood-curdling shrieks, followed by a confused outcry.

'Heavens!' said Harriet. 'Something's happened to Paul!' She shot through her own room on to the Privy Stair, which, by a subsidiary flight, communicated with the back bedrooms. Peter followed more slowly.

On the landing stood Miss Quirk in her nightgown. She had Bredon's head tucked under her arm, and was smacking him with impressive though ill-directed energy. She continued to shriek as she smacked. Bredon, accustomed to a more scientific discipline, was taking the situation stolidly, but the nursemaid, with her head thrust out of an adjacent door, was crying,

'Lor', whatever is it?' Bunter, clattering down from the attic in his pyjamas with a long pair of firetongs in his hand, pulled up short on observing his master and mistress, and, with some dim recollection of his military service, brought his weapon to the present.

Peter seized Miss Quirk by the arm and extricated his son's head from chancery.

'Dear me!' he said. 'I thought you objected to corporal chastisement.'

Miss Quirk was in no mood for ethical discussion.

'That horrible boy!' she said, panting. 'He put a snake in my bed. A disgusting, slimy snake. A snake!'

'Another erroneous inference,' said Peter. 'I put it there myself.'

'You? *You* put a snake in my bed?'

'But I knew all about it,' put in Bredon, anxious that the honour and blame should be equitably distributed. 'It was all his idea, but it was my snake.'

His father rounded upon him. 'I didn't tell *you* to come wandering out of your bed.'

'No, sir: but you didn't tell me not to.'

'Well,' said Peter, with a certain grimness, 'you got what you came for.' He rubbed his son's rump in a comforting manner.

'Huh!' said Bredon. '*She* can't whack for toffee.'

'May I ask,' demanded Miss Quirk with trembling dignity, '*why* I should have been subjected to this abominable outrage?'

'I fancy,' said Peter, 'I must have been suffering from in-growing resentment. It's better to let these impulses have their natural outlet, don't you agree? Repression is always so dangerous. Bunter, find Master Bredon's snake for him and return it carefully to the furnace-room. It answers to the name of Cuthbert.'

Notes to the Solution

I.I.   VIRGO: The sign of the zodiac between LEO (strength) and LIBRA (justice). Allusion to parable of The Ten Virgins.

I.3.   R.S.: Royal Society, whose 'fellows' are addicted to studies usually considered dry-as-dust.

IV.3.   TESTAMENT (or will): Search is to be directed to the Old Testament. Ref. to parable of New Cloth and Old Garment.

XIV.3.   HI: 'He would answer to Hi!
                 Or to any loud cry.'
                         The Hunting of the Snark.

I.5.   TRANS.: Abbreviation of Translation; ref. to building of Babel.

XI.5.   SCENT: 'Even the scent of roses
                   Is not what they supposes,
                   But more than mind discloses
                   And more than men believe.'
                         G. K. Chesterton:
                         The Song of Quoodle.

VI.7.   ICTUS: Blow; add V (five) and you get VICTUS (vanquished); the ictus is the stress in a foot of verse; if the stress be misplaced the line goes lamely.

I.8.   SPINOZA: He wrote on the properties of optical glasses; also on metaphysics.

IV.13. THIRTY-ONE: Seven (months) out of the twelve of the sun's course through the heavens have thirty-one days.

XIV.13. ET: Conjunction. In astrology an aspect of the heavenly bodies. That Cicero was the master of this word indicates that it is a Latin one.

X.14. BEZOAR: The bezoar stone was supposed to be a prophylactic against poison.

II.I. PLAUD: If you would laud, then plaud (var. of applaud); Plaud-it also means 'cheer.'

10.II. ALIENA: *As You Like It.* II.1.130.

I.III. R.D.: 'Refer to Drawer.'

4.III. CANTICLES: The Magnificat and Nunc Dimittis are known as the Canticles, but the Book of Canticles (the Vulgate name for the Song of Songs, in which the solution is found) occurs earlier in the Bible.

2.VI. EST: ὄν καὶ μὴ ὄν = *est* and *non es* – the problem of being and not-being. Ref. Marlowe: *Doctor Faustus* I.1.

12.X. TOB.: Add IT to get Tobit; the tale of Tobit and the Fish is in the Apocrypha (the book of hidden things).

I.XI. MANES: 'Un lion est une mâchoire et non pas une crinière': Emile Faguet: *Lit. du XVIIe siècle*. Manes: benevolent spirits of the dead.

I.XV. SAINT: Evidence of miraculous power is required for canonisation.

The solution of the
cross-word puzzle in
'The Fascinating Problem'

MACMILLAN COLLECTOR'S LIBRARY

**Own the world's great works of literature in
one beautiful collectible library**

Designed and curated to appeal to book lovers everywhere,
Macmillan Collector's Library editions are small enough to
travel with you and striking enough to take pride of place
on your bookshelf. These much-loved literary classics
also make the perfect gift.

Beautifully produced with gilt edges, a ribbon marker,
bespoke illustrated cover and real cloth binding, every
Macmillan Collector's Library hardback adheres to the
same high production values.

Discover something new or cherish your favourite
stories with this elegant collection.

**Macmillan Collector's Library:
own, collect, and treasure**

Discover the full range at
macmillancollectorslibrary.com